FATAL BETRAYAL

Bruce Forester

TwinBridges Pub. Co. L.L.C.

I

FIRST EDITION

The characters and events in this book are fictitious.
Any similarity to real persons, living or dead, is coincidental
and not intended by the author.

Library of Congress Cataloging-in-Publication Data

10 9 8 7 6 5 4 3 2 1

Printed in the United States of America
by
Sun Graphics Inc.

DEDICATION

To Erica,

For a continuing supply of Oxytocin,

Phenylethylamine and, of course, PASTE.

Prologue

Is this really happening? Is it possible this will actually turn out to be my big break? Tyrone Sawyer, the lanky 23-year-old with deep blue eyes that made the girls swoon whenever he played at a local gig, climbed the well-worn stairs to the third floor of the converted warehouse in Tribeca. At the second floor landing, he stepped over an empty can of beer, several discarded milk containers and a few pages from yesterday's Daily News. Not exactly the look he expected for a building that was to house his future. He expected the location to resemble those he'd seen on MTV and Hard Copy. But it's a start, he reminded himself. Eventually, if all worked out as he hoped, he'd have control over where he worked, but for now, this place, any place would do. The aesthetics could wait. They were irrelevant. To have his music wanted was all that mattered.

The unexpected phone call from Philmont Music came out of the blue. True, Philmont wasn't a household name. Certainly not of the reputation or the caliber of the big names; certainly not an Arista or CBS Records or Motown. But this was the beginning, his beginning.

Sol, his agent, constantly raved about his musical talent, the uniqueness of his beat, the melodious yet passionate sound of his voice. He was one of a kind, really special, Sol constantly reminded him. Yet, month after month passed and still no interest from the only voice that counted. The music industry.

All he needed was patience, Sol would reiterate. An 'in' would come and the rest would follow. But when? How patient could he be?

His demo was good. He knew that. He believed in his talents, his ability to both create and perform his music. Still, eight years of frustration was hard to take. Now suddenly, a well-known professional in the business was actually willing to gamble on him. It was simply too good to be true. Sol insisted the person had big bucks—that Tyrone's was exactly the unknown voice the company was looking for, a young man with a powerful sound that they could harness and would propel Philmont into the big leagues. This evening's audition, Sol believed, was a mere formality. A lucrative contract would soon be forthcoming.

The endless months of rejection from other studios—or worse yet, no response at all—suddenly were meaningless. He was finally going to get his chance. That's all he wanted. He was confident his voice would accomplish the rest.

Tyrone grasped the cross dangling around his neck and silently thanked God for this beginning.

He continued mounting the stairs, finally reaching the third floor. His eyes wandered to the peeling pink paint on the cracked walls and to the four wooden doors that dotted the hallway. All was quiet. A dim light bulb without a fixture and a sliver of sunlight that sliced through the small stained window on the stairwell were the only sources of light in the otherwise dark hall.

Tyrone's thoughts wandered momentarily to the group. He couldn't wait to tell them.

Beads of perspiration formed on his forehead. This was it. The door to the studio was directly in front of him with the name Philmont Recording Company posted in clear view. He took a deep breath, then knocked. There was no answer. He knocked on the door again, this time harder.

"Tyrone, is that you?" a voice called out.

"Yes," the young man replied anxiously.

"Come on in. The door's unlocked. I've been waiting for you."

A tall, lanky figure with graying hair greeted him.

Tyrone scanned the large room, his jaw dropping in awe. He had never seen such a well-equipped facility, not even on MTV. High-Tech, floor-to–ceiling, state-of-the-art speakers were in each corner of the room. In the circular area near the control room, Tyrone stared at the criss-crossing wires, a large drum set, and three electrical guitars. Several headsets sat on top of a small rectangular table. Long, thin microphones hung from the ceiling. He also noticed two standing microphones stationed near the drum set.

Tyrone walked to the walls; posters of vocal groups were everywhere. "Are these your clients?" he asked.

"Some of them. Soon you'll be up there with them," came the response. Tyrone moved toward the far corner of the room where a glass partition separated the musical compartment from the control room. He glanced through the clear windows at the synchronizers and mixers of different sizes and shapes.

"Impressive, isn't it?" the voice said.

"I'd say," Tyrone, his eyes bulging, replied.

"I'm sure Sol told you how much I loved your tape. We've been searching for a young male voice like yours for quite some time. Grab one of the electric guitars. Play one of your songs for me. Don't be nervous. You have nothing to worry about. We're already sold on your talent. It's just that I'd like to hear in person what we're going to be heavily investing in before I send Sol the contract."

Tyrone walked briskly to the center of the room and grabbed one of the guitars. He noticed the figure walking to the desk drawer and pulling out a small piece of metal.

Suddenly, Tyrone felt a stinging sensation in his right leg. It felt like a mosquito bite. He reached down to scratch the sensitive area. He raised his trouser leg to see where he'd been bitten. He started feeling light-headed, dizzy. His heart began pounding in his chest. Sweat began pouring down his face.

He was feeling weak, very weak. The guitar fell to the floor. Tyrone began to panic. He had never felt like this.

"What's the matter?" the smirking voice asked. "C'mon, I want to hear your music."

Tyrone's head began throbbing. He felt nauseated and faint. He began to lose his balance; began staggering. He was feeling fainter, more light-headed. The room became darker. It was starting to spin. Faster, faster. Then nothing.

The tall figure walked over to Tyrone, bent down to retrieve the small oval object lying next to the young man's still body, slipped it into a coat pocket and smiled.

1

Mort Yvars glanced across the desk at his wife Millie. Her slender fingers rubbed her forehead.

"What are you thinking about?" he asked.

"This evening's group. Over the past several weeks I've sensed something different between our patients in this particular group compared to those in our other groups."

"Such as?" Mort asked, a surprised tone in his voice.

"Vibes I'm picking up. I know I'm not being very scientific, but several members seem more hostile than I'd expect."

"Millie, we treat violent-prone patients. All of our patients are in treatment because they have had serious problems dealing with their anger. This group is different because they have difficulty in expressing anger."

Mort began pacing the floor. "Now that you mention it, I've observed a certain familiarity among several of the patients in this group I've never noticed in our other groups. You don't think they've gone against our agreement, do you?"

"I don't know? We were very explicit in our first session that any contact outside of our therapy meetings was strictly forbidden."

Mort looked at his watch. It was 6 p.m.

" The group should all be here by now. Let's pay close attention to each patient's body language and tone of voice. Hopefully, we've imagined it all."

****

Mort stared at his Swiss army watch. "It's six after. Let's start."

"Tyrone's not here yet. Let's wait a few more minutes," Jeff Osgood, a tall, well-built member of the group said.

"No way. Let's get started. Each minute costs money. We've wasted six minutes already," Steve Bass, seated across from Osgood, demanded.

"I'm sure Tyrone will be here momentarily. He's been a member of our group for almost two years. He's never missed a session without first calling." Mort's voice was tinged with obvious irritation and frustration. He glanced at his co-therapist Millie, seated directly across from him in one of the ten Breuer chairs that surrounded the walnut table. Her smile cut through his annoyance at Sawyer's lateness. How he adored and cherished her. She was his lifeline. He often wondered at times like these how he had been fortunate enough to have found such a wonderful woman who wanted him as much as he wanted her. The fact that she was his co-therapist to boot, was an added bonus. Millie, with her dark brown, deeply set eyes and sharp features, emanated strength.

Mort scanned the seven members of the group who were impatiently waiting to start their weekly 90-minute session.

"What happened to you?" Steve Bass, a tall, chunky man in his early fifties asked the woman seated next to him, her long angular arm in a sling. "Did Max do that to you?" "I only wish," Mary Hargrove, the assistant manager of a fashionable Madison Avenue boutique replied. "If only from your mouth to God's ears. If he struck me, even broke my arm, it would mean he cared enough to expend some energy on me. No! It was nothing like that. I fell in one of our mayor's potholes Saturday afternoon."

"Why don't you leave him? He'll never change," Doug Simons, investigative reporter for The New York Times, asked.

"It's not that easy. That's why I'm coming here," Mary replied, her eyes downcast.

Millie leaned over and patted Mary gently on her slim shoulder. "I understand. I know it's hard, but you'll get there. One day you'll do what you have to do. Until then, try to be more tolerant of yourself."

Mort patted his trim mid-section. He could still pinch an inch, per-haps two, but no longer seven or eight. "I can't emphasize enough what Millie was getting at; the importance of self-esteem and positive self-image. Give it time. As you slowly but surely start liking yourself better, you will feel you deserve better," Mort paused. "Have you told Max you feel neglected?"

"Not in so many words, but he knows."

"Maybe, maybe not. Why not tell him directly? You might be pleasantly surprised at his response," Yvars said.

"Enough of this," Lyle Stuart, the television soap opera idol of millions, barked. "I don't see where this conversation is heading. Let's move on."

Mort held his still beefy hand in the air. "We'll get to you, Lyle. We always do. Mary hardly ever talks. Let her finish."

"I am finished." The defeated woman replied sheepishly.

'Well, I'm not,' Millie replied angrily. "Mary, you just let Lyle bully you into shutting up. Just like you do with Max. I want you to do me a favor. Between tonight and next Monday's meeting, I want you to promise me you'll tell Max you don't think he cares about you. See what he says."

"He'll tell me he does. I'll feel like a fool." Mary Hargrove said.

"You might very well be right about his reaction," Mort began, "but you have nothing to lose. If he says he does indeed care, ask him how you are supposed to know that?"

"He'll say it's obvious," Mary replied.

"Mary," Mort gently said, "We all need to feel loved. You are enti-tled to feel loved. If Max keeps insisting he does care, but there is no change in his behavior that allows you to feel he does indeed care, then you'll have your answer."

"And what if I can't deal with that?" Mary asked.

"That's what we're here for." Meg Armstrong, the author of

romantic gothic novels, said. "We'll get you to build up your muscles like the heroines in my novels do. You'll be willing to start over. Believe me, I know. There's life after Max. Read my books. You'll see."

"Where could Tyrone be?" Mary Hargrove asked.

"I'm sure it's the traffic," Bass said, "I've never seen anything like it. There's a problem with the trains, and the construction on both Broadway and Columbus made getting here a nightmare. I almost got out of the taxi I was in and gave up. He'll be here. It's only 6:30."

Millie thought she spotted Mary Hargrove suddenly stare at Osgood. The tall, blond haired, muscular man then seemed to nod back at her. Was this a sufficient gesture to implement Mort's therapeutic decision. She glanced at Mort. He didn't appear to have noticed. She sighed; deciding a more obvious indicator was needed before she'd say anything.

"I'd like to confess something to everyone here," Osgood interjected. He reached for a glass of water. "I've been meaning to tell you this for months. I didn't have the courage. I've been made to feel by being in this group for over a year and a half that as long as I keep lying to you, I can't possibly expect to get over my problems. I've felt very badly not being honest with you, but I've been afraid. Afraid of what effect my telling you the truth about myself would have on my career."

Meg Armstrong leaned forward in her chair in anticipation.

"You queer or something?" Lyle Stuart asked.

"No. Nothing like that. I've been afraid that if you knew who I really was, my career would be ruined. Mort and Millie don't even know."

"Cut the suspense, Osgood. Get to the chase," Doug Simons exclaimed.

"I'm not Jeff Osgood. I'm really Judd Webster. Senator Judd Webster from Colorado."

Steve Bass leaned back in his chair and laughed. "That's the big secret? What's the fucking big deal about that? I fried many of you big shots on the hill for years. How else would I have been able to continually obtain special variances for my shopping malls? You guys have always

10

come through for me. One hand washes the other. That's life. Don't sweat it. Your secret is safe with me. I won't mention it to anyone."

Everyone else nodded in agreement.

"That's it? None of you really care that I lied to you for all these months?" Webster, obviously relieved, asked.

"We all have our problems. That's why we're here," Lyle Stuart replied. "Yours is trust. Join the club."

"Do we have to call you Senator Webster now?" Meg Armstrong, smiling, asked.

"No. Judd will do just fine."

Mort looked at his watch. It was 6:43 p.m. Still no Tyrone Sawyer. He was becoming increasingly worried. Sawyer even came when he was sick with fever. Not even a phone call. Nothing. "Do you think we should call his home? Tyrone's mother should know where he is." Mort said.

"Relax Mort," Millie said, placing four charts on the desk behind her. "I'm sure he'll be here any minute." She turned to face Stuart. "Okay, Lyle. We're all yours. You can now have our full attention."

****

Mort took a sip of brandy and then placed it on the coffee table in their Art Nouveau decorated living room. It was 10:45 p.m. Millie's review class for her LSAT's was over at 10. She should have been here by now. He downed the rest of his brandy. If he was this worried about Millie and she hadn't even applied to law school yet, what, he wondered, would he be like after she started going to night school. He had no objection to her wanting to continue as his co-therapist while attending law school at night. On the contrary, he admired her resolve. His passion was psychiatry. Hers had always been the law. They envisioned one day combining their two fortes. He'd evaluate her violent clients. She'd defend or prosecute them. She hadn't yet decided which route she'd take. However, he hadn't realized he'd be this much of a basket case. Suddenly, the phone rang. He wasn't expecting any phone calls. Something had happened to Millie. There wasn't any other possible explanation for his phone to be ringing this late at

11

night. He walked to the desk, his heart pounding in his chest.

"Mort. It's Ed Berger!"

"Ed!" Mort hadn't spoken to or seen Berger since their internship days at Bellevue. Berger was the Chief Medical Examiner there. Good God, his fear had come true. Something had indeed happened to Millie. He took a deep breath. "What is it?" he finally asked.

"We've got a D.O.A.. A young Caucasian male. He was found by a stranger on a deserted sidestreet in Tribeca. He had no identification on him. No wallet. Nothing but a card that we found in his trouser pocket. It was one of your appointment cards. We need you to come over to identify the body."

Mort sighed in relief. Millie was fine. His imagination had run away with itself. "I'll be right over," Yvars said, slamming down the phone.

****

Yvars parked his green Audi 100 in the crusty old garage on First Avenue. He hadn't been in this lot, or any part of the Bellevue complex, since his residency program ended. That was ten years ago. The place looked the same, he thought, as he walked toward the main hospital. The complex still spooked him. He passed unshaven men and tattered old women with shopping bags stuffed with their belongings.

The grimy old buildings where he had trained ran from 23rd to 34th Streets, south to north, all built of brick and stone, with years of accumulated New York soot. There were no lawns, no trees, nothing to brighten the surroundings. No wonder he never seriously considered staying at NYU after his training. His interview with Dr. O'Connor at Wentworth Hospital wasn't what sold him—rather, it was Wentworth's tall, glass and steel high-rise complex in the gentrified part of the upper West Side, its three-story atrium with imported Japanese maples, and the ultra-modern criss-crossing system of escalators.

Yvars began wondering who could be lying in the morgue with only his appointment card as identification. Obviously, either a patient or someone who'd been given his appointment card but had yet to call for an evaluation. He searched his mind, trying to think of who he was currently treating who might be self-destructive enough to have committed suicide. Suddenly, it hit him. Paul Nolan perhaps? He had admitted Nolan to Wentworth's psychiatric wing two months ago for a severe depression with recurrent thoughts of suicide. He was to see Nolan tomorrow afternoon. He hoped he was wrong, but the more he thought about Nolan, his depression, his family's history of suicide and his recent suicidal ideation, the more he started to believe Nolan would be the D.O.A. he'd shortly be identifying.

****

Yvars descended the steel spiral staircase with its green glowing lights, memories of his internship flashing before him. The morgue looked then as it did now: the long corridor in aquarium green, municipal green, bureaucratic green; the plaster cracked and the paint chipped. Those same green, moist tiles, freezing in the winter, sweating in the summer. Down he went into the soft green netherworld under First Avenue, past a dozing guard, and through the iron anteroom gate which moaned open and clanged shut behind him.

Yvars descended yet another short flight of stairs. He now found himself in the familiar, darker green sub-basement level. The heavy air was thick with vapors of formaldehyde. He never was able to feel comfortable in an autopsy room. Death and asafetida, formalin and fright. During that painful internship year, that odor imbued his clothing and saturated his skin and hair.

His pace quickened as he entered a cool area filled with the high-pitched electrical roar of refrigerator motors. On the left were a number of stainless steel trolleys, each bearing a lumpy, belted canvas sack, the remains of the last night's harvest of victims. Yvars stopped for a moment and gazed at the wall of refrigerated compartments that ran from floor to ceiling, temporary repositories for the unclaimed, the anonymous and the unwanted. Here the dead lay, all left to the cold impartiality of separate drawers, all succumbing to the pathologist's blade.

Finally, Yvars dropped down another three steps, pushed open a

13

pair of swinging doors and entered a bright white glow. Rapidly, he moved past several pans of cirrhotic livers and diseased lungs gurgling in a tub of formalin. The ever-thickening fumes were beginning to make him feel nauseated. The place was a hive of activity; twelve tables all going at once. Cadavers, naked, flayed open, sectioned. The whole procedure seemed so inhumane, so unreal: the pathologist cutting, weighing, evaluating: the police stenographers taking dictation from the doctors, scribbling on their pads and the dieners sewing up the cadavers with large needles and black thread.

He couldn't wait until he got to the end of the room. Finally, he spotted an older version of the Ed Berger he remembered from internship days. He greeted the large man with rugged features.

"Well, I'll be. Mort Yvars! I can't believe how great you look. We've all aged, started going to seed. That was you during our training years. You've gotten younger as we've gotten older. What's the secret?"

"Start taking off fat. Then trim down. I've lost about thirty pounds since Christmas. It tends to fool the eye. It's like Trompe l'oeil. I'm 39, same as you. It's that I looked 49 when I was 29. That was the problem."

"Whatever, you look great!" Berger replied.

"I finished the autopsy on the D.O.A. Acute Heart Failure," Berger said. "All his arteries are open. There is no evidence of any chronic disorder. We'll know after we do some frozen sections but as of now, I'd have to conclude the poor guy arrested. We've come a long way in medicine, but there are certain mysteries left for research to solve. I believe this case is going to turn out to be one of those. A sudden, unexplainable disruption of the autonomic nervous system's cardiac regulatory mechanism with sudden death resulting. We see this kind of case more often than you'd think. When this happens, it's always a tragedy, but especially when a victim is so young."

Yvars, relieved, stared at the sheet covering the dead man. At least Nolan hadn't committed suicide.

The pathologist slowly lifted the cloth from the victim's face.

Yvars gulped hard. His face turned ashen. He stood motionless, taking a deep breath, trying to regain his composure. He could not believe what his eyes were taking in. He was staring directly into the lifeless face of Tyrone Sawyer.

2

Senator Judd Webster glanced at his watch and smiled. It was just past noon, the entire day still ahead. He adjusted the rear-view mirror on his Ford Mustang convertible and cranked the handle above his head; the deep blue sky came into view. He accelerated past the waving guard and exited rapidly from the parking lot on Capitol Hill. What a beautiful day, he thought, as he deeply breathed in the warm, spring air. His destination: his white colonial house perched on a small hill in Chevy Chase. He hoped Jane would be home. He couldn't wait to see the surprised look on his wife's face. Why hadn't he thought of doing this sooner? What had possessed him through his life to always place career over loved ones? And his adorable precious little William. Only three, but he knew his daddy was somehow not like the other daddies in his play group. Their daddies would occasionally watch them at their activities, even drive them home. Be there while they ate their snacks. Not his father. His father, mommy would constantly remind him, was too busy, too important to get away during the middle of the day to be with him. How was a three-year-old to understand? How could Jane even understand? He now realized he didn't understand it himself. He was proud he told the group who he really was. It had taken a long time, but at least he finally was able to admit he'd gotten his priorities backwards. Sure, his position as chairman of the Senate Finance Committee on Banking was a pivotal and important post. But not at the price it was having on his loved ones. Never again would any venture, any political quest take precedence over his family.

Thank God for those Monday evening group therapy meetings. He was finally starting to see the light. His career had sapped his energies for too long. Mary Hargrove's plea not to be neglected was what finally made it clear to him. Then and there he realized he was as guilty as her husband, Max. True, his underlying motives might have been more altruistic, more important, but they were irrelevant nevertheless. He thought of his sister Ruth insisting he enter therapy. If it wasn't for her he was certain he'd never have seen the light.

Webster veered his sports car on to the Beltway and floored the accelerator. He was amazed at how little traffic there was when one didn't use the system of highways that encircled Washington, D.C. during peak hours. He could actually accelerate to 70 miles per hour. Hopefully, bumper to bumper from today on would be a thing of the past. He took in the warm breeze, basked in the bright sun and let himself enjoy the sensation of unlimited freedom.

Suddenly, he heard a cracking sound. He turned his head sharply to the left. The window on the driver's side had been shattered; fragments of glass were ricocheting off the dashboard; off his suit jacket. He quickly grabbed the steering wheel firmly with both hands. He began feeling his body shake, his head felt strange. He started feeling lightheaded, dizzy. His vision became blurred. Then a violent sensation shot through his chest and down his left arm, followed by a wave of intense nausea. He started retching. He had to pull off the road. His sight became dimmer. Everything looked distorted. He blinked once, then again. It was no use. All was becoming gray, hazy. He now could-n't see well enough to even pull off the road. He slammed his brakes down hard. He'd wait for this attack or whatever it was, to pass. Then he'd contin-ue driving. Get home. He was certain once home with Jane and William, all would be fine. But he had stepped on the brakes too late; his left fender smashed directly into the stone embankment. His head hit hard against the dashboard.

He tried to catch his breath. He couldn't. He was finding it more and more difficult to breathe. He began gasping for air. His heart was racing faster, faster. His vision became dimmer, everything now a blur…Then darkness.

17

Yvars, seated behind his large oak desk, was putting the final touches on his progress notes from last night's meeting. His quick shuttle flight to Washington, earlier in the day, to hear Dru Abramson's talk on his research into the psychological makeup of the criminal mind had invigorated him.

All was quiet. Completely still. He thought of his chosen profession and smiled. Oh, how he loved those sessions, the interaction between different psyche; the resistance, the justification, and the compliance. He even enjoyed the defiance. If it were humanly possible, he'd probably schedule patients back to back, leaving barely a moment in between to either take a leak or refill his ever-present glass of water. It was Millie who convinced him he couldn't work like that. It wasn't human. He'd get his cases mixed up. He'd wind up an irritable basket case. He sighed and returned to his notes.

Yvars came to Tyrone Sawyer's chart and started flipping through it's pages. His mind flashed back to the young man whose promising future would never evolve. The youngster had come to their group after a series of assaults and through perseverance and hard work, finally mastered the ability to channel his angry, destructive energies into creating passionate music.

Yvars checked his watch. It was still 90 minutes until his next patient was due to arrive. Millie was busy studying for her LSATs at home until 4:00. He was free for an hour and a half. Ample time to go back to Bellevue and speak to Berger. By now the results of tissue sections, blood and urine samples would be in. Berger would be able to pinpoint the cause of Sawyer's death.

Mort went into his small back room and pulled out his new, black, mountain bike, his pride and joy. He could ride through New York City with the best of them. Forget baseball, tennis, football and the rest of those competitive sports; after a lifetime of feeling like a male misfit, he'd finally found his niche. Screw those airhead jocks. When he was on his mountain bike, the world was his oyster. He felt ten feet tall.

Yvars pulled down hard on the straps to his helmet and shook his head. He edged the bike out the door of his brownstone office building and onto 88th Street and Central Park West.

By the time Yvars arrived at Bellevue, his long-sleeved, yellow, turtleneck shirt was saturated with sweat. He hadn't realized how hot it was. He had spent the 20-minute trip deep in thought, oblivious to the sounds around him. He kept envisioning Sawyer, vibrant and alive. His poor mother. Not married. No other children. Tyrone was her whole life. She lived for him. What would become of her now? It didn't make sense. It wasn't fair.

Berger was seated behind his desk in his office when Yvars entered the medical examiner's suite. On his desk were Sawyer's autopsy findings, microscopic slides and the results of various tests.

"Well, what do you think?" Yvars asked, pulling up a chair alongside the red-haired pathologist.

The tall physician leaned back in his seat. "I signed Sawyer out as a cardiac arrest secondary to anaphylactic shock."

"What?" Yvars asked incredulously.

"These things happen. His blood showed a far larger than normal number of eosinophils, which means that his system massively overreacted to an allergen. Which allergen we don't as yet know. But hopefully, we'll find out."

"That's impossible," Yvars replied. "I sent Sawyer to an internist three months ago. He wanted a routine physical. He had a complete work-up. A to Z. No allergies. No illnesses at all. He was completely well. Totally normal."

"There's no way to test a person for every allergen under the sun. Even the healthiest of us could be allergic to one thing, or a combination of things, without knowing it. Hopefully, after the microsections come in we'll know what triggered Sawyer's reaction. It could have been something he ate. Perhaps an insect bite in an area we've so far been unable to locate. Massive sudden anaphylactic reactions are unfortunately not that uncommon. Two weeks ago we had a 32-year old woman who dropped dead immediately after drinking a glass of milk. It turned out she was allergic to penicillin and somehow the glass she drank from hadn't been thoroughly washed. Traces of ampicillin were still at the bottom of the glass."

Yvars went over to the microscope and stared at a section of skin under the lens. "What's that?"

"The skin was very red, almost as if it had recently been burned. I had a section made. I thought, or rather I hoped, the allergen would be lodged somewhere in the area. As I said, perhaps an insect bite. Something like that. Maybe even a bee sting. However, on examining the section, there was no evidence for a heightened immune reaction, as you'd expect given the outcome. No inflammatory cells. Just your normal number of histamine cells." Berger paused and folded his hands across his expansive chest. "So you have as up to date a reading as possible. I wish I could have pinpointed the exact allergen that precipitated Sawyer's death by now…. but patience and persistence in both of our fields and not speed lead to our best results. "I'll eventually find the allergen."

Yvars stood up to leave. He shook Berger's hand. "Please call me as soon as you do. While it won't help bring Sawyer back, the knowledge will allow me to help his mother and the other members of our group start the difficult healing process."

"Will do, Mort."

****

Yvars removed his helmet and placed it on the rack above his mountain bike. His muscles were sore from the ride to and from Bellevue, but it was a good sore. His newly-found physical prowess truly amazed him. Who would have believed he could have pulled this off? Berger almost had a stroke when he first laid eyes on him after ten years. He couldn't wait until his next reunion to see others' equally flabbergasted reactions. Having achieved this goal convinced him that anything was possible. Sure, he was somewhat frightened weaving through the city streets

20

and darting to miss passers by, but as he kept reminding Millie, he needed these experiences if he were to overcome his lifelong fears of the unknown.

Yvars looked at his watch. He still had ten minutes until his next patient's appointment. He was about to take a quick shower when the phone rang. He quickly dashed into his main office and picked up the receiver.

The voice at the other end of the line was obviously distressed. "It's Jane Webster," the caller said.

"It's Judd. He's dead!"

"What? Judd dead? He was at our group last evening. He was in perfect health. How? What happened?"

"I don't know," the bereaved widow replied. "The police just left. They said Judd was killed in a car accident on the Beltway. He lost control of the car and crashed into the middle stone embankment." Jane paused. "I need your help."

"Sure, anything." Yvars, still reeling from the shock, replied.

"I need to know what really happened to Judd."

"I don't understand. You just told me what happened. Don't you believe the police?" Mort asked.

"It's not that I normally wouldn't believe them. Of course, I would. It's just that after they came, an agent from the FBI called."

"So?"

"The FBI doesn't get involved in investigating car accidents unless they suspect there might have been more to it than simply your routine car accident."

"Perhaps they investigate all sudden accidental deaths when they involve members of the government."

"That's not true. Last year, one of our friends in Chevy Chase, a member of the House, was killed on the Beltway. The FBI never once contacted anybody in his family. Why then would they call me?" Jane asked.

Yvars said nothing. He felt numb all over. He thought of the Senator, and how he had joined the group somewhat over a year ago after becoming severely depressed when he noticed his night vision failing. While never able to express his feelings as easily as the other seven in the group, he had over the past several weeks begun opening up, leading to last night's startling admission that he had been deceiving the group, and admitting he was not Jeff Osgood but Judd Webster, senator from Colorado.

After a month of therapy, Judd's depression had lifted. He had begun to learn that having a physical problem was not equated with one's manliness. His sex life improved dramatically. While according to the opthalmologist, his night blindness had significantly worsened over the year, he had indeed learned to put it into proper perspective; even twice joking about one day perhaps becoming the only blind senator from Colorado to ever seek re-election.

All had been going so well for Judd, -until today, -until this.

"Sure. Anything," Yvars finally replied. "I'm very sorry, Jane. Millie and I were very fond of your husband. How's your son?"

"He just keeps asking for his daddy."

"I'm going to call Mike Stanley at D.C. General. He's their chief pathologist. If there was anything out of the ordinary about Judd's death, Stanley will know."

"Thanks, Mort. Please keep in touch. I loved Judd so. I don't think I showed him how much."

"He knew how you felt," Mort said reassuringly. "He knew you loved him very much."

****

Shortly after Yvars finished seeing his three scheduled patients, he dialed Mike Stanley, Chief of Pathology at D.C. General. "Well I'll be. Mort Yvars. I thought you'd fallen off the face of the earth. How the hell have you been?"

"Pretty good."

"You sound very serious," Stanley replied. "What's up?"

"It has to do with a patient of mine, Senator Webster. I spoke to his

22

widow. She gave me the tragic news about his fatal car crash. I'm calling about the post on him."

"I did him myself. I mean how often do you get a chance to slice up a senior level government official and get away with it?"

Stanley sensed Yvars wasn't appreciating his sarcastic wit. "I know all about that doctor-patient confidentiality crap, but I'm curious. Why would a man in his position need to see a shrink?"

"It's a long story. I'd rather not go into the details now. Maybe next year at our reunion. How'd he die?" Mort asked.

"He had a massive coronary. His arteries were loaded with athero-sclerotic plaques. He was in excellent physical shape on the surface, but tell that to his inner arteries. They were incredibly narrow. Young guy, too. Early 40's. I'd guess not much older than we are. I hope you don't still eat those donuts like you used to. I wouldn't want to one day find you as my next subject."

"Any other finding?" Mort questioned.

"He suffered a severe concussion. Hit his head on the dashboard. The fool wasn't wearing a seatbelt. He'd have died anyway, but still. It doesn't set a good example for our youth when one they admire doesn't buckle up."

"So you are certain the heart attack preceded his head injury?" Yvars inquired.

"As certain as one can get in this inexact science. I'd say Senator Webster had a massive myocardial infarction. He then lost control of the wheel, hitting his head when the car crashed into the stone embankment."

"Any other finding?" Yvars queried.

"Not yet. The blood, urine tests and tissue sections aren't back. If anything out of the ordinary shows up, I'll call."

****

Millie carefully placed all of Monday evening's patient files, including those of Sawyer and Webster, back into their respective folders, alphabetically arranged, in the top desk drawer. She then lifted the charts containing the records of the eight violent prone patients they'd be seeing that evening from the drawer.

Mort's eyes wandered to the group of teenagers camped under their office window. Cheerful, laughing, like they didn't have a care in the world. He imagined switching places with one of them. It felt good.

"I can't believe how two healthy patients of ours could suddenly drop dead within 24 hours of each other," Millie said, snapping Mort back to the present. "It doesn't make sense. It's scary."

"I know how you feel. I have a sadness and emptiness too, but why are you afraid? Are you worried that I'm going to drop dead too? Maybe a year ago when I was thirty pounds heavier, completely out of shape and exercise consisted of munching on donuts. But now, relax. You'll be stuck with me for years to come," Mort replied.

"I wasn't thinking about your dying from a heart attack, having a stroke or even developing cancer. It's that I find it rather odd that two members of our group both died so suddenly and unexpectedly."

"Sure it's odd. A lot about life is odd. Shit happens."

"I understand that," Millie replied. "But two! Doesn't it strike you that the circumstances surrounding their deaths were both so peculiar? Sawyer, from an overwhelming allergic reaction. Webster, from a massive heart attack. I don't know. It just doesn't make sense to me."

"What are you getting at?"

"Nothing specific. I was just thinking."

"You can't possibly be suggesting that one of our group members was somehow responsible for Sawyer's and Webster's deaths. Give me a break!"

"Have you heard from the police?" Millie asked.

"No, and I don't expect to."

"You are so naïve. Sometimes you don't see things for what they really are," Millie said, shrugging her shoulders. "Maybe now you can understand better why I worry about you when you're bicycling through Central Park or when you're late getting home. I want you to be around when we're old and decrepit. I love you, Mort. I don't want to lose you."

"What do your feelings have to do with the police?" Mort asked, masking his irritation.

"The police investigate all sudden, unexplained deaths. They will investigate both Sawyer's and Webster's. Webster was a Senator."

"You've been watching far too many cop shows on the tube."

"That's what you think. You'll see. Once the police and the FBI find out that both Sawyer and Webster were patients of ours, they'll be calling us. We'll become part of their investigation."

Suddenly the phone rang. "I told you so!" Millie said, picking up the phone. A look of embarrassment swept across her face. "Hi, Mike. Mort told me he spoke to you. One second. He's right here. I'll put him on."

Two minutes later a stunned Yvars replaced the phone in its cradle, walked into the back room and reaching in the small refrigerator, grabbed a stale glazed donut.

He slowly made his way back to his main office, taking several bites out of his past passion. "I guess you were right," he said to Millie who had a puzzled look on her face as she watched Mort down the remains of the hard donut. "The FBI and the police will both be calling."

"What did Mike Stanley say?" Millie asked.

"Stanley is still convinced the Senator died from a massive heart attack with severe head trauma secondary to his collision. However, on careful inspection of Webster's body, he also found a small caliber bullet in the Senator's left arm."

3

Mary Hargrove rushed to the silver-haired man seated at a booth in the far corner of the crowded diner on 85th Street & York Avenue. "I came as soon as I could. It's a good thing Max went to the Mets game with a few of the guys."

"Doesn't he ever let you out of his sight?" the frail, older man asked.

"Only for my Monday evening group. What's so urgent?" she asked, sliding into the booth across from him.

"Webster's dead!"

"What?" Mary sighed, her face ashen.

"I heard it on the six-o'clock news. He apparently had a heart attack while on the Beltway."

Mary began to cry. "Judd dead?"

"I know how fond you were of him."

"Our talks were always so comforting. He was so kind, so easy to talk to. I can't believe he's dead."

"There's something else I have to tell you," he said gasping for air.

"Jim, are you feeling okay?"

"As well as possible." He paused momentarily to catch his breath. "We can't meet after tonight."

"What? You can't be serious!"

"I am, it's too risky."

"Why? We've never done anything wrong. It's not like we're having an affair."

"That's not the point. We can't, that's all. No more phone calls either."

"Why?"

The sickly man said nothing.

"You bastard. You're worse than Max," Mary, tears streaming down her face, said.

"Here, take this." Jim said handing her a napkin.

"I don't want a fucking napkin," she sobbed, rapidly rising from her seat and storming from the restaurant.

****

Yvars turned the brass knob and let himself into their spacious apartment 5 blocks south of his office on Central Park West. He walked past the Galle table, with its distinctive floral marquetry work, that stood on the long wall in the living room opposite the Majorelle sofa. Millie was seated on the Art Nouveau couch. "You received two phone calls while you were out", Millie said, staring directly into Mort's eyes. "Two calls from two different men. One was a detective named Davis, from the 20th Precinct. He told me that's our local police precinct. It's on 82nd Street. The other came from a FBI agent. I think his name was Jackson, Chris Jackson. Something like that. They both wanted to know when they could meet with you. They wanted to know your schedule. I asked if a phone call would do. They both said no. They both insisted on talking to you in person."

"When will they be calling back?" Mort asked.

"They both said they'll get back to you some time early tomorrow. They made it very clear they want to meet with you before the weekend." Millie paused, stood up and walked to the wet bar by the window. "What a nightmare!" she exclaimed. "I need something to calm my nerves." She poured herself a glass of sherry. "Do you want anything?"

"No, I'm okay, sad, but otherwise fine. I dread having to go over Sawyer's and Webster's histories." They both died from unfortunate accidents. Accidents occur. Why can't both the police and the FBI accept that?" He paused briefly. "Everyone has to earn a living, I guess. What are their names…Davis and Jackson? I imagine they need to write detailed reports."

"I'm scared," Millie said, walking back to the sofa. She sipped her Bristol Cream.

"About what? There's nothing to be frightened about," Mort replied, placing his arm around her quivering shoulders.

"I understand that's how you're forcing yourself to feel. Otherwise you'd be worried like I am."

"That's nonsense," Mort replied. "Accidents happen. Even two in two days. That they both happened to be in our Monday evening groups is a mere coincidence. It's weird, but a coincidence nevertheless."

"The senator had a bullet wound in his left arm. You cannot tell me that's accidental," Millie blurted out.

"Stanley insisted the bullet wound was an incidental finding during the post. It had nothing to do with the senator's death. Webster died from a sudden heart attack. These things happen, Millie. You know that. I know that. You read about it every day. Our friend, Bart Louis, was fit as a fiddle. He went jogging, and was found on the street dead from a massive heart attack."

"Bart wasn't shot when he had his heart attack," Millie replied.

"Webster was! I'm not a doctor, but I do know a bullet wound is a bullet wound. That's not an accidental event. That's not a natural event. Bullet wounds don't just happen. Somebody causes them to occur."

"Now you're sounding like Jessica Fletcher. Straight out of "Murder She Wrote." Stop playing detective!"

"I'm not playing detective," Millie angrily replied. "You're the problem here. You're in denial."

"Maybe you're right. However, I can't believe two of our patients were murdered. At least not yet. Not until we know more."

"Come to me," Mort said, placing Millie's head on his shoulder. We both need some oxytocin."

Millie laughed. "We definitely do. I would love some."

Last week Millie and Mort had attended a special lecture at

Wentworth Hospital on the evolution of a relationship, given by Dr. Lovejoy. At the time, Mort recalled saying jokingly how he was certain Lovejoy changed his name when he went into the love research business.

****

The stranger slowly walked to the brownstone on 88th Street off Central Park West, sidestepping a couple strolling with their golden retriever. The figure glanced in all directions. Other than the dog walkers, the street was deserted. The intruder reached for the key a locksmith had made from a mold taken from the door latch. The door opened immediately.

The visitor took a flashlight from a jacket pocket and walked past the empty waiting room into the large office directing the light onto the desk. Then slowly opened the top drawer, and removed all eight of the files listed under Monday's 6:00 p.m. group, jotted down the names and addresses of the six still needed to be contacted...the six who still needed to be dispensed with. Satisfied, the files were replaced.

4

Eileen Matthews stared at the wrinkles around her eyes. "Damn crow's feet," she muttered. She had to do it. The Retin A wasn't working. She'd put it off long enough. Today she'd finally relent and call Dr. Wilson's office for an appointment. Dr. Wilson was the plastic surgeon for the Jet Set. She had seen many of his successes. At thirty-five years old, Eileen was considered an "aging" model. It was submit to the scalpel or else resign herself to small assignments for the likes of Modern Maturity, Years and Longevity. The latter was repugnant to her self- image. She'd rather quit the fashion industry altogether.

She switched on the radio lying on the shelf next to the sink to full blast and began dancing to the rock beat of – who else? - "The Grateful Dead." Another reminder of the passage of time. She made a mental note to call her friend, Sunny, after her procedure. At 23, Sunny was hip to the present phenoms. If Eileen was to have a younger face, she'd better get with it in other areas as well. She entered the shower, closed the blue nylon curtain behind her, let the warm water cascade over her taut, lean frame. How silly to still care about the way she looked. And why continue modeling at all? For the past five years, her primary source of income had come from her work as an architect. Recently, she was hand picked to be the primary architect of the Port Authority's major renovation project at their main headquarters at the World Trade Center. Wasn't that sufficient glory? When would her vanity let up and allow her to use her designing skills to bring her the recognition she desperately sought? On second thought, maybe she'd wait. Not rush into this cosmetic overhaul so fast. At least not until next Monday night. Yes, that made sense. She'd poll the members of her Monday group. She trusted their judgment. She'd go with whatever they thought best. She knew what he would say, but screw him. Who cared about him anyway? It was the others advice she'd abide by.

To hell with Jeff Osgood or was it really Senator Judd Webster? She didn't need him. She didn't need anyone. Sure, she had a good thing going with him, or so she thought. Big deal if he couldn't get it up most of the time. He treated her well. At least in the beginning.

Thank God for Millie, Eileen thought. She helped her see how self-destructive she was, how easily she fell into the masochistic role of the victim. She felt badly she had never told Millie, either before or after one of their weekly group sessions, that she was having an affair with another member of the group. She knew the rules. Both Mort and Millie made the regulations very clear from the onset. There were never to be meetings between group members outside the office. They had learned through their own mistakes that allowing members to meet for coffee, or whatever in between weekly meetings, only served to confuse therapy and made reaching each patient's therapeutic goals difficult to achieve. She listened to them, but her heart desired him anyway. She loved the way he strutted into the room so majestically, with his dirty blonde hair, his tall, muscular body, that chiseled face. He emanated that raw sexuality she'd always craved; had never been able to pull herself from. She knew this magnetic draw was always her downfall, but what could she do? She fell for the Rhetts of the world. Millie tried to get her to want the Ashleys. It was hopeless.

Fortunately for Eileen, by the time Webster was about to toss her aside, she had met her new Rhett. A Rhett who would never drop her, punish her, victimize her. Or so she hoped. Luke Axinn seemed different. She was sure he was different. She prayed he was different. Fuck you, Osgood! Screw you, Webster!

Suddenly, the shower curtain snapped open. A stranger with a knife in one hand, stared directly at her. She began to scream. The sound of the water and the incessant loud beat of the "Dead" drowned out her cries. She saw the blade coming. Using all her might, she pushed the figure backwards. She jumped from the shower and raced into the bedroom. She had to lock the door, call 911…Pray the police would come before it was too late.

However, the stranger followed her too closely. She was unable to lock the bedroom door before her left arm was grabbed. She felt a plunging sensation in her back. Bright red blood poured onto her beige carpet. Then came the sound, like a firecracker. She couldn't catch her breath. She began gasping for air as her windpipe started to close in on her.

She was about to let out another scream when she exhaled for the last time.

****

Mort was digging into his plate of low-fat cottage cheese and peaches and Millie was standing by the kitchen counter when Detective Davis from the 20th Precinct called.

Mort picked up the phone on the third ring. "I'm sorry but I can't make it just now. I'm due at the hospital in an hour. It's an important departmental meeting. One of those I have to go to."

"That's okay, Doc," the pleasant male voice replied. "Our meeting can wait until later. I'm calling about Eileen Matthews. Was she a patient of yours?"

Mort shot Millie a surprised look. He pressed the speakerphone to the ON position. Millie sat down across from Mort. "Yes. Why?" Mort replied.

"I just returned from her apartment on Riverside Drive. She's dead."

"Dead! How? I mean…" Mort was speechless.

"Doc. You still there!"

Mort took a deep breath to regain his composure. "Uh, yes. Eileen dead? I just saw her Monday night. She was all cheerful and perky. She looked like the picture of health. What happened?"

32

"She was stabbed to death."

"Holy shit. Eileen murdered! How is that possible? She was the nicest person on earth. She never had an enemy in her life." Mort paused, his body still trembling. "Was she killed during a burglary?"

"That's what we initially thought. But her wallet wasn't touched. Neither were the usual items they go for. Her TV, stereo, and all her jewelry were in place. Her desk hadn't even been touched. There is no evidence to suspect a robbery. Her appointment card with your name on it was still placed neatly next to her calendar."

Millie began sobbing. Mort handed her a napkin to dab her tears.

"What can you tell me about her?" Davis politely asked.

"Give me a second," Yvars said, trying to clear his head. "Eileen is, uh, was a beautiful woman. A model. She was having trouble coming to terms with the aging process."

"There's a photograph of this handsome guy on a piano. Any idea who he may be?" Davis asked.

"I have no idea about the specifics of her life. I know she was seeing someone, but she never mentioned any of the particulars. The picture could have been a relative. She has a brother. Maybe it's him," Mort replied. "I don't think so. Its signed Love, Jeff." The detective paused. "From your profile on Miss Matthews, I doubt she'd engage in incest. The guy must have been her lover. In fact, he must have been another patient of yours."

"What?" a shocked Yvars blurted out.

"Underneath his name he wrote To our Monday evenings together."

"Why does that make you think this person, Jeff, is a patient of mine?" a bewildered Yvars asked.

"Your appointment card on Eileen's desk had Monday evening written on it. I added one and one together. Out came two. Eileen Matthews and Jeff. Monday evenings. Bingo. Dr. Yvars, level with me. It will make everything much easier for me, for you, for everybody concerned."

"I don't know what to say…"Mort began.

Millie interjected. "Excuse me, Detective Davis. I'm Millie Yvars. Mort's wife. We are co-therapists. My husband isn't deliberately hiding anything from you. He's been very upset. Jeff was Jeff Osgood. That's the name he used. He didn't want those in the group to know his real name. Mort and I didn't even know."

"Which was?" a skeptical Davis asked.

"Judd Webster. Senator Judd Webster. This past Monday he finally got the courage to admit to the group who he really was. He apologized for calling himself Jeff Osgood but explained he had been afraid some people, if they found out he was seeing a shrink, wouldn't understand. They'd view it as a sign of weakness and his political career and whatever future aspirations he might have would suffer."

"I can't believe it. Webster dead. Now Eileen Matthews murdered. Millie is right, detective. I'm not thinking straight. This is so shocking. So unreal. It never dawned on me when you mentioned the name Jeff, that you were referring to Osgood. I mean Webster. I'm sorry. I didn't mean to be difficult."

"I read about Senator Webster's death. A sudden heart attack. Well, if you've got to go, that's the way I'd want it. Here one minute. Gone the next. No prolonged suffering," Davis said. He paused briefly. "I remember there was something in the article about a bullet wound. Do you know anything about that?"

"Mike Stanley, a pathologist and personal friend from D.C. General, told me Webster was shot at the time he suffered his fatal heart attack. The bullet hit his arm. The shooting, Stanley said, was not connected with the Senator's death. Just a coincidence."

"I've been in the police force for 15 years. We don't believe in coincidences. If nothing turns up, then we conclude it was a coincidence. Not until then," Davis paused. "I hope for both your sakes that you're not keeping anything else from me. Two of your patients dead in the past two days. One is a definite murder. The other was shot while having a heart attack, or even before the heart attack. It might even be the real cause of his death. If it turns out both patients were murdered, then we really have a major problem on our hands."

"What do you mean by major problem?" Yvars asked.

"How many patients are in your Monday evening group?" Davis asked.

"Eight." Mort replied.

"That means only six are still alive. If it turns out your two patients were killed, then we have to change the focus of our investigation."

"Meaning?" Millie asked.

"Meaning we will then be dealing with a serial killer. I don't think I have to elaborate any further." Davis replied.

Mort mentioned Tyrone Sawyer's death. He didn't want to be accused of withholding information, especially if Davis suspected there was a serial killer out there slaying his Monday night group patients.

After Davis hung up, Millie persuaded Mort they had best call the five remaining members of the group and calmly but firmly insist, without alarming them, that they all come to their office for a meeting later that day.

Twenty minutes later, all five phone calls completed and the rest of their afternoon schedule canceled, they stared at each other, wondering how they were going to tell their patients what had happened and keep them from panicking.

****

It was shortly after 3:15 PM when Steve Bass finally strolled into Yvars office.

"Okay, let's begin!" Yvars said.

"But not everybody is here," Hargrove said.

"We'll come to that," Yvars replied.

"This better be important," Bass said, sitting down next to Mary Hargrove. "I left an extremely critical round of negotiations with the city to get here."

"I assure you this meeting is very important. I appreciate all of you taking the time to come," Mort began, facing Bass.

"It's about poor Senator Webster, isn't it?" Mary Hargrove, sobbing into her linen handkerchief, asked. "I read about his death in today's Times. I always read the obituary section. What a handsome picture of the senator. What a lovely article. He sounds like he was a wonderful family man; lived for his wife and child. How sad! His son is only three. I feel for the little boy. A boy needs a father. And his wife. So young."

"Do you feel sorry for everybody?" Bass asked. "Do you believe everything you read? How do you know he was such a great guy? He lied to us about his real name until Monday. What type of character strength does that imply? Not much in my book. It's no wonder he had a heart attack. If he kept a secret like that, he probably kept all his other emotions locked up also. He was always smiling, never seemed worried, nervous or down. Almost like Superman. He was unreal, not human. Besides, where there's one secret, there are always others. I've learned that in business. Once someone deceives you—regardless of their rationale—they've done it, and they'll do it again. It's no wonder his chest exploded. Mine would too if I lived that way."

"Shut up you bastard," Simons, the investigative reporter, said. "You don't know what the hell you're talking about. You shoot from the hip. You never check out your facts. Don't forget I've done several pieces on you. You're not exactly up front in your dealings."

Bass stood up. His fist tightly coiled. "Are you suggesting I'm a crook? That I've earned my money illegally?"

"Not at all," Simons replied calmly. "All I'm saying is, first check the facts. Then come to your conclusion. I've been an investigative reporter for a long time. Webster had a good reason to hide his identity from us. Washington is filled with snakes. They'd eat this news alive. We may think it's no big deal going to a shrink, but tell that to Middle America. They believe you have to be having a nervous breakdown or confined to a mental hospital before you see a psychiatrist. I believe Webster was right. If word leaked out, and he had any ambition to run for a higher office, he'd

36

have an incredibly hard time convincing the masses he was stable enough to handle the job."

Steve Bass sat down.

"Thanks, Doug," Yvars said to Simons. "It took a lot of guts for him to admit his true identity. There was no upside to it. But," Mort paused, "Webster's death is not the only reason we've called this meeting. A Detective Davis called earlier today. Eileen Matthews was stabbed to death in her bedroom sometime last night."

A look of horror filled the room. Everyone was speechless.

"Who'd want to kill Eileen?" Lyle Stuart asked, rubbing his face. Even a small slash could end his TV stardom in one moment.

"The police do not have a motive as yet. Nothing at all to go on. I told them Eileen was as nice as they come. I couldn't imagine she'd have an enemy in the world," Yvars said.

"What about the crazies she'd pick up in those bars she had a habit of going to?" Stuart asked, still stroking his face.

Millie stared at Mort. They both knew what the other was thinking. Matthews and Webster were having an affair, or had had an affair. Millie was about to speak. Mort shook his head. "What are you hiding from us?" Simons asked.

"It's not relevant," Millie reluctantly replied. Mort was probably right, she thought. Why add fuel to the fire, especially with both of them dead? What would telling the rest of the group about their suspicion accomplish? Nothing, she concluded.

Hargrove began crying again. "She died without ever having had true love."

"Are your tears for Eileen or for yourself?" Bass angrily asked.

"Stop picking on Mary," Stuart said. "Just because she and Max don't have the perfect relationship doesn't mean she can't genuinely be sad for Eileen."

"Can we go now?" Simons asked. "I think we need some time to think about what happened."

"In a minute. There's something else." Yvars said.

Armstrong looked at Mort's watery eyes. "It's about Tyrone, isn't it? He's always been punctual. Never missed a meeting. Did he call? Is he alright?"

Millie broke in. "I'm afraid not. Tyrone's agent called today. He hadn't heard from Tyrone since Monday. He said Tyrone was to have had an audition late Monday afternoon. Supposedly, a hotshot recording company loved his music. They were going to sign him to a contract. Now it's too late."

"What do you mean?" an alarmed Armstrong asked.

"Tyrone's dead! His body was found by a stranger on a sidewalk in Tribeca. According to the medical examiner, he apparently developed a severe allergic reaction and died within minutes."

"I don't believe this," Bass roared. "Three out of the eight of us have died in the past two days; one of a heart attack, one of some weird allergic reaction which sounds like complete bullshit to me. I've never in my life heard of dying from an allergy. And one murdered! Are we cursed?"

Suddenly, the telephone rang. "I'll take it in the other room," Mort said to Millie. "Hopefully, it's Berger."

Millied explained to the group that Berger was the Chief Medical Examiner at Bellevue.

Mort walked into the back room. He picked up the cordless phone. He began pacing as Berger spoke.

"What the hell are you doing to your clients? I have another of your patients in front of me," Berger said.

"I know. Detective Davis told me they were taking Eileen Matthews to the morgue for a post. I figured you'd be involved. She was stabbed to death."

"Stabbed to death!" Berger exclaimed. "Like hell she was. Yes, she was stabbed all right. Directly in the small of her back, but the knife wound wouldn't have killed a mouse. It wasn't very deep."

"What are you getting at?" Mort could hardly get the words out. "If the knife wound didn't kill her, what did?"

"I'm not certain yet, but her preliminary findings are identical to those we found on Sawyer. Lots of eosinophiles in the blood. A flaccid heart. A complete over-reaction of the immune system. She didn't die from a stab wound. She died from an anaphylactic reaction. Just like Sawyer."

Mort slowly put the portable phone down, and made his way back into the office. All eyes were riveted on him.

"Well?" Bass asked. "Don't keep us in suspense. Millie told us Berger is the pathologist who did the autopsy on Sawyer. What did he say?"

Mort repeated his conversation with Berger.

Millie gulped hard. "I think we should cancel all of our future Monday evening meetings. Nobody knows what's going on. Not the police. Not the FBI. Not the medical examiners. Until they do, I think we'd be foolish to continue our sessions."

"I agree with Millie. Better safe than dead," Meg Armstrong, the melodramatic, romance novelist said. "Monday evening there were eight of us. Now there are five. Remember Agatha Christie's 'Ten Little Indians' I strongly recommend we stop meeting until answers are found as to why three of our members have suddenly died in the last two days. I know you all think I live in a fictitious world, but I don't believe I do. I tend to exaggerate. It makes for better fiction. But I don't invent truths. Face it; somebody is killing us off one by one. I don't know about the rest of you, but I want to be around to finish my latest novel."

The other four members of the group agreed with Armstrong. They all felt frightened. "Whether we have anything to be concerned about doesn't matter. Fear is fear." Simons said, standing up.

"If any of you feel the need to speak to us, please call," Millie said.

Mort wanted to reassure them that they were not in any danger. That they'd be safe. That there was no reason to cancel any future meetings. However, how could he? He didn't know if they really would be safe.

He believed Sawyer, Webster, and Matthews would be fine. All three were now dead. He dared not risk a fourth.

5

Yvars couldn't wait until Wentworth Hospital's weekly multi-specialty Grand Rounds would be over. Usually, he was the only psychiatrist on the staff who relished the hours of preparation and being grilled by the audience. But not now. Not today. For the first time, he wished someone else in the department had opted to replace him. None would.

Fortunately, the hour flew by.

Yvars, feeling greatly relieved, was making his way to the doctors' locker room to swap his long white coat for his much preferred blue blazer when he spotted Mark Jacobs, a fellow psychiatrist and close friend.

"Great job, Mort," Jacobs remarked.

"Thanks," Mort smiled. For a split second, Mort thought about talking to Mark, letting him in on what had been going on over the past three days. Mark was a good listener. Mort knew that. He also knew that these feelings welling up within him needed an outlet. Instead, he decided against revealing his worries, quickly said goodbye to Jacobs and hastily exited the doctors' lounge.

Mort stepped from the hospital into the sun-drenched courtyard. He thought about the inner space that was all his. As much as he tried to get beyond his self-imposed barriers, he realized he never had. Unconsciously, he must prefer it that way or else he realized, he'd have blasted through it by now. Why, he wondered, hadn't he? The answer was apparent. He knew what lay underneath. That incredibly terrified little boy. He never wanted to feel that type of pain again. The agony of reliving those frightening times with his father was a nightmare too scary to plunge back into.

Yvars waved to Cliff Dunbar, the tall, white-haired founder of Wentworth, who while now in his 80's, still kept himself involved with his creation.

Red geraniums and multi-colored begonias dotted the path leading to the hospital's multi-tiered garage. It was spring in New York. The season of rebirth, of renewal. He knew he should feel excited, alive. Yet all he could think about were Sawyer, Webster, Matthews, and their eternal winters.

****

Yvars slipped his brass key into the door lock and twisted it to the right. It wouldn't move. He tried slowly jerking the sturdy piece of metal, trying to make the proper connection. The double-barreled latch was unyielding. The lock was jammed. There hadn't been any problem yesterday. He had entered his office easily. What the hell could have screwed up the mechanism overnight, he wondered?

Suddenly, he remembered he hadn't used his key yesterday. Mollie, the middle-aged woman who rented the upper floor of the brownstone, didn't work on Wednesdays. Yesterday, she was coming through the front door on her way out, when Mort arrived. She had let him in. He hadn't needed his key. He recalled her talking about the increased incidents of violence in the city, but because she loved her job so much and the fact that she was single and all, she felt she'd be lonelier living in the suburbs. He recalled her asking whether any of his patients ever became violent. He did not answer. If only she knew, he thought.

After seven more minutes of tinkering with the lock in the brass cylinder, the key finally made contact; the front door opened. He made a mental note to make sure to call the locksmith and have him check the lock. Whatever was jamming the mechanism wasn't something he would be able to fix. As Jackie Mason frequently joked, Jews and gadgets were like oil and water. The two didn't mix. Goyim Fix! Jews don't!

Yvars walked behind his desk, opened the top drawer and pulled out the records on the patients he had scheduled for the afternoon along

42

with the charts on the eight members of the Thursday evening group meeting he and Millie would be conducting at 7:00 p.m. Thursday evening's group members all shared in a common propensity to violent acting-out behavior as well as drug abuse. They were extremely high-powered executive types. Millie had photocopied an article in last Sunday's New York Times pertinent to the inherent stress on those who forced themselves to climb the corporate ladder. Mort placed eight copies of the article on top of the group's folders to ensure he'd remember to hand each member a copy to reinforce their therapeutic goals. The patients appreciated information on issues they themselves faced; frequently, assimilating the information contained worked far better then if either Mort or Millie voiced the identical facts.

Mort was in the bathroom washing his face when Millie arrived 15 minutes later carrying a shopping bag filled with vegetables from a local Korean grocer and shoved them into the small refrigerator in the back room. He heard the refrigerator close and walked into the small room. "What did you get?" he asked, his eyes beaming.

"Don't get so excited. It's for an herbal recipe I've been meaning to try for several weeks now. Cold veggies and curry with mustard sauce and low-fat yogurt."

Mort made a face.

"I told you not to get your hopes up. I'll prepare it for dinner tomorrow evening. If you don't like it, I promise never to make it again. It's supposed to lower blood cholesterol."

"All of this health craze is downright boring," Mort said.

"I agree, but you're the one on this health kick. I'm just doing my best to find enticing recipes to camouflage the foods I know you hate to eat."

Mort planted a kiss on Millie's forehead. They walked into their main office. "Can I see your key for a minute?" Mort asked.

"Sure", Millie replied, snapping her purse open and handing Mort her entire set of keys. He glanced at the various keys on her key chain until he found the one he was looking for. He then took his office key out. He placed them side by side on his desk. "They look identical to me. What do you think?" he asked Millie.

"Of course they have to be the same or they wouldn't open our office door. Mort, what made you ask me such a question?"

Yvars explained the problem he initially had in unlocking the entrance doorway. Millie brought both keys closer to her eyes and studied them carefully. They look normal to me. Call O'Neil. He fixed our lock last year when we had problems with it."

Millie put her keys back into her purse, walked to the desk, opened the large top desk drawer and pulled out the files on their Monday evening patients.

"What are you up to?" Mort asked.

"I'm not going to tell you. You'll think I'm paranoid." She began scrutinizing each file. "When did you last make an entry on our Monday evening's group session?" Millie finally asked.

"Sometime Tuesday morning." Mort replied.

"Are you sure? Are you positive you haven't rummaged through these files since Tuesday morning?"

"Of course I'm sure. Why?"

Millie stared at her husband. "Am I not the most anal retentive, compulsive person you've ever known?"

"Yes. You know I think you are. Why?"

"Why? Look!" Millie replied, pointing to the files strewn out in sequence on top of their mahogany desk. "I always have all of our group members' charts arranged in perfect alphabetical order. You know that. It's my nature. I get nervous when they are out of order. Look here. See for yourself. Monday's patients. When I put the files back in the drawer late Tuesday afternoon, they were lined up just so. Alphabetically in order. Armstrong, followed by Bass, then Elliott, then Hargrove, then Matthews, then Osgood, I mean Senator Webster. I hadn't gotten around to moving the senator's name down the list after he told us to call him Webster and not

Osgood, so he still came after Matthews. Then came Sawyer's chart." She paused for a minute, thinking of Tyrone. He was her favorite. "And then there was Simons."

"What are you getting at?" Mort asked, confusion obvious on his face.

Millie pointed to the file folders lined up from left to right on top of the desk. "Look at the order the files are now in.

Hargrove/Bass/Matthews/Osgood/Simons/Elliott/Sawyer/Armstrong."

"Yes, so?" Mort queried.

"The files are now in a different order from the way I had them arranged. Tuesday I had each file correctly alphabetized. Now they are not. You said you haven't moved them since I put the folders back in the drawer. If you didn't rearrange them, and I certainly didn't, then pray tell how they've gotten out of place."

"Maybe you made a mistake. Isn't it possible you didn't do your usual thing when you put the folders back on Tuesday? I mean you are human. You were understandably very upset following Sawyer's and Webster's deaths."

"Mort, you know all about compulsive behavior. The more stressed I get, the more important it is for me to repeat my compulsion, until I feel I have done them correctly. Sometime it gets embarrassing, like checking two or three times to make sure I've turned off the oven."

Millie paused and glanced at the front door to their office. She then walked over to the door and moved her hand over the brass lock. "I now know the reason you had trouble opening the door. Somebody broke into our office. Somebody came into our office sometime between Tuesday evening and this morning. Somebody who obviously wanted information contained in our Monday patient group file." Millie retraced her steps and faced Mort. "Meg Armstrong made a comment during our emergency meeting yesterday that has been plaguing me."

"I don't remember anything that Meg said that could have been so striking you'd keep thinking about it. She's always joking during sessions," Mort replied.

"She was damned serious when she made her remark. It was the one having to do with Agatha Christies's 'Ten Little Indians.' Three of our Indians, Sawyer, Webster and Matthews, have been killed. Whoever broke into our office came with one purpose in mind. And that was to get the names and addresses of our other Indians."

"Millie," Mort shook his head in dismay. "Your imagination is running away with itself. Nobody broke into our office. The door lock is slightly jammed. That all! O'Neil will have it repaired in no time."

"Mort listen to me. Whoever killed three of our Monday group members now has the addresses of the remaining five. He is going to kill them," Millie paused. "Oh, my heavens!" She placed her hands around her face. "Whoever broke into our files probably did it after he killed Sawyer and Webster but, before he killed Eileen Matthews. I'm sure he got her address from our files, went to her apartment and killed her. We better warn the other five that there is a maniac out there."

"Calm down, Millie please! Nobody has proven anything so far. Three of our patients have died. I can't deny that sad fact. But as of now, we have no reason to suspect the deaths have anything to do with our group. Please, Millie. Be reasonable. Detective Davis is going to be conducting a full-scale investigation. I've learned in psychiatry that patience, precision and non-panic leads to success. We need to relax, calm down, and think more logically. Just as we tell our own patients to do."

"And the door lock? Was that another of Mother Nature's natural acts?" Millie asked sarcastically. "And my alphabetically arranged folders out of order. Explain that, Sherlock!"

"Please, Millie." Mort replied, trying to control his annoyance at Millie's persistence.

"Mort, by the time you lift your head up from under the sand and realize I'm the one who's been completely logical, it could very well be too late. By then another member of our Monday evening group might have been killed."

****

Mort greeted Jane Webster at the entrance to his oak-paneled office and directed her to a comfortable chair alongside Millie. He pulled up another chair and sat down. He hadn't remembered how breathtakingly beautiful the Senator's wife was. Millie handed Mort and Jane each a glass of iced tea. Mort gazed at his wife. Millie, short, petite, with her dark complexion and inviting smile. That's the wife he always wanted. The Jane Webster's weren't his type. They were for the others. Was it his lack of self-confidence that the Janes would reject him, or worse yet, laugh in his face? No, that wasn't it. The Millies made him feel warm, cozy, and comfortable. You wanted to come home after a long, hard workday to Millie, not to a Jane.

"Thank you for seeing me on such short notice," Jane Webster said.

"It's the least we could do," Mort replied, sipping his cold beverage.

The hours since the senator's death were clearly etched across Jane's face, Mort observed, especially after she removed her sunglasses and patted her watery, bloodshot eyes. Dark bands had begun forming under her deepened lids. "I need your help." She finally replied.

"Whatever we can do, we'll gladly do," Millie smiled, handing her a box of Kleenex lying on a nearby table.

"Thank you," the widow said, dabbing her wet eyes. She took a few sips of tea and placed the glass back on the tray. "I never told you, but initially, I was very much against Judd seeing you. Not you personally, but any psychiatrist. It was his sister who finally convinced me Judd needed help. I fee so guilty now. Maybe if I hadn't put up such a fuss, he'd have started seeing you sooner. Maybe he'd still be alive. I never should have objected so strongly, but I was afraid of his going to see a psychiatrist. Gossip spreads in Washington faster than a forest fire. Remember poor Senator Tom Eagleton. He was actually forced off the Vice Presidential ticket when word leaked out that he had, in the past, suffered from depression and needed psychiatric help. I knew Judd was ambitious. A possible

47

future run for the presidency was not out of the question. Several colleagues had already tried whetting his appetite. I tried reassuring him that he'd eventually adjust to his visual problem and once he did, our sex life would be fine again. I told him I loved him anyway, with or without sex. He didn't hear me. I don't know, maybe it's the way I said it. Eventually, his depression worsened. He couldn't sleep. He lost his appetite. He kept insisting his problem was far deeper than his sexual impotency and even more serious than worrying about his visual problem. He opened up and told me he was beginning to lose all of his self-respect. Self-doubts were starting to creep into his decision-making. I began feeling his suffering, but I still resisted his seeing a psychiatrist. In retrospect, I realize I was such a fool. Then when he became violent after drinking too much at a Washington, D.C. bar, his sister became insistent. She believed nobody would realize Judd was a senator if he called himself by a different name. He liked her idea. I felt reassured and relented. I never should have misled you when we met. I should have told you who Jeff Osgood really was. Maybe then he'd still be alive. Now it's too late."

"You have nothing to feel guilty about." Mort replied. Millie patted Jane gently on her shoulder. "Unfortunately, your worries about mental problems and their effect on politician's careers are well-founded. Physical problems are tolerated in Washington. Everyone realizes they are part of life. Everybody's life. However, mental problems are still viewed by many in Washington and elsewhere as a stigma. Many are frightened about them. What can I say? It's pathetic, but true."

"How can we be of help?" Millie asked.

"A man named Jackson, Chris Jackson, from the FBI came to our home early this morning. We talked for almost three hours. He had endless questions about Judd, about us, about our relationship. He wanted to know if we were having marital problems. He even asked if Judd had any enemies I knew about who might hate him enough to kill him."

Mort picked up his glass of iced tea and gulped half of it down.

"Judd wasn't murdered. I spoke directly to the medical examiner at

DC General. He assured me Judd had a heart attack and then hit his head on the dashboard. Death was instantaneous. The only saving grace is that the senator didn't suffer."

"Jackson believes otherwise." Jane Webster replied. "Jackson is convinced Judd's entire episode started with the gunshot wound to his left arm. The agency has listed his death as probable murder. According to the FBI, whether my husband died from a heart attack or a concussion isn't the point. The only thing that matters to them is the bullet and that somebody tried to kill Judd."

"Jackson told me he has put himself in charge of the case and will do everything in his power to personally make sure he finds the murderer. I don't want the FBI involved." Jane said.

"I've worked with the FBI on many occasions. In my dealings with them, I found they always do one hell of a good job. If Jackson feels he must investigate, I don't see what's the big deal. It's a nuisance but nothing more than that. In a few days, hopefully, Jackson will be satisfied Judd died of a heart attack—nothing else—and he'll drop the matter," Mort replied.

"I'm frightened, not for myself, but for William," Jane said, tears again rolling down her pale cheeks.

"Why frightened?" Mort asked. Millie leaned forward in her chair.

"When I called earlier today to ask if you'd see me, it was after Jackson had left. If the FBI is going to get involved, I need your help. If there is any chance Jackson is right, I want you, and not the FBI, to find out who tried to kill Judd."

"Why? They're the experts. The FBI does this for their living. They're excellent at investigating and following up leads. It's their bread and butter," Millie replied.

"When William was one, he and I went grocery shopping at a nearby Grand Union in Chevy Chase. I had him sitting in the front of the shopping cart. I wheeled him to the meat counter to get some chicken breasts for Judd to barbecue for dinner. Anyway, it took me a few minutes to find the chicken breasts. After I finally spotted them and was going to put them into the cart, William had vanished. He was nowhere in sight. I panicked. Who wouldn't? He was a one-year-old. He was able to walk some, but certainly didn't have the muscular coordination necessary to climb out of the shopping cart by himself.

"I ran throughout the supermarket screaming. I don't know what possessed me to waste time looking for him. I knew he couldn't have walked out of the store by himself. I knew what happened. He had been kidnapped."

A shocked Mort and Millie sat dumbfounded. "Didn't you go to the police?" Millie asked.

"Of course. Since it was a kidnapping the FBI took charge of the case immediately and almost screwed everything up. After two days, the phone call we were waiting for finally came. We set up the time, place and date for the exchange; William for money. All was in order. The kidnapper demanded Judd and I come alone. We agreed. The FBI led us to believe they'd adhere to our wishes. They didn't. They had two agents seated in a car parked only a few yards from where we were to meet the kidnapper. I can still visualize the entire scene vividly. It seems like only yesterday. The kidnapper spotted the two agents in their car and took off. I heard William screaming. I burst into tears."

"God works in mysterious ways. The tire had a blowout and the car crashed into a tree. Fortunately, William was in the back seat and unharmed. One of the agents jumped from his car, ran over and pulled William free."

"So yes," Jane paused and took several more sips from her glass of iced tea. "It did have a happy ending but…I am afraid with the FBI getting involved with Judd's death, something will happen to William again. He's all I have left. That's why I flew here this afternoon. I'm asking you to do me a favor. I know I'm asking for a lot, but please, if not for me, then for Judd, for William!"

"I wouldn't know where to start, how to begin," Mort replied.

"Judd's dead. Nothing will bring him back. I know that. I just don't want the FBI around. I think you can now understand why. If you can convince the FBI Judd was not murdered, I won't worry anymore. That's all I ask. Please." Jane begged.

"But the FBI will be in charge of the investigation regardless of whether I get involved or not. There isn't anything I can do to stop them from doing their job." Mort said.

"I realize that. But I'll feel better if I know I can count on you." Jane paused.

"When is the funeral? I'll call you after you return." Mort said.

Jane hesitated briefly before replying, "I hope you won't think I'm a terrible person, but I'm not going to go to the funeral."

Mort looked startled. "Why not?"

"I know I should go, but until Judd's killer is caught I'm afraid to leave William."

"Who said anything about not taking William. I took it for granted he'd be going with you."

"It's not worth it. Mrs Webster will probably be relieved."

"I don't understand," Mort said.

"You don't know my mother-in-law. Judd's sister even agrees it's probably best if we don't go. Ruth will take Judd's body back to Seattle. She'll return after the services. I'll arrange a memorial for Judd at our church."

"Believe me, it will be best for all this way."

"Mother-in law problems are very common. But at a time like this, regardless of how she feels about you, she'd want to see her grandson." Mort replied.

"Not Mrs. Webster. Mr. and Mrs. Webster never wanted me to marry Judd. Only his sister Ruth did. They felt my family was beneath them. They did all in their power to prevent our getting married. However, as long as my father-in law was alive, our visits were almost tolerable.

"However, at Judd's father's funeral, Mrs. Webster glared at me and

51

then slapped me across the face, blaming me for her husbands death. 'You killed him when you married Judd and took him away', she screamed. Judd stood there in shock. He said nothing. He never could stand up to her. She told me to leave the funeral. That she never wanted to see me again. I thought after William's birth things would change, but she stood firm. She's never even acknowledged William's birth. Judd tried reasoning; even at times pleading with her to be a grandmother to William. It was always to no avail."

Mort shot Millie a look. Their patients were their babies, their children. Judd Webster's death had brought her into their family. She needed their help and understanding. How could they refuse to help?

"We'll be in touch." Mort finally replied.

****

Mary Hargrove slowly rose from the couch and stared at Max. He was snoring; an empty beer can in his hand.

She walked to the TV, turned the volume on the Mets game up louder. "Max, you awake?" she asked.

He groaned momentarily before continuing to snore. Once satisfied he was asleep, she quietly walked into their bedroom and opened her closet. She then reached above her head and pulled a phone out from under several sweaters.

She took a deep breath before dialing the unlisted number. After the eighth ring she carefully replaced the receiver back into its cradle and returned the telephone to its hiding place.

"Damn you Jim. You're not going to get rid of me this easily." She muttered to herself.

6

Immediately following the hastily-called conference, Chris Jackson and two detectives from the 20th Precinct returned to his temporary office on the 21st floor of the FBI building on Federal Plaza.

Within an hour after Magadan, the Chief of the main Bureau in Washington, had been notified of Senator Webster's sudden death, he had insisted that Jackson lead the investigation. He had bluntly told him, "This is a rather ticklish case. My ass is on the line because of our fuck-up with the senator's kid two years ago. No holds barred. Do whatever is indicated, prudent or otherwise, but get me the bastard who killed Webster. I won't ask how! Just nail him!"

Drug busts, Mafioso arrests, even terrorist attacks paled in comparison to the potential impact of this case. Magadan couldn't survive another major screw-up, another humiliating blast from the media. His tarnished image and the reputation of the once mighty Bureau hinged on his trusted, long-time buddy.

The unexpected death of a senator, always front-page news, was made far more significant by the presence of a bullet imbedded in the senator's left arm. "Bullshit." Magadan raged, when the official pathology report came back stating the senator's death was secondary to a massive myocardial infarction and not from the bullet. The Bureau Chief hadn't risen to his lofty perch by filing away autopsy results, especially when one included an unexplained bullet wound. For Magadan, that was more than ample evidence to believe Webster had been murdered. The only question was would a hot shot Washington Post reporter beat the FBI to the killer?

Madagan couldn't, wouldn't tolerate that possibility becoming a reality. His solution: Jackson, a 240-pound former all-American tackle.

Just as Jackson had fought on the gridiron, so he did in his current battlefield: risking everything, holding back nothing. The legality of his techniques was often shunted to the side. He always did whatever it took to sack the opposing quarterback. Magadan was counting on him to use similar tactics to bring down whoever murdered the senator, without regard to consequences, no matter whose feathers he ruffled in the process. And with Jackson's winsome smile and charismatic demeanor, he was perfectly typecast to deflect the inevitable outpouring of the media.

Jackson had decided to set up shop in the small office in downtown New York City rather than conduct the investigation from Washington, based on a series of coincidences revealed by a special investigative tool of his own.

Jackson had earned an advance degree in Psychology at Georgetown University, survived a stint in Vietnam, and then entered the Bureau. He was instrumental in setting up the Violent Criminal Apprehension Program, a computerized national master file with particular emphasis on serial killers.

The agent had just completed an information session with two detectives, Davis and Brady, both from the 20th Precinct, which serviced the geographical location where both Tyrone Sawyer and Eileen Matthews lived.

Jackson informed the two burly detectives that 'VICAP', as his program was dubbed, was able to establish patterns in what previously would have been considered isolated cases. "The master file in my program," he told Davis and Brady, " has alerted us to a possible connection between these three recent, unexpected, sudden deaths. Two of the victims, Webster and Matthews, were shot in an extremity; the third, Tyrone Sawyer, had a severe burn mark on his leg. While no bullet was found, the discolored area was characteristic of a bullet gone astray. However, and this is what intrigues me," Jackson paused briefly, "the medical examiners' reports in all three cases, both Sawyer's and Matthew's here in the city and Senator Webster's in Washington, all listed heart failure as the cause of death."

"That's quite fascinating," Davis said. "We checked out Matthews and Sawyer extensively. Eileen Matthews originally looked like a fatal stabbing secondary to a botched burglary attempt, but when we found out nothing was stolen or even out of place in her apartment, we were quite puzzled. With Tyrone Sawyer, his death seemed more routine. The medical examiner diagnosed Sawyer's death as the result of a severe allergic reaction. We talked to everyone we could find who knew either Sawyer or Matthews. We came up with nothing. The medical examiner reassured us we never would. He agreed that it was odd Eileen Matthews was stabbed and a bullet found in her leg, but he was adamant that neither contributed to her death."

"Who are we to dispute a doctor's finding?" he asked Jackson. "He's the medical expert. He explained how there are many causes of heart failure and that Sawyer and Matthews were unfortunately victims of two such types."

Jackson smiled. "And the pathologist at D.C. General gave me practically the same scoop concerning Webster. The bullet wound was incidental. The cause of death, acute heart failure. In the senator's case, the failure according to the medical examiner, was the result of a heart attack."

Jackson peered out his window overlooking the city's skyline.

"What's the link?" Brady asked.

"I don't know," Jackson replied, directing his gaze back at both detectives. "None of the bullets hit any vital organs, nor was anything found under microscopic examinations in the surrounding tissues to raise suspicion. I don't know," Jackson paused, "but gentlemen, we will. Believe me, in a very short while, we will find out."

"What haven't you told us?" Brady asked. "Nobody in your position at the Bureau would sound as positive as you do about the connection between these three deaths without having something substantial to go on.

What is it?"

"All three of our victims were members of a psychotherapy group on the upper West Side. According to our computer data base, all the insurance claim forms were mailed to a psychiatrist, a Dr. Mort Yvars."

"Eileen Matthews' girlfriend told us about Yvars," Davis remarked, "And Sawyer's mother also mentioned her son had been seeing a psychiatrist." Davis paused, took out a pad from his coat pocket and thumbed through several pages. "He was also seeing Dr. Yvars."

Brady interjected. "C'mon Jackson. You're not about to tell us Senator Webster came in from Washington every week to see Dr. Yvars too, are you?"

"He certainly did. I had a long talk with his widow. She was initially reluctant to discuss anything that personal. But eventually, after extensive prodding, she admitted her husband had been depressed for over a year, but was afraid to see a shrink in Washington, believing someone would find out and ruin his future political career. Somehow, he was referred to Dr. Yvars and began seeing him on a weekly basis."

"That's amazing," Davis reluctantly admitted. "All three victims were patients of Dr. Yvars at the time of their sudden, unexpected deaths. I've been trying to set up a meeting with Yvars."

"Yes," Jackson replied, rubbing his thick hands through his closely cropped gray hair. "I think a call on the good doctor is in order."

"What about starting instead by talking to other relatives and friends of the victims?" Brady inquired.

"Or perhaps meet individually with the remaining members of the group to see if they can tell us anything?" Davis said.

"In due time, gentlemen. In due time," Jackson paused and patted his expanding midsection. "Yvars was in Washington on Tuesday. Webster was killed on Tuesday. That's reason enough to speak to the good doctor before anyone else."

7

Yvars led Jackson into his office. The tall, muscular agent carefully eyed the details in the large room and walked over to glance at Mort's diplomas before sitting down on the chair at the side of his desk. "I thought all New York shrinks practiced on the Upper East Side. Isn't that where the money is?"

Yvars sat down on the swivel chair behind his desk. Millie had filed away all the patients' records and cleared off the various magazines and mail Mort usually let pile up. He had to admit there was something calming about the lack of the usual clutter that invariably covered his large mahogany desk.

Mort smiled as he chomped on a carrot stick. "Not all of us went into psychiatry for the money. Some of us actually became psychiatrists because we really care about our patients. I'm a West Side type. My patients are mostly all West Side types. My wife and I like it better in this part of the city. It's quieter, the people more real and less pretentious. The cost of housing is far less expensive. It allows me to charge my patients more reasonable fees. Now let's get on with why you're here."

Jackson plucked out a pad and pen from his jacket pocket. "I'd like a run-down, a short biographical sketch on all eight of the patients in your Monday evening group. The three who were murdered and the five who are still alive."

"Nobody has proven any of the three were murdered. All three were signed out by the respective medical examiners as having died from natural causes."

"You're too intelligent to be satisfied with that diagnosis."

"It's hard to believe three of my patients were murdered."

"I understand but, with what we already know there isn't any other possible conclusion."

"I'm sure you are right. However, I'm still hoping there's another explanation possible."

"Fill me in on your eight group members and I'll be out of here."

"You should have asked my wife to be present. She's a far better historian than I am. Why did you insist on our meeting without her?" Yvars asked.

"I've learned when taking a history in these matters, one on one works best. I'll talk to her later."

Yvars signed. "Basically, all eight are, I mean were, genuinely nice, well meaning, well intentioned men and women who as a result of various events in their lives, eventually became unable to successfully cope and sought Millie and I out for help."

"I need specifics. The whys. Their psychological make-ups. Where they live? How they spend their time? Anything and everything that you feel might be pertinent in my investigation."

Yvars glared strongly at Jackson. "You know I can't divulge that kind of information. It's all privileged communications. Without my patients trusting that all they told me would stay confidential, they'd never open up, never reveal their inner thoughts or feelings. There wouldn't be any point to psychotherapy. Everything would come to an abrupt halt. People wouldn't get over their problems. These eight people, all of my patients, basically have a deep-seated trust problem. The only reason they eventually start expressing their innermost feelings is that they begin to trust me. They'd never do that if they didn't completely believe everything they said would be kept in strictest confidence."

"You sound very convincing. I'm sure Mike Wallace would love to hear you pontificate about patients' rights. But that's not going to help me. I have an investigation to head. As far as I'm concerned, we're dealing with murder. You've already voiced your disagreement with my conclusion. I'm in charge, not you! You can make this easy or difficult for yourself. The ball's in your court. But before you run me out, think about the Tarasoff case in California. I'm sure you're familiar with all the details," Jackson said.

"Of course. A psychiatrist was sued and lost a malpractice case when an ex-patient of his murdered his girlfriend. I don't get the connection you're trying to make between my situation and the Tarasoff case."

"Tarasoff lost the case because he believed his patient was capable of violence, but he decided not to call the police."

"But he notified the girlfriend's family. And anyway, the case has nothing in common with my patients' deaths."

"Violence was involved in both Eileen Matthews' and Senator Webster's deaths. You can't possibly disagree with that. I mean bullet wounds are the result of violent behavior, are they not?" Jackson sarcastically asked.

"I get your point," Yvars angrily replied.

"Then start cooperating. Remember in the Tarasoff case the courts ruled, and the law still stands as of today, that confidentiality between a doctor and a patient must be waived if the public, without this knowledge, might somehow be harmed. In these incidents it's said the public good must prevail over the patient's right for privacy."

Yvars moved restlessly in his chair. Jackson was sharp. Quick. There was obviously no way he'd be able to talk his way out of revealing whatever the FBI agent demanded to know. Mort inched forward in his leather, high-backed chair and sighed. "Where do you want to start?" he reluctantly asked.

"Tell me all you know about Tyrone Sawyer," Jackson requested.

"Tyrone was a super kid. All spit and vinegar. Incredibly ambitious and according to those who heard him perform, a very talented, modern day type, rock singer. He got into drugs. Got wasted once and busted a cop in the jaw. The court let him off provided he seek counseling. He was doing so well. His demo had attracted some big wig in the record business. He was so excited. Sad, real sad…." Yvars voice trailed off.

Jackson, writing as rapidly as Yvars spoke, looked up as Mort paused. "Do you know anything about his friends, who he hung out with? Things like that?"

"No. In our group we have a cardinal rule to keep the conversations, as much as possible, between ourselves. It brings out our patients emotions more rapidly and intensely. Once they become aware of these feelings, changes within begin. Of course, occasionally we deviate from our usual practice. Life doesn't exist in a vacuum. When events outside the group effect a member of the group, they will hopefully discuss it, but on those occasions, we try and keep the names of the others out of the conversation. Somehow making it more anonymous allows them to open up more easily than they would if particular names were mentioned."

"However, with those patients I see on an individual basis, I follow an entirely different set of rules. The more personal the better. With those patients, I get to know the whole cast of characters in their lives," Yvars paused. "On occasion, when Millie and I conduct our intake interview, we sometimes meet with a significant other besides the patient. For example, we talked with Tyrone Sawyer's mother twice. She filled us in on some the details of Tyrone's childhood-facts we thought would help us help him. She's a lovely woman. He was her whole life, I feel very badly for her."

"Were any of your Monday group patients also seen individually by either yourself or your wife?"

"No. None of them. We saw all eight only in our Monday evening group."

"Is that your usual practice?" Jackson asked, still scribbling as quickly as possible.

"I've learned after practicing psychiatry for years now, that nothing is either usual, customary or normal. All is relevant. Each patient is unique and is evaluated accordingly. For example, in our Tuesday morning group, I see two of the eight members privately, one patient twice a week and the other one once a week. Millie sees another patient twice a week. The other five we only meet with during our weekly two-hour group session. It really totally depends on the needs of the particular patient, his or her set of problems. There are no hard or fast answers. In certain ways, psychiatry is more of an art than a pure science. Much depends on your own feelings, rather than following a medical recipe."

"What about Senator Webster? Why was he seeing you?" Jackson asked.

"He became very depressed after he started having trouble getting an erection. He started feeling sexually inadequate and began drinking heavily."

"Why was he having potency problems?" Jackson asked.

"His night vision was deteriorating. He went to his internist who referred him to an ophthalmologist. An extensive work-up revealed him to be suffering from a rare hereditary disease called Retinitis Pigmentosa. The disorder consists of a slow, gradual destruction of the retina, starting with the periphery of the eye and working its way towards the center. Eventually, the patient's entire field of vision can be affected. The disease, because it's carried on a specific gene and is inherited as a dominant rather than as a recessive trait, will affect three out of every four offspring. That's 75%. Judd was, therefore, not only worried about his deteriorating night vision, but also feared that his son, William, would more than likely inherit the same disorder. However, since the symptoms of failing vision don't start until adolescent years at the earliest, and in the Senator's case not until he was 40, the ophthalmologist was unable to reassure Judd that William would not one day be struck down by the same condition. To compound matters further, the doctor said there was also no guarantee where the deterioration would end. He said some patients he'd been following for years were left with only visual problems at night. Others, however, eventually became completely blind. There was no way to predict. There was no treatment. He 'just had to deal', the doctor declared."

"However, Webster couldn't 'just deal'. He felt he had let his son down and also took it as an assault on his masculinity. He started feeling weak and inadequate. That's when he became sexually impotent. He began drinking heavily. One night he got into a violent fight at a local pub in D.C. Fortunately, the owner of the bar recognized him and took him into the back room before the police arrived. This episode further terrified Webster and made him feel he was completely losing control of his life. According to his wife Jane, his sister was able, after this outburst, to convince him to see a psychiatrist. However, he feared his clout, as a senator would be severely compromised were he to see a psychiatrist in the Washington area. Others he knew had their political careers ruined from depression severe enough to warrant intervention by a shrink. Another of my patients, known by the senator, recommended him to me."

"After a month, Judd's depression had lifted. He had begun to learn that having a physical problem was not equated with one's manliness. His sex life improved dramatically. While according to his ophthalmologist, his night blindness had significantly worsened over the year, he had indeed learned to put it into proper perspective."

"He was a perfect example of what I was referring to before as someone who had trouble trusting. When I met him, he introduced himself as Jeff Osgood. It's ironic. This past Monday he finally decided to reveal his true identity and the next day he's dead."

"Did you ever suspect he was using a false name?"

"No. Perhaps if I watched the evening news I would have eventually seen him. Known who he really was. However, Millie and I don't usually get home during the week until 9:30 or 10PM."

"Is there anything else I should know about the Senator?"

"Yes, there is. I haven't told his widow. I don't think I ever will. I can't see what good it would do. The guy's dead. Let him rest in peace. However, Detective Davis told me he and another of the members of our group who is now dead, Eileen Matthews, either were in or recently had an affair. Millie and I were both shocked."

"You didn't know?" Jackson asked skeptically.

"No we didn't. We were talking just prior to the group's meeting this Monday about how we perceived something odd, something different in this group than in any of our others. There seemed to be more familiarity among some, more hostility among others than we'd experienced in any previous group. We were going to discuss our suspicions as soon as either of picked up one of these sensations. Unfortunately, none occurred this past Monday."

"What can you tell me about Eileen?"

"She was a lovely lady. Quite stunning. Not only a knockout model but with brains to match. She was selected by the Port Authority to be in charge of the architectural renovation of the World Trade Center. An amazing coup considering that all of the largest firms in the country were competing against her. She came to see me on her own accord after she suddenly felt a violent urge to throw her sister's baby boy out the window. She was always terrified of losing control. She had begun realizing the difference between thought and action. These two completely different processes are frequently misinterpreted as one by very competitive angry people. She was at the stage of accepting that her rage was borne out of her frustration in not being able to get the baby to stop crying."

Mort stood up, walked to his bookcase and pulled out his copy of 'The Obsessive Personality'. "You might be interested in reading this excellent portrayal of Eileen's character type. A few days before she came to me, she found the man she was engaged to in bed with another woman. She freaked. It's very possible her rage was displaced from her fiancé onto the baby. Obsessive people like Eileen use the defense mechanism of displacement frequently. I can't prove any of this, of course, but given Eileen's terrible track record with men and the fact her sister's baby was a boy makes you wonder whether her rage would have been significantly less had the baby been a girl."

Jackson placed the copy of the book on Yvars' desk. "Who are the other members of your Monday evening group?"

"Steve Bass, Meg Armstrong, Mary Hargrove, Lyle Stuart and Doug Simons." Mort replied.

"What's Bass's story?"

Yvars walked back to his desk chair and sat down. "A real hard ass real estate type, but under the bravado and façade, he's a pussycat. Nice, maybe overly so. He came because of severe migraine headaches brought on by intense rage at a partner of his who screwed him royally in some big deal. He was so enraged, he threatened to kill the guy. His degree of anger frightened him. He was another example of someone confusing a wish with what they actually do in reality."

"And Hargrove?"

"Ah. Mary. Good old Mary. She's the prototype victim the talk shows love to get their hands on. A wounded bird in the true sense of the word. She lets everybody step all over her. Her husband, Max, neglects her but she's too insecure to leave him. She's absolutely without an iota of self-confidence, preferring the known enemy to what she's convinced would only be a worse situation. She doesn't feel entitled to a good life. She was referred by a colleague because she started hitting the bottle a bit more than usual in an unsuccessful attempt to suppress her mounting distress. However, one day her anger still got the best of her and she threw an ash tray at Max, missing him but smashing her television set. She's harmless. As I said, a real wounded bird."

"And Armstrong?"

Yvars pointed to several books on the lower shelf of his walnut bookcase. "Those are hers. She lives in a fantasy world populated by gorgeous, wealthy, big-breasted women and handsome, international hunks. Her gothic romances have netted her a fortune. But her real life is diametrically opposite to the ones she depicts in her novels. She developed a huge ulcer rather than vent her continual anger at her mother who had always devoted all her love and affection to her four sons rather than to her. Her mother admitted to her it was because they were men. Sons were important. Daughters were irrelevant. It's no wonder she hates men. Yet she is obsessed with getting married. A neurotic conflict if ever there was one. Whenever she starts feeling close to a man, any man, she starts carping and nagging unmercifully at him, finally pushing him away. Her biological clock, as she often puts it, is rapidly running out. She finally realized she needed professional help if she was ever going to get over her anger at men. Otherwise, she'd have to give up on her fantasy of marriage with kids and a picket fence and spend the rest of her days in creating fictitious passion for others."

"What's the scoop on Doug Simons? I must admit, I've read many of his columns. He doesn't come across as an angry guy."

"That's part of the fascination with being a psychiatrist. The work is never boring. Just when you think you know it all, and the days are becoming routine, in comes a Doug Simons and your adrenaline starts pumping all over again. He's one tough customer. I wouldn't want to mess with him. He's one hell of an angry guy. He's in the perfect profession. He loves nothing better than to dig up dirt on big wigs and let them have it in beautiful prose, three times a week. He's damn good at his job. He came for therapy after being passed over for a promotion he was convinced he deserved. He almost choked his editor to death."

Jackson flipped to a new page in his pad. "That's seven of the eight." He began thumbing through his scribbled notes seeking the name of the eight member of Yvars group.

"You don't have to look over your notes. Lyle Stuart is the eighth. He's every woman's, married or single, heart throb. He lives in the Village. I think he's latently gay. I don't think he's ever consciously had a homosexual thought or fantasy, but he overreacts whenever a guy makes a pass at him. Invariably, when anyone reacts in an exaggerated manner, there's something below the surface fueling the response. With Lyle, I think he's repressed his homoerotic tendencies. He was sent here by the director of his show after he became violent at a bar and shoved the guy who made a pass at him against a wall, breaking the fellow's arm. The studio feared that if the women who made their soap opera number one in the ratings were to find out about this incident, his image would be irreversibly tarnished and with it their show's ratings would dramatically plummet. They paid off the bartender and the victim to forget about what happened. The studio took care of all the medical bills," Yvars rubbed his hands together. "The matter was dropped. It's incredible what money can accomplish."

"You've been very helpful. These bios will give us a head start on our investigation," Jackson paused. "I almost forgot. I need all eight of your patients' addresses and telephone numbers."

Yvars pulled out his folders on the Monday group. "All but Senator Webster live in the area bordered by West 60th and 109 Streets and between Central Park West and the Hudson River." He quickly provided Jackson with the exact addresses and the specific phone numbers he requested. "Detective Davis informed me his precinct services that entire catchment area."

Yvars replaced the file in the desk drawer and stood up. "You don't think one of our Monday group members is somehow involved in these deaths, do you?" Mort asked.

"All eight of your patients came because of a history of violent behavior. You've acknowledged that."

"Yes, but...so have many of my other patients."

"I'm not interested in any of your other patients. At least not yet. I'll talk at length to each of the five remaining members of your Monday group and their close friends and relatives. If I feel none of them had anything to do with the three deaths, then I'll move on. But I've worked on many violent crimes during my years with the Bureau. In roughly 80% of the cases, the killer is someone known very well by the victim," Jackson replied, still seated.

"And I've been in this field for quite some time and have learned that frequently what smells like a rose and tastes like a rose isn't necessarily a rose."

Jackson stood up and faced Mort. "That brings me to my final question of the day. Why did you decide to go into psychiatry rather than one of the other medical specialties?"

"I don't see the relevance of your question." Mort replied.

"You're the psychiatrist in the a group where 3 out of 8 patients have died under very suspicious circumstances in less than one week. I think that's sufficient reason to want to know."

"You certainly don't think I'm responsible for their deaths," Mort angrily replied.

"Just answer my question."

Yvars rested his lower back against his desk and momentarily tried to relax his tense muscles. "I had many fears and an extreme lack of self-confidence. You could say I didn't like myself very much. During my third year of medical school, I was mesmerized by our psychiatry class. The field sounded incredibly fascinating to me. The mind is so phenomenally complex and in many ways is still a mystery. Dr. Milstein's program at New York University was highly regarded. I was accepted and did my training there. In retrospect, I've gotten to realize the deeper reason I chose to specialize in psychiatry was because I thought that through learning about the inner workings of the mind, I'd overcome my own problems while at the same time helping others." Yvars smiled. "But, unfortunately, I think I've done a better job with my patients than I have with myself. I still have a ways to go. I still can't go to the top of the Empire State Building without feeling panic-stricken. Forget the Statue of Liberty. Any tall building or enclosed spaces get to me."

Jackson continued writing feverishly on his pad. "What made you decide to focus specifically on the violent-prone patient?"

"Is this really necessary?" Mort asked.

"Yes."

"My father was very abusive. He'd frequently physically beat up my mother. I'd try to stop him and intervene between the two of them, but I learned the hard way he was too big for me. I retreated, began withdrawing. I became very shy and introverted. I began developing my fears. My analyst and I discussed this many times. Everything I've told you is all connected. I've just never been able to put all the pieces together and free myself of the past. It still haunts me."

"I felt if I could help both those who were abused as well as those who did the abusing to become aware of the feelings that made them either victims or abusers and teach them to channel these emotions in a more constructive way, they'd all benefit. The abuse would stop. Feeling victimized would end. Everyone would develop an inner self-confidence and gain self-respect." Mort said.

"What you hope to accomplish sounds incredibly idealistic. You've been a psychiatrist for quite some time. Do you still believe what you've said?"

"What are you getting at?" Yvars, his muscles tensing again, asked.

Jackson didn't reply. Instead, he stared directly into Yvars' eyes, through his eyes and into the recesses of the doctor's mind.

"Damn you," Yvars said, his tone furious. He paced to the window and stared at an elderly driver unsuccessfully trying to fit a Mercedes into a spot meant for a Volkswagen. He then turned and faced Jackson again. "You're making me very uncomfortable. I'm getting the feeling you suspect me of these deaths."

"I never said that. You did."

"You didn't have to. It's in your tone, in your body language."

"You did go to Washington this past Tuesday, didn't you?" Jackson asked.

"Yes."

"Senator Webster was killed that day. Why were you in Washington?"

"To attend a special lecture at Georgetown Medical Center."

"What made the talk important enough to travel all the way to Washington to hear?"

"Dr. Abramson was presenting his research findings on the criminal mind. While I specialize in violent prone patients, I've never treated a patient who actually committed a violent crime. The differences between the two groups fascinate me. I took the 8:30 AM shuttle, attended Abramson's talk and flew right back home."

"Did you talk to anyone while you were there?"

"No."

"What time was the lecture?" Jackson asked.

"10 AM."

"When did the lecture end?"

"At about 11:30 AM."

"When was your return flight?"

"1:30 PM." Yvars angrily replied.

"According to the Medical Examiner, Webster died sometime between noon and one. That would have both given you time to attend and still.....,"

Mort interjected vehemently, "I can't believe this. Jackson, you need a good shrink. I'm as far away from the profile of a violent-prone personality as anyone you'll ever meet." Yvars paused momentarily to regain his composure. "Now if you are finished, please go. I have a patient to see."

Jackson stood and walked to the door. "I'll be in touch."

****

A dour-looking, stout, middle-aged female peered over her reading glasses, pressed down on the intercom and announced Jackson's arrival. She then pointed to the open door on the right-hand side of the reception room.

A tall, medium-built, gray-haired man with a long white coat greeted the FBI agent. "I'm Dr. Milstein," he said warmly. "Please come in. I'm sorry I've had to keep you waiting so long, but I've been swamped lately, even more than usual," the head of New York University's psychiatric residency program said.

Jackson looked at the furniture, which resembled remnants from the Salvation Army. "I know the aesthetics leave much to be desired. It's not like in the old days. But the budget squeeze is everywhere," Milstein said apologetically. "Cuts here and there. Not exactly how you pictured a prosperous New York shrink's hangout, is it? Those offices do in fact exist,

69

but primarily on the Upper East Side. Here we make do. It's like the Day's Hotel chain. No frills. We have a great staff, superior students and residents, but if it's glamour you're after, best head uptown. The Whitney Pavilion at New York Hospital gets four stars."

"Tell me about Mort Yvars," Jackson abruptly asked, interrupting the loquacious doctor.

"Ah, Mort!" Very smart. Diligent. Personable. A real hard worker. I've followed his career with great pride. Keeping abreast of our residents after they graduate is one of the really gratifying parts of heading the residency program year after year. You get a wonderful feeling from your students' successes, and Mort Yvars has had many."

"I'm sure he has. I don't mean to be rude, but I'm here for a particular purpose. Three of Dr. Yvars' patients—all, it so happens, members of one of his groups, were killed in the past week. I need to find out more about Dr. Yvars other than his conscientiousness and capabilities."

"You think Mort might be responsible for those three deaths?" a shocked Dr. Milstein asked.

"I didn't say that. I just want to know more about his psychological make-up. I figured who'd know better than his mentor during his residency years."

"Well," Milstein paused, "I'm sure it's nothing, but during Mort's second year of training I had to force him to go into analysis. Most of our candidates voluntarily decide to go into therapy during their three-year stint here. Mort didn't. I wasn't going to press the issue since going into therapy, while an excellent idea for a budding therapist, isn't mandatory. However, as his second year wore on, he started getting irritated at several of his patients and actually screamed at one particular young man who refused to listen to one of Mort's insights. The floor nurse overheard the yelling and came to see me. I spoke with several of his supervisors who all agreed that lately he had become hostile with those he was supposedly trying to cure. I met with Mort and demanded he seek professional help or I'd regrettably have to ask him to leave our program. I emphasized how we

70

tolerate a great deal here, but the staff were worried he was losing it." Milstein moved towards his wall-to-ceiling metal file cabinet. He quickly thumbed through many files in one of the lower drawers until he eventually pulled out a thick folder. He opened the record and flipped through several pages before continuing. "I sent him to a Dr. Hugh Schwartz. He's a top-notch analyst. He still practices full time on the Upper East Side. His address is 171 East 81st Street. I think he's the one you should direct your questions to. Hugh treated Mort for two and a half years. If anyone will know Mort's innermost dynamics, he will. I'll call Schwartz and tell him you'll be contacting him."

Jackson thanked Milstein, walked out of the medical center, sidestepped a sleeping, homeless woman propped against a wire-meshed, tall garbage pail and hailed a taxi.

8

Yvars, pulling his helmet down firmly in place, shifted the gears downward on his bicycle, and pedaled rigorously into the entrance of Central Park at 67th Street. He breathed in deeply, a fine mist wetting his hair and face. He relished rising early on Saturday mornings-the start of the weekend. All play no work! Millie's black glistening birthday gift, in less than two months, already registered over 210 miles on the odometer. "Why do you always have to be such an extremist?" his wife constantly asked. Moderation wasn't his thing. Whether food, or now bicycling through the park, he went all out. The middle of the bell shape curve bored him. "Sleep in," she'd admonish him. "What's the hurry? You have all weekend. Why the rush?" But she knew! He loved the early morning hours, quiet, peaceful, hardly any traffic, even on damp dawns, with the dark, ominous clouds above providing an almost surrealistic view of the greenery.

This morning he felt an increased need to mount his bike and accelerate it as fast as his muscles could endure. The more rapidly he rode, the less he thought about his anger at that damn FBI agent. The easier it was becoming to suppress his rage. How dare the bastard consider him a suspect in the deaths of three of his own, of harming anyone. Fearful, kind, gentle Mort! He continued climbing the steep hill; passing a large boulder on his left and several joggers and dog-walkers on his right.

His tires sped over an art graffiti scene on the pavement depicting a couple locked in an oral-anal embrace. Only in New York, he thought. What a city! He loved yet feared Manhattan. So many oddballs. So many who didn't value life; willing to snuff out others for a thrill. And that, he realized, he had felt well before the recent unexpected and bizarre deaths of his three patients. Since completing his residency, part of him wanted a more suburban, safer, more relaxed existence; but the side that wanted, needed excitement, that hoped to master his fears, dictated living in the city. Millie's desire to live in the city made the decision easier. Perhaps one day, after he overcame his fears, he and Millie would head for the burbs. But not now. Migrating north with his fears intact would symbolize cowardice; diminish his self-respect. He refused to let himself give in.

Yvars swerved, just missing a frail, elderly woman being led by five large assorted breeds of dogs, each pulling in different directions, honing in on their favorite spot to further wet the already saturated grass.

Mort weaved his way onto the dirt bike path adjacent to the paved road.

A figure peered out from behind a thick oak tree, 25 feet away. In the right hand, a small pistol. The stranger waited patiently as Yvars' bicycle approached. The stranger had observed the psychiatrist's every move for several days now; had his routine down pat. Mort was now ten feet closer. In five seconds, he'd be in range. The stranger cocked the gun. Yvars drew nearer. Then the trigger was pressed. Suddenly, a female jogger darted diagonally in front of Mort. Yvars instinctively spun his front wheel to the right. The bullet hit the thick front tire and all the air rushed out. Yvars fell from the seat. The spokes smashed into his left leg and his head hit the dirt.

The young woman immediately stopped jogging, rushed to Mort's side and bent down. "I'm terribly sorry. Are you okay?" She nervously asked.

Mort felt momentarily dazed, his left side aching. She slowly helped him to his feet. "Do you want me to get a doctor?"

"No, that's okay. I didn't see you coming. I took my eyes off the path. I must have run over a rock or a piece of glass."

Mort brushed himself off and stared at his front wheel. The tire was completely flat. He leaned over and began examining the tire, looking for the tear in the rubber. He couldn't find it. Maybe the tire could be repaired he thought, but he doubted it. He couldn't fix flats and the owner of the bicycle shop on 81st Street and Columbus would more than likely insist he needed a new tire. Oh well, he muttered to himself, that's what you get for living in the city. Grin and bear it or move out. He slowly stretched his aching left side. It didn't hurt that much. Big deal! He'd simply walk his prize possession to the rip-off artist on Columbus, buy a new tire and return for the rest of his morning ride. He reached for his wallet to make sure he'd brought enough cash. His spirits suddenly sank. He hadn't brought his wallet with him. He'd left if home. The owner demanded cash. He'd have to go home. Millie would demand an explanation. She'd convince him he'd had enough of an adventure for the day. He slowly began walking his wounded bicycle from the park. He'd have to wait until tomorrow to return.

The stranger kicked the large oak tree, replaced the revolver in a jacket pocket and quickly disappeared into the deep surrounding brush.

****

Jackson hopped out of the cab in the theater district, peered at the list of Yvars patients and headed toward West 43rd Street, to the editorial offices of The New York Times, and his scheduled visit with the investigative reporter, Doug Simons.

Jackson had hoped to be able to talk to the psychiatrist Mort had been treated by while a resident at NYU. However, Dr. Schwartz was busy with patients and wouldn't be available until 4:00 PM. It was now only 12:30 PM. The FBI agent reluctantly rearranged his priorities. He'd talk with Simons. If time permitted, he'd talk to another of Yvars patients, by then it would be 4:00 PM. Schwartz would be free.

The tense receptionist at the desk led Jackson into Simons' office. He scanned the room, appalled at the peeling paint and well-worn furniture. His eyes took in the myriad of photographs dotting the walls, depicting the smiling reporter shaking hands with dignitaries, the famous and the infamous.

Simons was screaming expletives into the phone when he looked up at Jackson. He quickly slammed down the receiver and turned to the agent. "So, what brings you here?" Simons asked. "My secretary told me it was important, but she didn't know what you wanted to talk to me about."

"It's about what's been happening with your Monday evening group therapy members. The FBI has put me in charge of finding out who's responsible for these murders."

Simons nodded his head. "I understand. Our two jobs are really very similar. To excel as an investigative reporter, I have to follow-up on all leads; some clear-cut, others I come up with on my own. You obviously must do the same. Five of our group are still alive. One of us might be the killer."

"Exactly. I'm glad you understand. It makes my work quite a bit easier. Why did you go into group therapy initially?" Jackson asked.

"What difference does it make why I went into therapy?"

"Obviously, the more information I have the sooner I'll be able to figure out who might have murdered all three patients."

Simons sat back in his moth-eaten, upholstered chair and laughed. "You got an example a few minutes ago. I have quite the temper. I became absolutely outraged when I was passed over for a promotion. I was sure I'd become chief of our New York bureau. I had the credentials. The experience. Everything!"

"How did you show your outrage?"

"I ranted, raved, kicked my desk. I fired my secretary. She's the one who let you in. She's the best. Naturally, when I regained my sanity the next day, I rehired her. It cost me another $1,500 a year, but she's well worth it. In the end, she was the one who convinced me to see a shrink. At the time, I thought what bullshit. But she pleaded with me to give it a shot. Mort Yvars evaluated me, thought my problems would best be solved in a group rather than in an individual setting and started me in his Monday evening group. I've been going regularly, mess up occasionally, things come up. You know modern life! It's not easy to pull yourself away from

75

your work come 6:00 p.m. every Monday to sit around a table talking about your feelings. At times it seems a waste but.." Simons paused.

"Can you tell if there's been any change within you since you started in the group?"

Simons smiled. "After my recent outburst, you probably don't think so, but seriously, the meetings have helped considerably."

"How so?" Jackson asked.

"Millie, Mort's wife, has been especially helpful. She got me to realize it's the big picture that counts. I can be the best investigative reporter in the world, but if I'm a pain in the ass and make others feel like shit, I have to expect shit in return. She calls it consequences for one's actions. It took awhile, but eventually her message sank in. I had a father who was a real screamer. We all submitted out of intimidation. It worked well. Things at home went peacefully. Mort got me to realize despite hating and fearing my father, I had unconsciously identified with him. In other words, my unconscious had permission to rail against whomever I felt I wanted to, regardless of whether I'd be blown out of the water or not. I had, without realizing it, become my father."

"Have you ever become violent?"

"You really zero in don't you?" Simons asked.

"It's my job."

"I almost strangled my chief editor when I was told I wasn't going to get his job. Does that qualify?" Simons laughed again. "But since I've entered therapy, as the others in the group are fond of telling me, I'm all bark and no bite. I give the Yvars a hard time, jerking them around with their bills, but I'm not really serious about that. They deserve what they get paid. My wife will attest to that fact. I don't really get angry much at all these days. And when I do, she simply puts cotton in her ears and waits for my tirades to end. The final proof that the group, or something, has clicked is that I recently had my annual review. My chief commended me on the changes he'd observed, wanted to know if I was on medication. He was so impressed by my new attitude, as he labeled it, that he was going to put me up for a promotion, to be head either of our office in the city or in our Washington bureau."

"What about Dr. Yvars? What's your read on him?" Jackson asked, getting to like Simons the longer they spoke.

"Mort. Pudge, as we now call him since he's trimmed down. He's a great guy. Warm caring. I'd do anything for him. Same for his wife. Wonderful people. Excellent therapists."

"Did you know much about the three patients in your group who've been killed?"

"I'd be one pathetic investigative reporter if I hadn't known. I recognized Webster immediately. I decided not to let on."

"Why didn't you bring it up. I thought group therapy was all about expressing, emoting, being honest, open."

"It is. I had my reasons for not wanting to reveal Osgood's true identity."

"Which were?" Jackson asked.

"I'm no saint. I was waiting for rumors about a scandal on the Hill to circulate. Then I'd strike a deal. My continued silence about his cover-up in return for some juicy information."

"You are a piece of work." Jackson replied nodding his head in disbelief.

"You better believe it. Since Webster's death I have begun my own investigation. Hopefully, I'll hit on something that might interest both of us."

"What did you know about Eileen Matthews?"

"Only that she was one hell of a sexy lady."

"Anything else?" Jackson asked.

"I suspected she and the senator might have been having an affair."

"Why was that?"

"Nothing specific. Mainly body language. The way they'd look at each other."

Jackson lifted himself from the uncomfortable chair. "One more question. What were you doing this past Tuesday?"

"I was waiting for you to get around to that. I was here at the Times all day. Ask my secretary. I almost drove her crazy that day. I had a deadline to meet and I was slightly unglued."

"Thanks for your cooperation. I'll be in touch if I need to talk to you again."

"Anytime," Simons smiled.

****

Jackson glanced at his watch. It was only 2:45 PM. He still had another hour and fifteen minutes until Schwartz would be available. He took his pad out from his jacket pocket and peered at the other names on his list. He began calling each of them. Hargrove and Stuart couldn't meet with him until tomorrow. Bass wouldn't be in the city until Monday.

Meg Armstrong was the only one able to see him on such short notice. He began walking uptown to her apartment. The light rain had let up. The gray thick clouds still lingered.

After four rings, a red-haired woman, tall and heavyset, opened the apartment door. "You Jackson?" she uttered, her eyes undressing him. She led him into her living room.

"Care for a cup of coffee?" she asked, holding a mug of black espresso in her firm right hand. "This stuff keeps me wired, fully awake. It allows me to stay up all night creating if I want to."

Jackson politely refused. He glanced around the small studio apartment on West 68th Street. The place looked like it hadn't seen a vacuum cleaner or a dust mop in months, perhaps years. There were even cobwebs on the faded draperies and coffee stains interspersed between the weave of the stark yellow throw rug in the center of the sparsely furnished room. The one modern, up-to-date piece of furniture in the far corner of the room was a black Formica desk with a computer and laser printer resting on its top. "I appreciate your seeing me on such short notice." Jackson finally said.

"It's no big deal. It's not like I had to cancel anything. I have all the time in the world. I live for my books. Other than that, I'm all yours."

Jackson moved back several feet. The large woman bothered him.

"I have no friends," she continued. "Just me and my stories. They are companions enough." She pointed to her unkempt long hair. "Don't get me wrong. I don't expect nor want self-pity. I like my life this way. My characters are far more entertaining than any real person I've ever met. You can shut them off whenever they start boring you. Better yet, you fine tune their character, slip in a quirk here, a wild desire there, and presto, they now perk you up and stimulate you again. Besides, they can't hurt you. They don't reject. You do all the rejecting." She paused. "Would you prefer a martini to coffee?"

"No. I'd just like to ask a few questions. I hope I won't offend you, but since you are aware three of the eight members of your Monday evening group have recently been killed, I think you can understand I need to talk to you on the off chance you might be able to help me sort things out. Were you at all involved with either Matthews, Sawyer, or Webster?"

Armstrong let out a booming laugh. "Right! A lesbian fling with Matthews. Pedophilia with Tyrone Sawyer. A whirlwind of an affair with one of the handsomest men I've ever met. You wouldn't know this, but when I thought he was that Osgood chap, I made him my male protagonist in a 'Gone with the Wind' type saga. He was quite a turn-on according to my fan mail."

"I didn't mean it that way," Jackson sheepishly replied.

"Ah, I get it now," Armstrong beamed. "I'm a suspect."

"I didn't say that."

"That's perfectly all right. I always wanted to be a suspect. Just like in my novels. What do you want to know?"

"Whatever you think might help me sort out what's going on."

"I love it. I'm sure by now you've spoken to Dr. Yvars and he's told you all about me. My detectives always check up on their suspects before confronting them."

"I have."

"What did he say about me?"

79

"I'd rather hear your comments about the others in your group."

Meg gulped down several large swigs of her bitter, hot brew. "Unfortunately, I never had anything to do with any of the three other than during our weekly sessions. They all seemed to be very nice and caring people. It's sad, but who in the Big Apple doesn't eventually get murdered, mugged or raped. I've already jotted down a few ideas on how I'm going to incorporate their deaths into a future novel. Anything else?"

Jackson was shocked. He couldn't comprehend how those slick, beautiful, affluent jet setters that populated Armstrong's romantic novels sprung from the woman standing in front of him. It didn't jive. Human nature, he mused, was still a mystery to him. "You never socialized with them, not even once, or knew of anyone in the group who might have?" Jackson finally asked.

"Nope. Don't you want to know if I had a motive to kill them?"

Jackson couldn't believe he was having this conversation. He couldn't believe this Armstrong woman was for real.

"Well, I didn't," she continued.

"What made you start therapy?"

"I went to Dr. and Mrs. Yvars because I was blowing another relationship. It was sort of a pattern of mine. That is before I swore off men and began sticking with my characters. You might not be able to tell by my outward appearance, but lots of guys are turned on by me. And this happens well before they find out I'm both fantastic in the sack and a famous writer. Anyway, Greg was starting to get to me. I slapped him several times hard across his face. Bloodied his lip. Scared myself. I called the American Psychiatric Association's Direct Branch here in the city, explained my problem, and they referred me to Dr. Yvars. I'm sure you know he's an expert on those, who like me, have short fuses. He and Millie made me realize how their love and caring contrasted dramatically with the cold neglectful way my mother raised me. My brothers were the princes. I was Cinderella. Greg, I came to see, represented my brothers. They took and took. They never gave. Greg even looked and behaved like they did. He

80

was the fourth in a row of similar type men. I must somehow attract them like bees to honey. Then after I start getting close, they stir up all of my hidden hatred for my brothers. Mort and Millie forced me to become aware that once I put these men in that slot, I'll destroy the relationship. Millie once put it in its proper context. Sooner or later, she said, I'd turn these men into my three brothers who I not only hate, but I'm also incredibly jealous of because they got all of mother's love, while I was shunted aside to do the cooking, the cleaning, the picking up after."

"Any more questions?" Armstrong asked.

"Where were you on Tuesday?"

"Sitting on my fat ass pecking away on my typewriter."

"Can anyone confirm your story?"

"You sound exactly like my detectives. No, no one can. I don't go out when I'm writing a novel. I also take my phone off the hook during the week. Nobody can vouch for my alibi. It's up to you to decide whether I'm telling the truth or if I'm hiding something."

Jackson checked his watch. It was 3:30 PM. If he left now, he'd arrive at Dr. Schwartz's by 4PM. "Not right now. How can I reach you if I have any further questions?"

"If it's a weekday, you'll have to come back to this apartment. On Saturday or Sunday you can call and I'll pick up."

****

This was more like he envisioned a shrink's office, Jackson thought, as he sat on a thick, brown leather chair in Dr. Schwartz's well-appointed waiting room. The office reeked of money, paid for no doubt by well-heeled clients.

Within two minutes, a friendly looking, frail, elderly man with a short-cropped, gray beard feebly walked towards Jackson. "What do I call you, Detective? Agent? Sir? I've never talked to anyone from the FBI before."

"Jackson will do just fine," the agent replied. They headed slowly into Dr. Schwartz's oak-paneled office with it's 19th century Regency desk

81

and a group of four matching 19th century Regency chairs. In the far corner of the room, Jackson glanced at the typical shrink's couch as portrayed countless times in the movies. He noticed the old man had a severe head tremor and that his hands shook uncontrollably.

"It's Parkinson's. Getting old sucks, but as they say, it's better than the alternative. Dr. Milstein filled me in on why you wanted to see me. Don't bother reminding me of the Tarsoff case; I'm well aware that I have no choice but to answer your questions. I'll try to summarize Mort Yvars as succinctly as possible. Hopefully, what I'll tell you will be helpful."

Dr. Schwartz spoke softly about the nervous, heavyset young resident. He never felt he was totally able to penetrate through the mental wall Mort had erected around himself. "It doesn't happen often. As a psychiatrist, I have many techniques I utilize to pry the difficult cases open. However, on occasion, nothing works. It becomes very frustrating. Mort was one of the more frustrating ones. I felt sorry for him. Frustrated, but sad. I always sensed an emptiness, a loneliness hidden under his ever-present smile. Mort had a tough time with his father. According to Yvars, his father frequently abused him. He mentioned several times being tied to a chair and once being locked inside a closet. Grim stuff. When the father drank, things even deteriorated further. He would physically hit his mother. When Mort tried to intervene, he'd get walloped but good. Once, his mother had to take him to the hospital with a dislocated shoulder caused by his father shoving him against the wall."

"Even his one warm memory of his father was pathetic. He and his father were out buying groceries. His father accidentally locked the car with the keys still inside. He pulled out a large paper clip and showed his son how to use it to pop open the lock. He told him to always carry a similar type paper clip wherever he went. When he relayed this story, he reached into his pocket and pulled out a large paper clip. Streams of tears rolled down his face."

His therapy wasn't a complete failure. He made progress, significant strides. He slowly began realizing how much rage and anger lurked behind his smiling veneer which occasionally erupted. For example, I'm sure Milstein told you about the patient who refused to accept his pearls of wisdom. Mort lost it and began verbally abusing the poor guy.

While, as I said, I never felt Mort fully resolved his anger towards his father, he did learn to channel his anger well; learning to become aware of the emotion and nipping it in its early stages before it built up strength to seethe over. He did gain 25 pounds during the course of treatment, so perhaps he displaced some of his anger through excessive eating," Schwartz concluded.

"Tell me, doctor, if you can—what might happen if Yvars stopped channeling his anger well, or as you said, stopped displacing in into overeating? Is it possible Yvars could turn violent?"

Schwartz shuffled his stiff legs slowly before replying. "If the conditions were frustrating enough and at the same time Yvars also stopped displacing his anger, for example, say he went on a strict diet, then yes. I'd say he's the type who could then blow, could become extremely angry!"

"Angry enough?" Jackson asked.

Schwartz burst out laughing. "Mort kill! Never!"

"You just said he could become extremely angry."

"Angry, yes. Pound his fist against a wall perhaps. Yell and scream maybe. But kill? Never! I hope I have answered your questions sufficiently. I have to excuse myself, my 4:30 PM patient is waiting."

"You may be hearing from me again," Jackson replied.

"Any time," Schwartz said shuffling to the door.

9

Jackson was showering when the phone unexpectedly rang. He stubbed his big toe on the raised piece of metal as he hurriedly stepped out of the diminutive stall, cursing the Bureau for the tiny apartment they'd rented for him in Battery Park City for the duration of his investigation into Senator Webster's death. His momentary anger was suddenly lifted by the voice on the other end of the line. It was Millie Yvars calling. She apologized for the lateness of the hour. However, she was terrified. Millie pleaded for him to please come to their apartment as soon as possible. Mort had fallen off his bicycle while riding through Central Park earlier in the day. Her voice trembled as she recounted the details of her husband's accident. Mort was convinced his tire had had a blowout when pierced by either a jagged stone or a piece of glass lying on the dirt path. She was equally as certain the rubber was punctured by a bullet. It was too coincidental, she maintained. Three of their patients killed. Mort's freak mishap. She was frightened that Mort was soon to be the killer's fourth victim.

He hadn't removed his thick finger from the buzzer when Millie, in a brightly colored Laura Ashley print dress, greeted him. Mort, in his bathrobe, reluctantly nodded to the agent while Millie led him into their spacious living room.

Jackson eyed the lovely pieces of Art Nouveau furniture in the tastefully decorated room. "I can see you've done all right for yourself, even if you do practice on the West Side," he said to Mort, trying to slice the obvious tension in the air.

"Thank you, but Millie deserves all the credit. It's her doing. The place looks far more expensive than it really is."

"I feel foolish Millie dragged you here so late at night. But you know women. I couldn't reassure her no matter how hard I tried. She insists I was shot at while bike riding in the Park earlier today. She is firmly convinced that a bullet missed hitting me, but struck my front tire instead. She wouldn't shut up until I relented and let her call you," Yvars said, still inwardly seething over Jackson's insinuations on Friday.

"It's no bother". Jackson replied.

Millie approached Jackson. "If you were only here yesterday when Mort came home after the accident. He had the saddest look in his eyes, cradling the bike as if it were a baby. The bike is in one of the guest bedrooms." she said. The FBI agent followed her into a small rectangular room decorated in the French provincial style. The mountain bicycle was lying against the four-poster bed.

Jackson bent down and carefully scrutinized the tire. He asked Millie for a large glass of water and a thick towel. She walked briskly into the bathroom, returning with both items. Jackson laid the towel over the carpet. He then poured water over the tire's entire surface and methodically combed the area looking for the hole in the rubber. He finally spotted it.

"I told you, Mort," Millie said to her husband as the agent pointed to the tear in the tire. "Three of our patients were killed this week. I don't want to lose you. Mr. Jackson has just found proof that your tire was flattened by a bullet." Millie paused and turned to the agent. "Will you please tell my stubborn husband how serious this is? That whoever killed our three patients is also obviously out there trying to kill him." She paused and turned towards Mort. "Good God. How much more evidence do you need before you'll be convinced your accident wasn't caused randomly?"

Jackson stood up and eyed Millie. "I haven't said this flat tire was caused by a bullet. You did. I think your husband is probably right. The hole looks far too small to have been the result of a bullet. I've seen every type of bullet hole in my time, all caliber bullets, from every conceivable type of gun. Bullets invariably make far larger holes than this one. I agree

85

with Mort. The flat most likely occurred when his tire ran over some natural object, such as a stone. These tires are very fragile. I know the manufacturers tell you otherwise, but they are, especially if you ride on dirt paths."

Mort felt relieved. Millie still wasn't reassured. "How many flat tires have you previously checked out?" she asked.

"Several," Jackson replied.

"Car tires? Bicycle tires? Both?"

"Well, not both. Only car tires. But rubber is rubber and bullets are bullets. I understand your concern, but there's nothing to worry about. Nobody shot at Mort. It was only an accident. Nothing more. Fortunately, Mort wasn't injured."

They all walked back into the living room.

Jackson then turned and faced Mort. "I spoke to Doug Simons today. I didn't expect him to have such a high pitched voice."

"He's very sensitive about it."

"What did he have to say?" Mort asked.

"He's quite clever. I can see why he's so good at his job."

"Meaning?" Mort inquired.

"He's always known who Osgood really was."

"Why didn't he mention it in group?" Millie asked.

"He was waiting for the opportunity to make a deal with Webster. He'd maintain his silence in return for information concerning a hoped for scandal that was ready to erupt on Capital Hill. Something sufficiently juicy for his readers. Unfortunately, he never heard any rumors circulating that warranted his confronting the senator during the time he was in your group."

"That was probably one of the vibes I sensed," Millie said.

"There's more," Jackson continued. "Simons is also very perceptive. He felt something was going on between Matthews and Webster."

Mort nodded his head in disbelief. "This is all so ironic. To start a therapeutic relationship with a patient I have to fully trust him. Simons on the other hand enters therapy suspicious of everyone. Suspiciousness has it pluses. It forces you to develop antennas. You then pick up signals others, including trained psychiatrists, either miss altogether or don't catch for quite sometime."

Millie interjected. "That's true Mort. However, I wouldn't want you to become a paranoid therapist."

"I also spoke to Meg Armstrong. What a character." Jackson said.

"Was she helpful?" Mort asked.

"She was entertaining. Whether she will turn out to be more than that remains to be seen."

Mort was about to thank Jackson for coming and head for bed when the FBI agent resumed talking.

"I met with both Dr. Milstein and Dr. Schwartz. They were very informative. Why didn't you tell me you entered therapy because of your fears?"

Mort's muscles tensed. He said nothing.

"I found out the real reason you went into therapy. Milstein forced your hand. It was that or leave your residency post. They both told me all about your explosive temper. Schwartz was quick to point out he wasn't at all certain you had conquered your problem prior to terminating therapy."

Millie couldn't believe her ears. "Mr. Jackson. I have known Mort for nine years. We've been married for eight. I've never known a kinder or a more gentle man. He gets angry at times. We all do. Getting angry is normal."

"I agree. However, three of your patients have been killed this week. Your husband has a history of not handling his anger well."

Millie interrupted, "There is a big difference between anger and murder."

"I have never accused your husband of murdering his three patients. He's a suspect. All of the remaining members of your group are also suspects."

"Am I suspect, too?" Millie asked.

"Not unless I find out something that might cause me to suspect you. However, your husband is a different matter. Not only does he have a history of a violent temper, but he was in Washington at the time Webster was killed."

Jackson turned to leave. "After I see Hargrove, Stuart and Bass, I'll hopefully have more to go on. Then we'll talk again."

*　　*　　*　　*　　*　　*　　*　　*　　*

Mort and Millie walked into their bedroom. "At least Jackson agrees I wasn't shot at while bike riding in the park. Now you don't have to worry about me."

Millie shook her head in disbelief. "Jackson has tunnel vision. He sees only what he wants to." She paused. "What are you thinking about?"

Mort pulled off his trousers before replying. "My reputation. I have to clear my name."

"Clear you name?" Millie sounded puzzled.

"Yes. Jackson believes three of our patients were murdered. So do you. It's getting harder and harder for me not to agree."

"That's a relief."

"However, he thinks I might be behind these killings. I have to prove he's wrong."

"Meaning?" Millie asked.

"I have to find out who killed our three patients." Mort faced Millie.

"Not for Jane Webster's sake only, but also to clear my name."

"Mort. Please. You're not making sense. You're not a cop. Nor are you in the FBI. You're a doctor. A psychiatrist. You're damn good at what you do, but you're not a detective."

"As Jackson talked to me, he reminded me of my father, of some of my medical school professors, of some of the kids in my neighborhood while I was growing up, mocking me, making fun of me. I have to prove them all wrong. I have to prove to myself I'm a man."

"Honey," Millie said rubbing her hands down his back, "you're all man to me. I've always been proud of you."

"I know, Millie. But somehow that's different. It's not sufficient. I have to believe it for myself. Once and for all, I have to stop submitting to these bullies. That's probably what my fears are all about. My fears are most likely my present day bullies. As long as I keep giving into them, I won't have any self-respect. I won't like myself. I won't have anything."

Several minutes passed. Finally Millie broke the tense silence. "I think I'm finally starting to understand how you have always felt. I now realize I can't stop you. I wish I could, but I can't. I need to have you like yourself. But please Mort, don't get carried away."

"I won't."

10

What a place, a wide-eyed, speechless Jackson thought, as he entered the posh East Side Health Club. He mentally contrasted the ultra-luxurious fitness center with the club he belonged to in Washington. The equipment was the same; the various Nautilus machines, even the Olympic-size swimming pool, the saunas, the Jacuzzi; the list of aerobic classes posted on the bulletin board adjacent to the reception area. The differences were all in the trimmings, the lush carpeting, the plush locker rooms, the thick new towels and, of course, the hordes of people. This was Sunday. When he went to his club on Sunday, which in itself was a rarity, it was mainly to read a sports magazine. The walls were his main companions. The center was otherwise invariably deserted. Here it was bedlam. All machines were in use. The instructors barked out exercise commands to an aerobic class that overflowed into the hallway. The noise in the crowded swimming pool reverberated throughout the glass enclosed area. He couldn't understand who in their right mind would want to work out on Sundays. Sundays were meant for vegging. Even God vegged Sundays. Jackson could barely summon up the motivation to actually utilize his club's exercise facilities more than twice a week, and that was with resentment. Yet the faces dotting the large center were beaming, smiling. It was almost as if they enjoyed punishing their bodies, regaling at their self-inflicted leg cramps. They kept at their machines, at their individualized exercise regimens, without regard to the extreme agony he envisioned they had to be experiencing. However, as he was quickly learning, New Yorkers were a breed apart. Separated from mere mortals by some strange inner drive.

They seemed to be compelled to maximize every minute of every hour of all of their days. Mondays, Wednesdays, Sundays. The days didn't appear to matter. God rested on Sundays, but New Yorkers, never!

"Hi, you must be Mr. Jackson," an incredibly handsome, blonde-haired man with a picture-perfect physique greeted him. He was garbed only in a short white towel. "I'm sorry I didn't dress for the occasion, but I'm running late. I have to meet with my agent at 3:00 this afternoon and had to quickly figure out how I was also going to be able to get in my 100 laps and 20 minutes in the sauna," Lyle Stuart said.

They walked to the health bar. Stuart ordered a greenish vegetable concoction Jackson had trouble looking at. He begged off.

"So you want to know if I killed them?" Stuart came right to the point.

Jackson was taken aback by Stuart's directness. No artful dodging. No beating around the bush. Right to the jugular. He admired that.

"Do I need an attorney?"

"That's up to you."

Stuart smiled. "I'll chance talking to you without one."

"Well, did you kill them?" Jackson asked.

"Of course not. My career hinges on my image. I don't have any false illusions about being the next Sir Lawrence Oliver. I am who I am, a matinee idol to millions of women and gay men. I get off on my leading role as Tray in 'The Reckless and the Passionate.' I wouldn't risk ruining my career for anything. I love it too much. I can't afford to lose my cool, let alone murder anyone."

"Then how do you explain the fight you were involved in at the bar the night that led to your starting therapy with Dr. Yvars?"

"John Feldman, the director of the 'The Reckless and the Passionate', is a patient of Dr. Yvars. I respect John very much. He's become the father I never had. I told him what happened at the bar. He thought my reaction was far too extreme. He convinced me that if I over-reacted once, I probably would again unless I found out the underlying

91

causes for my outburst."

"What actually happened at the bar?" Jackson asked.

"I was minding my own business and sipping a Perrier."

"Don't you drink any of the hard stuff?"

"Not usually. Occasionally I'll have a Coors or two. I already had a few beers. That was enough. I like Perrier, the bubbles, especially the lemon-flavored variety. I was waiting for a friend. This guy approached me and offered to buy me a drink. I politely refused. He kept insisting. Then he put his hand on top of my groin. I freaked and decked him."

"What did Dr. Yvars think?"

Stuart shrugged his shoulders. "Well it's sort of complicated. You have to admit I'm exceptionally good-looking. My mother's friends would make up reasons to come over to our home just to stare at me. Being this handsome has both its up and down sides. Not only do women want me, men do too. I always knew I got turned on by good-looking bodies, be they women or men, but before I started talking to Yvars, I never put it together. He explained I had an unconscious hatred for gays because secretly I feared I was one of them myself."

"Are you?" Jackson asked.

"Who knows? I do read some of the gay magazines and stare at the nude men in the centerfold. I also stare at some of the hunks here in the club. However, I've never had an actual homosexual experience if that's what you want to know."

"I can understand why you decided to get into individual therapy. But why group therapy?"

"Mort thought it would be more beneficial for me if I let this hidden part I had never discussed with anyone else out of the closet, so to speak. Initially, I refused. Eventually, he convinced me to give it a try. He told me I could always quit the group and start individual therapy again if I felt it was too uncomfortable. I didn't open my mouth for the first five sessions. Eventually, I did. Nobody in the group thought it was a big deal. Meg Armstrong admitted she'd had a crush on me for months. She had never missed an episode of my soap. Eileen Matthews was the same. They both admitted they fantasized being with me."

"Did you ever take either of them up on their offer?" Jackson pressed.

"No. Neither was my type, but if one of them had been, perhaps I would at least have given it very careful consideration." Stuart paused for a moment. "Now you are starting to sound like a real investigator. We always hire a detective whenever we are about to shoot a storyline dealing with murder. He goes over the script for credibility. He makes it a point to have all possible suspects questioned for an alibi."

"What's yours?" Jackson asked.

"I was on the set all day. Call Feldman, our director. He'll vouch for me," Stuart replied.

"How can you be sure he'll be able to distinguish Tuesday from any other day last week?"

"Because on Tuesday he was a madman. He told us we couldn't act. He even accused me of not kissing passionately enough. He apologized on Wednesday. He'll remember." Stuart paused. "Are you finished? My agent gets impatient if I'm late."

"That's enough for now. If I need to talk to you further, I'll let you know." Jackson lifted himself from the health bar, thanked Lyle for his time and walked out into the warm air. All this psychology was getting to him. He was glad he abandoned psychology, after he'd gotten his Ph.D., for a career in the FBI. Sometimes it was perhaps better not to know everything about yourself, he concluded.

****

"I'm getting old," Jackson muttered as he dragged his heavy frame to the fifth floor walk-up, stopping at each landing to regain his breath. He thought of the rigors Lyle Stuart put his body through every day of the week and quickly decided that wasn't for him. He would have to allow the aging process to evolve without his attempting to hold back Father Time. He had cut out cigarettes and stopped eating red meat. That was enough.

93

He didn't have the necessary incentive to put in the time and effort keeping trim would require.

The door to the dimly lit apartment was opened by an irritated, pot-bellied, middle-aged man sipping a Budweiser. "This better be something important. The Mets have the bases loaded and only one out. I don't want to miss any of the action."

Jackson quickly reached into his coat pocket and flipped open his wallet, flashing his badge into the ornery man's pudgy face.

Mary Hargrove nervously approached Jackson. "Max, please try and be nice to Mr. Jackson He's from the FBI. He called yesterday. It's about those three members of my group who were killed last week."

"Don't tell me who I should or shouldn't be nice to," Max Hargrove, crushing the empty beer can with his beefy hand, said. "Get me another Bud."

"Excuse me, I'll be right back," Mary said, returning from the kitchen within two minutes with a full can of her husband's favorite brew. Max grabbed the unopened beer, twisted off the aluminum lid and gulped down several mouthfuls. He wiped the foam running down his chin with his undershirt. "I told you not to join that garbage. It's all rubbish. Now look what a mess you've gotten yourself into," Max replied, moving his bulk and plopping it back into the overstuffed armchair near the blaring voice of the Mets' TV broadcaster.

"Maybe today isn't a good day for us to talk." Mary said.

"I have to question you Ms. Hargrove. The sooner, the better."

"Max, is it okay if Mr. Jackson and I talk for a few minutes?"

"He can ask you whatever he wants, but not in this room. I want to watch my Mets without listening to bullshit. Go into the bedroom and shut the door. I don't want to be disturbed."

Jackson and Hargrove walked into the small, orderly room.

"Now you've met Max. He's the reason I'm in Yvars' Monday evening group. I love Max, at least I think I do, but he doesn't love me. It's as plain as day. You saw how he treated me. Like I'm his maid. Not like a wife whom you love. In the summer, it's the Mets. In the fall, the Jets. In the winter, it's the Knicks. And in the spring, he and some of his friends from the post office go fishing someplace upstate. I'm an afterthought. Sort of like an asterisk, Millie Yvars recently told me. That's not a very flattering comment to hear, especially from somebody like Millie whose opinion I value greatly."

Mary walked to the window and peered at the cluster of elderly women seated outside the nursing home across the street. "I don't feel comfortable talking about myself, especially with Max in the next room."

"Take your time. I'm not in any rush. What made you initially go into therapy?" Jackson asked.

"According to both Mort and Millie, my situation with Max finally got the best of me. I started drinking. Never that much. Maybe a Scotch or two. But for someone like myself, who never touched alcohol before, the booze really did a number on me. One afternoon last fall, Max had the Giants game blasting on the television. He'd already watched the 1:00 p.m. Jets game. I was hoping we would go out, get some Chinese or something, anything. I just wanted to get out of the house for once. He said if I wanted Chinese food, I should go and get it myself. He was fine with his pretzels and peanuts. He didn't want anything else. I pleaded with him to come with me. We'd go for a walk and bring the food home. It was no use. He turned the volume up. The noise was deafening. I had another scotch. Then I snapped. I picked up an ashtray and heaved it at the television, smashing the screen. There was glass all over my nice clean carpet. I never knew I had so much anger inside me. I scared myself to death. The next day I called a friend. She recommended her psychiatrist. I immediately called her and explained the situation. However, she was all booked and wouldn't have any openings for at least a month. She referred me to Dr. Yvars, insisting I was probably better off going to him anyway, as he specialized in helping people who had trouble handling their anger."

"How did Max take to your decision?"

"You heard him. He said he was against it, but that's not true. He didn't really say much of anything; he didn't care what I did. It was up to me. If I was stupid enough to spend my hard-earned money on talking to a group of strangers, that was my business. He just wanted me to know he wouldn't pay for it and never wanted to hear a word of what the group discussed. Fortunately, I earn good money as Assistant Manager of a lovely boutique on Madison Avenue."

"Have the sessions been helpful?" Jackson inquired.

"I'm not sure. It's still too soon to know. The other members of the group tell me I have to be patient. That self-confidence takes time to build up. It just doesn't develop overnight."

"How will having more self-confidence help? Max loves his sports, that's obvious. I don't get how your having increased self-confidence will change that."

"Millie wants me to confront Max and demand he shape up and start paying more attention to me instead of the Mets or else ship out."

"How does this confidence develop?" Jackson asked.

"I don't know. Call me in about a year. Hopefully, I'll have the answer by then."

"I have to ask you one more question." Jackson said.

Mary's heart skipped a beat. Her palms began sweating. "What is it?" she asked.

"Where were you on Tuesday?"

"In my apartment all day."

"I thought you have a full time job?" Jackson asked, a surprised look in his eye.

"I do. I wasn't feeling well, I decided to stay home."

"Was Max home with you?" Jackson asked.

"No. He was at work all day. Then he went out with the boys. I was asleep when he came home."

"Did you see or speak to anyone that day?"

Mary thought about her meeting with Jim. She didn't want to tell Jackson about that part of her life. "No," she said.

Jackson eyed Hargrove skeptically. There was something about her demeanor, about her apparent fragility that spooked him. He handed her a card. "If you remember anything anyone in the group ever said that might help me in finding out who killed Sawyer, Webster, and Matthews, please give me a call," he said turning to leave the bedroom. He made a mental note to make sure to question her again. Only next time he'd act like Max. If Hargrove were indeed hiding anything, she'd never be able to maintain her composure. She'd talk.

****

Mary's conversation with Jackson had unnerved her, made her feel more isolated, more lonely. She glanced into the living room. Max was still absorbed in his game. She had to call Jim and plead with him to reconsider his decision. With Webster dead, she needed him more than ever.

After the third ring a voice answered. However, it wasn't Jim's voice. It was a woman's voice. "The number you have dialed has been disconnected," the recording said.

Damn it, she screamed to herself. He refused to ever tell me his last name. I never asked him where he lived. There's no way I can contact him. First Webster. Now Jim. How can I still be such a fool? Mort Yvars is no different from all other men. He lied to me. He told me I'd change. I'll never change.

****

11

The immaculately dressed older man reached across his large mahogany desk and rigorously shook the special agent's hand. "I'm in between meetings, so let's get on with it. One can never start early enough. Days are too short. God, or whoever concocted the 24-hour day, certainly goofed. If I were asked, I would have opted for a 45-hour day. Eventually, we die. We have all of eternity to catch up on our sleep. Why do we have to waste so much valuable time while we're alive? Yup, I'm sure of it. Somebody missed the boat on that one. So let's get on with it," Bass, the motor-mouthed real estate tycoon said. "It's Chris Jackson, isn't it? Can I call you Chris? Please call me Steve. I hate these formalities."

The still half-asleep agent, suppressing a yawn, nodded in agreement.

"How can I be of help?" Bass asked.

"By telling me as much as you know about the members of your therapy group."

"No way. I can't do that. What goes on in our meetings is confidential."

"Not when a violent crime has occurred. Then the public good takes precedence over your privacy rights."

"Are you shitting me?"

"No. If you don't believe me, call your attorney. Ask him about the Tarasoff case. He'll tell you you must answer my questions."

"Then let's get on with it. Time is money. Where do you want to start?"

"With the three who were murdered.."

"I liked the kid, the woman grated on my nerves. She was always whining, but then again, so does my wife. Maybe all women do. But we want the sex. It's a trade-off. All deals are like that, don't you agree? But that Matthews woman, she wasn't my type. She flirted constantly, but I'd look the other way. I mean who'd want to screw someone like that? She probably was the type who kept talking through her orgasms. Anyway, I'm too busy these days to bother with anybody but my wife. It's getting harder and harder to make deals. It's not nearly as easy as it used to be. Bring back the 80's I keep saying. The Reagans. Those were the days. Junk bonds! Financing with a snap of your finger. Shopping centers, malls built in no time. Investors knocking on your door carrying suitcases filled with cash. Today, everything's different. It's a whole New World. Your books are scrutinized by the banks before they'll loan you a dime. All they care about is your credit rating, your bottom line. I still love the action, but it's getting harder and harder to hit the jackpot."

"If you're like this and it's not even 8:00 in the morning, what are you like by noon?" Jackson inquired.

"A madman. Completely daft. Three calls handled simultaneously. Sending faxes with one hand and jotting down new ideas for future transactions with the other, while incessantly dictating letters and memos to Daisy through the speakerphone. It's all in a day's work. I love the action, can't you tell? I go crazy on Saturdays and on Sundays. Leisure time is for the birds. Fishing, golf, tennis. Absurd activities. Foolish inventions of mankind. My internist tells me to slow down. That I'm going to suddenly run out of fuel and drop dead. That I'd better change my way of life. My whole modus operandi. No way! So I'll keel over one day. Big deal! Don't we all. I'd rather go my way. High stakes rolling one minuet; six feet under the next."

Jackson took an immediate liking to the no nonsense way the Seville Row tailored man in his early-60's approached life. Bass knew how he wanted to live and no one was going to veer him off his chosen course.

Not even a fear of death. The older man reminded him of himself.

"What about the senator?" Jackson asked.

"He seemed like an okay fellow to me. I didn't know he was a senator until last week's meeting. He had us believing he was an attorney, Jeff Osgood, from a small town in Bergen County, New Jersey. He didn't talk much. I'd occasionally wonder why he came to the meetings. I mean I knew he had a problem. His pecker stopped working. Something about going blind at night. A genetic disorder, Yvars told the group. Webster was terrified his eyes were only a precursor of what lay down the road. He was convinced his hearing would soon go and then the rest would just slowly deteriorate. God knows why he let himself think that way. I never let my mind wander. It would only mess me up. It caused his dick to stop functioning. But he never allowed himself to open up to the others in the group. Stuart, the kid Sawyer, and myself, we talked much more freely than did the senator. I mean why else spend the time and the money. Of course, none of the men in the group went on like those women would. But then again, regardless of what the women libbers say, there are basic differences between men and women. Women talk endlessly. Men don't. Maybe that's why Mort and Millie had an equal number of men and women in the group. You know, to show equality of a sort. However, without exaggerating, I'd say the women talked 80% of the time. They'd moan and groan about one thing or another. I'd tune out after a bit and think about what I had to do at the office later that evening, hopefully conceive of a new idea for a deal while they were rambling on."

"Why did you continue going to the meetings if they were a waste of time?" Jackson asked."

"I didn't say they were a total waste of time. I got a lot out of the meetings, especially when either Mort or Millie spoke," Bass replied.

"What made you go to begin with?"

"Is all this personal stuff necessary to talk about?"

Jackson nodded.

"I was always aware I'd get frustrated too easily, especially when others I'd work with didn't get the point fast enough. My frustration would mount. I started getting migraine headaches. Real bad ones. My neurologist, a Dr. Barrett, tried every pill out, then Caffergot suppositories. Those are the worst. I mean shoving those things up you ass. Gross! And they had no effect. My headaches kept getting worse and worse. Some days I couldn't work. That's how bad they'd get. Dr. Barrett was well aware I was a workaholic. I mean you didn't have to be a rocket scientist to figure that out. He used my love for work to get me to see Yvars. He guaranteed me that after being in therapy for a short period of time, I'd be able to work to my heart's content, without having to miss days with a headache. How could I refuse such a prescription? I called Yvars immediately and demanded to meet with him that very same day. He rearranged his schedule. We met at his office two hours later."

"Has the group helped?"

"The headaches are better, but I don't really know if it's a result of being in the group or because the economy has picked up and deals are coming along more rapidly. I never feel as frustrated when I'm able to wheel and deal to my heart's content."

"What's your read on Mort Yvars?"

"Surely you don't suspect Mort has anything to do with this."

"I have to cover all bases," Jackson replied.

"He's a smart fellow. Not quick like I am. He's more like a tortoise. I'm a hare. I think his wife is more like I am. She gets the point faster than he does. But he's very thorough and extremely methodical. He also is a very nice guy and makes you feel cared about. Those qualities matter to me. You don't find them very often, so I can tolerate his slower pace."

"Have you ever seen him get frustrated? Maybe even lose it?"

"Jackson you're barking up the wrong tree. Mort is the furthest thing from a murderer I've ever seen. Of course he gets angry. We all do. I'm sure you've even gotten angry yourself."

"I didn't say I thought he was a murderer. I asked if you'd ever seen him get angry."

Bass spun in his swivel chair rapidly before coming to a halt after completing a full circle. He then stood and walked to his window and peered across the street at Rockefeller Center. After a few minutes, he returned to his seat.

"Well, there was this one time. I pride myself on punctuality. I hate being late. I'm sure this doesn't come as a great revelation to you. Late, early, both waste valuable time. Anyway, Mort tends to run late. Once a meeting I chaired ended sooner than I expected and I arrived at his office 20 minutes earlier than usual. I rang the bell. There wasn't any answer but the door was open. I was sitting in Yvars waiting room making several phone calls on my cellular phone when I heard this loud commotion coming from the street. I walked to the door and there was Mort screaming at some poor fellow from Federal Express who obviously had screwed up some delivery. Yvars took the package and heaved it against the guy's truck. I was shocked. This wasn't the Yvars I knew. He saw me and looked quite embarrassed. Other than that one incident, though, I'd say no. As I said, he's usually a model of calmness and serenity. Those qualities pay off. They rub off on those in the group. We tend to chill out in his presence. His voice, his entire demeanor, the way he carries himself. You get the picture."

"Can you account for your whereabouts last Tuesday?" Jackson asked.

Bass thumbed through his calendar. "I was at an all day meeting with the CEO at Logan's International in Hartford, Connecticut. I'm negotiating with him about one of his subsidiaries. I want to purchase it. However, he wants too much for the company. I told him to either significantly lower his price or we'd have no deal."

Before the agent had a chance to shake Bass's hand, the business tycoon had his hand pressed hard on the intercom. "Daisy, get Murray in here immediately. Conrad from Citibank will be here in less than five minutes."

****

Detectives Brady and Davis from the 20th Precinct listened intently as Jackson recounted each interview he had had starting with Dr. Milstein, Mort Yvar's mentor at NYU, and ending with his conversation with Steve Bass.

Brady stood up and gazed out the window from the 1st floor of the FBI building on Federal Plaza. "Well what do you think?" the heavyset officer asked.

"At this point each one should still be considered a suspect."

"Have you been able to come up with a motive yet?" Davis asked.

"No. However, all of the surviving members of the group have an alibi except for Mary Hargrove. She also seemed the most difficult to read. I'm going to press her further."

"What about Dr. Yvars?" Brady asked.

"His shrink told me he went into therapy during his residency because of problems handling his own anger. Couple that and his being in Washington on the day Webster was killed puts him right up there on the list."

"What about considering whether somebody other than Dr. Yvars or a member of the group might be the killer?"

"I've thought of that possibility. However, it's too soon to broaden our investigation. I've called Butler, my assistant in Washington. He's going to do a computer search on all our suspects to see if any of them have ever had a problem with the law. While Butler's doing that, I'm going to call on each of our suspects again. However, this time I will be more forceful. Confront them more directly. Stir up some fears. Fear works wonders. People become unglued. They slip up. That's when I have them where I want them."

"What would you like us to do?"

"Interview each of our suspects' neighbors, friends, an co-workers. Everyone and anybody you can find who has had contact with them. I'll be in touch."

103

12

"Jackson? It's Doug Simons." The high-pitched voice on the other end of the line said.

"Who?" Jackson, still asleep, asked.

"Don't you remember? I'm one of Dr. Yvars' Monday evening group therapy patients. We talked the other day. I'm the investigative reporter from the Times."

"Oh, yes. I'm sorry. What time is it?" Jackson asked, searching for the alarm clock alongside his bed.

"It's almost 7:30."

Jackson yawned. Another crazed New Yorker who had no concept of how to balance a day. "What is it?"

"When we talked Saturday morning, I told you I'd check my sources and see what I could come up with. Well, I've found the smoking gun you were looking for."

Jackson, suddenly alert, sat up in bed. "I'm listening. Go on."

"You were right on the money. I dug a little deeper, called in a few favors. Yvars is your man. There is absolutely no doubt about it. None whatsoever."

Jackson stood up and slid on his bathrobe. "What exactly did you find out?"

"I'll tell you when we meet," Simons replied.

"You have my home address on the card I gave you. I'll be here until 9:00."

"That's not possible."

Then meet me at my office. I'll be there all day," Jackson replied. "No. I can't do that either. I've got a meeting with Parsons, the Deputy Mayor. I've found out he's deeply involved in the city's current police scandal. I want to give him a chance to tell me his version of it before I break the story."

"Then I'll come to your office at the Times. When will you be finished with Parsons?"

"Before noon, but we can't meet there either," Simons replied firmly.

"Why not?"

"Are you serious? I've gotten to the top of my field by working behind the scenes. Digging where others don't. My colleagues are as incredibly competitive as I am. There's no privacy there. They'll overhear our conversation and run with the story. I'd be left high and dry. I know because I would do likewise. It's dog eats dog in my field. There's no way we can meet at my office. This is my story. I call the shots!"

"Then where do you want to meet?"

"Where I'm meeting Parsons. It's a small park on 97th Street by the Hudson River. It's my favorite spot. I've met with many informants and exchanged information there."

"Why there? New York is such a mammoth place. Surely we can meet somewhere that's more convenient."

"I told you I have information. If you want it, then you play by my rules. The park is quiet. Nobody will be there to possibly snoop around. I know that this way what I tell you will remain between us. You'll get what you're after. I'll get to print the story once you give me the go ahead. Seems like a fair exchange to me. Well, what do you say?" Simons calmly replied.

"You haven't give me much choice. I'll be at the park at noon."

"Don't get alarmed if I'm a few minutes late. After I finish with Parsons, I'm going to a coffee shop on 97th Street and Broadway to jot down a few thoughts I might otherwise forget once we start on Yvars. It's part of my routine. Then I'll head right back to the park."

"I'll be there," Jackson reluctantly replied.

"Great. I'll see you in a few hours," Simons replied.

****

Jackson climbed out of the taxi, felt generous and handed the driver a whopping tip. He hadn't felt this ecstatic since he'd sacked Morrison with 30 seconds to go in the championship game against Clemson. What a thrill that was. He was feeling it now, once again. That rush. That excitement. This is what he lived for. Ever since Nancy left two years ago, life had been without meaning. No cases to thoroughly hurl himself into; not until now. Not until Simon's phone call alerted him to specific evidence linking Yvars to the murder of his three patients. It was almost too good to be true. Jackson briskly walked into the park, passed several older Italian men preoccupied in their bocci game and a group of two older couples picnicking on a wooden bench. All was quiet, peaceful. New York did indeed have at least one remote tranquil spot after all, he thought.

Jackson, focusing exclusively on his meeting with Simons, did not notice a metallic-colored Chevrolet near the entrance to the park, its driver hunched behind the wheel.

The agent stood by a maple tree in the midst of the greenery and waited for Simons.

The thin figure slowly emerged from the car and threaded past the partially opened wrought iron gates and into the park. When the figure was about 30 yards from Jackson, the stranger pulled out a small revolver equipped with a silencer from a jacket pocket. There were no obstructions. The agent was now clearly in view. The stranger quickly raised the automatic and fired.

The bullet hit Jackson in his right hip. "Shit", the agent screamed, falling to the ground, writhing in pain. The four older people seated at the picnic bench, relishing their fried chicken, jumped up without delay and rushed to the fallen agent."Are you OK?" one of the four asked. Jackson tried to respond. He couldn't. He began feeling lightheaded, nauseated.

The bright sun was becoming dimmer. His breaths were more labored, coming with more difficulty. He attempted to stand but couldn't. His legs were too wobbly, too weak.

"Let me help," another of the four said, offering Jackson his hand.

A third barked. "There's a pay phone at the corner. I'll call 911. Tell them to come to the park immediately. There's a guy here dying."

Jackson faintly heard the beginning of their conversation, but not the rest. He coughed once, then again and again. Then stillness.

****

13

"I came as soon as I could reach Tobias and cancel his session," a shaken Yvars, kissing Millie on her cheek, said. Millie had interrupted Mort's 7:00 p.m. session as soon as she'd gotten word that Chris Jackson had been murdered in the small park they occasionally walked through during hot summer nights.

They ambled into the living room. Mort fixed himself a Bloody Mary.

"Our patients are starting to get annoyed at all of these unexpected cancellations this past week. It's a good thing our annual two-week vacation starts next week. Otherwise, if we kept having to cancel their sessions, pretty soon they'd get fed up and find another shrink in Manhattan. I can sense their annoyance already. Who can blame them? They come for help, besides our expertise they need consistency, stability. Unfortunately, since all this madness started last week, I haven't been available to give them what they need most, and with Jackson's death," Mort shrugged his shoulders and downed his drink. "Ah, that's better. It really takes the edge off. It may even beat food. I'm surprised we never got into having a drink every evening. No wonder millions long for their before-dinner cocktail."

"Mort, we're Jewish. Jews eat. Goyim drink," Millie said. "I understand how you feel. Believe me, our patients do too."

"I hope you're right. Besides loving my work as a psychiatrist, we need the income to pay our monthly bills."

"Mort, get a hold of yourself," Millie commanded. "Three of our patients murdered within the past week and this morning Jackson killed.

You mean far more to me than money. If our patients can't drop some of their incredibly self-absorbed worries and care about what you're, we're, going through, then so be it. Let them find another psychiatrist. You're a great therapist. You'll get new referrals, other patients. If worse comes to worse, I'll go back to my old job at New York University. Whenever I bump into my former director, he's always telling me whenever I want a slot, there's always one waiting for me. Working as a social worker at Bellevue wasn't all that terrible and face it, the money and the perks were better than I get working for you," Millie replied smiling.

"How was Jackson killed?" Mort asked, refilling his glass with another Bloody Mary.

"I don't know. All I was told by the FBI agent, I think his name was Butler, was that he and Jackson were working together on Webster's murder. After he found out about Jackson's death, he flew to New York and went directly to Jackson's office at Federal Plaza. He looked through his log. Apparently Jackson had received a phone call from our patient, Doug Simons, who insisted he had proof that not only were our three patients murdered, but that you were the one who killed them."

"I can't believe this!" Mort replied incredulously.

"Why not?" Millie said. "Simons, after all, is a renowned investigative reporter. What else do those types do but snoop around looking for stories that will hopefully add to their reputations."

"That's absurd. Simons is not that type of reporter. He goes after white-collar crime, political corruption. Murder isn't his bag. He's told the group that."

"Regardless, he must have sounded very convincing. Jackson bought into what Simons had to offer. They were to meet at our park on 97th Street near the river. A group of four were having lunch at the time. They saw Jackson go down. They tried to help. They called 911. The paramedics came, but it was too late. Jackson was already dead. Eventually, a detective from the 20th precinct arrived. The detective found Jackson's I.D. on him and notified Butler."

"What about Doug Simons? I can't believe he's a murderer. Ego-crazed perhaps, who'd do anything for a lead, even at times known to blur the line between right and wrong, but a killer?"

"Butler doesn't think Simons is the killer either. Apparently, Doug has an airtight alibi. He was on the Cape, in Woods Hole, doing a story on the possible corruption at the Institute at the time Jackson was murdered."

"Where does that leave us?" Yvars, finishing his second drink, asked.

"I have no idea. Butler said he wanted to see us tonight. That's why I called and insisted you cancel the rest of your evening's patients. Otherwise, I would have waited to tell you about Jackson until after you came home. It's almost 8:30 now. Butler should be here by 9:00."

Yvars thought for a moment. "The police had to have brought Jackson's body to Bellevue for a post. Berger will be home. I'm going to call him. I want to find out what the autopsy showed."

****

"Berger, it's Mort Yvars. I was hoping you did a post today."

Ed interjected. "I do autopsies every day of the week. Do you want to know about the floater, the old lady found chopped into small parts in a garbage bag, or the baby with a baggie tied over it's head?"

"None of those. I'm interested in Jackson. He was an FBI agent. I was sure your department would have gotten to him by now. I guess you're like the rest of us. All backed up. I'll call tomorrow."

Berger paused. "That won't be necessary. I did do a post on a Jackson. Real weird, that one!"

"How so?" Mort, leaning forward in his living room chair, asked.

"He was a real muscular type. Must have been a jock in his day. He was still in reasonably good shape. A bit of a gut, but that's par for the course. It happens to the best of us, except for you, that is. You already went through that phase. You're now contracting while the rest of us are into expansion."

"Why does Jackson's physical condition matter? He's dead.

110

Murdered! I'm calling to find out what happened."

"His physical condition matters tremendously. Yes, he was brought in DOA as a gunshot wound. However, at post I found the bullet. It was lodged in his right hip. I've seen a lot in my day, but never have I witnessed, read, or heard about anyone dying from a bullet wound in the hip. I carefully went over the entire body looking for another bullet wound, one that would have killed him. There was none. There were no markings that could explain his death. None whatsoever. However, his heart was a total disaster. Flabby. His vessels, especially his aorta, in a completely collapsed state. What I'm getting at is I don't think Jackson was murdered. I believe he died from heart failure, most likely secondary to a sudden heart attack. That's what's so puzzling to me. That's why I've gone on and on about his seeming to be in fairly good physical shape. I never would have predicted a man looking as fit as he did, could have a heart that was obviously in such horrendous condition."

"A healthy, middle-aged man, one moment fine, the next dead. I'm about his age. I wonder what my coronaries look like?" Yvars, gulping hard, asked.

"I can understand how you feel. I'm also about his age. You're a psychiatrist. You don't get to see these cases often. Unfortunately, I see this every day. I watch the joggers, all the health nuts, and wonder. Does it really help? Is there something yet to be discovered that we carry within us that regardless of how well we take care of ourselves, will do us in at a specific age. If you dwell on these things, you can drive yourself nuts. I try not to think about it. I've come to the conclusion that when you time's up, it's up. That there isn't all that much you, or I, or anyone else can do about it. It's all in God's hands. Maybe sometime in the future, perhaps in the time of 'Star Trek', the Next Generation', answers will be found that will allow us to circumvent God's will. But not today. Now, we are all potential Jackson's."

These mortality conversations always made Mort uncomfortable. "Anything unusual about the bullet?" Yvars asked.

"No. Just your garden variety small caliber.44."

"Have Jackson's blood chemistries come back from the lab yet?"

"Yes. They are all normal. I took a frozen section of the area around the right hip where the bullet struck. However, other than the mild inflammatory reaction you'd expect surrounding a foreign object, nothing out of the ordinary turned up." Berger replied.

"Your findings and diagnosis concerning Jackson seem incredibly similar to your conclusions related to Sawyer's and Matthew's deaths. I'm sure you remember they were both patients of mine who died suddenly last week. You did both of their autopsies. Do you remember Mike Stanley?"

"Sure. He's Chief Pathologist at D.C. General. I meet him each year at our American Pathology Association's meeting. Why?" Berger asked.

"A third patient of mine, Senator Webster from Colorado, also died suddenly last week. Stanley performed that post. His findings and diagnosis were strikingly parallel to yours. A bullet wound in an extremity, an incidental finding in the actual cause of death, which in his case and in the three others, was due to heart failure brought on in two of the cases by a probable heart attack, and in the other two from acute anaphylactic reactions. Jackson was the FBI agent investigating Webster's death. That makes three patients of mine and the forth victim, Jackson, all previously healthy yet all dying suddenly from acute heart failure within the past week. Doesn't that strike you as very odd?" Yvars asked.

Berger paused. "Yes and no. Stanley and I see so many deaths from bizarre natural causes, accidents, murders, both here and in Washington, D.C. each week that you get to realize both of these cities are hard to survive in. Both of us fantasize whenever we meet, that working as a pathologist in Maine or Vermont might be preferable." Berger replied.

"Are you telling me that you are convinced that these four deaths are unrelated? That they were all victims of random, unfortunate accidents? Terrible tragedies, but not murder? That there are no connections? No links whatsoever?" Yvars asked.

"I've learned after thousands of autopsies that nothing is certain."

"You've been very helpful. I've had one hell of a week." Mort said, replacing the phone back into its cradle.

****

"Berger doesn't believe Jackson was murdered, but that he died from acute heart failure," Mort said, walking towards Millie.

"So I gathered form hearing your end of the conversation. If Berger believes all four deaths could conceivably have been accidental, it's no wonder it has taken you longer than me to realize the truth," Millie replied. "Fortunately, you now are convinced. That's all that matters."

"I'd still like to believe Berger will eventually turn out to be right."

Millie stared at her husband; a somber mood engulfed her. She was so in love with Mort, yet now more than ever, she was frightened she was going to lose him. Sawyer, Webster, Matthews, now Jackson, next Mort. The thought caused her head to throb. She remembered the first day they met. The teddy bear in long whites, the social workers at N.Y.U. dubbed him. Cute, cuddly, warm, and tender. Growing up in rural upstate New York, the only child of the only Jewish family in town was a horror. She always felt an outsider. Until Mort, her loneliness from childhood lingered deep within. She didn't feel she belonged. Now she did, and she wasn't going to let anybody or anything take Mort from her.

Her reverie was interrupted by the jarring sound of the doorbell. She watched Mort as he opened the door. A tall, thin, youngish looking man wearing a dark blue suit walked in. He flipped open his wallet to flash his I.D. "I'm Fred Butler. You must be Dr. Yvars. I spoke to your wife earlier today. I know the hour's inconvenient, but…"

"That's okay." Millie said, greeting the angular-faced FBI agent. They walked into the living room.

"Care for a drink?" Mort politely asked.

"No thanks. I don't drink on the job. It tends to dull the senses, but if you want one, go ahead. I take it your wife has filled you in on the unfortunate details."

Yvars was about to pour himself another Bloody Mary, thought

113

he'd better not, and plopped himself down on one of the chairs that flanked the sofa.

Millie and Butler sat down on a nearby couch.

"You have a very unusual looking place here," the agent said to Millie.

"Thank you."

Butler faced Yvars. "I'm sure you sensed Jackson believed you were the one who murdered your three patients."

"I know he did." Yvars said.

"What now?" Millie asked.

"Jackson filled me in on his interviews with all five of the surviving members of your Monday evening group as well as his meeting with your former therapist. I'll begin by going over his notes. Other then that," Butler shrugged his shoulders. "It's a brand new case. We will have to start from scratch. I'll meet with Senator Webster's widow tomorrow."

"And then?" Mort asked.

"I'll talk to each member of your group again. Davis and Brady, the two detectives initially assisting Jackson, have been reassigned to other matters so I'll be working alone."

"Four murders and they've been taken off this case. That doesn't make sense." Millie replied.

"Unfortunately, with all large cities having severe budget problems, we run into this all the time. Once the FBI gets involved, local precincts feel justified in this policy." Butler paused. "With all the crime on the streets I can't blame them. I'd probably make the same decision. I spoke to Ed Berger who did the autopsies on Sawyer, Matthews and Jackson and Mike Stanley who did Webster's. All four died from heart failure. Neither of the medical examiners believed any of the four were definitely murdered. What the medical examiners frequently put down on the death certificates and what finally turns up as their final diagnosis aren't always the same," Butler said.

The agent stood up. "I've bothered you enough for one night."

Mort and Millie rose from their seats and were about to say good-night when Millie suddenly had a thought. "Do you have a minute? Mort had a flat tire while riding his mountain bicycle in Central Park on Saturday morning. Jackson checked the tire out and told us the rubber had been severed by a rock or a piece of glass. Fortunately, Mort hasn't had the time to bring the tire in for repair. It's still in our apartment. Would you mind looking at it? I'd feel more comfortable with a second opinion."

"Butler's tired. He's had an exhausting day," an embarrassed Mort replied. "There's no need to waste your time. A flat's a flat," he said to the agent.

"That's okay. I'd very much like to look at your tire." Butler said.

Millie led Butler into the guest bedroom. Mort followed slowly behind. The bike was still leaning against the bed.

Butler bent down. "Can I have a flashlight?" he asked.

Within a few minutes, Millie reappeared with the strong light.

Butler slowly and deliberately examined the tire, letting his fingertips gently encircle the ripped area. He then pulled the entire piece of thick rubber from the wheel. "Do you mind if I take the tire with me? I'd like our lab to have a look."

"Of course you can take it. But why do you want the lab to see it?"

"Because the rubber around the hole in your tire is charred. A rock or a piece of glass doesn't cause burn marks. I want the lab to confirm my findings."

"What would cause charring?" Millie asked, her heart rate accelerating. Suddenly she wasn't sure she really wanted to hear Butler's response.

"A bullet! Only a bullet has the force on impact to generate the amount of heat needed to sear the rubber on the tire the way it's been seared."

Millie looked at Mort. Her worst fear had been realized. She pictured upstate New York. Rural New York. Life before Mort. Life without Mort.

Butler stared at Mort.

"You didn't have an ordinary flat tire. It was deliberately shot at."

Millie eyed Mort. She said nothing.

"At least that removes me from your list of suspects," Mort replied, forcing back a sudden surge of anxiety.

"I didn't say that. Even though you have a tire with a bullet hole, you could have easily put it there yourself."

Millie looked at Butler in disbelief. "Mort couldn't have. He doesn't own a gun."

"I can't rule out anybody yet. That includes your husband." Butler paused and faced Millie. "If it's any comfort, I don't believe as Jackson did that Mort is one of the primary suspects. However, there is a killer out there. A cold-blooded murderer who's killed four times. All in an eight-day time span. He's not about to stop now. I don't know who he is or why he's doing this, but I will find out."

****

Millie began crying. Mort groaned, running his hands helplessly over her heaving shoulders and down her back, trying to console her. "I'll be fine don't worry." Threading his hands through her hair, he turned her tear-streaked face up to his, his thumbs moving tenderly over her cheeks. "Come to bed with me," he murmured.

Millie wrapped her arms fiercely around her husband's neck and Mort swung her into his arms. He put his knees on the mattress, lowering her gently and following her down, his lips clinging to hers in an unbroken, scalding kiss.

He finally lifted himself off her to tear off his shirt and unbutton his pants. He felt her arms encircle him from behind. He then rolled onto his side and pulled her into his arms.

She rolled him onto his back and brushed her parted lips over his, sweetly offering him her tongue. Without thought, she moved her hips against his engorged manhood, circling herself on him, faint with the pleasure she was giving him and taking for herself.

116

Beneath her she could feel the pulsing of his rigid shaft, the fiery touch of his heated skin, the violent hammering of his heart against her breasts.

Millie arched herself upward in a fevered need to share and stimulate his burgeoning passion, pressing her hips hard against his pulsing thighs, crushing her lips against his, while waves of sensation shooting through her built into a frenzy and began exploding through her entire body in piercing streaks of pure, vibrant ecstasy.

A shudder shook Mort's frame as he felt the spasms of her fulfillment gripping him, and he plunged into her one last time. His body jerked convulsively, shuddering again and again. She drained him of everything and replaced it with joy.

"Wow," Millie, after catching her breath, eventually said. "That was really something!"

"It sure was," Mort replied. "I guess science isn't 100% perfect in its predictive ability."

"What do you mean?" Millie asked.

"Remember the recent lecture we attended on romantic love? Well, we're supposed to be, according to the charts, in the cuddling part of our love life. Our 'oxytocin phase', as the researchers called it. Well tonight, we reversed the script. We shifted back in time to our 'amphetamine stage'. Our 'phenylethamines' clearly shot back up in rare form." Mort replied.

They both were startled at the irony, that through their suddenly engulfing nightmare, passion had been rekindled.

****

117

14

An hour had passed since Jane Webster had called and pleaded with Mort to press forward and discover who killed her husband. Her fears for her son's safety, three members of his group and FBI Agent Jackson's probable murders, not to mention Butler's insistence his tire was punctured by a bullet while sufficient in themselves, Mort knew, wasn't the real reason he eventually agreed to help Jane. It was his need to clear his name; to prove he wasn't the killer. He asked Jane to go through her husband's address book and fax him all their names and numbers. Then he'd spent minutes canceling the remainder of today's scheduled patients.

Fortunately, his annual vacation was coming up. He'd simply start his time off earlier than he originally planned.

Mort reached for the phone on his desk and dialed his colleague and friend Art Schore, asking his fellow psychiatrist to please cover his practice. He told him he and Millie were wiped out, needed a breather and were going to take the next seventeen days off. Almost a week earlier than they'd originally thought, but they desperately needed a change of environment and five more days was too long to wait. Art Schore was a fantastic psychiatrist and, more importantly, a genuinely good person. If he was available he wouldn't refuse Mort's request. He'd gladly agree to cover. Art's reply came immediately. "Absolutely. No problem. You and Millie just go and enjoy yourselves. After what you two have gone through over the past nine days, I think I'd have already left the city. Three patients dead, probably murdered. Forget the city! I'd have gotten on the space shuttle to Mars. Anything to get out of here. Where are you and Millie going?

"We haven't decided as yet. All we want to do is leave New York for awhile. Where we actually go has become unimportant."

"Go enjoy! You'll come back nice and refreshed. Have Millie give Val a call when you get back. We'll set up a date to go out together."

"We'd love that," Mort replied. "Thanks a lot. Millie and I really appreciate it."

"Hey what are buddies for! Now shut up and start packing. Time is awasting."

After Yvars hung up the phone, he walked over to his Fax machine at the far corner of the room and switched on the modern contraption. Jane Webster had been busy gathering the names and numbers from the senator's New York City and Washington address books. She said she'd be ready to begin faxing in about an hour. That gave him twelve minutes.

He poured himself a glass of ice water and walked over to his window. He stared at the passersby, some chattering aimlessly, while others frantically zoomed toward their urgent destinations as only Manhattanites could race. He thought about Jane and this morning's conversation. Jane discussed her visit earlier in the day with Agent Butler, who filled her in on Jackson's death. "I didn't want the FBI involved," she reiterated, "Jackson was killed while investigatin Judd's murder. Now you can better understand why I'm afraid for my son. He means everything to me. It took us eighteen years to conceive him. He's all I have left of Judd. My husband kept all of his important papers, his address books, everything he deemed significant in his office on the second floor of our house. I was the only one he completely trusted."

Judd's address book contained names of all their mutual friends, relatives and everybody in Washington he had had dealings with, Jane had emphasized. That would be sufficient for now. He'd interview all those closest to Senator Webster. If he came up with evidence Webster was indeed killed, then he'd decide how to proceed.

Suddenly, Yvars heard the humming sounds of the Fax machine. Within five minutes, papers were strewn all over the carpeted floor. Mort walked over to the pages and pages of paper, bent down and scooped them up. Holding them firmly against his chest he stood up, carried them back to his desk and sat down. He couldn't believe the enormous number of papers he was going to have to sift through. He was amazed at the incredible volume of people Judd Webster had listed in his address books.

He began by separating them into two different piles, those whose addresses and phone numbers were in New York, and those who resided in Washington. He then took out a yellow pad and pen from his desk drawer and, as in a Chinese menu, he listed all those from Washington under Column A and all those from New York under Column B. That seemed like the scientific approach. Make lists. Check variables. Then compare and contrast. But which variable or variables was he looking for? Then it struck him. He'd go down the list of all those under Column A and all under Column B and see if any name appeared under both columns. At least that would be a start.

Ninety minutes later, bushed and with a throbbing headache, he felt frustrated. He had gotten nowhere. There was not a single name that appeared on both columns. That would mean he'd have to interview everybody on both lists. The task was insurmountable. The numbers on both lists equaled the population of a small village. Millie was right. He wasn't a detective. This was a job for professionals, not for an amateur. Who did he think he was kidding?

He was about to call Jane Webster and convince her that as reluctant as she was to cooperate with the FBI, they were in fact the best of all possible alternatives. That they would eventually find the killer, Mort's name would be cleared, all would be fine. Then suddenly it hit him. There was one phone number, 212-889-3243, listed under the New York City column which didn't have a corresponding name alongside it. He glanced at the Washington column. Every name had a corresponding phone number next to it. He had no idea what, if any, significance this phone number might have. But he had no other lead to work with. Whether this would turn out to be a dead end or open up a Pandora's box, he didn't know.

Yvars called Lillian, the research librarian at the Midtown Library. He had come to her assistance when her son tried to commit suicide. He was sure she'd be willing, if the information was at the library, to find out the name and address corresponding to the phone number.

Within 5 minutes she supplied him with what he needed. Barbara Leckie, 520 Riverside Drive. The name sounded familiar. He searched his mind for several minutes. It was to no avail.

Millie looked up from the newspaper. "You're not going to call her, are you? How do you know she might not be the killer?"

"I don't but still….."

Millie interrupted, "and after you call her, what then?"

"I'll go over to her place. Ask some questions. Don't worry."

"It will be safer if you at least meet her at a public place, rather than at her apartment."

"That might be. But I'll learn far more if I visit her at her place. Trust me. I'll be careful."

Yvars reached for the phone and dialed the number. A high pitched, downcast sounding woman answered.

"My name's Dr. Mort Yvars. I'm sure you don't have any idea who I am, but I think we need to meet. I knew Senator Webster well. He said I should call you if I was ever in the neighborhood. The voice at the other end of the line didn't answer immediately. Yvars? She recognized the name. Why? Then suddenly she gasped. She did indeed know who Dr. Yvars was. The realization caused her muscles to tighten. Her head began pulsating. "I think you are right. We should meet," she replied, her voice cracking.

"I'll be over in a few minutes." Yvars said, replacing the receiver.

****

Yvars entered the dark, well-appointed two bedroom apartment. The woman greeting him looked vaguely familiar. He didn't know why. She feigned a smile, but her bloodshot eyes and trembling hands showed she was noticeably upset. Mort decided he'd don his psychiatric demeanor.

Be patient. Not inquire. Let the woman gradually open up.

She led him into the living room decorated in a variety of chintz patters. "I'm going to fix a bourbon and water for myself. Do you want anything?" she asked.

"A bloody Mary if it's not too much trouble, but no snacks please."

Barbara, a nice looking woman in her mid-forties, with dark rings under her brown eyes, handed Mort his drink while taking several sips from her Jack Daniels.

She was about to speak when Yvars noticed an 8" X 10" colored photograph resting on the bookcase. It was a picture of a woman, a man and a young boy. The boy looked seven, nine at the most. Mort walked to the bookcase and grabbed the frame.

"Don't! Please don't look," Barbara pleaded.

But it was too late. Yvars had seen what Barbara Leckie wasn't quite ready to let him in on. The man in the photograph was a slightly younger version of Senator Judd Webster. His eyes darted to another photograph on the bookcase. The senator dressed with black tie and tails and a woman dressed in a long lace wedding gown. He blinked once, then again. He couldn't believe his eyes. There, near the photograph of Judd Webster and Barbara Leckie with a young boy between them, was a wedding picture of the senator and Jane Webster. "What gives?" Yvars pointing to both pictures, asked.

"It's a very long, very complicated story. Please take a seat."

They both sat down.

"Jane and I were best friends. We roomed at Smith together. I dated Judd long before she ever set eyes on him. I was madly in love with him. I thought he felt likewise. However, he fell for Jane. I was Maid of Honor at their wedding. I never thought things would turn out this way. I can't believe what's happened." Barbara, bursting into tears, said.

Yvars took a deep breath, trying to maintain his composure. He downed his drink. He then took another deep breath and forced his mind back into its psychiatric detached mode. "I'll have another and some potato chips if you have any," he said.

Five potato chips and two sips of his Bloody Mary later, he felt better, armed, calmer. "Go ahead. I'm listening," he softly said.

"Well, passion as I'm sure you are well aware, does strange things, even to an incredibly driven man like Judd. He and Jane were living in Colorado. I think, at the time, he was clerking for the assistant DA in Denver. I was also living in Denver, staying with my parents while trying to save money for my own place. One evening Jane invited me over to their apartment for dinner. The fire began blazing again. He called me, and I him. We tried to keep our relationship confined to frequent telephone calls. We used all of our will power, our logic, our common sense, not to go beyond that level of involvement. However, not even our mutual love for Jane could keep us apart. We began lunching together, soon we were sleeping together," Barbara paused. "I can't believe Judd's dead. I could accept he would never be totally mine. He occasionally considered leaving Jane. I'd always be the one to say no. Don't get me wrong. I'd have loved nothing better than a life with Judd, but not at Jane's expense. What we were doing was harmful enough. At least she didn't know. At least I don't think she ever did. I wanted it to remain that way. We'd get together whenever we could. I mean life is a tradeoff, at least that's how I thought, until now. I can't believe I'll never feel his touch, hear his voice again," she said, shaking uncontrollably.

Yvars sensed she was holding back, that there was more to her story than she'd so far admitted. Then she said, "How can I go on without my baby, without my Tyrone?"

Tyrone. Yvars was stunned. Tyrone wasn't your garden-variety name. There only one Tyrone he ever knew. Tyrone Sawyer. His patient. A sickening feeling began welling up in him.

Yvars quickly rose from his chair and walked rapidly back to the bookcase. He reached for the photograph of the man, woman and young child. He stared at the picture for several minutes, disbelief turning to shock and then to sorrow. There was no doubt about it. The young boy in the picture standing between Barbara and Webster was Tyrone Sawyer. "Tyrone was your son. I had no idea. I'm so sorry," he said.

Barbara sobbed uncontrollably for several minutes before she finally was able to pull herself together long enough to speak. "I became pregnant shortly after we began our affair in Denver. After I found out, I was going to have an abortion. Judd however, wouldn't stand for it. He begged me to keep the child. I knew I'd never have Judd, but in a child I'd have a constant reminder of Judd. A link between us that nobody could take away. A connection that would last forever. I reluctantly agreed to go along with Judd and have our baby. I never regretted my decision for a moment. Tyrone gave me all the joy a mother could hope for. Now he's gone. Judd's dead. What's the point of my continuing to go on? The only two people in the world I truly loved and who truly loved me are dead."

"Are you sure Jane didn't know about you and Judd, or about Tyrone?"

"I haven't seen Jane for years. I've always tried my best to believe she didn't know about us, but she's very perceptive, so perhaps she did. Judd and I were always very discreet, but you never know. I moved to Manhattan shortly before Tyrone was born. Judd bought me this apartment. He got me my present job. I think his family are the principle owners of the company I work for. I never asked. I like my work. But now. Please, just promise me one thing. Don't ever tell Jane about us."

"I won't unless," Yvars voice trailed off.

"Unless what?" Barbara shocked, asked.

Yvars recounted all that had happened over the past nine days, culminating with FBI Agent Jackson's death. "If they don't eventually catch the killer on their own, I'll be forced to tell them whatever I know. Only then will Jane find out about your relationship with Judd and about Tyrone. That's the best I can offer."

"I guess I can't ask for more than that," Barbara replied.

"How'd you get the name Sawyer?" Yvars asked.

"Sawyer's my maiden name. I tried marriage after Tyrone was

born. I thought a normal family would be better. A boy needs a father. I gave it a fair shot. It just didn't work out. We lasted less then three years. His name was James Leckie. I kept my married name but never changed Tyrone's. Now it all seems so meaningless." Barbara paused. "How's Jane doing?"

"Not well. She's terrified William will be killed," Yvars said.

"I can understand why she'd be so worried," Judd told me about the kidnapping two years ago."

"There are so many creeps out there."

Barbara turned and forced a smile. "I am grateful for one thing."

"What's that?" Yvars surprised asked.

"Tyrone and Judd had a wonderful relationship. Regardless of how busy he was in Washington, he made it his business to spend time with Tyrone at least once or twice a month. He completely supported us. Barbara motioned across the well-decorated living room. I never could have lived like this without Judd's help." She paused before continuing. "He was so proud of Tyrone, of his musical ability. He was his biggest booster. And on the night of his big audition," she gulped hard, "It doesn't make sense. Who would want to kill Tyrone and Judd?"

Yvars nodded sympathetically.

When you called I didn't immediately make the connection," Barbara said. "But then after a few minutes I remembered. You were Tyrone's therapist. I'm sorry I didn't recognize your name right away. You helped him so much. You really gave him a shot of confidence no one else had been able to do. When he started on drugs and then hit the policeman, I never thought things would turn around. Not even with Judd's love and support. But you did it! You made him care more about his music than those damn drugs, so I owe you a great deal. You were a Godsend."

Yvars looked shocked. "I always wondered how a senator from Colorado ever sought me out. I knew he wouldn't go to a psychiatrist in Washington, but in New York City there are thousands of us. He never did actually tell me why he wound up in my office. So that's how it happened.

Good God! Father and son! I never would have guessed. They behaved friendly towards each other, but Judd never gave off any paternal type signals, and Tyrone certainly never reacted to Judd as if he were his father. At least not during our weekly sessions.

15

"This is the life! When was the last time we slept in?" Mort asked, slowly rising from the king-sized bed in their peach colored bedroom. Millie pulled open the thick draperies; the morning sun streaming through the windows, further brightening the already cheerful floral décor.

"This is how the idle rich do it. It seems like a wonderful way to live. Rise late, do lunch with friends, check out an opening at either the Whitney or the MOMA, and then dress to the nine's for your nightly charity ball. True, they don't accomplish much, but then again what's so great about having to do so much? Of course you need a purpose, a goal to strive for, but why can't the goal be less consuming, allowing lots of time to just be," Millie said, stretching her stiff back muscles. "But, we are on vacation for the next seventeen days. We can be like them for two and a half weeks. Float, drift, plan, whatever. Guilt free time." She breathed in deeply. "The best. Two and a half weeks from now we can deal with what our goals should be."

"Whatever you say," Mort said, donning his cotton bathrobe and walking into the bathroom. "You seem to come up with this theme on the first morning of our vacation each year. Somehow we never pick up and pursue the issue once we're back in our regular routine." Mort paused while brushing his teeth. "So where to this year? I was thinking of Israel."

Millie's eyes lit up. She raced into the bathroom and kissed Mort on the lips. She wiped the green gel from her lips with Kleenex. She had always wanted to tour Israel. To visit her heritage. To see Masada, the Wailing Wall, and numerous other historical sites she'd read about for years come alive. "Really! You always come up with a reason for us to postpone Israel for another year. It's either too much turmoil in the Middle East, or you get me all hot and excited about another part of the world I hadn't previously considered. I thought you never really wanted to go to Israel. That these were all justifications you'd know I'd go along with." Her excited tone suddenly was dashed, replaced by a saddened expression. "Do you really think we can? I mean, shouldn't we stay around the area this year in particular? I don't think FBI Agent Butler is going to want us to leave the city. He wants us for his investigation. And besides," Millie paused and sighed, "I think I'd be nervous myself leaving home this year. At least right now. I mean what with this maniac out there. I've looked forward to going to Israel for too long to finally go and not be able to fully enjoy it. And I know I wouldn't. No. This year I'm the one who would rather not visit Israel. I appreciate your wanting to take me there, but I think I'd feel safer here. I know Butler is around. He gives me a certain feeling of safety. If we left the country, we'd be completely on our own. What if the killer followed us?"

Yvars finished shaving. "Let's table this discussion until later. Get washed. I'll put up some coffee. We'll spend the day walking around the city, maybe take in a movie. Play it by ear as the teenagers say."

Nine minutes later Millie was dressed in a short navy skirt with a yellow tank top. "I'm ready. How do I look?"

Mort smiled in approval. He poured each of them a cup of coffee and filled up two large bowls with a hardy amount of Crackling Oat Bran. "I'm pissed off at myself," Mort said, chomping on the hard grains of round oats. "I can't believe it never crossed my mind that Tyrone Sawyer and Judd Wesbter had some type of relationship together, one that reached beyond our Monday evening sessions. How did I miss something so obvious, so apparent? Sawyer and Webster both must have periodically sent off some vibes I just didn't catch."

"I never suspected anything either. Neither of them ever brought up anything during any of our sessions to suggest they knew each other, let

128

alone that Judd was Tyrone's father."

"But we, I mean, I should have been able to pick something up. Good God. I mean what in hell was my psychiatric three-year residency all about if I'm not able to pick up the subtleties, the nuances, and the innuendoes. Those nonverbal gestures we were constantly told were always in the air, ready to be plucked and frequently, it was more these nonverbal signals rather than those verbally expressed ones that would reveal vital insights into the patient and allow us finally to enter their world. Then real therapy and eventual recovery could begin."

"Mort stop berating yourself. I'm not. We knew there was something about the vibes in our Monday evening group that was different. We just never got to the bottom of it. In retrospect, we obviously missed important signals, we screwed up. However, we have to accept that we aren't perfect. You've always told our patients to learn from their mistakes. We have to do the same," Millie replied.

Mort was about to grab a huge blueberry muffin purchased last night at the all night Korean Deli near his office, thought better of it, and threw it into the nearby garbage pail. I don't need any further temptations."

"You didn't have to throw the muffin out," Millie replied.

"Yes I did. I'm stressed out. You're stressed. When you're stressed you talk endlessly. When I'm stressed I eat too much as if you didn't know. I worked hard to lose these thirty pounds. Right now my willpower is shot. Goodies are too tempting. I can't even look at them."

Millie was patting her husband empathetically on his hand when the phone rang. She reached for the telephone. "It's Jane Webster." She said.

Mort grabbed the phone. Millie pressed the speakerphone button.

"Mort, Ruth and I have gone through all of Judd's personal papers. His records. All his correspondence. His bills. I've been up all night. I've found something that I think might turn out to be very important."

"What is it?" Mort, startled asked.

"Judd's phone bills since January. Those he made from his office in

129

Washington and those from our home in Maryland. He made an incredibly large number of calls to a particular number in New York City. According to the bills, some of the calls lasted only a few minutes. However, there are several that ran for two to three hours?"

"Do you recognize the number?"

"No. Both Judd and I have many friends who live in Manhattan. However, none of them has that phone number."

"Are you sure? I don't know about you, but I can barely remember my own number let alone anybody else's." Mort said.

"I'm certain. I looked through our personal phone book. Nobody we know has the number 849-7241," Jane replied.

"Judd was probably involved with certain government matters that required all of those calls to that particular number. You have all of the files and papers at home?" Mort asked.

"Yes. They are scattered all over this desk."

"Look through them. I'm sure you'll come across the phone number along with whomever he kept calling. Millie and I are going out for an hour or two. Leave us a message on our answering machine when you find out the name. We'll get back to you when we return home at about noon."

"I can't do that," Jane said. "I'm afraid to talk on the phone about anything specific that might be important. I'm terrified more than ever, especially now that FBI Agent Jackson's been murdered. I know I am imposing, but I trust both of you and really need to feel the matter will be kept confidential."

"What do you want us to do?" Mort asked.

"Fly to Washington. Come to my place in Chevy Chase. We'll go over Judd's records and papers. We'll find out about that number in Manhattan together. Please Mort. Please Millie. I need both of you. William needs both of you."

Mort hesitated.

"Well Mort, we are on vacation," Millie broke in. "I love Washington, especially at this time of the year. What do you say? We haven't been to Washington since we took your cousin Ben there five years ago. I'd love to see the new Eakins exhibit at the National Gallery. You adored the Smithsonian on our last trip. I'm sure there's lots more at the Institute you've never seen."

"I thought you insisted we stay close to home. That we should let the FBI handle everything," Mort said, hanging up the phone.

"That was before Jane called. I can feel her fear." Millie pleaded

"Okay, okay," Mort said. "I'll never understand you women. First it's no, then it's yes. Soon it will probably be no again." He looked at his watch. It was 10:40 A.M. "We should be able to make the noon shuttle to National."

****

The Wesbter's palatial, ninety-eight year old Georgian brick house was spread out along Bradley Lane in the posh section of Chevy Chase between Connecticut and Wisconsin Avenues. The magnificent greens of the Chevy Chase Country Club abutted the back of the property.

The exclusive area was rumored to have originally been the summer residence of President Grover Cleveland and several members of his cabinet.

Mort and Millie were greeted at the front door by an attractive, trim, middle-aged woman. "Hello. I'm Ruth, Jane's sister-in-law. You must be Dr. & Mrs. Yvars."

"Please call us Mort & Millie," Millie said.

Ruth smiled and ushered them into the English Regency-style living room. "Jane will be back in a few minutes. She's dropping William off at a friend's for the day. She thought it would be best if we were alone. She didn't think you'd be able to get much done if he was constantly under your feet."

"I'm sorry about your brother," Millie said.

"Thank you."

"How is Jane holding up?" Millie asked.

"Better than I'd expect. She cries a lot. I try to comfort her but...."

131

Ruth's voice trailed off.

"I don't know what Jane has told you, but Judd was a patient of ours," Mort said.

"My brother never talked much. Silence runs in our family. However, he mentioned you on several occasions. He liked the sessions".

"He was a very nice man. We will miss him," Millie said.

"That's very kind of you to say," Ruth replied, motioning them to the Regency sofa. "You have already expressed more emotion about Judd's death than either my mother or any of our relatives did. Nobody even cried at the funeral. It's as if nothing happened."

"I'm sure they were upset," Millie replied. "Everybody handles grief differently."

"The Websters don't grieve. My family doesn't emote. Being with them made me realize why I never returned to Seattle after graduating college. The Websters give a new meaning to the definition of WASP coldness."

Suddenly the front door opened. Jane Webster with her long, blonde hair flowing down her back came into view. She walked into the living room and kissed both Millie and Mort on the cheek.

"I was telling the Yvars about my family and their inability to feel," Ruth said.

Jane nodded her head in agreement. "They are definitely a different breed. Mrs. Webster didn't even ask about William."

The four moved into the dining room and sat across the table blanketed with the senator's bills, personal memos and private papers. "Everything is here," Jane said. "All of Judd's papers both from his offices in the Senate and those he kept in the study upstairs."

Jane handed the pile of phone bills to Mort. He slowly and methodically, page by page, went through the list. "There are 14 calls to that number on his January bills, 19 in February, 13 in March, 15 from April and 16 last month. That's 78 calls in 5 months. That's an incredible number of phone calls to make to one party."

"I know. I don't understand it." Jane replied.

Mort looked puzzled. Millie was equally so. "Unless," Mort looking up from the stack of bills, began.

Millie broke in. "Unless what?"

Mort turned to Jane. "What Senate committee did Judd serve on?"

"The Senate Finance Committee. He was the chairman of the subcommittee on banking."

"There's our answer. Judd and his committee were undoubtedly working on financial matters related to the banking industry in New York. The phone number must be located at one of the large banks. Perhaps even the Federal Reserve."

"Did he go to New York often since January?" Millie asked.

"As far as I know, only for your weekly sessions. He'd take the 3 p.m. shuttle to New York every Monday and the 11 p.m. back to Washington. However," Jane paused, "he was a very private person. He didn't talk to me much about either his work in the Senate or even our lives together. How is it possible that I could have loved him so, and he me and yet we couldn't talk. No matter how hard I tried, he couldn't communicate about much of anything."

The Yvars stared at one another. "That's why he went into therapy." Millie said. "We all develop physical problems as we age. We don't usually fall apart from them. He did. Eventually, he began talking during our group meetings. The more he opened up the better he became at dealing with his failing night vision."

"Besides," Mort interjected. "As both you and Ruth have said, the Webster's conditioned Judd to repress his emotions very well."

Yvars began scanning several other papers strewn on the finely polished, rectangular, dining room table. "Let me see that phone number!"

Jane handed the number to Mort. Yvars walked to the phone at the far corner of the room and began dialing. He couldn't believe his ears. He dialed the number again. The response was the same. Then a third time. The results identical. Yvars gulped hard.

"What is it?" Jane asked.

"The phone number has been disconnected."

Jane handed Millie her husband's diary from his office on Capitol Hill.

"No! Not that one. That's his official date book. I want to see his personal diary."

Jane shuffled through more bills and papers, finally retrieving Judd's personal appointment book.

Millie flipped through Judd's entire log. She was about to hand the book back to Jane when her eyes focused on an entry made on Friday, May 31. "I've found something."

"What is it?" Mort asked.

"Judd made a notation on that Friday."

Mort stared at the Senator's note. Alongside the phone number 849-7241 he had written—WILL END IT TODAY—in large capital letters. He read aloud Judd's declaration.

"What do you think he meant?" Jane asked.

"I don't know." Mort replied.

"Judd was killed 4 days after he wrote that. Do you think there might be a connection between his death and that entry?" Jane asked.

"It's our first lead. Let me see if I can find out whose phone number he kept calling, then we can take it from there," Mort said grabbing the telephone. He dialed Lillian at the Midtown Library.

"I'll call you when I find the telephone number in one of my reference books," Lillian replied.

Two minutes later the phone rang. Mort pressed the speakerphone button down. "The number isn't in any of my books," Lillian said.

"What!" Mort exclaimed bewilderedly.

"Our reference books only contain numbers that are listed. 849-7241 is an unlisted number."

"Now what?" a downcast Jane asked.

Mort didn't know what to think. The more time that had passed since Webster's sudden death, the more facts had surfaced which made him realize that Jane wasn't the only one who didn't know Judd. He didn't. Millie didn't. He was beginning to feel nobody did.

Suddenly it struck him. "Doug Simons. I'll call Simons."

"Who is Doug Simons?" Jane asked.

"He's an investigative reporter for the New York Times. He's also a patient of mine. He was a member of Judd's therapy group," Mort replied.

"Will he be willing to help?" Ruth asked.

"I'm sure he will. His arrogance is a cover. Underneath he's a caring person."

"Get real Mort," Millie replied. "Simons might be many things, but caring he's not."

"Believe me he'll want to get involved. He's a reporter. He'll smell the potential for a big story," Mort said.

****

135

16

Jane Webster's eyes wandered out the window to her peaceful garden with its tall shrubbery, neatly lined begonias and manicured lawn. All so perfect. All in peace. So serene. So still. All in contrast to her inner turmoil. She had been convinced Judd was murdered as soon as she'd been informed he was dead. But 78 calls all made to a phone in New York City. A phone both unlisted and now disconnected. A phone she knew nothing about.

Were there more secrets, other hidden deceptions waiting to emerge? And if there were, would they endanger William's safety? Poor William. Her sole concern. Now, more than ever, she had to rely on Mort and Millie to help her. The more others became involved, as she painfully learned in the near tragic ending to Williams's abduction two years ago, the more the chances of a leak, a mishap. She feared her child, her only reason to continue, would be taken from her. This time, not for days, but forever.

Jane turned away from the window. "Are you sure Simons can be trusted?"

"Yes," Mort and Millie both agreed.

"Please stay for dinner," she pleaded. Ruth seconded the offer.

"Don't be ridiculous," Millie said. "Cook! After all you've been through. Never! I won't hear of it. If anything, we should take you out."

"It's no problem. I already have a roast chicken defrosting." Jane replied. "Besides, you mentioned on the phone you were starting your vacation today. Unless of course, you've already made plans."

Yvars laughed. Plans, he thought. What plans? Ever since Tyrone

Sawyer's death ten days ago, plans and schedules had gone out the window.

"On one condition. No real cooking. We'll stay only if you have something that you can easily heat up in the oven."

Jane thought for a moment. "I've got something that's perfect. I bought several small pizzas at Grand Union last week. They're in the freezer. I'll have them zapped in the microwave in two minutes."

Mort's face dropped. "I'm on a diet. Pizza won't do."

Jane smiled. "These pizzas are dietetic. Non-fat gooey cheese, everything you demand in a pizza, yet low in calories and without fat. You can't beat that combination. What do you say?"

"Fine." Mort said, after looking at Millie. "We'll stay."

The Yvars set individual place settings around the breakfast table while Jane whipped up a large tossed green salad.

"You look in good shape to me," Jane said, placing the overflowing greens in the wooden bowl on the white Parsons table. "I hope you're not one of those New Yorkers who weigh themselves five times a day and become practically suicidal when they gain a pound."

Mort laughed. "Hardly. I've been on a diet for the past several months. Millie's right to be on my back. I need reminders or I tend to slip up."

Jane carried in four individual-sized pizzas and plopped one down on each of their ceramic plates.

They ate in relative silence while a classical cassette disc quietly played Wagner's Tristan in the background. Finally, Jane broke the stillness. "Since you're both on vacation for the next two and a half weeks, why not stay in New York City and work with that investigative reporter. Do whatever it takes. I can't have peace of mind until Judd's killer is caught."

Ruth finished her crust and glanced at Mort. "I'd feel better too, if I knew you were going to be involved in helping find out who murdered my brother."

Yvars turned to Millie. "I like the idea. You've always wanted to indulge yourself on Madison Avenue, visiting all the boutiques and art galleries. Besides, listening to 'Tristan' while we've been eating dinner reminded me that the Metropolitan Opera is putting on Wagner's 'The Ring' in its entirely throughout this month. All four parts. You know how I flip over Wagner. True, we've seen 'Siegfried' twice and 'Das Rheingold' once, but that's far different than seeing Wagner's complete 'Ring' cycle. And to think Wolfgang Schmidt will play Siegfried and Gwyneth Jones, Brunhilda. It's a once in a lifetime opportunity."

Millie stared at Jane and then at Ruth. "Mort and I are therapists, we aren't detectives. We've never solved a crime in our lives. I understand your reservations about the FBI, but Butler seems different. We've met him. Jackson was impulsive, careless and cocky. Butler seems analytical, logical, and careful. He's sharp. He can be relied on."

"I'm afraid to take the chance," Jane began sobbing uncontrollably.

"Well what do you say?" Mort asked Millie.

Millie shrugged her shoulders in resignation.

"I'll call Simons tomorrow morning."

Jane signed in relief. "Thank you. Thank you both."

****

138

17

Mort was listening to the beginning of Act 3 of 'Das Rheingold' when the bell rang. It was Doug Simons. The sun sliced through the living room draperies causing him to squint.

"So this is where my money goes," Simons said.

The reporter walked over to the Galle table.

"Did I pay for this?" he said, pointing to the piece of Art Nouveau furniture. "This is the first time I've ever been inside my own shrink's home. It's a funny feeling. Until now I could only picture you in your office, sitting in your chair, leading our sessions. He paused before continuing. "Being here makes you more human, more real."

Millie entered the room, greeted Simons and then sat down on one of the three upholstered chairs surrounding the coffee table. Mort and their patient sat down on the other two.

"When you phoned an hour ago I was very surprised," Simons began. "I never imagined you'd ever call on me for help. I came to you for my problems. Now the shoe is on the other foot." He smiled. "I like this reversal of roles."

Mort looked directly at Simons. "The FBI are convinced we are dealing with murder. The medical examiners are equally convinced all three patients died from natural causes. They feel the bullets were an incidental finding in each case. It took me awhile, but after Jackson's death I'm forced to agree with the FBI that we are dealing with a killer. Someone's who's already killed four times and might well kill again."

"Who is in charge of the investigation now that Jackson's dead?" Simons asked.

139

"An agent named Butler. He seems like he knows what he's doing," Mort replied.

"That's a relief." I'm sorry Jackson was killed, but the guy wasn't all that swift. I question many people to get my stories. Invariably, I have to press them or they won't divulge any important information. Jackson didn't press much at all."

"Butler will. He's going to question all the remaining group members. He said he's going to be far more forceful than Jackson was."

Simons shook his head in disbelief. "When I found out the killer used me as a cover to manipulate Jackson into meeting him in the Park, I was shocked."

Mort handed Simons a piece of paper. "That's the phone number I told you about."

Simons stared at the number and then shoved the paper into his jacket pocket. "There's a senior vice president at Verizon who owes me a favor. I shouldn't have any trouble getting him to find out whose number this was."

"It's that simple?" Mort asked.

"Yeah. I promised I'd leave his name out of a piece I was writing. It had to do with a major scandal at Verizon. He was very appreciative."

Millie glared at Simons. "Do you often make deals like that?" she asked.

"I do whatever it takes to get my story." Simons said.

"You mentioned on the phone you had already begun your own investigation. What have you found out so far?" Mort asked.

"I don't share my information."

"You have to. Otherwise how can we work together?"

"Wait a minute," Simons replied. "Who said anything about a team effort. I was under the impression when you called, I'd be working alone. I always have. I always will."

"I have to be involved!" Yvars exclaimed.

"Why?"

"I promised Webster's wife. She's afraid for her son's safety," Mort replied.

"I know all about the kidnapping. Fortunately, the boy was found alive. Why is she worried now?" Simons asked.

"He was found alive in spite of the FBI. They screwed up. He was almost killed. She's terrified once they get involved in investigating her husband's death, they'll screw up again. This time she won't be so lucky. She'll lose her son. Then she'll have nothing. After Jackson's murder, she's more convinced than ever she can't rely on them."

"But the FBI will be involved anyway," Simons said.

"She knows that. However, she feels there's a better chance of her husband's killer being found, and at the same time protecting her son, if I'm also involved. I told her I couldn't do it alone. I thought of you. That's why I called."

Simons paused briefly. "That's very altruistic of you. However, I've learned everyone has a personal, a more selfish motive, one that goes beyond just wanting to help another. What's yours?"

Yvars hesitated briefly. "The FBI suspects I could be the killer."

"So in other words you want to clear your name. Great! I can relate to that motive better than I can your doing all this for the senator's widow. However, I still have to work alone."

"We have to work together. Believe me, I can be of help," Mort said.

"How?" Simons asked.

"Because of my particular specialty. You were referred because of your temper. Why did you come to me and not go to another psychiatrist?"

"You were recommended. You're supposedly the expert on people like me who have violent prone personalities."

"That's exactly my point. If the FBI is correct and we are in fact dealing with a murderer who's already killed four times and might very well kill again, my knowledge of the type of person capable of these murders, I'd think, would be invaluable to you."

141

Simons thought for a moment. "Okay.... but only on one condition."

"What's that?" Yvars asked.

"You agree that I have exclusive rights to the story," Simons replied.

"I'm the psychiatrist. You're the writer. Why would you even think I'd want to write an article for the NY Times about what we find out?"

"I'm not talking about the article I'll write for the Times."

"Then what are you talking about?" Yvars, exasperation in his tone, asked.

"A blockbuster book deal. Truman Capote made a ton on 'In Cold Blood.' I'm hoping for millions out of this one."

Yvars shook his head in disbelief. "I have no interest in writing a book."

"What about the millions?"

"Help me solve this case and you can have your millions."

"I'd also want to be the one on the TV talk shows."

Yvars stared at his patient in astonishment. "You're incredible. What grandiosity."

"Well?" Simons asked.

"Fine. Whatever it will take. What have you found out so far?"

"Nothing as yet. I haven't had the time. I've an important deadline to meet before this afternoon's over. Then I'll work on this. I'll plow through our worldwide web network to find more on the other four group members. If there's anything in their past worthy of note it will be in our data base system." Simons paused. "It'll be very helpful, if we are to work on this investigation together, for you to give me a general thumbnail description of the type of person we are looking for," Simons said.

"Four murders all having the same M.O. points to a serial killer," Mort said.

"Meaning?" Simons asked, taking out a notepad and a pencil and starting to write feverishly.

"Serial killers all have a pattern. They all leave their individual signatures at the scene of the crime."

"In our four cases that would be the bullets, correct?" Simons asked.

"It would seem so. However, we don't have any connection as yet between the bullets and the deaths." Yvars paused and stared at Simons.

"In all four cases the medical examiner concluded death was caused not by the bullet, but by heart failure."

Simons stood up. "What else should I know?"

"We are probably dealing with a man," Yvars replied.

"Can't a woman be a serial killer?" Simons asked.

"Yes, but in the vast majority of cases men turn out to be responsible for the killings."

"What else?" Simons asked.

"He's probably single."

"Why can't he be married?"

"He can be, but again, that's a rare finding in these cases. Usually he is a loner, very shy, no close friends, and lives in a fantasy world."

"What type of fantasy world?" Simons asked.

"That's always one of the most intriguing aspects. Each serial killer has his own imaginary world."

"Surely there must be some similarity among their worlds?"

Mort thought for a moment. "Well revenge fantasies are common, righting past wrongs, things like that."

"Are there any other similarities other than a fantasy world?"

"Yes. They frequently have parental permission. They have witnessed a parent being violent. That gives them license to do likewise if provoked."

Simons gulped hard. "You are making me nervous. I frequently am out for revenge. That's what led me to seek help. I also had a mother who'd get drunk and on occasion come at my father with a knife. I'd never kill another human being, yet I seem to fit the profile you've just described."

"Good point," Yvars smiled. "The difference is, you have a conscience, a super-ego that won't permit you to commit murder. The person I'm describing has what we term super-ego lacunae. He has gaps in his conscience. He doesn't feel guilty when he should. He's a type of psychopath. There are all degrees. Some psychopaths commit white-collar crimes. Others merely go through red lights. Our man kills."

"In other words I'd feel too guilty to ever kill anyone?"

"Exactly," Mort replied. "However, you have your own gaps."

"I do?"

"Yes. Otherwise you'd never blow up like you do, nor would you be able to bribe others for information. However, fortunately you would feel guilty if you'd killed someone. Therein lies the difference between a violent prone angry person like you and our killer."

Simons walked to the door and was about to leave when he suddenly turned around. "One further request. Don't tell Butler what we're doing. The FBI doesn't take well to anyone invading their turf."

"That's too dangerous. There's a killer out there. We need Butler." Millie said.

"Trust me Millie. I'm a pro. If you tell Butler, they'll stonewall us at every turn. We'll get nowhere."

Millie reluctantly agreed.

Simons paused and patted his jacket pocket. "I should know whose phone number this was in an hour or two."

"We'll be home," Mort replied.

****

Mort and Millie were having a sandwich in the kitchen when the phone rang. Mort picked up the phone.

"It's Butler. I've set up meetings with each of the five remaining members of your Monday evening group starting later this afternoon."

"When will you have finished seeing them all?" Mort asked.

"By 1 p.m. Monday."

"Good. Millie and I will probably be out. Leave a message. I'll get back to you as soon as we return." Mort replied.

18

"You definitely look more like the FBI agents in my novels than Jackson did," Meg Armstrong, puffing white plumes of smoke in the air, began. "He was even too large for his clothes. My agents are always fit and trim." She paused. "Like you."

"You write romantic novels don't you?"

"That's my genre."

"Why would there be a need for an FBI agent in your type of book?"

"Do you ever have sex?" Armstrong asked.

Butler blushed.

"Need I say more. So why the visit? I told Jackson everything I know."

"Jackson is dead. I've taken over the case."

"Jackson's dead? What happened?" Armstrong asked.

"He was murdered."

"This is getting very exciting. How was he murdered?"

"The killer had Jackson meet him at the park by the river at 97th Street. He supposedly had information relating to the murder of the three patients in you therapy group. Obviously it was a setup. Jackson got there. He left in a body bag."

"You definitely have a way with words. I'm going to use that line in my next novel."

"Let's get to the point. You never told Jackson you had a gun," Butler declared.

"He never asked me. My characters don't divulge information

unless asked. Neither do I," Armstrong replied.

"According to the police files you were arrested on a gun charge two years ago."

"This neighborhood isn't exactly what you'd call upscale. There are crack dealers on every street corner. Shooting and stabbings are commonplace. I'm a single woman. I have to protect myself. I bought a gun from one of the drug dealers. I knew I should have gotten a permit and then gone out and purchased one, but I hate hassles. I'd be asked why I needed a gun. I don't have time for that. My characters need me. One night there was a robbery across the hall. I heard screaming, took my gun with me and went to see what was going on. Unfortunately, when I got there, the police had already arrived. They saw my gun. I didn't have a permit. They took me to the precinct, confiscated my gun and booked me. I was so embarrassed."

"You have a gun now?"

"No." Armstrong replied vehemently.

"Level with me. Do you or don't you? You'll be in deep shit if I find out you're lying."

Meg opened her top desk drawer, reached inside and pulled out a small automatic.

Butler grabbed the gun from her hand. "All four who were killed were shot. You have a gun. I'm going to run your bullets through ballistics. For your sake, you better hope the caliber of your bullets and the bullets retrieved from our four victims do not match."

****

"Damn it! My source at Merill Lynch won't return my call. The world's gone fucking crazy," Doug Simons said, directing Butler to a chair alongside his desk.

"The words out another derivative scandal is about to break. Brazil will likely declare bankruptcy in less than 24 hours and I can't write the fucking story without my source's compliance. I need him for the details." He reached into his jacket pocket, plucked out a bottle of pills and swallowed two of them. "No wonder I have an ulcer. These Zantac don't even help any more." Simons paused. "I get so frustrated. I just want to do what I'm paid to do and I don't get any cooperation."

"I know the feeling. Folks don't cooperate with me either." Butler replied.

"I'll do my best. How can I help with your investigation?" Simons asked.

"I went over the notes Jackson took during your meeting together, I noticed he didn't have any notation concerning your having been court-martialed when you were in the army."

Simons stood up and paced the floor. "How the hell did you find out about that?"

"The same way you find out your information. You have your sources. I have mine."

"I thought that was all behind me. Besides, what does my army experience have to do with your investigation?"

"I don't know yet. Maybe nothing. Perhaps something. What happened?" Butler pressed.

"Well if you really must know, I was a wild kid. I had a wicked temper even back then. My parents couldn't control me. When I was fifteen they shipped me to a military academy in upstate New York. I wasn't exactly a model cadet there either. I was suspended for repeatedly breaking curfew. My parents gave me a choice. Either join the army or get a job. However, on no condition could I live at home again until I shaped up. I got off to a bad start in the army from day one. After that it all went downhill rapidly."

"What did you do?" Butler inquired.

"I got messed up with drugs. Mainly cocaine. I got busted one night and sentenced to five months in the brig. One month after I was out, I got busted again. I was count-marshaled, given a dishonorable discharge and sent packing."

"What turned you around?" a curious Butler asked.

"One night I went to a sleazy motel with a hooker. I got completely drunk and passed out. When I woke up the bitch was gone and so was my wallet. I decided then and there I either had to shape up or I'd be dead before long. I moved to Manhattan, got my high school diploma and then went to N.Y.U."

"What made you decide to become a reporter?" Butler asked.

"Several friends of mind went directly from N.Y.U. to either Wall Street or to one of the investment banking houses. We'd frequently get together for a drink. They'd tell me stories about what went on behind the scenes that made me cringe. It wasn't that I had become a born-again Christian or anything like that. However, finding out many extremely wealthy and respected people were involved in incredible schemes, all for their own personal greed, intrigued me. Several of them had been people my parents admired and wanted me to emulate."

"One morning I woke up and realized how ironic it would be if I became an investigative reporter. I'd spend my life ferreting out these characters and forcing my parents to read about their fallen idols. I was accepted at Columbia's School of Journalism, graduated with high honors and was tapped by the New York. Times. I've been here ever since," Simons said.

Butler got up to leave. "I'm going to talk with the others in your group. Then I'll be back. In the meantime, perhaps you'll think of other important parts of your past you've conveniently overlooked."

****

The trim, tense, gray-haired woman carefully smoothed the creases from the designer dress and then hung it on a hook on the nearby wall. "It's an Anne Klein. Do you like it? I might have one in you wife's size," Mary Hargrove said to the tall muscular man.

"I'm not here to buy anything," the agent replied, flipping open his wallet to reveal his I.D. You told me yesterday when I called that this would be a good time for us to talk."

"I'm sorry, but today won't work. My assistant is out sick and I'm the only one here to wait on the customers," Mary said.

"We'll only be a few minutes."

"I already spoke to Mr. Jackson."

"I told you on the phone that Jackson was dead. I've taken over the investigation."

"I discussed with him everything I know about the three patients in our group who were killed. I also answered all of his questions about my personal life. I don't have anything to add."

"Ms. Hargrove, I'm dealing with four murders. I have more questions to ask. I can make this easy or hard on you. Either we talk here or we'll go to my office at F.B.I. headquarters. It's your call."

Mary sighed and reluctantly led Butler into her small, neatly arranged office. There was something about her that bothered him. What was it? He stared at her briefly. Suddenly he realized what it was. It was her eyes. There was something about her oval-shaped, brown eyes that had unnerved him.

He glared into her dark eyes. She momentarily looked away. He continued staring at her eyes, through her eyes. He had learned over the years that eyes often were very revealing, at times even more telling than what the suspect had to say.

"Are you sure you have nothing to add to what you and Jackson discussed?" Butler asked firmly.

"I'm sure." Mary, her eyes wandering across the room, replied.

"Jackson's notes indicate you have violent tendencies. Have there been any other incidences you're hiding? It's better if you tell me rather than if I find out myself."

"I told you I have nothing else to say." She said in a tremulous voice.

Butler kept staring at Mary's eyes. They spoke differently. Finally she broke the silence. "One night last year, my upstairs neighbor's dog finally got to me. The damn thing never stopped barking. I had, on several occasions, gone to the apartment and asked him to do something about his dog. He'd smile, pat the damn dog he always held in his arms, and told me he would get him to be quiet. He never did. Between that and his blaring TV and the constant barking of the dog it got to be too much. I asked Max to intervene. He told me the barking didn't bother him. It was my problem. If I wanted the dog to shut up, I'd have to deal with it myself," Mary said.

"What did you do?" Butler asked.

"I went upstairs with a frying pan. I held it behind my back. When the owner opened the door, I took the pan and smashed it over the dog's head."

"What happened to the dog?" Butler asked.

"I don't know. The barking stopped. That's all I cared about."

"Didn't the owner call the police?"

"No. He'd never do that. The landlord doesn't allow pets in our building."

"But surely others must have been bothered by the dog's barking besides you."

"Of course. Every tenant complained to the landlord. However, the dog's owner is his son-in –law. He'd never make his son-in-law get rid of the dog, but if the son-in-law called the police, their private pact would no longer work. The landlord would then have had to force him to get rid of the dog."

"Have you ever gotten that angry any other time?" Butler asked, staring directly into her eyes.

She began blinking. He kept staring. "Well."

"No," Mary finally blurted out.

"I hope you are not hiding anything else from me or I'll be back," Butler said walking from her office.

****

"That bastard," Simons screamed into the phone.

"Calm down Doug," Yvars replied. "What are you talking about?"

"Butler came to see me today. He did a complete search into my background. He found out about something that happened to me years ago.

151

Something I've tried to erase from my mind."

"Is it anything you never told us about?" Mort asked.

Simons recounted all he had discussed with the FBI agent.

"Why didn't you tell Millie and me? That's what we're here for. I can understand you're not feeling comfortable telling the entire group about your court-martial and all that, but not telling Millie and me...."

Simons interrupted. "I know I should have, but I wanted the past to stay in the past. I didn't want to dredge up those bad times and have to feel those emotions again." He picked up the dictionary on his desk and heaved it against his bookcase. The heavy book crashed into a decorative vase, sending slivers of glass throughout the room.

"What was that noise?" Yvars asked.

"I lost my cool. It's nothing. I'm fine," Simons said. I'll call you as soon as my source at Verizon gets back to me."

Mort hung up the phone and turned to Millie, seated by the living room window, a copy of New York Magazine stretched out on her lap. "I can't count on Simons as much as I originally hoped."

"Why's that?" Millie asked.

Mort repeated his conversation with their patient. "If he still loses his temper that easily, I can't trust him not to lose it again. And the next time could be the critical time, the time when we are set to confront our killer. If Simons erupts, then our killer will clam up. We'll lose him before he confesses. We'll have blown it."

"Mort, if you can't rely on Simons, then get Butler more involved."

"No, I can't do that either. Remember what Simons told us about the FBI. They won't let me help them. They work alone."

"Then what are you going to do?" Millie, her anxiety mounting, asked.

"I'll have Simons gather the information I wouldn't be able to get myself, but I'll do the confronting."

"How will you manage that? He's a hands-on person. He'll never agree to that," Millie replied.

"I'll figure out ways to keep him away. I have to. I now see I don't have any other choice."

19

Butler had spent Saturday afternoon in Washington, D.C. interviewing Webster's widow. While talking with her, he also had a chance to discuss Judd with Ruth, his sister. Jane had appeared guarded, resistant to talk. However, Ruth was far more open and answered the agent's questions as best she could. She explained the reason for Jane's reluctance to talk freely to the FBI and promised she'd help in any way possible. She couldn't believe anybody would want to kill her brother. He had spent a lifetime doing good for others; the virtue she admired most.

Butler stepped over the thick television cables that snaked across the floor and approached a tall, thin man who was redirecting a large, overhanging floodlight. "Is that better?" he asked.

"Yes," came a deep booming voice from the side of the stage.

Butler pulled up a bridge chair and watched while the crew taped the final segment for a future episode of 'The Young and The Restless.'

"No, no Lyle. Not like that!" came the loud piercing voice again. "Stronger and with more passion."

The FBI agent gazed at Lyle Stuart as the actor pressed his thick lips against the beautiful young blonde lying on the couch.

"Cut," came the angry director's order. "Lyle, we aren't paying you thousands of dollars a week to kiss like that. Get into it more." The director then turned to his head cameraman. "One more take and we'll call it a day."

Butler watched in awe as the handsome actor pressed his muscular body against the blonde and then passionately kissed her succulent lips.

"That's more like it. That's what we're paying you big bucks for," the director smiled. "See you all here tomorrow at eight. We're running behind schedule. We have five episodes to shoot this week instead of four." The weary ensemble groaned in unison.

The FBI agent approached the sweaty actor. "I'm Fred Butler. Where can we talk?"

"Follow me. My dressing room is a mess, but we'll have privacy. Sorry you had to wait, but Sid's not satisfied until he feels we've got each scene down perfectly. That's why we're behind schedule."

The two men entered the room cluttered with clothes strewn across the entire floor.

Stuart tossed a bathrobe off the couch. "Take a seat." He paused and poured a glass of water. "I'm sorry about Jackson. He seemed like a very nice fellow. I don't understand why you want to talk to me. I answered all of his questions."

"I've been put in charge. I have my own questions to ask," Butler replied.

"Do you think I'm in any danger?" Stuart nervously asked.

"Perhaps."

"Should I get a bodyguard until the killer is caught?"

"That's up to you." Butler paused. "Can we begin?"

"Sure. It's just that I'm pretty scared," Stuart replied.

"That's understandable. Now, tell me anything about yourself that you neglected to tell either Jackson or Yvars."

"What makes you think I've hidden anything from any of them?"

Stuart reached for a towel lying on the floor and wiped the sweat from his forehead. I was engaged four or five years ago. One afternoon we finished shooting early and I went home to our apartment. I caught my fiancee in the sack with another guy. I went ballistic. She landed in the emergency room. I beat her up pretty bad."

"Did the hospital notify the police?" Butler asked.

"Yes. It was a terrible scene. They were going to press charges, but my fiancee persuaded them not to. I gave the police my word I'd never do such a thing again."

"Have you?"

"I never lost it like that before then and I haven't since."

"Anything else I should know?" Butler inquired.

"Only that I hope you find the killer soon. My nerves have been a mess since this all started. I'm forgetting my lines. You saw yourself that I couldn't even get into kissing today and believe me I've never had a problem in that department before."

Butler handed Stuart his card. "If you remember anything that might be of help give me a call."

****

"Watch you head," Steve Bass said as he led Butler into the trailer.

"We'll be able to talk better in here. It's quiet. Construction sites and conversations don't mesh well together."

"We could have met at your office," Butler replied.

"I like my men to see me on the job. They work harder. Everything gets done faster. So why the need for another meeting. I talked to Jackson. He seemed satisfied."

"I'm harder to please. If you have any hidden skeletons in your closet I'll find out."

Bass walked across the narrow trailer. "Care for a drink?"

"No."

The real estate tycoon poured himself a large scotch and downed the liquid quickly. "Ah, that's better. Sure I can't tempt you?"

"No."

Bass rubbed his thick neck. "There was a police captain. His name was Terry Glenn. He worked at the 17th precinct. Seven years ago we worked out a deal. That's it. Nothing more."

"Why would a police captain be interested in making a deal with a real estate developer?" Butler asked.

Bass sighed deeply. "I owned two townhouses on 63rd Street between Second and Third Avenues. I wanted to knock them down and

156

build a high-rise. However, there was one small problem. There was another brownstone between the two I owned. The asshole wouldn't sell. I couldn't build without having his property. I offered twice the market value. He didn't give a shit, said he didn't care about the money. He liked where he lived and didn't want to move."

Bass poured himself another stiff Dewars.

"What's the connection between you and Glenn?" Butler asked.

"I'm getting there. Be patient," Bass, gulping down his second drink, replied. "I didn't know what to do to get the owner to sell. Finally, I decided to scare him. I hired a hit man to stalk him wherever he went. To threaten him. Not to kill him, but to use whatever tactics his type utilizes to frighten the guy sufficiently so he'd be more than willing to sell. It took about three weeks. Finally, he called and accepted my offer."

"I still don't get where the police captain fits in," Butler said.

"After selling the brownstone to me, the bastard called the police and told them what he thought I had done to get him to sell. They investigated and found the guy I hired. They promised him immunity in return for my name. The police took me to their station and grilled me for hours. After eight or nine hours I was exhausted. I told them everything. Fortunately, I had previous dealings with their captain. He liked cash. I asked Glenn what it would take to squash the report and to drop all the charges. He said a three bedroom condo on West End Avenue in the 70's. I got him his apartment. The incident miraculously vanished. As they say, one hand washes the other."

"Did you ever mention this to either the Yvars or anyone in your group?"

"No, it never seemed relevant. I went into therapy for my temper, not for the way I conduct my business."

"Did Glenn ever help you out of other difficulties?"

Bass paused. "You mean like murder?" The barrel-shaped man asked. "I'm a lot of things, but one thing I'm not is a murderer."

"Where does Glenn live? I'd like to ask him some questions."

"You can't. You're too late. He died of cancer a year ago."

****

Butler walked to the corner and hailed a cab. He'd interviewed all five remaining members of the group. Each had given him sufficient reasons to make him feel each was capable of murder. His thoughts then shifted to Yvars. Jackson had interviewed Dr. Schwartz. Now Butler realized he should talk to Mort's former analyst. He was about to direct the driver to the psychiatrist's office when he realized Schwartz hadn't seen Yvars for over ten years. Ten years seemed too long ago to help him with what was going on now. He'd have to figure out another way to find out more about Yvars.

"Where to Mac?" the driver asked.

Butler thought for a moment. Mary Hargrove's eyes began haunting him again. He checked his watch. It was 1:30 p.m. She'd be at work. He'd catch her off guard and confront her further. He knew her type. It didn't take much to get them to crack. "935 Madison," he replied.

****

Mort dialed Jane Webster's number. "Have you found anything else in Judd's papers?" he asked.

"Just several more places where he wrote down that same phone number. Has your investigative reporter found out whose telephone number that was?"

"No. Not yet. I expect to hear from him later today. I'll call you back soon as I find out."

****

Butler walked into the upscale boutique and approached a frazzled looking salesperson. "Can I help you?" the attractive woman asked.

"I'm looking for Ms. Hargrove. Is she around?" Butler asked.

"No she's not. Are you a friend of hers?"

"Yes. I told her I was going to be in the neighborhood one day this week and I'd drop in. Do you know where she is?"

"No I don't," she replied. "I called her home. There was no

158

answer there."

"Mary always struck me as very conscientious," Butler said.

"She is. We've worked together for four years. Till last Tuesday she never missed work. She even worked once with a 103-degree fever. This is so unlike her. I hope she's okay." The salesperson paused. "What's your name? When I see Mary I'll tell her you stopped by."

"That's not necessary. I'll catch her at another time." Butler replied. He slowly turned and exited.

The agent stepped onto the sun-drenched sidewalk and smiled. His conversation with Mary had obviously unnerved her. It was time to meet with the Yvars, fill them in on what he had found out and get their feedback. After that, he'd start digging deeper into Mary's past. If there was any evidence Mary was involved with the four murders he was investigating, he'd find out.

20

Millie, sitting next to Mort on the couch, pointed to Butler's ring finger. "Does this mean you're available?"

"If you mean am I single, the answer is yes," the agent, seated across from them, said.

"Have you ever been married?" Millie asked.

"Wait a minute. I'm here to investigate four murder cases. I'm not here to be cross-examined."

"It doesn't seem fair. You are getting to know all about us and we don't know anything about you," Mort replied.

"That's the way this works. You don't tell your patients about yourselves do you?" Butler asked.

"It depends on the circumstances. If revealing something about ourselves might help them understand themselves we might." Mort said.

"Okay. I'll answer one question." Butler reluctantly replied.

"What made you go into the FBI?" Millie asked.

"My father was in the agency. He loved his work. I admired him very much. After college I went to business school. I never liked it. He encouraged me to try the FBI. It was a perfect fit. I never regretted my decision." Butler paused. "If I ever need a shrink I'll come to you. I'll tell you everything you want to know. Now, let's get down to why I'm here. I've spoken to all five of your patients. Each of them told me about a very important part of their lives. A part, according to Jackson's notes, they apparently never told you."

"Such as?" Millie asked.

"Bass hired a hit man to threaten the owner of a townhouse in the city who wouldn't sell regardless of the amount of money Bass offered him. Eventually, the hit man was caught. He told the police what Bass hired him to do. Men like Bass are well-connected. He bribed the captain of the precinct to lose the police report in return for an apartment."

"I remember your asking Bass if he had ever gotten into trouble with the law," Millie said to Mort. "He said he never had."

"Why did Bass seek your counseling?" Butler asked Mort.

"He threatened to kill a partner of his who had swindled him in some real estate deal. The intensity of his anger frightened him sufficiently to seek help."

Butler then turned his attention to Stuart. "Your soap opera hero was once engaged. He caught his fiancee in bed with another guy. He beat her up so badly she had to go to the emergency room. However, she never pressed charges," Butler paused. "Did Stuart ever mention that incident to either of you?"

"No." both Mort and Millie replied.

"What reason did he give for starting therapy?" the agent asked.

"He was approached by some gay man at a bar and freaked. He broke the guy's arm."

"Isn't that quite an overreaction?" Butler asked.

Mort thought for a moment before replying. "For us it would be. But for these incredible hunks it's not that uncommon. Some of them are latently gay. A man makes a pass at someone like Lyle. He unconsciously gets turned on, panics because his hidden desire is tapped into. He then reacts in an explosive way. His anxiety stops. He then feels ashamed and guilty because he isn't consciously aware of any of this."

"And what can therapy do for someone like Stuart?"

"The power of the unconscious is greatly diminished when you know what is going on within it."

"Has therapy helped Stuart?" Butler asked.

"Yes. Two men have flirted with Lyle recently. He told us he felt a little nervous. However, both times he didn't feel any anger. He politely smiled and walked away."

"Okay, now we come to Simons. He's got quite a past," Butler said.

"What do you mean?" Millie asked.

"He was a behavior problem. His folks sent him to a military academy. The school couldn't even whip him into shape. He tried the army. He spent most of his time either high on drugs or alcohol. One night he was drunk and stabbed another soldier. He was court-martialed. After that he told me he turned his life around. However, he's seeing you, so obviously he doesn't exactly have it all together."

Mort looked horrified. Not only was he treating a patient far more violent then he'd realized, but the same patient was the one who was helping him investigate the murders.

"Why did Simons start therapy?" Butler asked.

"He was turned down for a promotion. He became enraged and was afraid he might strangle his editor."

Now it was Butler's turn to look surprised. "According to Jackson's notes, Simons mentioned that when he wasn't given the promotion he yelled at his editor and fired his secretary. There was nothing in Jackson's report about Simons choking his editor."

"I'm not surprised. We only know what we are told. You've found out things that we didn't know about Bass, Stuart, and Simons. We knew something about Simons he never told either you or Jackson." Millie said.

"Now we come to your patient Meg Armstrong. She keeps a gun in her apartment," Butler said.

Millie gulped hard. "Meg, a gun. Why?"

What concerns me isn't that she has a gun. If my mother lived alone in New York, I'd feel more comfortable if she had a gun. You both might be accustomed to living in Manhattan, but I'm sure you'd agree it's not one of the safest places to live. What bothers me is that she never obtained a permit. She just went out and bought one."

"What made her tell you about the gun?" Mort asked.

"She didn't. Before I called on each of your patients, I ran their names through our computer system. Armstrong was arrested two years ago."

"What happened?" a shocked Mort asked.

"Apparently there was a lot of commotion in her hallway. She went to check out what was going on. There had been a robbery at one of her neighbor's apartments. The police were already there. She came barging out of her apartment holding a gun. They asked her if she had a permit. She said no. They took her to the precinct and booked her. She pleaded guilty. When the police found out she had no past record, they fined, reprimanded her and let her go. However, she went out and bought another gun without a permit."

"She just came right out and admitted that?" Millie asked.

"Of course not. I frightened her into telling me. I've met her type before. They are very stubborn. They do what they want. I had a hunch she'd purchased another gun. I told her she'd be in big trouble if she was lying. She went to the desk and handed me the weapon." Butler paused. "Can I use the phone? I sent one of her bullets to ballistics. If her bullet matches the one found in our four victims, she becomes our primary suspect."

Two minutes later Butler replaced the phone in its cradle. "Armstrong's lucky. She had a .45 caliber bullet in her gun. Our four victims were each hit by a .44."

Mort and Millie sighed in relief.

"Why did Armstrong start therapy?" Butler asked.

"Her anger at men interfered with her desire to get married." Mort replied.

"Finally, we come to Mary Hargrove. I found her the most intriguing member of your group. She's covering up something. What it is I don't know. But she knows more than she's letting on," Butler said.

"That's hard to believe. She's our most fragile patient. She's afraid of everybody. She'd be too afraid to keep a secret," Millie said.

"If she's so fearful, why did she come to you? You specialize in violent-prone patients. Why wasn't she referred to a psychiatrist who specializes in the fearful types."

"Mary is terrified of everybody. However, she, like all of us, is only human. All of us have a boiling point. If we are pushed beyond that point we get angry. Unfortunately, when Mary finally got fed up with her husband ignoring her all the time, instead of expressing anger verbally, she threw an ashtray at Max's television set. She became horrified that she lost control like that. She called for an appointment a few days later," Mort said.

"Do you know of any other time when she has lost control like that?" Butler inquired.

"Well she has. Mary's another patient who's kept something important from you," Butler said.

"What did she do?" Millie asked.

"She smashed a frying pan on an upstairs neighbor's dog. It seems there was a dog who barked all the time. She tried reasoning with the dog's owner to get the dog to stop barking. The other neighbors also continuously complained. The dog's owner did nothing. The dog kept barking. All the other tenants somehow were able to tolerate the noise. Mary couldn't, so she popped the dog with the heavy metal pan." Butler paused. "So your fragile fearful patient has another side to herself. A very violent side. She reminds me of a case I worked on several years ago. There was a series of murders. All the victims were men. They turned out to be either ex-lovers, or ex-bosses of this seemingly nice, kind, gentle, woman. However, this sensitive quiet gal also had this other side. A violent side. She bludgeoned all five men with an ax."

"Are you suggesting you suspect Mary of killing our three patients and then murdering Jackson?" Mort asked.

"No. I'm only filling you in on what I've learned about your patients. Events in each of their lives that are not only violent in nature, but events they never discussed with either of you," Butler said, scratching his thickly cropped hair. "It's hard to understand how you didn't know any of this. I've spoken to several psychiatrists around the country," Butler said, his eyes set on Mort. "They've all heard about you. Most of them have read your articles on the violent-prone patient. How could someone as well-regarded in your specialty miss such important facts about your patients?"

"Jackson asked us the same question." Mort replied. "For several months Millie and I have talked at length about the sensations we had been picking up among various members of this group. We've had many groups we've treated throughout the years. This was the only group where we have felt these strange vibes. We decided before our last session to pay close attention to these nuances and non-verbal gestures. As soon as either of us perceived any undercurrent whatsoever, we were going to directly confront the patient involved. Unfortunately, neither of us sensed anything out of the ordinary that evening. In retrospect, it's obvious we had misjudged this group very badly. The information you've gathered is additional proof of just how off we were on all of the members of this group."

"So you are in effect telling me this group was significantly different from any other group you and Millie have ever treated?"

"Yes. Quite different." Mort replied.

"How do you explain this?" Butler asked.

"We can't," Mort replied.

"How do you select the patients for you groups?" Butler inquired.

"We interview every referral and evaluate whether or not they are suitable for a group."

"And all eight were?" Butler asked.

"So we thought. We were obviously mistaken."

"How detailed a personal history do you take on each prospective patient?" Butler asked.

"It all depends on the nature of their problem. We are willing to try to help all who are referred, provided none of them had ever had a police record. If they tell us they haven't had a police record, we place them into one of our ongoing groups."

"But each of the five patients I interviewed had committed a violent act that was either reported to the police or should have been," Butler said.

"We now know that. However, we didn't then." Millie said.

"Don't you check with the police before you let a new patient into one of your groups?"

"No. We ask them. If they deny any problems with the police, we let it go at that," Mort replied.

"Isn't that naïve?" Butler asked.

"It's not naïve. We have to trust that our patients are telling us the truth. All patients who come to us have a deep-seated distrust for authority. Some of them border on overt paranoia. If we were to go behind their backs and check to find out whether they had misled us, we'd lose their trust before we had a chance to try helping them."

"So you have treated murderers before?" Butler asked.

"Not to our knowledge. We won't treat any patient if we know they have a criminal record. However, as is now apparent, some patients inadvertently slip by our evaluation process. Treating violent-prone patients is risky to begin with. Most psychiatrists won't take them on for this reason," Mort replied.

"Until this group, as far as we are aware, we've been fortunate. We've never had a patient accused of a violent crime, let alone murder."

"I'd call it lucky," Butler replied. "How are you going to prevent this from happening again?"

"There's not much we can do, except perhaps be more direct in our initial screening and confront our patients when we sense they're sending out non-verbal signals to one another. However, we can't change the overall way we conduct our groups. We still have to wait for each group to evolve to the point where each individual member will feel comfortable enough to trust each other. Then, and only then, will they reveal parts of themselves they've kept hidden from the others." Mort paused. "And at times also from us."

Butler checked his watch. It was 5:15 p.m. "That's enough for now. If you want to reach me for any reason, I'll be at headquarters for the next several hours. I want to access our central computer and get into the Internet system."

"What do you hope to find out?" Mort asked.

"I'm going to feed it Bass', Simons', Armstrong's, Stuart's and Hargrove's names. Hopefully, the search will provide me with additional information that will point me to the murderer."

"Don't you have any other suspects?" Mort asked.

"Except for you, not yet," Butler quipped.

Ignoring Butler's comment, Mort asked, "What if you don't find any connection between any of our patients and the murders?"

"Then I will broaden my investigation to find the link I'm looking for. I'll start by asking each of your patients to draw up a list of those they are in contact with on a regular basis. I'll question each of them."

"You've given yourself quite a task," Mort said.

"I don't have a choice. We are dealing with a killer who has already killed three of your patients and our agent. I have every reason to believe he will strike again." Butler paused. "Remember there are five group members still alive.....and that doesn't include their two group leaders. Until our murderer is caught, all of you are in danger, and all of you are suspects."

"Is there anyone you suspect more than others?" Mort asked.

"Not really," Butler hesitatingly replied.

"There is someone you suspect more than the others. Who is it?" Mort asked.

"There is something about that Hargrove woman's eyes that keeps haunting me. Hopefully, I'll find out tomorrow. I plan on calling on her first. Will you and Millie be home tomorrow afternoon?"

"Probably not. I promised Millie I'd take her to the Big Apple Parade on Fifth Avenue. Why?" Mort asked.

"I should be finished seeing all of your patients again by late tomorrow afternoon. I was hoping we'd meet after that to discuss what I've found out."

"If we're not in, leave a message on our answering machine. I'll call as soon as we return."

Thirty minutes had passed since Butler had left their apartment. Mort and Millie had spent the time discussing Butler's findings.

"After the killer is caught, do you think we will be able to continue our therapy with this group?" Millie asked.

"I don't know. It will be interesting to see. While therapy demands complete openness and honesty in each patient before significant changes can be made, they might all feel too exposed and too vulnerable to be willing to deal with each other again. However, that's for a later time. For now we have a far more urgent problem to attend to," Mort replied.

They were about to discuss dinner plans when the phone rang.

"It's Doug Simons. My contact at Verizon traced the phone number. The number 849-7241 belonged to Mary Hargrove."

Yvars stunned was momentarily speechless. "Mary?" He finally blurted out.

"Yes. I was surprised as you are." Simons replied. "What's her address. I'll confront her and find out why Webster called her 78 times since the beginning of the year."

"Hold on," Mort said firmly. "I think it's better if I speak to her myself."

"You called me in to help. Now you are pushing me away. I don't get it," Simons said.

"I'm not pushing you away. I still need your help. You're a great investigative reporter. You've come up with our first lead. However, your approach will terrify her. She'll clam up. She won't divulge anything. I'll have a better chance of getting her to open up."

"Why?" Simons asked curiously.

"For the same reason you feel more comfortable talking to me than

168

you do to others. I'm trained to put people at ease. Once they feel relaxed, they are far more willing to reveal parts of themselves they otherwise wouldn't. I'll talk to Mary early tomorrow morning. Then I'll call you and we'll take it from there."

21

Mary's hands trembled noticeably as she sat in the leather chair across from Mort Yvars. "Why did you insist I come over this morning?" she asked.

"We have some important things to talk about." Mort replied. He swiveled in his Eames chair to face Mary.

"I missed work yesterday. I can't afford to get fired."

"You won't get fired. Didn't you call your manager and explain you had a doctor's appointment?"

"Yes, but I still feel guilty. Tracy needs me. I get off at 5:00 p.m. on Tuesdays. Why couldn't we meet after that?"

"Because what we have to talk about is too important to have waited until then." Yvars paused. "Otherwise Butler would have barged in on you while you were at the store. I don't think that would have been very pleasant."

Mary's hands starting shaking uncontrollably.

"Calm down," Mort said. "Would you like a glass of water."

"No thanks. I'll be okay. Why do you think Butler would want to question me again?"

"Because Millie and I met with Butler yesterday and were shocked when he told us about the incident with your neighbor's dog. As a result, he thinks you are very capable of violent behavior. Why didn't you tell us about this incident?" Mort asked.

"I felt you wouldn't have let me into the group if I told you. You and Millie made it very clear you didn't treat patients who either had a police record or should have had one. You would have referred me to another psychiatrist. I had heard great things about you. I didn't want to go to anybody else. I knew it was wrong not to tell you. I was just too afraid."

"Have you ever withheld anything else from us?" Mort inquired.

"No. I told you about my throwing an ashtray at Max's television set. That's the only other time I've ever behaved violently. It scared me. I'd never let myself lose control like that ever again."

Mort fidgeted in his chair. He stared at Mary for several moments. The stillness in the air was having its desired effect.

"Dr. Yvars. You're making me nervous. Why are you so quiet?"

Mort kept staring at Mary saying nothing.

"Stop it. I can't take this silence. What's going on?" Mary asked.

"That's what I want to know," Mort replied.

"You sound like that FBI agent. You're scaring me."

"I need some answers and you're the only one who has them."

"Answers about what?" Mary asked.

"About your relationship with Senator Webster."

Mary suddenly began crying. Mort handed her a box of tissues.

"I'm waiting," Mort replied firmly.

"How did you find out about Judd and me?" Mary asked.

"After Judd died, Jane Webster asked me to investigate her husband's death. I agreed to help. We went through all of Judd's papers and bills. We noticed Judd made 78 phone calls over the past several months to 212-849-7241. I called the phone number. The line had been disconnected. I had to find out whose number Judd had called on all those occasions. I asked Doug Simons to find out. He did. He traced the number to you. However, it wasn't the phone number you gave me for my records."

Mary continued crying. "I can't believe Judd's dead. That we'll never talk again. That I'll never see him again. He was so warm, so kind, so understanding."

She dabbed the tears from her eyes. "When Judd and I decided we wanted to talk to each other, I took out an unlisted number. It was his idea.

He said it would be safer for both of us that way. I had the phone installed in my bedroom closet under a pile of sweaters so Max would never find out about our conversations."

"How did you arrange that?" Mort asked.

"I didn't. Judd came up with the way," Mary replied. "He asked me to jot down both my daily schedule as well as Max's. I handed him my list before one of our Monday evening sessions. I wrote down both our work schedules. I also included on my list a schedule of the Rangers, Knicks, and Mets games. During the week, Max either goes to a ball game or watches one at a neighborhood bar. Judd took my list and came up with our system. It worked perfectly. He'd call on my day off and whenever he knew Max wouldn't be home. He always did the calling. I wasn't ever to call him. I never did. I had the urge on many occasions, but a promise is a promise. He also made me agree not to tell anybody about our talks. He was afraid Jane would find out. He never wanted to hurt her. He loved her very much."

"If he loved her, why were the two of you having an affair?" Mort asked.

Mary looked startled. "We never had an affair. Of course, I'd fantasized about him. He was gorgeous. I'd envision us making love, his leaving Jane, my leaving Max. Our eventually getting married." Mary paused. "However, I knew nothing like that would ever happen. He was a family man. Besides, I'd seen Jane's picture in the newspapers. She's very pretty. I'm so plain and ordinary looking. Our relationship was strictly platonic. It all took place on the phone. We never even had a drink or dinner together."

Mort nodded his head skeptically. "You can't expect me to believe that. The senator was an extremely busy man. Seventy-eight phone calls are a hell of lot for him to have to made over the past several months if nothing was going on between the two of you."

"I know it sounds impossible, but it's true. We were two very lonely people. Max completely ignored me. Judd and Jane lived very separate lives. They were hardly ever together. He did his thing. She raised William and was very involved in the community. He never understood why, but somehow even when they were together, he never felt he could talk to her. He felt he could with me."

"What did the two of you talk about?" an incredulous Mort asked.

"Judd did most of the talking. I mainly listened. He'd talk mostly about his work."

"Seventy-eight calls, some lasting over an hour or two and all he discussed was his work?" Mort asked.

"Dr. Yvars, you didn't know the real Judd. He actually loved to talk. He needed a captive audience. I was that audience. He'd talk about what was going on in the Senate, various legislation his committee was dealing with, things like that. At times he'd share his future dreams with me. He had his heart set on one day running for President."

"What else did you discuss?" Mort asked.

"His frustrations at some of the egomaniacs on the hill, and of course, William. He'd go on and on about his son."

"Did he talk about Jane or other personal matters?"

"Not much. He was a very private person in that way."

"He never mentioned either Tyrone Sawyer or Eileen Matthews to you?" Mort asked.

"No. He never discussed anyone in the group."

"And you? What did you talk to him about?"

"I told you already. I mostly listened." Mary said.

"Surely you occasionally talked."

"Of course, but mainly about him. I kept pleading with Judd to tell the group who he really was. At times I'd complain about Max, but I did lots of that in the group. I didn't feel the need to talk to him much about Max. In fact I didn't want to. I wanted our relationship to be special. Talking about Max too much would ruin it for me. I was so proud of Judd when he finally opened up and told the group the truth about himself. Then the next day he died. I don't know how I'm going to go on without him. Our talks were all I had. Now I have nothing."

Mort leaned forward in his chair. "We also found a notation in his diary on May 31st. Next to your phone number he had written down Have to stop these calls."

Mary smiled weakly. "Judd repeatedly would call and tell me we had to stop having our conversations. That he was feeling too guilty for us to continue talking."

"You've said nothing was going on. Why would he feel guilty?" Mort asked.

"He was afraid Max would find out and make my life even more miserable than it was. I'd tell him not to worry. He'd be reassured and our talks would continue."

"Did he call May 31st?" Mort asked.

"I don't know. I didn't keep a record of when he called. However, he did call several times that week. During one of those calls he needed reassurance. I gave it to him. That could well have been on the 31st. I just don't remember."

"Did he call you after that?"

Mary thought for a moment. "I don't think so. That must have been the last time we talked." Tears welled up in her eyes again.

"When did you and Judd start this arrangement? Both of you were in our group for over a year and a half, yet according to Judd's phone bills your phone calls only began this past January?"

"I guess you could say we were matched up." Mary said.

"By who? How?" Mort asked.

"After our meetings I'd walk back to my apartment. Sometime last fall I started noticing this older man standing by the corner. I didn't think anything of it. However, after I saw him four or five times, he approached me. He was smiling and appeared very nice. He had a lot of trouble breathing, so I asked him if he was okay. We started talking. He introduced himself. He told me to call him Jim. He invited me for coffee at a nearby diner on Columbus Avenue. Max was at a Knick's game and wouldn't be home until after ten, so I agreed. We talked for about an hour. He seemed very

174

nice and sweet. He told me his wife had recently died, that he was very lonely and wanted to know if it would be all right if we did this again. I gladly agreed. We began having coffee at the same diner after my group sessions every Monday evening."

"What about Max?" Mort asked.

"Max never gets home on Mondays until after ten. If he's not at a ball game, he watches one at a bar with buddies. I've always cherished Mondays, even before joining the group. Monday is the one night Max is always out. I know I won't have to look at his face or have any contact with him at least on that one night each week."

"What did you and Jim talk about?" Mort asked.

"Jim mainly wanted me to talk. He asked me all sorts of questions about myself, my work, even about our group. After several weeks, I got up the courage to tell him about a crush I had on one of the members of the group."

Yvars thought of the five men in the group. "I take it you were talking about either Webster or Lyle Stuart," he finally said.

"It was Judd. Lyle Stuart's not my type. He's too taken with himself. Jim said he wished he had someone he felt strongly about. He asked me to describe Judd. I did. When we met on the following Monday, he told me he had made a point to wait near your office at 8 p.m. when we'd all be leaving. You can't imagine how surprised I was when Jim told me he not only recognized the man I had a crush on, but knew who he was. When he told me who Jeff Osgood really was, I almost fell off my chair. I asked him how he knew. He refused to tell me. However, he asked if I'd like to get to know Judd outside the group setting. I jumped at his offer."

"How was he going to orchestrate your getting together?" Mort asked.

"Jim said he was quite friendly with a colleague of Judd's in congress. I was so excited at the possibility of our getting together. However, the idea of a handsome senator wanting anything to do with me seemed preposterous."

"What happened then?" Mort asked.

"Jim insisted that I was mistaken. He said his friend had assured him Judd was a very lonely man and wanted companionship desperately. He'd have his friend talk to Judd and set things up. In return, Jim wanted me to do a favor for him. I figured I had nothing to lose, so I agreed. I almost fainted after group about one month later, when Judd stopped me as I was leaving your office. We began talking. It was amazing. Here was this handsome senator all excited about having a relationship with me. We worked out the ground rules. It was then that he came up with his plan. He asked me to get an unlisted private line that would be just for him. From then on we talked at least once a week until...." Mary's voice trailed off.

"What did Jim want from you?" Mort asked.

"He wanted to know what Judd and I discussed, especially about his work."

"Did he want information about his personal life?" Yvars asked.

"Not usually. He was mostly curious about Judd's daily routine, his comings and goings. What time he usually arrived at the Senate and when he left for the day. Trips he'd take. All of his coming plans with specific dates. He also wanted to be notified whenever Judd's plans unexpectedly changed."

"Such as?" Mort asked.

"For example, he was to meet with a bank president in Connecticut one day in April. He had a flight booked at one, returning at six. The day before he was to go, his Banking Committee called an urgent meeting. Judd had to postpone his meeting with the bank president until the following week. Things like that. He had me write everything down and give the notes to him each week."

"Why did this fellow Jim want to know all these details?" Yvars asked.

"I asked him on several occasions. He would never reply."

"Didn't his lack of a response seem odd to you?" Mort asked.

"Very," Mary replied.

176

"Then why didn't you press him for an answer?"

"I had a good thing going. For the first time in my life, I had in Judd a man, who for whatever reasons, valued me and liked to talk to me. I counted on him. I was afraid to rock the boat. I was frightened that if I pushed Jim too hard he might get his friend to intervene and get Judd to stop calling me. I didn't want to risk that happening. I needed Judd in my life. I still do," Mary replied tearfully.

"What is this fellow Jim's last name?" Yvars asked.

"I don't know. He never told me."

"Didn't you ask?"

"Of course. But again I was too fearful to make a big deal out of it. Besides, I didn't really care. I had Judd. That's all that mattered. Then Judd was killed and suddenly I felt lost, without anybody who cared for me, without anybody I cared for."

"What about Jim? Didn't he care?" Mort asked.

"I thought so. What a fool I was. I'll never learn," Mary said.

"What happened?"

"After our last Monday evening group session I met Jim like I always did. I answered all his questions about Judd's whereabouts. However, the next day he called me at my home. I didn't feel well and had taken the day off. He wanted us to meet again. This time at a different diner, one on York Avenue, rather than at our usual spot near your office. I met him there. He told me Judd had been in a car accident and had been killed. I was shocked. I couldn't speak. Then he announced this was to be our last meeting, that he didn't want us to meet anymore. He also was insistent I never call him again."

"Did he say why?" Mort asked.

"I was so shocked. I don't remember," Mary began crying once again.

"Have you tried calling Jim since?" Yvars asked.

"Yes. I called several times. Each time there was no answer. I kept calling, hoping he'd pick up the phone, that we'd talk, that I'd convince him that without Judd I now needed him more than ever. Then one day, it must have been several days after Judd's death, I called again. This time the phone was answered. However, it wasn't Jim who was on the line. It was the operator on a recording. Jim had had his phone disconnected."

"Do you know where Jim lives?" Mort asked.

"No. That was something else he never would tell me." Mary said.

"Fortunately, you have his phone number. That's important. What is it?"

"238-7423, but I don't see how the number can help you. I told you Jim disconnected his phone."

"The midtown library has a reverse phone directory. I'm friendly with the research librarian. She can locate anybody's name and address provided she has their phone number and their number is listed."

"It's no use. Jim's number was unlisted."

Yvars thought for a moment. "Doug Simons will be able to find out who this Jim is."

"How is that possible?" Mary asked.

"He's one heck of an investigative reporter. He has his methods. He found your name by knowing your phone number. I'm sure he'll be able to track Jim's last name and address the same way." Mort paused. "Once Simons finds out who Jim is and where he lives, I'll meet with him. Hopefully, he'll have some of the answers we're looking for."

"Do you think Jim killed Judd and the others?" Mary asked.

"I don't know. However, with Simon's help, if he did, or if he is in any way involved, we'll find out." Yvars stood up. "Do you have any family?" he asked Mary.

"Yes, a niece in Rochester. Why?"

"I think it's a good idea if you go and stay with her until the killer is caught."

"You don't think whoever killed Judd and the others would want to kill me, do you?" Mary asked.

"I don't know, but I don't want to take the chance he might. Can you get away from Max?" Mort asked.

Mary looked up at her therapist. "Not if I ask him."

"What about if you just go while he's at work?"

"I could do that."

"Would Max be able to find out where you are if Butler or anyone else asked him where you went?"

"No. He knows I have a relative, but he has no idea who she is or where she lives. They've never met," Mary replied.

"That's good," Mort said.

"What about my work? I can't leave Tracy to handle everything at the boutique by herself. The manager will get furious. I'll be fired."

"No you won't. Tell both your manager and Tracy you have to go out of town immediately. That an elderly family member who lives alone suddenly became very sick and she needs you. They'll understand. Everything will work out fine."

"What will I tell my niece? She'll think it's very strange that after all this time I am going to visit her. She knows all about Max. She knows he wouldn't let me go."

"Does she know how angry you are at Max?"

"Certainly. She's been begging me to leave him for years."

"Then tell her what she wants to hear…..That you've finally gotten your courage up and you're leaving him. She'll be thrilled."

Mary rose from her chair and faced Mort. "You don't think I killed Judd or the others, do you?"

Yvars sighed. "I don't, but all those phone calls and Judd's notation in his diary next to your phone number on May 31st that he was going to 'stop it,' are very incriminating. Once Butler digs deeper, and he will, he'll find the phone number in Judd's diary and that all those phone calls were made to you. He'll also, sooner or later, discover Tyrone Sawyer was Webster's son and that Eileen Matthews and the senator had an affair. He'll link all of this together. He'll conclude Judd rejected you and in revenge you killed him, his son and his mistress."

179

"What are you talking about?" Judd never told me Tyrone was his son or that he was seeing Eileen Matthews?"

"He never told us either. Millie and I didn't find this out until after Tyrone and Eileen were both dead."

Mary began shaking. "I don't want to believe Judd·was no different from Max. From Jim. From every other man I've ever known."

"I'm sorry I had to tell you this, especially now, but we all have to face these hard truths. I tried denying that three members of our group were murdered, but after Jackson was killed, I couldn't keep duping myself."

"I didn't kill anybody," Mary whimpered.

Yvars nodded his head in agreement. "However, after Butler finds out everything you've told me, he might have sufficient circumstantial evidence to issue a warrant for your arrest. The killer will still be out there ready to kill again. He'll be afraid you know something and might talk. He won't be able to take that chance. He'll likely come after you." Mort paused.

"Now go home and pack."

*

Shortly before leaving his office, Mort dialed Simons at the Times and recounted his conversation with Mary Hargrove.

"Holy shit. Meek, timid Mary involved in Webster's murder?" Simons asked incredulously.

"I didn't say that. I only repeated what Mary told me. We need to find out who this fellow Jim is and where he lives in the city. He had an unlisted phone number. It was 238-7423. Please ask your contact at Verizon to get this information for us."

"I'll get on this right away. I think we're finally getting somewhere," Simons gleefully replied. "Let's hope so," Yvars said, hanging up the phone.

22

Mort and Millie climbed the marble steps of the African Embassy on Fifth Avenue near 75th Street to have an unobstructed view of the ongoing parade.

The warm midday sun bathed a twenty-four-piece band as they marched briskly past the onlookers. They briefly stopped, directly in front of the Embassy, to play a John Sousa classic.

"This is more fun than I expected it to be," Mort said, leaning over and kissing Millie on her cheek.

Millie pointed to the float slowly making its way down Fifth Avenue. "Aren't they cute?"she said as she looked at the performers. "Promise me you'll take me to see 'AIDA' soon. The show isn't going to run on Broadway forever."

"You know I don't like musicals. Why can't you go with one of your friends."

"Because I want to go with you. I don't like opera, but you do, so I go. What's the big deal?" Millie asked.

"Okay. I promise I'll get us tickets for a matinee one afternoon during our vacation," Mort reluctantly replied.

Millie squeezed Mort's hand. Give and take. That's what marriage was all about.

Mort spotted a hot dog vendor on the corner of 75th Street. "I'm hungry. How about a frankfurter?"

Millie smiled and took Mort's hand. They treaded their way past a group of four bearded, literary types deeply embroiled in a debate over the merits of spending taxpayers' money on something as frivolous as a parade, and a young couple staring romantically in each other's eyes. "The turnout is much smaller than I thought it would be," Millie said. "In past years I've been told the avenue is lined two and three deep with people jammed together like sardines. It's too bad there isn't more of a crowd today."

Mort ordered two hot dogs covered with a mound of sauerkraut, handed one to Millie and then asked for a large pretzel. "Now this is heaven," he said, sinking his teeth into the juicy frankfurter. "I've decided to loosen up a bit. If I gain a few pounds, what's the big deal? I'm not going to let myself balloon out again and be like others I know who keep a thin and a fat wardrobe. I've decided I've been overdoing this dieting thing."

Millie smiled. "Enjoy," she said.

Suddenly, two muscular men dressed in long white coats and carrying large black bags crashed into them. "Sorry," the taller one said.

"It's okay. I was once a resident myself. I was always in a rush," Mort said.

"We've been on call for 36 hours," the shorter of the two said. "We're starved."

"The hot dogs are great," Mort said, biting down hard on his roll.

They parted company. Millie and Mort began heading back to the Embassy.

"Let's stop here," Millie said. "Isn't 'The Lion King's' float beautiful?"

*

A trim, well-dressed figure carrying a black attaché case stood in Central Park beside a thick oak tree directly across the street from Mort Yvars. The stranger's eyes darted in all directions. Those on the sidewalk were engrossed in the parade. None watched as the stranger walked toward an isolated small patch of greenery shaded by a tall tree. The figure planted both feet behind the broad, expansive trunk and carefully placed the attaché case on the ground. A heavy, effeminate man stopped momentarily by the tree, while his equally overweight poodle lifted his hind leg. "Good boy Frankie, come on," the high-pitched voice said as he patted his white fluffy creature. The man and his dog quickly disappeared in the park.

The figure kept staring at Yvars, slowly bent down, snapped open the attaché case and lifted out the revolver equipped with a silencer. The stranger then stood and waited for the perfect opportunity to press the trigger.

*

Mort and Millie were riveted on a juggling act from Big Apple Circus, when a large group of young men and women carrying PRO-LIFE banners raced onto Fifth Avenue disrupting the jugglers and sending their tennis balls careening in all directions.

Several police on the scene immediately pushed the PRO-LIFERS back to the side. "No wonder I thrive in New York. There's never a dull moment," Millie said.

Mort pointed to a float nearing 74th Street. "Look at all those actors in animal costumes. What show is that?"

Millie glanced up the street. "That must be 'Beauty and the Beast'. Another show I'd like us to see."

*

The thin figure appeared from behind the mammoth tree and eyed Yvars, now munching on his pretzel. The stranger recognized the woman with the doctor and smiled. They were standing alone. The nearest person was ten feet from them. The stranger finally had a completely unobstructed view of Mort Yvars.

The figure quickly lifted the automatic, took careful aim at Mort's chest and fired. Suddenly, three hippies on black Harley Davidsons appeared from nowhere and accelerated down Fifth Avenue.

The bullet ricocheted off one of the motorcycle's fenders and struck Millie in her right arm.

Millie let out a shriek, put her hand to her arm, and began gasping for air as she fell to the ground. Mort moved to her side. Her face was rapidly turning ashen gray. He felt for her pulse. It was weak. He breaths were coming in short, quick spurts.

Immediately, the two white-coated physicians standing nearby, ran over to the stricken woman. The taller of the two pushed Yvars aside and began administering mouth to mouth resuscitation. The other doctor reached into his medical bag, pulled out a needle and syringe, grabbed a small vial, filled the syringe with the liquid and plunged the fluid into Millie's cold, limp arm.

Mort bent down again. "She's my wife. What happened? Is she all right?" he asked, his voice shaking.

"I think so. A few more minutes and she'd have died. The adrenaline I injected saved her life." The doctor felt for her pulse. It was stronger now, more forceful. A pink hue reappeared on her face. "Is you wife allergic to anything?" the taller doctor asked Mort.

"Not that I know of. Why?" he asked.

"Because she was in anaphylactic shock," the doctor said.

The taller resident scooped Millie into his arms. He then paused and faced Mort. Your wife's a lucky woman. We work two blocks away at Lenox Hill Hospital. I'll carry her there. Once we're in the emergency room we'll give her intensive treatment. She should pull through."

Mort stared at his unresponsive wife. Her breathing was quieter, more normal. All rales and wheezes were gone. She let out a moan, then another. She was coming to.

Mort signed in relief. He was about to follow the two residents when he spotted a small, metal object where Millie had been standing. He bent down to retrieve it. It was a small caliber bullet. His hand shaking, his face now white, he placed the bullet into his pocket and began running to catch up to the two white coats in the distance.

*

The frustrated stranger replaced the revolver into the attaché case and rapidly disappeared into the park.

23

"We both know that bullet was meant for me," Mort, seated at the foot of Millie's elevated hospital bed, said.

Millie propped upright, with three pillows under her head, took Mort's hand in hers.

"How are you feeling?" Mort asked. "You look incredibly good for somebody who was in shock just yesterday." Yvars glanced around the modern, well-equipped hospital room. The cardiac monitor was no longer on. Her intravenous was out.

"I feel fine. I can't remember what happened. The mind really is great at self-protection, isn't it? I remember eating a frankfurter while watching the Parade. Then I go blank. The next memory I have is your leaning over me in this bed late last night."

"God does work in mysterious ways. I get upset every time I relive what happened to you. If it wasn't for those two residents from Lenox Hill at the Parade, you'd never have made it." Mort said, his body tensing once again. "Are you really leveling with me? Do you actually feel completely fine."

"Absolutely. Like nothing ever happened. I was up walking the hall several hours ago. I even ate a normal breakfast."

Yvars walked to the window overlooking a floral garden dotted with multi-colored begonias and impatiens. "You've got a beautiful view. I've never been to Lenox Hill before. It's quite a lovely facility. Not as state-of-the-art as Wentworth Hospital is, but definitely more than adequate." He turned and walked to a nearby table where a dozen long-stemmed red roses stood in a tall glass vase. "Do you like them?" he asked.

Millie smiled, "I've never known you to be a romantic. Maybe I should get shot every day."

Mort ambled to a brown vinyl armchair near the corner of the room and sat down. "Have you seen Dr. Evans yet this morning."

"I most certainly did. He was in before seven," Millie paused. "We think of ourselves as workaholics. He makes the two of us look like pure unadulterated hedonists. He gets to the hospital by six every day and that includes Sunday," Millie said.

"How does he feel you're coming along?" Mort asked.

"Excellently. Since I'm not a doctor, I didn't catch all the technical details. You can call him for the particulars. He said all my blood tests were normal as were all of the other tests they did on me last night."

Relief swept across Mort's face. "What is Evan's game plan for you from here on in?" he asked.

"Evans believes I can be discharged and continue recuperating at home. We're still on vacation. You can go to your operas. Once the doctors say I'm well enough to carry on as usual, I'll take you up on your promise. We'll go to the theater. I'll finally get to see 'AIDA'. Until then we can rent some X rated movies from Blockbuster's and practice their techniques."

"While you're recuperating, hopefully, Simons will start getting somewhere with our investigation."

Millie looked astonished. "What do you want to accomplish? Get yourself killed. This isn't our problem anymore. Neither is it yours. It's the FBI's. Perhaps the CIA's. Maybe even another one of our government agencies, but it's certainly not ours. You're in way over your head. If Doug Simons is crazy enough to want to carry on with his own investigation that's his business," Millie pleaded.

"You're probably right Millie. However, I can't stop. Not now. I agreed to get involved initially because Jane Webster pleaded with me, then to clear my name. However, after yesterday afternoon I feel compelled to continue. Somebody is out there to kill me. He almost killed you. He's going to try again. I can't trust others to make sure that we stay alive. I've got to ensure our safety."

"Are you certain you aren't just being sucked into proving you're macho?" Millie asked, reaching over to the nearby night table and picking up a glass of water. "Aren't you doing this to once and for all prove to yourself that you're a man? That you can finally defeat your father…your fears. Please Mort, find another remedy to feel good about yourself. Not this one. I don't want you to get killed. I want us to get old together."

"I understand how you feel, but I can't turn back now. You've always accused me of being stubborn to a fault. Once I zero in on something, I go all out. Perhaps you're right. Whether it's my macho needs, or to clear my name, or to save our lives, or perhaps even some other hidden motive, I'm not even aware of, I don't know. I don't care. All I know is that I have to do whatever it takes to stop whoever he is from further wrecking our lives."

Millie began sobbing. "It's all my fault. I never should have forced you to face what was happening. I should have let your denial win out. I should have kept my big mouth shut and not have asked Butler to look at your bicycle tires."

Mort moved closer to Millie and gently rubbed his fingers through her brown wavy hair. "Don't get down on yourself. I love you. All of you. Even your big mouth."

"But I'm now more afraid than ever," Millie replied, taking a sip from the glass before returning it to the night table.

"I know." Mort took a deep breath. "Hand me Dr. Evans' number. I want to know what his findings were."

Yvars dialed Evans' extension. "It's Dr. Yvars, Millie's husband. We met in the emergency room yesterday. How is she doing?"

"She is an extremely lucky woman," a tense, deep voice replied. "A few seconds more and she would have been dead. Now look at her. Doesn't she look great?"

"Yes," Mort replied. "Amazingly so. I can hardly believe how normal she seems. It's almost as if yesterday never happened." Yvars paused. "What tests did you run?"

"Everything you can think of. Initially, as we discussed in the emergency room, her symptoms all pointed to her having had a myocardial infarction. We hooked her up to a cardiac monitor, put in a femoral arterial cutdown in case she went back into shock and kept a defibrillator in her room to be on the safe side should she arrest. We kept her dopamine intravenous drip running until her blood pressure eventually stabilized. We took several vials of blood, ran every conceivable blood test, all the while concentrating on those tests such as the erythrocytic sedimentation rate and the transaminase levels, which as you are aware, are indicative of an evolving heart attack. All the tests came back completely normal. We repeated them twice more. Each time four hours apart. All results were still normal. Her EKG's and the constant printouts from the cardiac monitor kept showing a normal sinus rhythm. She didn't even have any preventricular contractions. We decided to do an angiogram. All her cardiac vessels were completely open. No blockage. Nothing. For the time being there's no need for further testing. She is totally fine."

"What caused her to go into shock?" a puzzled Yvars, asked.

"I discussed your wife's case with several of my colleagues," Evans replied. "We've all reached the same conclusion. Your wife developed an overwhelming allergic reaction starting at the site of the bullet wound. All her symptoms, in retrospect, point to her immune system pouring forth massive amounts of histamine causing her to go into shock. The adrenaline administered directly into her vein, by one of our residents at the Parade, saved her life. It counteracted the excessive histamine. There is no other possible explanation. She had a severe, nearly fatal, anaphylactic reaction."

"She was fine one moment. Then she was shot. Could she have developed such an allergic reaction to the bullet?"

"My colleagues and I believe that very likely something was on the bullet that precipitated her body's violent reaction."

Still confused, Yvars pressed on. "Such as?"

"We don't know. The forensic pathologist is in the process right now of analyzing the bullet you gave me yesterday," Evans replied.

"What should Millie and I do now?" Mort asked.

"Help your wife get dressed for discharge."

"Millie mentioned you told her that. I didn't believe her. You can't be serious," Mort said. "She practically died less than 24 hours ago. How can she possibly be well enough to be discharged?"

"I understand your concern." Evans replied, lighting a cigarette and inhaling deeply. "Our bodies are incredibly fragile on one hand, but extremely resilient on the other. When Millie was brought in she was in anaphylactic shock secondary probably to the allergen on the bullet. The allergen is now completely out of her system. That's why she isn't in any further danger. This morning we gave her a booster shot of 50 milligrams of Benadryl intramuscularly as a precautionary measure on the off chance her system might still be harboring a minute quantity of the allergen. Other than that, we haven't given her any other medications. She hasn't needed any. She won't need any. She's fine. As weird as it sounds it's true. She's made a complete recovery. Believe me, I wouldn't discharge her if my colleagues and I didn't all agree it was the proper course of action to take. Trust me. Her symptoms cannot reoccur. However," he paused briefly and took another deep puff from his cigarette before continuing, "Your wife told me Dr. Clarke is her internist. I'm going to give him a call and ask him to examine her thoroughly sometime within the next few days. One can never be overly careful in matters like these."

Mort glanced at Millie resting comfortably. "Thanks for all your help," he said, replacing the phone in its cradle. He then asked the operator to ring the forensic pathology laboratory. A Dr. Uppmann picked up on the fifth ring. "Ah yes, the bullet case!" he replied to Mort's question in a matter-of-fact tone. "We could not find anything unusual on the bullet. It was clean except for some black paint markings, probably caused when the bullet hit the motorcycle before striking your wife. We analyzed the bullet very carefully. We could not find any trace of a chemical, nor toxin. Nothing but your garden variety .44."

Mort slammed the phone down. He stood up and paced the hospital room.

"What was that all about?" Millie asked. "What did Dr. Evans say? Am I being discharged or not?" Please tell me what's going on," Millie asked apprehensively.

Mort didn't respond. Instead he grabbed the telephone once again and began feverishly pressing numbers.

"Wentworth Hospital," a melodious female voice answered. "What extension do you want?"

"Dr. Leeds. Pharmacology Department please." Yvars replied.

Two minutes later a hoarse voice answered. "This is Dr. Jerome Leeds. What can I do for you?"

"Jerry! It's Mort Yvars. I'm calling from Lenox Hill Hospital. Millie was shot yesterday while we were out watching the Parade on Fifth Avenue. The bullet only grazed her skin yet she went into shock. She almost arrested. Fortunately, there were two doctors nearby, one of whom injected her with adrenaline. She's fine now. Tell me Jerry, in your experience, have you ever come across anything that sounds vaguely similar to what I've described?"

"Which one, being shot or going into anaphylactic shock?"

"Being shot, without the bullet penetrating very deeply, yet still going into shock."

"No. I haven't," Leeds paused and thought for a moment. "But I can speculate if you want me to."

"Yes. Please do. Anything! The forensic pathologist I spoke to analyzed the bullet for chemical poisons and whatever else they test for. He found nothing," Mort said.

"That's not surprising," Leeds rapidly responded. "There are many chemicals which can cause sudden massive collapse of the cardiovascular system, precipitate anaphylactic shock, and cause sudden heart failure.

191

Each of these chemicals has different mechanisms of action. From your description I'd guess that the bullet was probably coated with a chemical that precipitated a massive allergic reaction with cardiac arrest following almost instantaneously," Leeds replied.

"But there were no traces of chemicals either on the bullet or in Millie's blood or urine," Yvars replied.

Leeds thought for a moment. "I can't be certain of course, but if you want an educated guess I'd say you are dealing with a chemical that acts immediately on impact and is rapidly metabolized. This way there can't be evidence of any chemical either on the bullet or in the victim's system. Furthermore, by the time the chemical is metabolized, which I'd imagine would occur via the kidneys and not the liver, whatever metabolites might still be present are undetectable with our present technology."

"Thanks Jerry. You've been very helpful," Mort said, hanging up the phone.

"Will you kindly tell me what all these phone calls and medical lingo have been all about?" Millie asked.

Mort recounted the contents of his phone calls with Drs. Evans, Uppmann, and Leeds. "The parallel is striking between all four murders and what happened to you," Mort said as he started packing Millie's nightbag.

She stared at him and her spirits sank.

*

Mort poured the hot tea into a cup and brought it to Millie seated at the kitchen table. He then went into the den and played back his messages. There were two calls from insurance brokers, one offering a free cruise to the Bahamas in exchange for a five hour tour of the City, a planned community somewhere in rural Pennsylvania, and five calls from FBI agent Butler.

Mort felt his pulse quicken as he dialed Butler's number.

"It's about time. Where the hell have you been? I've been calling since yesterday afternoon," the angry agent said.

Mort recounted what had happened to Millie.

"How is she doing now?"

"The doctors say she is fine. They discharged her about an hour ago. We just got home. With all that's happened I forgot to check my machine until now."

"I'll call the forensic pathologist myself. I think you and Millie are in grave danger until the killer is caught. I've got some very interesting news for you. I can't find Hargrove anywhere. I went to the store where she works. The salesperson told me she hadn't come in all day. I asked if she knew where Mary was. Unfortunately, it was her first day at that particular branch. She didn't even know who Mary was. I then went to her apartment. Nobody was home. I waited for her husband to show. After three hours, when he still wasn't home, I went back to headquarters. I accessed Max Hargrove's file, found out where he works and paid him a visit this morning. I warned you about those eyes," Butler said.

"What did Max have to say?" Mort asked.

"He was furious. He got home from a bar after the ball game last night and Mary wasn't there. He went into the bedroom and noticed her dresser drawers were open and many of her clothes were missing. Need I say more!"

"What did Max do then?" Yvars asked.

"Nothing. He called her a lot of names. That's about all. I asked him if he had any idea where Mary might be. He didn't. He didn't seem to care. It's like nothing happened. I asked if Mary had any family or friends she might have gone to visit. He thought she might have a niece, but if she did, he didn't have any idea where she lived."

Mort felt his tension lift. His plan had worked. Mary had left town before Butler could confront her.

"Do you know where she might have gone?" Butler asked.

"No I don't," Mort replied.

"Well, she can't disappear forever. I'm going to send out an APB describing Mary to our various headquarters throughout the country.

Sooner or later she'll surface and one of our agents will pick her up. Then we'll find out exactly what those eyes know."

After hanging up the phone, Mort returned to the kitchen. Millie was putting her empty cup in the dishwasher. "I overheard your end of the conversation. What did Butler have to say?" she asked.

Yvars repeated his conversation with Butler, omitting the agents concern for their safety.

"Does Butler know about all those phone calls Mary had with Judd Webster?"

"I doubt it. If he did I think he would have mentioned it."

"Why didn't you tell him?" Millie asked.

"For the same reason I didn't tell him I'm responsible for Mary's leaving the city."

"Mort, trying to solve these murder cases is one thing. Obstructing justice is another. You're playing with fire. I don't want you killed, nor do I want you in jail."

Their conversation was interrupted by the phone in the nearby foyer. Mort grabbed the receiver.

"It's Dough Simons," the investigative reporter said. "How's Millie?"

"She's fine. The doctors discharged her a few hours ago. She's sitting in the kitchen right now."

"My contact at Verizon came through again. He found out Jim's name as well as his address."

"Who is he?" Mort asked.

"I don't think it's a good idea to talk about this on the phone."

"You're not getting paranoid on me, are you?" Mort asked.

"Not at all. When we meet it will be very obvious why I'm being so cautious."

"Come here then. Millie and I aren't going anywhere. I'll see you in about thirty minutes," Mort said.

"That's too soon. I'm still finding out information about him."

"When do you think you'll be finished?" Mort asked.

"In about two hours. However, I don't want to meet at your place."

"Why not?" Yvars asked.

"I'm too wired. When I feel like this I need to unwind. Only a sauna will relax me. Go to my health club on 57th Street and Eight Avenue. I'll call the receptionist at the desk and tell her you'll be coming as my guest. She'll let you in. Meet me inside the sauna at four."

"I'll be there," Mort replied, hanging up the phone.

24

What lengths one had to go to, Mort thought as he entered the sauna room at the Westside Health and Racquet Club, removed his terry cloth bathrobe and hung it on a nearby hook. What could Simons have found out that unnerved him to the point he refused to discuss his findings on the phone. He'd known Simons to be hot tempered and flare up in anger....but to behave cautiously, until now, never.

Mort sat on the hot damp wooden bench in the small oven alone for seven minutes. No one else would have agreed to such an outlandish request, he thought, as the heat was beginning to make him feel dizzy.

He climbed from the wooden seat and was about to leave the hot room and wait over by one of the nearby cool swimming pools, when Simons opened the heavy door and came in.

"Thanks for agreeing to meet me here. I'm already starting to loosen up. Sorry I'm late. I kept getting more and more information on Jim. Facts I believed might be too important to overlook."

"What did you find out?" Yvars asked.

Sweat began pouring heavily down Simons face and over his entire torso.

"Ah, the cleansing body. What a wonderful feeling. The pores opening up. The angst flowing out."

The heat was taking its toll on Mort. "I'm waiting," Yvars said impatiently.

"I spent all the time hooked into our Internet system at the Times. Have you ever used the Internet? The information it has at its disposal is mind boggling."

"No I haven't. I'm very old fashioned that way." Yvars said.

"Well one day you'll come to my office. We'll access your name. Wait until you see how much data the system has on you. On all of us," Simons replied excitedly.

"Who is Jim?" Yvars perspiring profusely, asked.

"Forgive me. I've gotten carried away. You'll remember why after I finish briefing you on all I've learned." Simons paused. "My contact at Verizon traced 238-7423 to 625 Madison Avenue. The office of a Jim Carlin. The unlisted number was disconnected on Saturday June 10th. Does that name Jim Carlin sound familiar?"

Mort thought for a moment. "No. Should it?"

"He was a former United States Senator," Simons replied.

"I guess I spend too much time reading my psychiatric journals and not enough time to keeping up with current events," Mort replied. "Please come to the point. I'm about to faint from the heat?"

"Jim Carlin was not only a former senator, but he was a senator from Colorado," Simons said.

"I still don't get what you're driving at."

"Judd Webster was a senator from Colorado. Do you know how he became senator?" Simons asked.

"No," Yvars replied.

"He defeated Carlin in the primary five years ago. Webster then went on to win the election. In other words Webster took over Carlin's senatorial seat."

"Why would a former United States Senator from Colorado want to have anything to do with Mary Hargrove?" Yvars asked.

"I don't know," Simons said. "However, you told me Carlin arranged for Mary to talk to Webster, didn't you?" Simons asked.

"Yes," Yvars replied.

"You also told me that according to Mary Hargrove, in return for setting them up so to speak, Carlin wanted her to report to him on Webster's specific activities."

"You think Carlin used Mary as a go-between?" Yvars asked.

"Yes, I think so," Simons replied.

"But why?" Yvars asked.

"That's a question for later. Right now let me tell you some very interesting facts on the former Senator from Colorado. The hypertext linking in our computer allowed me to access all documents related to Carlin. All I had to do was type in his name and the fact he was formerly a United States Senator and within seconds my screen displayed a large article dated August 21, 1992 in the Denver Tribune. In 1992 Carlin had been selected as Colorado's Man of the Year. The article detailed Carlin's entire life, from his roots in Colorado through his years as a congressman and then a senator. After his defeat in his reelection campaign, he moved to Manhattan where he became a well-known and respected philanthropist. He is currently serving on many corporate and non-profit boards." Simons paused. "Ah that heat. This beats sex any day of the week. I then accessed every charity mentioned in the article to find out if I knew a member on any of the boards he served on. Fortunately I did. Edith Rudolph, my editor's wife, served with Carlin on the board of the March of Dimes. I called her. She went on and on in glowing terms about all Carlin had done for children's causes over the years. She made mention of his wanting to donate a wing for the children's center at Beth Israel Hospital in his name."

"That's takes a lot of money. Did the article in the paper allude to his coming from a wealthy family?"

"On the contrary. He worked his way up the hard way. He came from a working-class background."

"And his entire life was spent in politics?" Yvars asked.

"Yes, until he went into philanthropy," Simons replied.

"I'm sure you investigated whether he was ever rumored to have been involved in any kickback schemes or any other illegal activities that would have provided him with the sizable amounts of money we are talking about."

"Edith mentioned he married well. His wife died a few years ago."

"So you think his wife had all the money?"

Simons shrugged his shoulders. "That's how it seems," he replied. "She also told me Carlin's a very sick man."

"What's wrong with him?" Yvars asked, his lips now dry. He felt spent. Completely dehydrated. "Do you think we can continue this conversation outside the sauna?"

"Just a few more minutes. I'm almost finished." Simons paused. "I accessed the health insurance claim forms Carlin had submitted through the Internet."

"Isn't anything private any longer?" Yvars asked.

"No. All information on everybody in our country who has a social security number is fair game for the computer. I found out about Carlin's health problem," Simons said.

"What's wrong with him?" Yvars asked.

"Something called end stage heart disease. His claims totaled $29,000 last year. Wentworth Hospital billed his insurance company for $5,500."

"I work at Wentworth. What doctor did he see there?"

"I don't remember," Simons said.

"That's probably not important anyway." Yvars replied. "I still don't get it. Why would a highly respected philanthropist, a former senator, court Mary and then arrange for her to carry on a relationship with Webster. And why would Webster want to talk to Mary on the telephone 78 times during the past several months. None of this makes any sense to me?" Yvars said, shaking his head.

Simons stood up. "I'm ready for a nice cold shower. How about you?"

Yvars leaped at the offer. Five minutes later, wrapped in a dry towel and feeling refreshed, they both sat down on the bench adjacent to their lockers. "Edith Rudolph told me even though Carlin's very ill, he still works until eight or nine every day." Simons opened his locker and grabbed a card from his jacket pocket. "Carlin worked at 625 Madison

Avenue." Simons checked his watch. It was 4:49 p.m. "Let's hop a cab and talk to him. I'll press him. He'll be too physically weak to withstand my questioning for very long. We'll find out why he was using Mary Hargrove."

"We can't just go and barge in like that," Mort standing up and putting on his khaki trousers, said.

"I don't see why not. I've gotten many of my best leads that way. You catch them unexpectedly and they reveal things they otherwise wouldn't."

"I don't think your method will work on Carlin," Yvars replied.

"Why not?" Simons asked.

"He's undoubtedly incredibly clever and cunning."

"How can you tell? You've never met the man."

"Because of Mary," Yvars said.

"How so?"

"The way she described how skillfully he ingratiated himself into her life."

"She's so needy. She'd fall for anybody who paid any attention to her." Simons replied.

"You might be right. However, the more masterful we believe him to be, the better prepared we will be to figure out a way to get him to tell us what's going on."

"What do you suggest we do?" Simons asked.

"We have to think of a plan that will catch him off guard. Once he's hooked, our questions will unnerve him and he'll be far more likely to talk."

"You really think all this subterfuge is necessary?" Simons inquired.

"Yes, I do. However, we need to come up with a plan that will work."

Simons thought for a moment. Suddenly his eyes brightened. "We'll play on his being a philanthropist."

"How so?" Yvars, slipping into his blue blazer, asked.

"Edith Rudolph described his involvement in various children's charities. She said he is now thinking of donating money for a pediatric wing at Beth Israel. You're a psychiatrist at Wentworth. Tell him you are spearheading a large fund-raising campaign to build a new pediatric wing at you hospital. Play up to him. Even agree to name the wing after him. If he is as sick as he sounds, he'll want to be remembered after he's dead. I've never met a senator who doesn't want to be immortalized in some way or another. This will be his way."

"He's too clever to fall for that," Yvars said.

"I agree he will eventually realize he's been had. However, if we move fast enough, we'll have found out what we need to know before then." Simons paused. "There's something else you'd better think about before we pay Carlin a visit."

"What now?" Yvars asked.

"He's probably seen you outside your office while waiting for Mary Hargrove. Therefore, he has a general idea of what you look like. Hopefully, he won't recognize you. However, he knows your name. You can't go there and introduce yourself as Mort Yvars."

"Shit, I never thought of that."

"Think of another name. One you'll remember."

Yvars thought for a moment. "Tom Laster. We roomed together in college. There's no way I'll ever forget his name."

"Great," Simons replied standing up and starting to get dressed.

Yvars' spirits were suddenly dashed. "Carlin will run a check on me. He'll find out there isn't any psychiatrist at Wentworth named Laster."

"You're probably right. However, by the time he finds that out and also eventually uncovers he's been duped about Wentworth Hospital and their new pediatric wing, he'll have supplied us with the information we're looking for."

"We're taking a big risk," Yvars said.

"We don't have any other choice." Simons paused. "Now Dr. Tom Laster, let's get a move on."

They both walked from the health club and onto the street. Doug

Simons waved his arm to hail a taxi.

"I think it's better if I talk to Carlin by myself," Mort said.

"You're not serious!" an angry Simons exclaimed.

"I am. Believe me this isn't an ego thing. It's exactly as it was with Mary Hargrove. You're an investigative reporter. You've done another great job. Look what you've now uncovered. I'm a psychiatrist. It's again time for me to do what I do best."

"Damn you Yvars. It was your idea to involve me in this case to begin with. Now you want to shove me aside again just as things are starting to get interesting."

A medallion cab pulled up and stopped. "I understand how you feel. Trust my judgment again. Believe me I know what I'm doing."

"Okay," Simons reluctantly replied. "But this is the last time."

Yvars opened the door and slid into his seat. "Meet me at my home at 7 p.m. I'll be back by then. I'll fill you in on everything I find out."

25

Yvars sat impatiently in the well-appointed waiting room at 625 Madison Avenue for his meeting with Jim Carlin. Simon's ploy had worked. Mort called Carlin's secretary from a pay phone directly across the street from the former senator's office. He apologized for the relative lateness of the hour and lack of advanced notice and then launched into his pre-thought-out script. He rehearsed it several times during his cab ride across town.

He introduced himself as Dr. Tom Laster, a pediatric psychiatrist at Wentworth Hospital and mentioned his recently concluded conversation with Edith Rudolph a long time acquaintance and benefactor of Wentworth Hospital. Yvars told the receptionist Edith insisted he call Carlin and meet with him, that the well-known philanthropist would be very receptive to the idea of helping Wentworth's capital drive to raise the necessary funds to build a new pediatric wing. Carlin's secretary relayed the message to the former senator. 'Any cause Edith Rudolph is involved in deserves my immediate attention,' was his reply. The secretary told Yvars Carlin would be free at 5:30 p.m. She realized that wouldn't give Yvars much time to get to the former senator's office, and that she'd gladly set up a time later in the week for them to meet. Yvars assured her he'd have no problem getting there by 5:30. It was now 5:49 p.m. Where was Carlin?

Yvars was squirming in his leather chair when the stocky, middle-aged receptionist called to him. "Mr. Carlin is ready to see you." She ushered him into a large room decorated with Biedermeier sofas and chairs and an upright secretary. A high-pitched soprano voice reverberated throughout the office, with an intensity and force that could not be significantly muffled by the thick carpeting.

A balding, emaciated, older man with obvious shortness of breath and a grayish pallor introduced himself. "I'm Jim Carlin. I take it you're Dr. Tom Laster," he said. "I'm sorry to be running so late, but my March of Dimes Benefit hit a snag." Carlin adjusted his black tie. "I don't have that much time to talk. I'm due at the Metropolitan Opera in thirty minutes. However, when I heard that Edith Rudolph sent you to see me, I felt we should at least meet. I owe her a lot. She's been incredibly helpful in many of my charitable endeavors. If we don't have time to get enough accomplished now, we'll set up a meeting in a few days and hammer out the rest of the details."

Carlin walked slowly to his stereo system located in the walnut bookcase and turned down the volume. "That's better. We'll be able to hear each other now," the former senator said as he carefully lowered himself into his chair.

"Is that Jessye Norman as Sieglinde?" Yvars asked.

Jim Carlin leaned back in his chair and smiled. "You must be a true Wagner lover to know that. And a doctor? I can hardly believe it. I don't remember the last time anyone came into my office and commented on my musical selections. Everyone comes asking for my money for their various charities and then leaves." Carlin paused and flattened the lapel on his tuxedo. "You look familiar. Have we ever met?"

Yvars' heart began racing.

"No," Mort blurted out.

"I don't' recognize your name. It's something about your face." Carlin paused. "Please forgive me, I'm an old man. I've met so many people through the years that everybody looks familiar to me."

Yvars forced a smile. He realized Carlin was clever, even sharper than he had suspected. He had to quickly absorb Carlin into his fundraising scheme before he could confront the former senator about Hargrove and Webster: and do so before Carlin realized who he really was. To

accomplish that, he had to lull Carlin into a false sense of security. The Wagnarian music would hopefully do that.

"I love Wagner. Tristan. All of his operas, but I have a special fondness for 'The Ring.' My wife and I make sure to catch at least one of the four parts to 'The Ring' whenever it's performed at the Met. Unfortunately, the costs of mounting the production are so enormous, what with the complicated, intricate sets and the magnificent costumes, the Met rarely puts on 'The Ring' these days. You can imagine how excited we are that the Met has come up with the funding necessary to produce the entire Ring cycle throughout this month. We are on vacation. We hope to be able to watch some of the performances, providing all the tickets haven't already been sold out," Yvars said.

Carlin's eyes lit up. "You Dr. Laster are a fortunate man. I don't know if Edith mentioned it to you, but I'm on the Board of the Metropolitan Opera. In fact, I'm chairperson this year. I'm responsible for persuading our annual subscribers to ante up a bit more than usual so we'd have sufficient funding for 'The Ring.' I check with our ticket office daily. All the seats are sold out. The scalpers are having a field day selling tickets that normally go for one hundred dollars for more than five hundred dollars a pop. However, I have two house seats set aside for each performance. I'll call the ticket office and tell them to leave my two tickets each night for the duration of 'The Ring' cycle, for both you and your wife. You'll be able to catch all four parts of 'The Ring' at least twice before the season ends."

"That's very kind of you but, ..." Yvars said.

"Have I offended you? I've been warned I occasionally come on too strongly," Carlin asked.

"No. It's not that. It's that my wife and I have decided to spend the next two weeks of our vacation taking advantage of all the various things our city provides. Unfortunately, I'm the opera buff. My wife reluctantly attends performances with me a few times a year. I'm the one who's passionate about the opera. I wouldn't feel right insisting she spend so much

205

of our vacation pleasing me by watching Wagner. It wouldn't be fair. She prefers Broadway musicals and some drama. More of a variety. I'm sure you can understand," Yvars said.

"Of course I can. My late wife tolerated many of my passions. Opera was one of them," Carlin wheezed. "I'll tell you what. I'll leave two tickets for each performance at the box office anyway. I'll leave word with the office that if you don't pick the tickets up fifteen minutes before curtain time, they are free to sell them to the general public. Believe me, they will not go unused. There have been lines waiting for last minute cancellations at every performance. Whenever you and your wife don't show, you'll make two opera fanatics very happy." Carlin paused and poured himself a glass of water. He glanced at his watch. It was 6:14 p.m. "I'm sorry Dr. Laster. I've gotten so carried away with our conversation that I didn't realize the time. My driver is to pick me up in fifteen minutes. Please tell me about Wentworth's pediatric expansion plans."

Yvars thought for a moment. Carlin was peering into his eyes in the manner his paranoid clients often did. He was skillfully listening to Mort, while simultaneously observing his every movement and each of his gestures. Mort realized he would never be able to lull this ex-senator in the few minutes remaining. He knew Carlin's type well. If he now revealed his true purpose, the old man would feign ignorance, become outraged and deny all. Mort would lose his opening forever. Mort reluctantly was forced to conclude he had to heed his psychiatric evaluation of the frail man. This was not the right time to bring up his real intentions.

Mort hooked into Simons' ruse. He went into great detail about the need to expand the children's services at Wentworth, especially in the neonatal unit and for the treatment of various childhood malignancies. He finished with how urgent it had become to build the facility and obtain the funding needed to keep their prized research physicians who were being lured away from Wentworth by the deeper pockets of Harvard, Duke and Stanford.

Carlin nodded his head in agreement. "I'm intrigued by your

hospital's plan. Do you have a primary benefactor as yet?"

"No we don't. We are still searching."

"Would Wentworth be willing to name the wing after the primary donor?"

"I would think so," Yvars said.

Carlin smiled. "Life is quite ironic. If you'd come to see me six months ago, I probably would have thrown you out I was so angry at the time. I hadn't been feeling well for about a year. My internist wanted me to be evaluated at Wentworth. The doctors at your hospital agreed my condition warranted intervention, but they decided I was too old for their cardiac transplant program. It took a few months before I could accept their decision. I'm still upset by their refusal to help, but I now understand their reasoning. Rules are rules. I have mine. They have theirs. I'm simply too old for their program. I can now look at this with less emotion. If, as you have said, Wentworth really would be willing to name the new pediatric wing after the main fundraiser I'd be interested, very interested indeed."

Carlin coughed several times and clutched his chest. He then reached into his tuxedo pocket, took out a small pillbox and tossed a round white tablet under his tongue. "Damn pain. Ah, that's better. The miracles of modern medicine. I dread the day these drugs stop working their magic."

Yvars took a deep breath. It was 6:25 p.m. In five minutes Carlin would be leaving for the opera. Mort had succeeded in whetting Carlin's appetite for their trumped-up plan. He was wondering how another window of opportunity would present itself for him to confront Carlin when the former senator unexpectedly provided the opening.

"By the way," Carlin said, slowly rising from his chair. "Tonight I'm throwing my annual party for the 'The Ring's' entire production company. We start shortly after the end of the performance, at about eleven. Everyone will be there. All decked out in their costumes. It's great fun. How about coming? I'd be pleased if you and your wife would join us," Carlin paused briefly. "Who are your favorite characters?"

"Woton's warrior daughter, Brunnhilde."

"Of course, Gwyneth Jones. What a delight, and a voice you could die for. She'll be there. Who else?"

"Wellgunde."

"Jane Bunnell. Absolutely. She's a class act. A real riot. Always one of the earliest to arrive and one of the last to leave. Really loves parties. Any other favorites?"

"Siegfried," Yvars replied.

"Certainly! William Johns, a superb tenor. You'll get a kick out of him. You'll also get to see the other two carefree daughters of River Spirit, Woglinde and Flosshide. As I said, everyone comes. Even Alberich the dwarf. He's quite shy, but in costume he comes out of his shell and is quite an amusing sort."

"I think my wife has other plans for this evening. However, I have a very good friend who loves the opera and would also enjoy your party."

"That would be fine. Bring him along."

"Are you sure your cast won't mind two outsiders on such a special evening?" Yvars asked.

"Absolutely not. The cast enjoys anyone who is passionate about Wagner. And, once they find out you're a psychiatrist, they won't leave you in peace. They'll bombard you all night with their angst."

Carlin took his wallet from his tuxedo pocket and handed Mort his business card. He pointed to the left side. "That's my home address and phone number. I live in a brownstone on 69th Street near Muscadet. Have you ever eaten there?"

"No I haven't," Mort said.

"You'll like it. Try it sometime." Carlin paused. "Enjoy Das Rheingold with your friend. I'll see both of you at my place at about eleven. We should have plenty of time to discuss your hospital's new pediatric wing then. I look forward to seeing you there."

* * * * * * *

The stranger leaned against the office building directly across the

208

street from Carlin's office and watched the doctor as he briskly walked onto the street. It wouldn't be long before the stranger would be able to stop worrying about Yvars meddling into the masterfully crafted plan.

* * * * * * *

Mort leaned over and kissed Millie on her cheek.

"Now look who is late," Simons, seated next to Millie on the couch said.

"How did it go?" an anxious Millie asked.

"Quite well," Mort replied.

"Was Carlin involved in Webster's death?" Simons asked.

"I don't know yet."

"Did you at least find out why Carlin wanted Mary Hargrove to give a run down on the senator's weekly schedule?"

"No. The timing wasn't right. I only had thirty minutes with him. Carlin was in a rush to leave his office."

"What! Give me a break. Thirty minutes was more than enough time to have found out what we needed to know. I should never have listened to you. I should have insisted on talking to him myself," Simons said.

"You would have blown everything with your approach. He is a very suspicious man. He thought I looked familiar. Fortunately, I think he was thrown off by my using Tom Laster as my name. If I'd introduced myself as Mort Yvars, he probably would have figured why I wanted to see him."

"How can you say things went well? You didn't find anything out."

"Because I passed the most difficult hurdle. He believes I'm a pediatric psychiatrist at Wentworth and he is very interested in getting involved with our hospital's expansion program. He became very excited when I suggested we might even name our new wing after him."

Millie stood up and faced her husband. "I don't like any of this. Now you're making up stories. Carlin sounds far too cunning for you to handle. He'll catch on to what you're up to. Then what? I don't want to be a widow. Mort, please call Butler. Fill him in on what you know. Let him do the rest."

"Don't worry Millie. I have everything under control. Carlin is now mentally set up. The next time we meet I'll come right to the point. He'll unravel. We'll have our answers," Mort said.

"Did you set up another meeting?" Simons asked.

"Not exactly," Mort replied.

"What do you mean?" Simons asked.

"He invited us to attend a party at his townhouse, for the entire cast of 'the Ring', after tonight's performance. He'll be distracted. We'll catch him off guard. He'll talk," Mort replied.

"What's 'The Ring'?" Simons asked.

"Richard Wagner's operatic masterpiece. Carlin's left two tickets at the box office for us. We'll go to the opera and then to the party. We'll confront him there."

"I hate the opera. Forget it. You go to the opera. Tell me what time the party is set to begin. I'll meet you in front of Carlin's home. We'll go in together," Simons replied.

Yvars shook his head. "We don't want Carlin to get any more suspicious than he already is. He's going to be at the opera. He'll see me there. Either we both go to the opera and then to his party together, or I'll go both places alone. Otherwise, he'll surely suspect something odd is going on. He'll never open up. We'll never find anything out."

"Those operas are endless. I'll never be able to spend four hours listening to that crap," Simons said.

"You don't have to listen. You can sleep for all I care. The important thing is Carlin will see you are with me. Yvars checked his watch. It was 7:00 p.m. "The opera starts at eight. We'd better get dressed. It's black tie."

Simons sighed in relief. "Then I can't go to the opera. My tuxedo is at my apartment. I'll never be able to get home and still get to the Met by eight. I'll meet you outside Carlin's townhouse at eleven."

Mort smiled. "We're in luck. There's a rental store two blocks from here. They carry all sizes of tuxedos, shirts, black shoes, the works."

Millie walked to the closet in the foyer, removed a large box and opened it. "Take your cellular phone with you." She grabbed two extra batteries from the box and handed them to Mort. She then copied down the phone number on a piece of paper. "I'll feel better knowing I can reach you if I need to."

"You'd better copy the number down for me too . . . just in case," Simons said.

Millie jotted down the phone number, handed the piece of paper to Simons and then slid the phone and batteries into Mort's pocket.

26

Yvars and Simons climbed out of the taxi in front of the Muscadet bistro adjacent to Carlin's townhouse. Several night owls passed them and went into the posh eatery for a late supper.

"I hate these monkey suits. I feel like I'm in a straitjacket," Simons said, pressing down hard on Carlin's front doorbell.

The former senator, looking far more frail than earlier in the day, greeted Mort at the door. "Ah, Dr. Laster. I'm glad you made it. Did you enjoy 'Das Rheingold'?"

"Yes. The entire performance was magnificent. The sets and costumes were truly spectacular," Yvars replied.

"Forgive me," Carlin said turning to Simons. "I'm Jim Carlin. Dr. Laster told me he'd be bringing a friend."

"Thanks for inviting me," Simons replied.

"Did you enjoy the opera as much as Dr. Laster?"

"Yes. It was everything Tom said and more."

"Good. There aren't enough people who genuinely appreciate opera." Carlin paused. "You look familiar. Have we met?"

"Not that I'm aware of," Simons replied.

"Adam Johnson is a colleague of mine at the hospital," Yvars said.

"Not another psychiatrist!" Carlin smiled.

"No. Dr. Johnson's a dermatologist," Mort replied.

"I was in the middle of a discussion with our treasurer when you arrived," Carlin said. "Why don't you get yourselves a drink. I'll be back in a few minutes to show you around."

Simons stared at Yvars. "He recognized me."

"I doubt it," Mort replied. "He also thought I looked familiar. He thinks everybody looks familiar."

"I'm serious. I looked at Carlin's eyes. It's as if he saw right through my charade."

"Calm down. I didn't notice anything," Yvars said.

They walked to the bar and each ordered a Jack Daniels on the rocks. "Mort I'm telling you he knows who I am. Each year before Christmas, the Times spotlights 100 of New York City's neediest. Our month-long drive ends with a benefit. Last year Carlin was our guest speaker. Afterwards we were introduced to one another by my editor. We must have talked for more than thirty minutes."

"Now you tell me. Hopefully, he won't make the connection," Yvars replied. "There's nothing we can do about it now. Let me do the talking and ask the questions. If you don't open your mouth, there's far less of a chance he'll remember you since reporters never shut up."

"And if you're wrong," Simons said, gulping down his drink and then placing the glass back onto the table.

"I'll come up with something. I'm getting good at this game."

Carlin approached his two guests. "I hope you are enjoying yourselves."

"Yes," Mort said, savoring his final sip. He handed his empty glass to the bartender.

"Let me show you around. I think you'll enjoy seeing the apartment before meeting the cast. My wife collected many beautiful early 20th century pieces." Carlin paused. "There are advantages in marrying well. I'm sure as a psychiatrist you can understand I'd rather have Katherine still alive. However, I get a certain amount of comfort in being surrounded by what made her so happy."

Carlin pointed out the numerous Bauhaus pieces that dotted the living room. The Wagnerian ensemble were drinking champagne and congratulating each other on tonight's performance.

Carlin maneuvered Yvars to the far corner of the room. "Those," he shakily pointed with his index finger, "are original Mies van de Rohe chairs that Mies personally designed for the Tugendat House in Bruno, Czechoslovakia, made with flat steel legs and arms with leather cushions instead of the customary tubular steel prevalent at his time. They are rare pieces."

"My wife Millie would kill to see those magnificent pieces," Yvars said. "She is especially interested in furniture of the late 19th and early 20th century."

They threaded their way between the Mies Van de Rohe steel and glass coffee table and one of his Barcelona chairs. Carlin suddenly stopped in his tracks, his breaths coming in short bursts after walking less than fifteen feet. He waited until he regained his breath and then pointed to the area under the window. "That's another van de Rohe masterpiece. It's a chaise longue. A splendid work of craftsmanship. It was designed for his protege, Philip Johnson's apartment."

When in God's name would Carlin stop salivating over the furniture, Yvars wondered, or was it conceivable Mort had been so successful in pretending to be enthralled by the period pieces that Carlin would be caught off guard when Mort finally confronted the old man.

"Come Dr. Laster. It's time for you and your friend to meet some of your favorite characters," the ex-senator said to Yvars.

Simons interjected, "It's been a long day. If you wouldn't mind I'd rather have another drink first."

"Suit yourself. This is a party. You're here to have a good time," Carlin replied.

Carlin introduced Yvars to a tall, muscular figure dressed in a metallic blue gown with a patch over his left eye, holding THE RING on his extended right hand. "You must be the psychiatrist with old world tastes," Woton, the leader of the gods said. "My name's Robert Hale. I'm honored to meet a member of the intelligentsia."

Yvars was speechless for several seconds. He'd adored and idolized

214

Robert Hale, the magnificent tenor masked as Woton for years. He never in his wildest expectations believed it possible he'd ever find himself in the same room with his operatic idol; no less in a face to face conversation

"Do your tastes run to Mozart, Verdi, Brahms, Debussy or are they primarily confined to Wagner's music?" Hale asked.

"Mostly to Wagner," Yvars replied.

"That's most interesting. American patrons usually go for the lighter more melodious operas. In Europe it's the reverse. Is there any particular reason you find yourself preferring Wagner over the other composers?" Hale asked.

Yvars broadly smiled. "You're asking a psychiatrist so be prepared for a psychological answer. As far as I'm concerned, everything one likes, dislikes, does or doesn't do is somehow rooted in one's childhood. Wagner obviously was an extremely sad melancholic man. A solitary figure who detested authority. I was an incredibly lonely child. An only child. My father was a tyrant. Fortunately, I had a very loving mother. I don't know what would have become of me if I hadn't had her as a support while I was growing up. Mother obviously wasn't enough to offset my father's destructive effects on me, but she helped as much as she could. She had one passion. One burning interest that I'm sure saved her. Kept her sane. It was opera. She'd lose herself for hours every day listening intently to whatever opera was on her classical FM radio station. Eventually, she bought herself a record player. We're talking before the advent of tapes let alone compact discs. Fortunately, our town's library was well stocked with opera selections. She never ran out of operas to listen to. She constantly searched for ones she'd never heard, but was content to hear her old favorites again and again.

When my parents would go out and I'd be left all alone, I realized I not only loved the same type of music as my mother did, but that I seemed magnetized toward Richard Wagner's operas in particular. In retrospect, I'm sure even at that young age I connected on a deep level to Wagner's own inner sadness and loneliness. I'd listen and not feel as sad or as alone.

He was in effect my therapy."

"Heavy stuff," Hale replied.

"The best part of my childhood, fortunately had to do with the fact it was time limited. Eventually it ended. I stayed interested in opera during my college and medical school years, but I was frequently so busy studying that I rarely had the time to actually sit quietly and do nothing but listen to the music and the lyrics of my favorites. When I finished my psychiatric residency and began practicing psychiatry, I became enthralled with 'The Ring'. I still enjoyed Wagner's other works, but 'The Ring' began taking on a personal meaning. It began fascinating me."

"Why 'The Ring' in particular?" Hale inquired

"Wagner seemed to select a specific characteristic of the human condition and create each of the characters in 'The Ring' to symbolically portray that particular quality," Yvars replied.

"What characteristic does Woton symbolize?" Hale asked.

Yvars, always uncomfortable talking about himself, paused briefly before replying. "Because although you play God, you aren't perfect. You are constantly searching throughout 'The Ring,' always questioning who you are. It's almost as if you are, as we'd term it in psychiatry, on a never ending struggle to establish your own personal identity. I feel I still don't know all I should know about myself. In this way Woton and I are kindred spirits."

"Although I've played Woton more than one thousand times, that's a concept I hadn't thought of," Hale replied. The tenor turned to Carlin. "Thanks for inviting Doctor Laster. He's adding an interesting new dimension to your annual party," Hale paused. "Hey Franz, come over here for a minute."

Franz Mazura, who played the role of Alberich, the dwarf, walked over. "Yes Woton my master," he laughed.

"I'd like you to meet Doctor Laster. He's a student of 'The Ring,'" Hale said. "What is there about Franz's character that stands out?"

Yvars tried hiding his embarrassment from all this attention. "I love your role because you are the catalyst. The initiator. I have a problem initiating anything. I'm more a follower than a leader. By your theft of the Rheinegold, you precipitate the plot of the sixteen hour tetralogy. I call that initiation on a large scale. I think of you whenever I find myself procrastinating when initiative is called for."

Carlin began to cough. Again and again. He had trouble maintaining his balance.

"Are you okay?" Freia, played by Hei-Kyung Hong asked, handing Carlin a glass of water.

Carlin reached into his burgundy velvet smoking jacket, took out a vial of small white pills and placed one under his tongue. "I'll be fine in a minute," he gasped.

"What's the matter?" Hei-Kyung Hong reiterated.

"It's my heart. These pills stop those terrible chest pains. They also make my breathing easier," Carlin wheezing, replied.

"Shouldn't you lie down and rest," a concerned Woton asked.

"And miss what we all have been looking forward to. Never!" Carlin, regaining his strength, replied. "I don't want anything to ruin tonight's party. You have all worked so hard. You deserve this celebration. If I get overly tired I'll go to bed. However, promise me if I do you'll continue partying."

The cast members surrounding the frail man nodded their heads in agreement.

"What about my character Freia," Hei-Kyung Hong asked Laster.

"You're the goddess of youth. Look at your outfit. There you stand holding your golden apple that is essential for the gods' continual rejuvenation. Without you, they lose their eternal youth. Everyday I look in the mirror and see wrinkles where none existed. I'm always obsessed about getting older. To me you represent Ponce de Leon, except you have indeed discovered the Fountain of Youth," Yvars replied.

Carlin's eyes lit up. "This is absolutely fascinating. Personal identification with each of 'The Ring's' operatic characters. When I invited you, I had no idea you'd make the party. I've never viewed opera other than from a strictly musical point of view. In the future I'll be able to focus on the performance from an entirely different vantage point.

"You're very flattering, but on an unconscious level I'm sure you've realized this. You just don't know you have. That's what psychiatry is all about. Bringing to the conscious what before was unconscious."

"Your work must never get boring," Loge, the demigod of fire and master mischief maker, said. "What is it in my makeup that invites personal identification, Graham Clark, who played Loge, asked.

"You hatch schemes, symbolize the willingness to take risks that many of us, I for one, am invariably too frightened to do," Yvars replied. "I envy your daring nature."

Carlin suddenly let out a loud deep yawn. "I've had it. I'm exhausted," he said as he slowly walked to his bedroom. At the entrance to the door he turned and faced Hale. "Remember your promise. The party, like the performance, must go on!"

Hale nodded. He and Hei-Kyung Hong assisted Carlin into his bed.

Yvars shot a glance at Simons. The investigative reporter shrugged his muscular shoulders as if to say 'Now what?'

Mort started cursing to himself. Perhaps he should have let Simons do it his way. He realized in all probability Carlin would have denied everything, but at least there was a chance he'd somehow slip and reveal something, anything. Now they were left with nothing. What, he wondered, could he do now? There was no conceivable way he could storm into Carlin's bedroom and demand answers. The former senator was now far too weak to respond to questioning.

Yvars stared dejectedly into the bedroom, at the old man propped up on two pillows with both Hale and Hei-Kyung Hong by his bedside.

The enormous presence of Brunnhilde brought Yvars back to the ongoing festivities. Woton's favorite child, dressed in her metal helmet, breastplate and spear, tapped Mort gently on his shoulder. "It's my turn. What about my character is appealing to you," Gwyneth Jones asked in her thunderous voice.

Yvars took a deep breath to regain his composure. He looked at the large soprano and feigned interest. "You are a daughter, a sister, a warrior, a maiden, a lover, a bride, besides also being a wronged wife and a widow. When you decide to put an end to your suffering and take your own life by committing suicide, your self sacrifice serves to redeem all mankind. The old order of the guard passes and a new era will now begin. We all want things to be better. We all desire world peace, an end to starvation and plagues. For example, we all want a cure to be found as quickly as possible for AIDS. All of us have this altruistic side. Your final noble act symbolizes this. However, I, and I'm sure all of us in this room tonight, frequently find our charitable side hidden behind our insatiable appetites for personal riches, power and happiness. It's very difficult for us to keep in the forefront of our minds a better tomorrow for others; for a new era for all."

Wolfgang Neumann, dressed as Siegfried, in his tan tight-fitting, leather, head to toe outfit, with his father's sword in his hand, approached Yvars. "What can you say about my character?" the Adonis looking tenor asked.

"I love your innocence, your noble nature. You are a hero without a semblance of fear. I have so many different fears that I envy your courage. While your character and Loge's are similar in that respect, you also possess another facet to you personality that I identify with. It's your incredible impatience with elders. I frequently have problems with authority figures of all types, be they senior members of my department at the hospital or even the policeman on the street. My impatience, as does yours, has often cost me dearly."

Suddenly, an ear piercing shriek emanated from Carlin's bedroom. Hale immediately rushed toward Yvars. "Doctor come quickly. I think Carlin's had a heart attack."

Yvars, with Simons following closely behind, raced into the

bedroom. Carlin was clutching his chest, his eyes were rolling back into his head.

Mort quickly pressed his left ear against Carlin's bony chest. "He's filling up with fluid. He's in acute heart failure."

Hale picked up the phone to call for an ambulance. Several other members of the cast dashed into the stricken man's bedroom and surrounded the bed.

"We don't have time to wait for an ambulance," Yvars said. "His heart will give out before then. Does anyone have a car parked downstairs? New York Hospital is only a few blocks from here. He'll have a better chance to make it if we can get him to the hospital ourselves."

"Yes," Hale replied immediately. "I was lucky. I found a space right across the street."

"Good. Get your car and bring it to Carlin's front door."

Hale tore out of the bedroom.

Yvars scanned the fear lined faces of the onlookers.

"Somebody go into the living room and get Fasolt and Fafner," he yelled.

Within seconds the two giant earthly brothers came into the bedroom and approached the bed.

"Fasolt grab Carlin's shoulders. Fafner you take his legs. Everybody else clear out of the way."

Quickly the two mammoth figures carried the semi-comatose former senator from his home and into Hale's waiting car.

Mort took a deep breath and glanced at Simons. They both realized they could do nothing now except hope Carlin would survive, not only long enough to get to New York Hospital's Emergency Room, but long enough for him to recover sufficiently to reveal what was going on.

27

New York Hospital's Coronary Care Unit was housed on the eighth floor of the ultra modern glass and steel annex abutting the older massive facility on York Avenue.

Mort had just finished speaking to Millie for the fifth time since they had arrived at the hospital. He walked back into the CCU.

Jim Carlin was lying comfortably in bed. His color was now pink, the direct result of the constant flow of oxygen streaming into his nostrils from the large metal tank adjacent to the nightstand. Carlin felt energetic; not weak, nor fatigued. He hadn't recalled feeling this alive since his severe heart attack six months ago. It was then that Dr. Lance Wagner evaluated him at Wentworth Hospital in New York City as a possible candidate for a cardiac transplant. Then came the decision. Concise and to the point. 'The committee has decided to reject your application for a transplant. The reason is your age. Fifty-five is our present cutoff mark. Anybody older is excluded from a cardiac transplant. There are just not enough donors to go around. We feel we owe it to those who are younger and still have more of their lives ahead of them.'

After six months, Carlin still felt frustrated that none of his supposedly powerful, well-connected friends in Washington were able to use their considerable clout to force Wagner and his colleagues at Wentworth to make him an exception to their arbitrary rule . . . To force them into reversing their decision and place his name on top of the list for a new heart . . . For a new lease on life.

How long he had left he did not know, Carlin thought, as he listened to the beeping sounds of the electrocardiogram machine attached to the nearby wall. Hours earlier, when he felt the onset of that crushing stabbing chest pain, he doubted he'd ever see the light of a new day, let alone feel as energetic and as strong as he now did. He laid his head back onto his pillows and basked in just being alive. He wouldn't even allow the cardiac monitors with their constant annoying sounds, nor the pain in his arms caused by the intravenous needles, to distract him from focusing on how much he valued life. How much more he cared about staying alive, regardless of what it took, than even he had realized. His powerful role in important charitable causes still meant a great deal to him. He desperately wanted to continue his efforts in helping others.

Immediately on his arrival into the emergency room, he was whisked into the one private room in the entire unit. He was relieved not to find himself forced to lay next to other heart patients. All patients, but especially those with acute cardiac problems, only served to remind him of his own mortality. The way he was feeling on admission, the last thing he wanted to face was what he knew was only lurking around the corner. Death might still be hovering around him, but at least in the privacy of his own room he could periodically manage to suppress the gravity of his own condition.

Dr. Madison, a tall, thin man with a gray mustache accompanied by Dr. Yvars and Doug Simons entered Carlin's room. Madison stared at the normal heart rhythm registering on the fluorescent screen and smiled, pleased his patient had responded so rapidly to his medical efforts.

Madison grasped Carlin's frail wrist and felt his pulse. It was weaker than he'd anticipated judging from the monitors tracings. He grabbed the stethoscope from his white jacket pocket and placed the rubber tips into both his ears. He then pumped air into the sphygmomanometer and slowly released the valve. His smile abruptly turned to concern. He opened the IV drip further sending more dopamine into Carlin's bruised vein. "This should raise your pressure. It's a bit too low." He paused and glanced at his patient's healthy complexion. "You look good. How do you feel?"

"I was feeling fine until you made me realize my blood pressure isn't high enough. That means my heart really isn't functioning nearly as well as I thought," Carlin disappointedly said.

Madison waited three minutes before taking Carlin's blood pressure again. "110/60. That's better. It's still not quite what we'd like but it will have to do."

Carlin interjected. "Did I have another heart attack last night?" he asked Madison.

"Not according to your blood tests or your EKGs," the physician replied.

"Then why did I have such severe chest pain? Why did I collapse?" a bewildered Carlin asked.

"You were in acute heart failure. Ever since your heart attack you've been in borderline failure. Your physician, Dr. Brooks, informed me that the various medications he's been giving you allowed you to continue functioning as well as you have been up to now. In retrospect, the anticipation and the excitement of your party last night was undoubtedly what tipped the scales and sent you into severe heart failure."

Carlin glared at Madison. "Something as trivial as my cast party almost killed me!"

"Nothing you ever do is trivial given the extreme weakness of your heart muscles. Mr. Carlin, I know you don't want to believe it, but you have endstage heart disease. That's the reason Dr. Brooks consulted Dr. Wagner at Wentworth Hospital last year. Brooks and I have been on the phone frequently since you were brought to our Emergency Room. He's filled me in on all the details of your particular heart condition. Unfortunately, Brooks told me you didn't meet Wentworth Hospital's criteria for a heart transplant. I'm sorry your heart is in as weak a state as it is but," Madison shrugged his shoulders, "I've done all I can for you."

"That's easy for you to say. You're not the one dying," Carlin replied.

"You're right. I wish there was more I could do."

Suddenly, a slight quickening of the beep on the monitor brought Madison's eyes to the fluorescent screen. Carlin's heart rate was accelerating. "What's his blood pressure?" he called out to the young male nurse.

"90/60," the nurse replied, his gaze also focused on the monitor.

Yvars looked back at the EKG. Carlin's pulse was still rapid but even more disturbing, there were now ectopic beats interspersed between the normal rhythm.

"What's the matter?" Carlin cried out.

Madison's eyes were riveted on his patient; watching, waiting, realizing that if he didn't succeed in regulating Carlin's heart rate immediately the former senator would go back into failure and this time he'd probably die. "Give him 4cc's propranolol stat," Madison finally ordered. Henry, the male nurse, quickly filled the syringe with the potent medication that was frequently used to convert an irregular heart rate back to normal. However, Madison realized that for this particular patient he was taking a gamble, a calculated risk in using such a powerful drug on an already severely damaged heart. A heart he knew couldn't handle being strained further.

Madison nodded at the freckle faced nurse who quickly plunged the needle into the IV.

"What are you doing?" Carlin, his voice now noticeably weaker, asked. He glanced around the room. All eyes were fixed on the monitor. He was about to call out again when he began coughing and gasping for air. Pink frothy material began oozing from both sides of his mouth.

"We're losing him," Madison called out. He glanced at the screen. The irregularity instead of decreasing had increased, becoming more frequent, too frequent.

"His blood pressure is falling. It's down to 70/50," Henry shouted.

Suddenly the monitor went blank. The fibrillation had ceased. All the rhythm had stopped. Carlin had gone into cardiac arrest.

"Code 99," Madison shouted out. There followed an immediate

frenzy of activity. The Cardiac Unit's arrest team, pushing their fully equipped cart, crashed through the doorwell and began to work immediately.

Madison directed Yvars and Simons out of the room. He then stared at Carlin. His patient wasn't breathing. "Mr. Carlin, can you hear me?" the doctor shouted.

Yvars and Simons, exhausted from their all night vigil leaned against a wall in the hall. They stared at one another, saying nothing. They were helpless. All depended on Madison successfully resuscitating Carlin.

"Carlin, can you hear me?" the doctor screamed.

There was no answer.

Evans pounded on Carlin's chest. Still no response.

He pressed harder and harder on his ribcage. Still nothing.

Lewis, a medical resident, inserted a short oval airway into Carlin's mouth and began providing respiration with an ambu breathing bag. Madison continued the external cardiac compression.

Two minutes later Dr. Fox, a trim anesthesiologist arrived and replaced Lewis at the head of the bed.

"Tube him," Dr. Madison ordered Fox. Madison then turned the job of cardiac massage over to another of the residents and walked to the cardiograph.

"Give me a 7.52," Fox said to the attractive nurse assisting him. The clear plastic tube with a diameter of three-quarters of an inch had a dilated plastic balloon wrapped just above the top. The meticulous physician skillfully slipped the tube between Carlin's vocal cords into his trachea. He used a long syringe to blow up the balloon, sealing the area along the tube to prevent air from leaking. He then attached the black breathing bag to the outside of the tube, connected oxygen to the bag and began supporting Carlin with breaths at a rate of 20 per minute. All at once Dr. Madison, his eyes still riveted on the EKG machine, noticed a slashing up and down of the stylus. There was a rhythm. He studied the finely lined paper flowing from the machine. "His rhythm looks like fibrillation,"

Dr. Madison said, his voice firm but calm. "Continue pumping the bag." He then turned to Henry, the nurse, standing by the defibrillator. "Get set to give him 400 joules."

Henry turned the dial on the machine to 400 and then squirted contact jelly on the two steel paddles before handing them to Dr. Madison.

Madison motioned everybody to move away. Then he quickly pressed one paddle along the inside of Carlin's left breast and the other one six inches below his left armpit. "Ready? Here goes!" He pressed the red button on top of the right hand paddle. A dull thunk sounded as 400 joules of electricity shot through Carlin's chest and throughout the rest of his body. His entire torso arched rigidly while his arms flailed in different directions. Then he was perfectly still – No rhythm. Nothing.

The resident resumed chest compression while Madison ordered medications to be given through Carlin's arterial cutdown: adrenalin to stimulate cardiac activity, followed by bicarbonates to counteract the rising lactic acid in this blood. No change. Another shot of adrenalin followed by three more 400 joules countershocks. Still nothing. Then Madison injected calcium, more bicarbonate and administered a fifth shock. Suddenly a moan was heard from the bed. Then another. Then a third, this one louder, more forceful. Madison glanced at the monitor. The cardiograph was showing a rhythm. Carlin's heart had started beating. Madison kept staring at the monitor. Fibrillation soon gave way to premature ventricular contractions and then, in less than three minutes, to a normal sinus rhythm.

The doctor sighed in relief. Somehow, someway, the fifth shock had worked its magic. He had succeeded in bringing Carlin back.

Everyone in the room watched silently, fearful of Carlin arresting again. After ten minutes a calmness settled over the room.

Madison waved for Yvars and Simons to return to the room. "He's out of danger for the time being," he said.

Carlin's right arm was motioning to his throat, to the tracheal tube. He wanted the tube removed.

Madison eyed Yvars, then glanced back at the monitor. "What's his blood pressure now?" he asked Henry.

"130/70. It's held steady for five minutes."

Madison then nodded for the anesthesiologist, Dr. Fox, to remove the tracheal tube.

After the tube was removed, Carlin whispered for a glass of water. He slowly drank the entire contents of the paper cup and asked for another.

"No. Not now. One cup is all for now," Madison commanded.

"My throat's killing me. It's incredibly dry. Why can't I have another cup. It's only water, " Carlin asked.

Madison explained to Carlin, in as gentle a manner as possible, that he had suffered a cardiac arrest and had to be resuscitated. His parched sore throat was an unfortunate, although benign, by product of the procedure.

"I almost died?" Carlin asked bewildered. "How is that possible? I wasn't doing anything!"

"I know," Madison replied. "That's what we mean by you having endstage heart disease. Your pump is completely shot. It doesn't take much to tip you into failure."

"Isn't there anything, any medications that will prevent me from arresting again?" Carlin pleaded.

"Unfortunately, not when your heart muscles are in as precarious a condition as yours. A new heart was your last hope. Dr. Brooks did all he could. He'll still do all he can. He'll be with you the rest of the way but . . ." Madison's voice trailed off.

Suddenly Yvars eyes brightened. Mort had inadvertently stumbled on the hook he needed to force Carlin to reveal what was going on.

"Dr. Wagner and I both work at Wentworth Hospital. I know him well."

"I appreciate your interest, but as you've heard, I've already been turned down by your Dr. Wagner and his transplant team. I'm also well acquainted with most members of your hospital's board. They tried their best. Apparently Dr. Wagner is God at Wentworth. None of them could budge him to reverse his decision. What makes you think you can do what they couldn't?"

"I know Cliff Dunbar. He founded Wentworth Hospital. What he wants, he gets."

"I also know Dunbar. He couldn't do anything," a suddenly more energetic Carlin replied.

Yvars suppressed his mounting excitement. He knew Carlin had no choice but to grab Mort's bait. It was now time to reel him in. "I'm your only hope, but if you don't want it that's fine with me. I hate being melodramatic but I'm not the one dying, you are."

Madison faced Carlin. "If Dr. Laster believes he can intervene and get you a new heart, what do you have to lose. It's worth a shot. In the past six hours you arrested once, almost died twice. The third time can't be very far off. I don't know if I'll be able to save you again."

Yvars walked over to the phone on the nightstand. "Well!" he paused and stared down at the weak, older man. "What do you say?"

Carlin feebly nodded his consent.

Mort began dialing Wentworth's phone number. Halfway through he abruptly stopped.

Carlin became alarmed. "Why did you stop dialing?"

"I want answers to certain questions. Then I'll call Dunbar."

"What is Dr. Laster talking about?" Madison asked his patient.

Mort stared at Carlin. "Yesterday at your office you thought I looked familiar, didn't you?"

"Yes."

"Do I still?"

Carlin nodded his head in agreement.

"That's because both Mary Hargrove and Judd Webster were patients of mine."

Carlin's face tensed. "You're Dr. Yvars?" he asked.

"Yes." Mort then pointed to Simons. "I think you also knew Dr.

228

Johnson. He's another patient of mine."

"Are you a doctor?" a bewildered Madison asked.

"No. I'm a reporter for The New York Times."

"Damn it. What's going on," Madison barked. He pointed to Simons. "You'll have to leave. Only doctors are allowed in this unit."

"Simons stays or I won't call Wagner." Yvars calmly replied to Madison.

"That's impossible. It's against hospital policy."

"All rules can be broken. It all depends on how important the matter is. I wouldn't think anything is more important than saving Carlin's life. However, if you feel differently, we'll leave," Yvars replied.

Madison glanced at Carlin, then at Simons, before coming to rest on Mort.

"I have one other request," Yvars began. I must ask you to please wait outside the room. If your patient cooperates and gives me the information I'm looking for we shouldn't be long. The nurses can monitor his cardiograph through the glass partition." Yvars pointed to the glass enclosure on the wall opposite Carlin's bed. "If his EKG suddenly changes or if he begins to go back into failure or arrests I'll alert you immediately."

Madison said nothing. His cherubic face turned bright red. He stared at his patient.

"Please do as he says," Carlin weakly pleaded.

Madison reluctantly turned and angrily walked from the room. "I'll be in the nurse's station tracking your cardiac monitor through   the glass partition. If I see any change on the screen I'll be right back   in here."

"Of course," Yvars replied.

Madison slammed the door behind him.

Carlin's eyes darted to Yvars. "Call Dunbar. Then I'll tell you everything I know."

Yvars grabbed the phone and immediately dialed Dunbar's private line at Wentworth Hospital. On the fourth ring Dunbar picked up the phone. He greeted Mort warmly.

"How are you feeling?" Yvars asked.

Dunbar replied. "I'm very tired but Kitty Blaker keeps insisting these symptoms are only temporary. In two weeks my last round of chemotherapy will be over and she insists in less than a week after that, I'll feel like my old self," Dunbar paused. "I appreciate your interest in my health. However, I can't believe that's the only reason for your call."

"I need a favor from you," Yvars said.

"Just ask. If it's at all possible I'll do it. I owe you a great deal. If it wasn't for your invaluable assistance during our horrendous cardiac transplant crisis two years ago, our hospital's reputation would have likely been irreversibly ruined. We'd have been hit with lawsuits by the hundreds. We might even have had to close our doors. Then last year you were incredibly helpful in pulling Lillian out of her deep depression following her husband's tragic death. I will always be indebted to you," Dunbar said.

Yvars quickly recounted in chronological detail all that had happened since Tyrone Sawyer's death seventeen days ago.

Dunbar thought for a moment. "I remember Jim Carlin. I did my best. Unfortunately Wagner has his rules. Lance admitted that while Carlin definitely needed a heart transplant, so did countless others, and that at 67 he was simply too old to be given one. Fifty-five was the magical age. He explained it had to do with the limited availability of donor hearts. I couldn't argue with him. I mean if it's a choice between someone 33 with a young family to raise and a man of 67 who's basically lived a full life, there's not much to argue about. I accomplished one thing, although it obviously hasn't been enough. I persuaded Wagner to put Carlin on UNOS I, rather than on UNOS III. UNOS I is compiled of the names of those who get first crack whenever a donor heart becomes available. However, Wagner would only put his name way down on UNOS I's list." Dunbar paused. "What's Carlin's blood type?"

Yvars sifted through Carlin's chart. "O Positive," he eventually replied.

"That should make finding an appropriate donor easy. His blood type makes Carlin compatible with any donor. I'll call Lance Wagner. He's probably still in the operating room. I'll explain everything to him. I'm sure he'll come through. He owes you ever since you were instrumental in helping his cardiac transplant department during their disaster two years ago. Give me your number. I'll get right back to you."

After replacing the phone back in its cradle, Yvars eyed Carlin. "It's done. I did it. Dunbar will take care of all the particulars. Now let's hear what you have to say."

"What I could make out from your end of the conversation left a lot to chance. I want a guarantee that a donor heart will be at Wentworth when I arrive. Then I'll talk," Carlin adamantly replied.

Simons jaw muscles tightened. He felt like pummeling the old man to force him to talk. Carlin glanced at Yvars. Mort smiled calmly. "As you wish. We'll wait. It's your heart, your life. You're the one with limited time, not me."

"You bastard," Carlin said. "You're blackmailing me." He became noticeably more short-winded after his angry outburst.

"Call it what you wish," Yvars said shrugging his shoulders.

Suddenly the telephone rang. Yvars grabbed it on the first ring. It was Dunbar. Relief swept over Mort's weary face. He pressed the speaker phone button down.

"It's done. I spoke to Lance Wagner and explained your predicament," Dunbar began. "He's agreed to help you out. He'll make the necessary arrangements. Tell Carlin Wagner has moved his name to the top of the UNOS I list. That means he will receive the next available donor heart. Lance is certain that because of his O positive blood type and his medium sized frame the needed donor will be easy to find. Lance explained to me that a heart remains viable for up to four hours after it's removed from the donor. He assured me that will give him more than enough time to have a suitable heart waiting. Wagner also mentioned since Carlin has already undergone all of Wentworth's pre-transplant testing procedures, that he will be able to start the operation immediately on his arrival." Dunbar

231

paused. "What time can I tell Wagner to expect you?"

Yvars looked at his watch. It was 4:21 p.m. "If Carlin cooperates we should be at Wentworth between 6:30 and 7 p.m."

"I'll give Lance the information. He'll be at the emergency room when you arrive. And Mort," Dunbar paused. "Good luck."

Yvars smiled. "You've heard my conversation with Dunbar. Everything is settled. Now," Mort raised his voice. "What the hell is going on?"

28

Carlin asked Yvars to crank his bed up higher. "That's better. Now I can breathe easier." He paused briefly. "I hated Webster. He ruined my life. However, I didn't always feel that way. For years we were very close. He was the son we never had. He and Jane would often come over for dinner. They'd spend many of the holidays at our home."

"How did you meet Judd?" Yvars asked.

"His father originally asked me if I'd hire Judd, after he graduated Yale law school, as one of my assistants. I was a congressman from Colorado at the time. Judd's father had helped me when I began my political career. I figured one hand washes the other. Besides, I could always use another smart young aide, so I agreed. Judd was incredibly competent. In less than a year he was running my office in Colorado, which allowed me to be able to carry on my work in Washington without having to constantly make sure everything was going smoothly in my district back home. I had no inkling how shrewd he and his father were. During all the time that I thought he was helping run my district, he was really furthering his own career . . . doing everything for his own purposes. One day, completely out of the blue, he announced he was going to run against me for my seat in congress. I was shocked. However, I didn't believe he could win. Was I wrong! He defeated me in the primary. He then went on to win the election."

"I eventually got over my loss. I didn't think of the why's. I began campaigning for senator. I won the election and began serving my term."

"I started observing Judd in the House. Although still young and inexperienced, he was incredibly focused and determined. He seemed to understand exactly what his district's priorities were. I believed he won the election on merit alone."

Carlin began coughing. The monitor began registering an irregularity in his heart rate. Madison rushed in and adjusted the Dopamine drip. Within two minutes the former senator's rhythm returned to normal. "How long will this take?" Madison asked Yvars.

"It all depends on your patient," Mort replied.

"I don't know how long we can maintain him," the doctor said, shaking his head and closing the door behind him.

"Five years later I ran for reelection," Carlin continued.

"My victory seemed a certainty. My record was outstanding. Colorado had flourished during my term. However, two months before the primary, Judd announced his candidacy. He was going to run against me again. I felt angry and betrayed. How could someone I had treated as a son want to do this to me again. However, once again I didn't believe he had a chance in the primary. Once again I underestimated the Webster clout. The old man turned the screws on all of the State's bigwigs. They owed him. He called in all favors owed, demanding they do all that was necessary to ensure Judd's victory. He didn't care how. All he wanted was the result. I lost the primary. Judd went on to win the senatorial election in November. I was angry and stunned, not because I lost the election: after all politics are politics. That's life. It was the way the old man manipulated the race. However, money and power are unfortunately all too frequently what politics are all about. Eventually I got over my defeat. My wife convinced me it was time to move on. We'd always wanted to live in Manhattan and get involved in various philanthropic activities. Now we'd have the time, and with her family's funds, the means to achieve our new goals.

"For the next three years all went well. I never forgave Judd for the way he went behind my back to defeat me, but I didn't spend much time thinking about it. That was the past. This was now. Then two years ago my wife developed cancer and within a few months was dead. I carried on for both of us. I buried myself more and more into our various charities." Carlin paused and took two deep breaths. "Then came the phone call last year and everything changed. After that call my hatred for Judd knew no bounds. It was unlimited. He suddenly became my Judas."

"Why? What happened?" Yvars asked.

"The caller informed me what had happened behind the scenes in both those elections. Webster's father hadn't just called in favors. Judd had convinced his father that unless the old man was willing to bribe key city officials to rig the voting machines, he'd never win either election. The caller told me I had actually won both elections before Judd's father forced the officials to change the results."

"What made you believe the caller?" Yvars asked.

"I didn't initially. I demanded proof. The caller supplied it. Judd's father had died two years ago. Sometime after that, my informant obtained written records of all that had transpired on those primary days. The old man kept a diary listing each and every person and every step taken to reverse the popular vote, turning my victories into defeats."

"Who was this informant?" Yvars asked.

"A man named Jerry Rollins," Carlin said.

"How did Rollins get his hands on Webster's father's personal notes?"

"I don't know. I asked. He wouldn't divulge his source."

"Have you ever actually seen the written notes Rollins described to you?"

"Yes. Jerry Rollins came to my office one day last fall and showed me everything."

"Who is this Jerry Rollins?" Simons asked.

"He's a real estate tycoon who began by developing much of Vail during the time I was Senator. Since then he's relocated to the northeast and is responsible for building many of our large, industrial parks in this part of the country."

"Why did he come to you?" Yvars asked.

"He had just had it out with Webster. The bastard betrayed him like he did me."

"How so?" a curious Simons asked.

"Judd was the chairman of the Senate Subcommittee of the banking industry. The committee basically set the guidelines banks are forced to comply with. Rollins wanted to purchase several acres of a deteriorated part of Bridgeport, Connecticut and gentrify it. Webster wanted the banks to change their image and parcel their larger loans to developers who were interested in building low-cost housing for the poor rather than dole out loans to make the rich even richer."

"That sounds commendable," Yvars said.

"On the surface it certainly does. However, remember Webster never was what he seemed. He was all charm, a facade, always covering up his ulterior motive."

"Which was what in Rollins case?" Simons asked.

"Webster, rumor had it, was in the running to become Secretary of the Treasury. He knew the President genuinely believes our country's downfall has greatly been caused by unscrupulous, greedy, business types who only care about personal profit. Webster wanted to create the image of a man who detested those types, who heralded those who sacrificed personal profit for the good of the common man. Webster chose Jerry Rollins as the archetype of all that was wrong with America. His strategy undoubtedly had begun working. The President, on several occasions, had dropped Webster's name as his choice for the Secretary of the Treasury once Perkins stepped down. Needless to say, it was bullshit. Webster never cared for the poor. He made millions himself in his family's real estate ventures in the Seattle area. His family had a notorious reputation for not having sympathy for the have-nots, evicting them from their buildings whenever possible." Carlin began feeling faint and lightheaded. He reached for a glass of water, took several sips and sighed deeply.

"You want to wait a bit before we continue?" Yvars asked

236

"I don't have time." Carlin replied. "Rollins was turned down for all of his loans by the banks. The president of the National Bank in Stamford, Connecticut, a personal friend, told Rollins it was all Webster's doing. Webster made no bones about it. Either the bank president would reject Rollin's requests for a loan or, he'd personally make sure his bank wouldn't get the federal help it needed. Rollins became enraged, flew to Washington and confronted the senator. Rollins threatened to go to the media and expose Webster's tactics. The senator told Rollins flat out that if he went to the papers, he'd personally see to it that all of Rollins' outstanding loans were immediately called in. Rollins would have no recourse but to declare personal bankruptcy.

"Rollins refused to submit. Judd made good on this threat. He called the various presidents of the banks throughout the northeast demanding that all of Rollins' outstanding mortgages and personal loans be immediately called in."

"Why would these bank presidents give a damn about an angry senator wanting to get even? This kind of behavior seems to go on in Washington all the time," Simons said.

"Because Webster ran the Senate Banking Committee as if it was a one-man operation. Whatever he said went. He came right out and told these presidents that the decision was theirs, but if they didn't call in all of Rollins' loans, he'd see to it that legislation would be passed to severely restrict their profitability."

"The banks called in Rollins' huge loans. There was no possible way Rollins could borrow enough money from his numerous contacts and friends to pay off such a large sum. He offered to pay the banks a higher interest rate. They all refused. One month later he filed for bankruptcy."

"Rollins was furious. He flew to Seattle and then to Colorado. That's when he found out everything I've told you. He called me and we met. We both had had our careers ruined by Judd Webster."

Carlin coughed again. His breaths were coming in shorter bursts. "It was at this time I was turned down by Dr. Wagner at Wentworth

Hospital for a heart transplant. My cardiologist told me if I was fortunate I'd live another year. That's when Rollins came to me with his plan. He asked if I'd like to see Judd get his just due before I died. I didn't know what he was getting at initially, but after we talked I realized he was discussing a plan to kill Webster. I had nothing to lose. I'd already been given a death sentence. I still wavered for a few weeks. I mean Judd was a bastard, but I never believed in an eye for an eye. However, Rollins knew my Achilles' heel. He offered me five million dollars immediately and one million dollars each month until Webster was killed. Once Judd was dead, I'd receive another five million dollars. All monies were to be deposited in a Swiss bank account. All monies I'd be able to use for my philanthropic work."

"I don't get it. You just told me Rollins was bankrupt."

"He told me the money was coming from someone who wanted Webster dead even more than we did."

"Who was that?" Mort asked.

"He wouldn't tell me." Carlin began coughing again. He took another deep breath before continuing. "Rollins wanted me to find someone close to Webster who knew his comings and goings. He knew Webster was seeing a psychiatrist in New York City. My part in the overall plan was very simple. He knew my wife had died and that I was usually free in the evenings. All I had to do was wait outside your office every Monday evening at 8:00 p.m., after your group therapy meeting ended, and select one of your female patients who seemed more lost and lonely than the others."

"How did Rollins know Webster was seeing me?" Yvars asked.

"I don't know," Carlin replied, his pallor returning. Yvars turned up the oxygen flow.

"After four weeks I spotted her. She looked so needy and frail, yet at the same time attractive in her own way."

"That's how you met Mary Hargrove?" Yvars asked.

"Yes. She had left the rest of the group and was near the corner of the street when I approached her. I invited her for coffee. She was very hesitant at first. I promised her she needn't be afraid of me. That I had sensed her loneliness. I told her I was a widower and was also very lonely. She smiled. We hit it off very well. I told her to call me Jim. I refused to ever give her my last name. It was obvious she didn't recognize me.

"We'd meet at the same diner every Monday evening after your group session. She told me about Max and how neglected she felt. I told her about Katherine, our lives together and how much I missed her. She said I was very fortunate to have had a wonderful marriage for so many years.

"After about a month Mary began telling me about a crush she'd developed on one of the members of the group. After she described him, I knew she was talking about Webster. However, she kept referring to him as Jeff Osgood. She'd tell me about her hours spent daydreaming. How she'd envisioned life if she had been married to Osgood instead of Max. And at times she'd blush, tell me she felt guilty about spending most of our time talking about Osgood. I'd assure her I looked forward to our weekly evenings, that I only wanted her to feel happy. If talking about Osgood was what did it for her, that's all I cared about. She fell for my line. I knew I had her.

"One Monday evening I decided to make my move. I told Mary I had been waiting outside your office and recognized Osgood. I informed her he really was Judd Webster, a senator from Colorado, and that we'd worked together on many charitable activities and I had gotten to know him very well over the years. She was, needless to say, startled. I told her Judd, although handsome and married to a beautiful woman, was a very lonely man. I mentioned many affairs he'd had over the years, all with beautiful women, but that the women he really enjoyed were those like Mary. Women who were warm, caring and sensitive. Those who'd want to listen rather than do all the talking."

"Was this true?" Yvars asked.

"Yes. When Judd was my assistant he ran around with many women, one more beautiful than the next. However, he'd confide in me what he missed most was a companion. Someone he'd be able to open up to rather than a woman he had to play a role with."

"What was Mary's reaction?" Yvars asked.

"She couldn't believe anyone as handsome and famous as Webster would ever want anything to do with the likes of her," Carlin replied. "I reassured her he most certainly would. However, I told her I'd set things up between them only if she was willing to make a deal with me. She also had to promise never to tell Webster I was the one who initiated the contact. Furthermore, I emphasized, their relationship would in all probability be completely platonic, confined to phone calls."

"How did she respond to your offer?" Yvars asked.

"She was thrilled. Being able to have an ongoing relationship with Judd, regardless of the conditions, was more than she could ever have dreamt possible. I gave her Judd's number on Capitol Hill and convinced her he'd be very receptive to her calling. My predictions came true. They hit it off beautifully."

"What was her part of the deal?" Yvars asked.

"Mary was to write down everything she and Judd talked about, with the emphasis on his daily routine. Each Monday evening over coffee she'd hand her notes over to me."

"What did you do with this information?" Yvars asked.

"On my way home I'd drop her notes in the mail," Carlin replied.

"Where to?" Yvars asked.

"To a pharmaceutical company in NYC."

"Who in the company did you send the notes to?" Yvars asked.

"No specific person. Just to the company," Carlin replied.

"What's the connection between Rollins and this so-called pharmaceutical company in NYC?"

"I don't know," Carlin replied.

"What's the name of this company?"

"The Nesbitt Pharmaceutical Company."

"Where are they located?"

"Someplace in Manhattan," Carlin replied.

"What's their address?" a still skeptical Yvars asked.

"Get me my wallet. I have the company's business card in it."

Yvars walked to the closet, reached inside Carlin's trouser pocket, pulled out a thick black wallet and handed it to the former senator.

Carlin snapped open one of the side compartments. "Here it is. The Nesbitt Pharmaceutical Company. 233 Duane Street."

"How do I know you're telling me the truth? Jerry Rollins name isn't on the card. There isn't anybody's name on this card. The card only contains the name of the company, their address and phone number," Yvars asked.

"You believe me. I know you do. You're a psychiatrist. From your insights into Wagner's operatic characters at my party last night, I'd say a very clever one at that. You realize full well I am telling you the truth. I have nothing to gain from lying to you."

"Did you kill Webster?" Yvars asked.

"No."

"Did Rollins?"

"I don't know," Carlin replied.

"Who was this person who wanted Webster dead even more than the two of you?" Yvars asked.

"I told you I don't know."

Yvars paused for a moment. He realized Carlin was indeed telling the truth, or at least the truth as he knew it. "Where does Rollins live?"

Carlin reached inside his wallet again and pulled out another card. "At 103 Burne Drive in Demarest, New Jersey. It's a big old house. He's lived there for years."

Yvars handed Simons Rollins' card. "Go to Rollins' home and question him your way. Make him talk! I'm going to go with Carlin to

Wentworth." Yvars glanced at his watch. It was 6:31 p.m. "I should be back home by 7:30 p.m., 8:00 p.m. at the latest. If I'm not home by then you can reach me on my cellular phone."

Yvars walked into the hallway, grabbed the pay phone and dialed Millie.

"Butler's been calling here all afternoon. He's furious. He's sure you're intentionally avoiding him."

"If he calls again, tell him I'll speak to him as soon as I get home." Yvars paused. "How did your physical with Dr. Clarke go?" Mort asked.

"Fine. He said I'm in perfect health."

Mort then recounted in detail all he had learned from Carlin since they had last spoken.

"Where are you now?" Millie asked.

"I'm still at New York Hospital."

"I know you're going to think I'm being a nag again, but please Mort come right home after you drop Carlin off at Wentworth Hospital. Don't go to that drug company. You don't have any idea of what you'll find. You've done enough. Give all the information to Butler. Let the FBI do the rest."

"I'm sorry, but I can't promise you that. I'm too involved to just stop now. I have to go. I'll call you when I get to the Nesbitt headquarters. Don't worry. I'll be fine." Yvars paused. "One more favor. If Simons calls don't tell him I've gone to the Nesbitt Company."

* * * * * * * *

The stranger's frustration mounted. New York Hospital personnel were everywhere. The intruder peered at Mort Yvars.

The figure watched intently as Yvars helped wheel James Carlin, his face covered by a plastic oxygen mask, into the waiting red and white ambulance.

The stranger knew exactly where Yvars was heading. This time Yvars would be alone. This time Yvars wouldn't escape alive. The plan would remain intact.

29

The newly painted ambulance was speeding through Central Park when suddenly it slowed to a crawl. Yvars peered through the front window. A traffic snarl. He glanced at Carlin lying restlessly on the stretcher, hooked up to both an IV and a cardiac monitor; his color no longer pink but ashen despite a constant flow of nasal oxygen.

Finally, the traffic jam ended. What was stop and go had miraculously cleared up. Cars were now moving at a brisk clip. Then came a detour for construction and swerving to dodge potholes. At last the 72nd Street exit. What should have taken twenty-five minutes tops, had taken an hour.

The ambulance swerved into Wentworth Hospital's emergency room entrance.

Lance Wagner, dressed in his surgical scrubs, greeted Mort. "I thought you'd never get here. What took so long?"

"Don't ask!" Mort moaned, grabbing Claire's custard filled chocolate donut from her hefty hand. He bit into the delicious gooey dough and devoured half of his favorite delicacy. He was about to shove the remainder of the donut into his mouth when he hesitated and handed the remains back to the 275 pound charge nurse.

"Since when have you stopped eating the whole thing?" a surprised but pleased Claire asked, as she quickly munched the rest of the donut before Yvars had a chance to change his mind.

"My diet, remember?" Yvars proudly replied.

"Oh yeah, right!" Claire said. "I've lost eighty pounds, gained fifty, taken off twenty more, put ninety back on. It's all this stress working here. You'll find out. Mark my words. Next time you'll eat the whole donut. Willpower only works so long. Soon the desire becomes too overpowering. Don't throw your fat clothes away. Believe me you'll need them again before long."

"I haven't put in all this effort to lose thirty pounds to ever gain them back," Yvars replied.

"That's what I thought. Let's see what you look like in a year. If you manage to keep the weight off, I'll rethink my philosophy. I'll try again," Claire said.

"Can we stop the chit chat," Wagner said impatiently.

"He's all yours," Yvars replied as Wentworth's two burly attendants carefully hoisted Carlin's frail frame from the ambulance and into the emergency room.

"Everything is all set," Wagner said. " A nineteen year old DOA. Hit and run three hours ago. Matching blood type. Similar body build. His heart's on ice. Carlin should do fine."

Yvars thanked Wagner for circumventing the customary bureaucratic channels and propelling Carlin to the top of the UNOS I list. Carlin would get his new heart. A new lease on life. Did he deserve another chance? Was this right? A nineteen-year-old boy with his entire life ahead of him, innocently crossing the street, minding his own business, run down, killed. Thanks to the advance of modern medical science his heart would be used to allow another to live. Ethical, moral questions. No clear cut answers. Issues he could dwell on at another time. All Yvars knew was he had had no choice but to do all in his power to have Dunbar persuade Wagner to cooperate, to give Carlin a new heart. Otherwise Carlin wouldn't have revealed what he did. What all this meant, Yvars didn't know. Where all this would eventually lead, he likewise didn't now. Hopefully, all his questions would be answered once he arrived at Duane Street.

Yvars waved down a taxi and climbed in. "233 Duane Street," he said to the driver.

"Where is Duane Street?" the thin, middle-aged, man with a thick Russian accent asked.

"Are you serious? You don't know?" a disgusted Yvars replied. Mort shifted nervously in his seat. Suddenly, he remembered the cellular phone in his tuxedo jacket. In all the commotion, he'd forgotten his promise to Millie. He reached inside his pocket and pressed the phone to the on position.

"Forgive me sir, but I've only been in the States four months. My English is good, no?" the Russian proudly asked.

"I have to get to Duane Street. It's somewhere downtown."

"No worry. Wait a minute," the cabby said reaching into his glove compartment and taking out a map. He unfolded the large sheet on the empty seat by his side. "The whole borough. It's here. We'll find it. No trouble," he proudly said.

They drove straight down Broadway without any problem. The enigmatic city never ceased to amaze Mort. He had expected the drive from New York Hospital to be a breeze. It was anything but. Traveling down Broadway was invariably a different story. Bumper to bumper on good days, gridlock on the others. But this evening, smooth sailing. There was barely a car on the Avenue. They reached Houston Street when the driver slammed on his brakes.

"Let me look at the map. We're here," he said pointing to Broadway and Houston. He studied the crisscrossing multi-colored lines intently. "Ah, here it is. I see Duane Street."

Trying not to think about what lay ahead, Yvars glanced out the dirty window. The area looked like the Bowery. He and Millie had taken a guided walking tour of lower Manhattan with a group from the 92nd Street Y last spring. Soho, Noho, Tribeca. All distinct geographical sections of lower Manhattan's maze. The lecturer on the grueling three hour walk described how this entire area had until recently been a total disaster. However, over the past two decades a partial renaissance had occurred.

Gentrified stretches with intimate bistros and renovated apartment buildings owned by well-heeled residents, juxtaposed between abandoned warehouses, graffiti illustrated brick façades, drug dealers and derelicts. A real hodgepodge. The lecturer explained that the district in the nineteenth century was a paradise of the gay life and the heart of nocturnal frivolity, along with its being the seat of enormously successful manufacturing plants. That was another time. Another century. Years of decay ensued. However, as Mort peered through the grimy window, the revitalization and the renewal of the entire expanse, while not complete, was well on its way. He wouldn't want to live here, nor work here. It was still too run down. He and Millie had gone to a Christmas party two years ago at a colleague of theirs who had purchased a converted warehouse. While a magnificent building inside, it was sandwiched in between deserted structures with boarded up windows and camped out homeless. Too spooky for the way he wanted to live, he said to Millie after they had left the party. 'Each to his own,' was her retort.

"We're here," the thick accented driver cried out in glee. "233 Duane Street."

Mort stepped from the cab. The street looked very familiar. Suddenly it dawned on him. He and Millie had parked their car on this very street the night they celebrated their first anniversary at the elegant Bouley Restaurant located a few blocks away. They had dined on deliciously prepared duck a l'orange while sipping a bottle of Moet and Chandon Champagne.

He glanced at the nearby buildings. Most were in dire need of repair. Many were abandoned. But 233 Duane had obviously undergone a facelift. It had a beautiful new red brick exterior, Anderson windows, and neatly trimmed bushes that dotted the walkway to the entrance. He recalled the tour leader mentioning this area as part of the Tribeca section of lower Manhattan. The Triangle below Canal Street, he had said.

"What do I owe you?" Mort asked the driver.

"Seventeen dollars and fifteen cents."

Yvars paid the fare and asked if the driver would wait.

"You pay I'll stay," came the immediate response.

Mort thanked the driver. A group of weirdos with assorted colored hair walked past the taxi. "Promise you'll be here when I come out," Mort asked

"The meter will be running. I'll be waiting."

Mort stepped over a pile of garbage strewn over the curb. He glanced upward at the remodeled five story building as he walked to the front door. He turned the knob. The wooden door was locked. There was no doorman. He looked around the door frame, his eyes focusing on a vertical metal box firmly attached to the right of the entranceway, listing the names and apartment numbers of all the occupants. He gazed at the list; doctors and businesses. No families. He couldn't find the Nesbitt Company. Where the hell was the Nesbitt Company? His eyes continued scanning the names, his frustration mounting. Shit, Carlin had lied.

He continued staring at the black plastic strips on the metal box. Suddenly he noticed something odd in the middle of the list of occupants on the left side of the box. All the black strips were perfectly lined up. One exactly under the other, except for one; the Philmont Music Company. Apartment 3C. He pressed his fingernail under the black plastic. There was another piece of black plastic beneath. He pushed the Philmont strip to the side. He stared in disbelief. There, directly in full view, was the name he had been looking for. Carlin hadn't deceived him after all. The Nesbitt Company did indeed exist. The pharmaceutical company was located at 233 Duane Street exactly as Carlin had said it would be. But what was with the Philmont Music Company? And why was the music company's plastic nameplate covering up Nesbitt's? Mort shrugged his shoulders. He quickly pressed the buzzer adjacent to apartment 3C.

There was no answer.

He pressed again, this time more forcefully.

There was still no response.

Was it possible for an office to be closed so early on a work day?

He checked his watch. It was 7:53 p.m. No wonder there was no answer. It was dinnertime. All the employees of the company had more than likely left for the day.

Now what, he wondered. He glanced back at the list of occupants. He spotted the name Dr. Levy. Perhaps the doctor would still be seeing patients. Mort invariably worked until 9:00. Might not Levy!

Yvars was about to press Dr. Levy's button when the door opened. A young woman carrying a sleeping infant in her arms emerged. She smiled at Mort. He smiled back, slipped past her and stepped inside. He glanced at the peeling, stained walls and the dull, gray, threadbare carpeting in the lobby.

What a contrast between the refurbished outside and the still dilapidated condition of the inside of the building. With all the commercial real estate available in Manhattan, Mort couldn't understand why a pharmaceutical company would have its headquarters in such a rundown dwelling. However, he wasn't here as an architectural or design critic. He had enough on his mind to deal with as he began his climb to the third floor.

30

Yvars huffed as he passed the grimy, large, Anderson window that faced the deserted courtyard cluttered with empty beer cans and a discarded baby carriage.

He reached the third floor landing, beads of perspiration saturated his collar and fell onto his already stained and wrinkled tuxedo.

He approached apartment 3C. In the middle of the green metallic door, on a large brass name plate, was printed in bold letters PHILMONT MUSIC COMPANY. Not again, Mort thought. Where was the sign for the Nesbitt Pharmaceutical Company? His eyes scanned the door frame. There was none. Was it possible both the Philmont Music Studio and the Nesbitt Pharmaceutical Company were two arms of the same company, one part involved in the manufacturing and the marketing of medications and the other with the music industry? He pressed the buzzer to the left of the door in the hope the downstairs buzzer was out of order and someone was indeed still in. No such luck. There was no answer.

However, he couldn't let himself turn back now. He had come too far in his journey. There had already been four deaths and a potentially limitless number of future deaths. He couldn't let a locked door stop him. But how was he going to figure out a way to open the locked door? Then suddenly it hit him. He reached into his pants pocket and pulled out his ever present paper clip. Thank God my father left me with something, Mort thought. The man whom Mort blamed for all of his adult fears and insecurities had at least taught him one lesson in life . . . to always keep a paper clip with him.

He carefully pulled the large paper clip apart and slid the sharp edge of the metal object into the keyhole. Suddenly he heard a click. The door swung open. Yvars paused, visualized his gaunt father lying in his open coffin, his body ravaged by cancer, and for the first time felt a sadness, an empathy for the angry man whose bitterness with his lot in life cost Mort dearly.

Yvars snapped on the light switch adjacent to the door and gazed in awe at the incredible display of musical equipment that filled the ten foot by twelve foot room. Hi-Tech floor to ceiling state of the art Dolby prologic surround optima speakers at each corner of the room. The Philmont Company must do one hell of a business he thought, as he glanced at the circular area equipped with crisscrossing wires, a large drum set and three electrical guitar units. Several head sets sat on top of a rectangular table cluttered with sheet music. Tall thin microphones hung from the ceiling. There were also two stationary standing microphones in the middle of the assortment of musical instruments.

He stared at the walls. All were covered with posters of various rock groups, each group dressed more outlandishly and seductively than the next. Mort quickly realized how rapidly musical tastes changed.

Tyrone Sawyer would call Mort 'over the hill,' whenever they discussed their musical preferences. Mort opted for jazz, rhythm and blues and an occasional Beatle tune, while Sawyer insisted nothing could top Guns and Roses or U2. He once persuaded Mort to watch MTV. Sex and violence along with the dissident beat horrified him. What was the world coming to? A planet inhabited by sex crazed, knife-wielding adults walking down the streets of Manhattan with ghetto blasters puncturing their eardrums, he told Sawyer during the following Monday evening's group meeting. It was in retrospect, Yvars realized, his willingness to spend that hour glued to the unpleasant sounds of MTV that finally brought Tyrone Sawyer out of his self-imposed withdrawal. "You cared enough to do that for me?" the shocked young man had asked. From that day on Tyrone began trusting Mort and opening up to the group. His anger dissipated and his music flourished. Mort shuddered as he recalled Sawyer on the slab at the city morgue. His mind immediately shifted back to the Nesbitt Company. Where the hell was the Pharmaceutical Company? There weren't any research facilities, no cases of ready to ship drugs. Nothing in the room but musical equipment. He walked to the far corner of the room where a glass partition separated the musical area from what looked to Mort like a control room. He glanced at the multicolored six by twelve foot area overflowing with synchronizers, mixers of various sizes and shapes and a long row of chairs behind a rectangular formica table. The entire look was identical to the photographs of the RCA, CBS and Motown recording studios in the several issues of Rolling Stone Magazine that Tyrone Sawyer periodically brought to the group meetings for Mort to read.

Mort scratched his head in disbelief, his frustration intensifying. Apartment 3C housed an exquisitely furnished music studio. Nothing else. He'd been deceived. Carlin had outsmarted him. He continued walking closer to the control room, staring at the various pieces of equipment behind the partition. The closer he came to the large pane of glass, the more something about the scene in front of him appeared odd.

Suddenly it hit him. Nothing beyond the partition looked real. Rather, all looked exactly like a photograph of an authentic control room blown up in size to simulate a genuine recording studio.

Yvars pressed firmly on the glass partition and stepped back. He couldn't believe his eyes. The enormous partition fell on its left side. The entire control room collapsed. He stepped over the fabricated creation and bent down. The mock control room had been constructed from sheetrock. The entire space was a sham of pictures and photographs that to the unobservant eye appeared completely genuine. Why would anyone go to such lengths to create this illusion? It didn't make any sense. He glanced behind the fallen panels. In the far corner of the room was a desk with a large metal file cabinet alongside it.

Yvars walked rapidly to the desk, opened the top drawer and pulled out all the contents. He sat down on the nearby swivel chair and began sifting through the various papers. There were letters from the Federal Drug Administration, and requests from the editor of the Physicians Desk Reference Annual's sixteen hundred page manual for a thorough list of all side effects of each of Nesbitt's drugs. Mort sighed in relief. There really was a Nesbitt Pharmaceutical Company! The drug company actually did exist. It wasn't like the Philmont Music Company. It wasn't a sham. Carlin hadn't deceived him.

He then opened both side desk drawers and pulled out large stacks of papers. Most were blank pieces of stationery with the company's letterhead printed in bold type. However, scattered in among the stationery were several handwritten notes detailing Judd Webster's routine, his daily schedule, his comings and going. Each page was dated on the top right corner. There was one from January, two from February, one from March and another from April. However, none since April. He stared closely at the handwriting and immediately recognized who'd written them. The writing was identical to handwritten notes he received each month attached to his monthly check for his psychotherapy services. The handwriting belonged to Mary Hargrove.

He remembered Carlin's deal with Mary. A favor for a favor. A relationship with Judd in return for frequent updates on the senator's daily itinerary.

However, he recalled Carlin insisted on weekly reports. He glanced once again through the piles of paper on the desk looking for Mary's other weekly reports. He couldn't find any. There weren't any notes for three weeks in January, two weeks in February, three weeks in March, three weeks in April and absolutely no notes whatsoever since April. Where were Mary's other weekly notes? And why weren't there any notes since April? Webster had been killed June 6th. That left many more weekly notes from Mary unaccounted for. Where could these missing weekly notes be? He rummaged through the entire stack of papers looking for the missing weekly notes once again. There were none.

Yvars then glanced at the company's letterhead. 233 Duane Street, New York. 212-472-2132. Suddenly his eyes hit upon a curious finding. Another phone number. This one however, had a 303 area code, but without a corresponding address.

He reached for the phone and punched in the numbers next to the 303 area code. On the third ring a non-descript voice began talking. Shit, Mort realized, the voice was a recording. He had reached an answering machine. The message: "You have reached the Nesbitt Pharmaceutical Company. Our company closes at 5 p.m. No one is presently available to answer your call. Kindly leave your name, the name of your company, your phone number and your message and we will return your call on the next business day."

Now what! Yvars ran his hands through his thick wavy hair. He thought for a moment. The operator. He'd call information. He'd find out which geographical locale area code 303 served.

"That would be Colorado sir," came the pleasant voice at the other end of the line.

"Colorado!" Yvars exclaimed in disbelief. "I'm a doctor. A patient gave me this phone number but I don't have a name or any address."

"Give me the number. If it's not unlisted, I'll get the information on my screen."

"303-342-2173," Yvars replied.

"That number is listed. Wait a minute. Let me bring up the name," she paused briefly. "Here it is. The Nesbitt Pharmaceutical Company."

"And the address?" Yvars asked impatiently.

"There isn't an address sir. Just a post office box."

"What town is the post office box in?"

"Leadville sir," came the reply.

"Thank you." Yvars replied hanging up the receiver.

Colorado! 303 – Colorado. Judd Webster was a senator from the state of Colorado. Why hadn't he made such an obvious connection sooner? His eyes wandered back to the stationery on the desk. Amid Nesbitt's bland pieces of stationery were several pieces of stationery imprinted with Jane Webster's name. Suddenly things began to click.

He tapped his hands on the desk for a few minutes, deep in thought. Going over each event, every conversation as best he could remember since it all had started two and a half weeks ago.

Jane Webster, that woman, he cried out. She must have been behind everything all along. No wonder she pleaded with him to get involved in the investigation. Sure she had been frightened ever since her son William had been kidnapped two years ago. But that wasn't why she really wanted him to help her. That was her excuse, her hook to persuade him to help. The real reason was not quite obvious. She insisted on his help rather than the FBI's not because she feared Jackson and now Butler would foul things up placing her son's life in jeopardy again. No, that wasn't it at all. It was exactly the opposite. She knew he would be far less likely than trained FBI agents to figure out why her husband was killed.

What a fool I've been. He reached into his tuxedo pocket, behind the cellular phone, and pulled out his address book. He dialed Jane Webster's number.

"Oh Mort. Thank God you called. I've been a wreck since we last spoke. What have you found out?" she asked.

"Everything! I'm at 233 Duane Street at the Nesbitt Pharmaceutical Company. It's been you all along. You killed Judd. The Philmont Music Company was a clever ploy. A phony recording studio. You almost had me fooled. I found some of Mary Hargrove's weekly notes. You had Carlin get them from her every Monday evening after our group therapy sessions. I also found many pieces of stationery belonging to the Nesbitt Company as well as several sheets of your own personalized stationery. Did you also kill Sawyer, Matthews and Jackson?"

"Mort I don't understand. What are you talking about?" A shocked Jane Webster asked.

"What is your connection with Jim Carlin and Jerry Rollins?"

Mort asked.

"None. Mort I still don't know what you're talking about?"

"Why did you kill your husband?"

"Me kill Judd? Have you completely lost it? I loved Judd. Why would I want to kill him?" Jane bewilderedly asked.

"I've believed you until now, but no longer. You diverted me by using William as an alibi. I can't believe you've conned me so well. Why did you do it?"

"Mort, please. You have to believe me. I didn't kill Judd. I really don't know what you are talking about. I keep wishing this was all a bad dream. That I'd wake up one morning and Judd would be asleep next to me."

"I'm not about to get sucked in again," Mort replied. "I'm going to call Butler and hand everything over to the FBI. I should have listened to Millie from the beginning."

"Please Mort, please," Jane pleaded. "Maybe I'm not all I pretend to be. Who is? In Washington, having a pretty face, quick wit and knowing the latest fashions and trendy places are all important. If those are crimes then I'm guilty. But not what you are accusing me of. I'd never kill Judd. I'd never kill anybody! You must believe me."

"How do you explain your own stationery being mixed in among all these papers?"

"I have no idea how my stationery got there."

"What's your involvement with the Nesbitt Pharmaceutical Company?"

"None. I've never even heard of that company," Jane replied.

Mort's tone began to soften. Maybe she was telling the truth. Maybe she didn't have anything to do with her husband's death. Perhaps she was guilty, but only of the same crime he was . . . burying his head in the sand. Perhaps she also didn't know about Tyrone Sawyer, his illegitimate son, or of Eileen Matthews, his mistress. He had to step back and rethink again . . . to use his psychological skills, his knowledge of others' psyches. He had to stop allowing his anxiety to overtake his objective perceptions. He had initially thought he understood Jane and her motives. They were pure and simple – to protect her son William. Her personality profile was consistent with those stated desires. The more he thought, the more he realized his first impression was most probably correct. She, at least for now, deserved the benefit of the doubt. If he found facts specifically linking Jane to Judd's murder or to the drug company and not simply blank pieces of her personal stationery he would turn everything over to the FBI. For now he'd go with his intuition. He'd trust her. He hoped he wouldn't regret his decision. "Forgive me," Yvars finally replied. "This detective business isn't for me. I'm a psychiatrist. I do best sitting back in my chair and listening to others."

"Then you do believe me! Thank God," Jane said, sighing in relief. "What are you going to do?"

"I don't know just yet," Yvars replied. "I'll tell you when I figure that out myself."

Mort hung up the phone and shoved Mary Hargrove's notes, along with a few pieces of both Jane Webster's and the Nesbitt Company's stationery, into his pants pocket.

He was about to leave the fabricated recording company when he suddenly remembered he'd promised Millie he'd be home before 8 p.m. It was now 9:15 p.m. She'd be frantic, imagining the worst.

"You are lucky you have such an understanding wife," Millie barked into the receiver. "Any other wife would have had the police out looking for you by now."

"There was a lot of traffic. It took forever to get Carlin to Wentworth."

"Where are you now?" Millie, her tone warming up, asked.

"I'm still at the Nesbitt Company," Mort replied. "I'll tell you everything when I get home."

"Butler called again. I gave him your message. You've got to tell him what you've found out," Millie said.

256

"I will . . . eventually," Mort replied.

" I hope you are hungry. I'm making you your favorite dinner."

"Meatloaf?" Mort, his mouth watering, asked.

"With mashed potatoes and thick gravy."

"I can't wait," Mort replied. He was about to hang up when an idea struck him. "Do me a favor. Call Wentworth Hospital's 24 hour Pharmaceutical Hotline. Ask to speak to Jack Feinstein. He's on call all this month. Find out if there really is a company named Nesbitt Pharmaceuticals. If so, find out all you can about the company. Who owns it. The name of the CEO. The president. What drugs they make? Everything you can," Yvars paused. "I have a taxi waiting downstairs. If there's no traffic I'll be home within the hour."

Yvars had made up his mind. He suddenly realized what he had to do next.

31

Doug Simons swerved his Mustang into the long dark driveway. The drive to Rollins' home proved far simpler than he'd anticipated. The Mobil attendant in Demarest knew where the house was located: two lefts, a right at the blinking light and 100 yards later, on the left, a large white colonial, straight out of 'Gone With the Wind'.

"You can't miss it," he reassured the reporter. "The guy keeps the outdoor lights on all night. Word has it he lives alone, is terrified of burglars and is willing to shell out an extra fifty dollars a month to the electric company for peace of mind."

Simons approached the front door. The darkness surrounding the house was in striking contrast to what the gas attendant had told him to expect. He felt for the doorbell but couldn't find it. It was too dark to see anything. His fingers moved in all directions, finally grabbing hold of a brass knocker which he slammed against the wooden door.

There was no response. He knocked again. This time harder. There was still no response. He peered through a side window. It was completely dark. Maybe Rollins was out for the evening. Simons was prepared to wait until Rollins returned home, when he accidentally leaned against the door. The knob moved. The door was not locked. Simons grasped the round knob and entered the foyer. He was enveloped by total blackness.

He immediately smelled a repulsive odor that momentarily made him feel faint. Simons felt for a light switch, found it and snapped it on. A bright, overhead, glass chandelier illuminated the parquet floor. The smell was becoming stronger, more overpowering. Simons walked toward the penetrating odor. It was coming from somewhere near the back of the house, probably the kitchen. Damn, the reporter thought, Rollins was probably away on vacation. The putrid smell was undoubtedly rancid food.

Simons entered the kitchen, turned on the lights and immediately stepped back in horror. Lying face up was a fully clothed, middle-aged man. The smell in the kitchen was rapidly overtaking him. The odor penetrated his clothes, his skin, his lungs. Everything. He began feeling light-headed, dizzy.

He bent down, took a deep breath and held it. He had come this far. He couldn't turn back. He had to make certain the decaying body in front of him was Jerry Rollins.

Simons stood and began walking from the kitchen. However, the stench engulfing him proved too much to withstand any longer. He started gagging and then vomited uncontrollably.

*   *   *   *   *   *

"Turn off here," Mort commanded his newly found buddy. The yellow cab exited the West Side Highway and headed east.

"Now what do I do?" Marchov asked.

"Don't you know your way around any part of the city?" an incredulous Yvars asked.

"Yes. Tell me how to go. I drive. That's it," came the accented response.

"Go to Central Park West. Make a left. I'm on the corner of 83rd Street," Yvars, irritatedly replied. "On second thought, hook a left on Broadway."

Marchov slammed on the brakes. A black Jaguar swerved just in time to miss smashing into the taxi's front end. "Central Park West. Now Broadway. You get mad at me for not knowing where I'm going and I'm from Russia. This is your city. What's your excuse? You Americans! I don't understand any of you!"

At 83rd Street and Broadway, Yvars ordered Marchov to make a U-turn, drive to 82nd Street and wait. "I'll be right out."

"That's what you said at Duane Street," the hairy-armed foreigner said. "It's your money. Take your time."

"Tell me about it. This has to be the most expensive cab ride of my life," Yvars replied slamming the door shut. He had to take three large steps before he reached the curb. "You could at least let your passengers off next to the sidewalk. Why don't you practice parallel parking while you wait?"

"More instructions. You Americans are so bossy. Just do what you have to. The meter's running," Marchov replied.

Broadway was bustling. People of all ages, races and sizes almost colliding as they passed each other.

It was mainly, at times like these, that Yvars was grateful he lived in the city. The city never slept. The shops on Broadway and Columbus kept their doors open until at least eleven. Restaurants until two. Bars until dawn. Manhattan was Millie's idea. His dream was to live someplace less urban, less crowded. Lower Westchester perhaps. Nothing fancy. A small house, a parcel of land. A tree or two. Maybe a flower garden in the back. He'd commute the thirty or forty minutes to work. But Millie persisted. He eventually relented. If they had children Millie would say she'd be more amenable but . . .

Yvars pushed open the doors to the Barnes and Noble superstore. He quickly walked to the travel section. If he was going to actually fly to Colorado, drive to Leadville, wherever and whatever that was, he'd better be prepared. Until yesterday, Colorado was 'Butch Cassidy and the Sundance Kid.' A state consisting of thousands who needed analysis, but instead hurled their frost-bitten selves down treacherous God-forsaken mountain slopes in the dead of winter, rather than lay on a warm Caribbean beach soaking up the sun's warm rays, sipping Planter's Punch and listening to calypso sounds.

A salesperson handed Mort a Rand McNally roadmap of Colorado and a guidebook for the state. Pretty thin book, he thought. He was about to pay the cashier when he noticed, adjacent to the cash register, a huge stack of Stephen King's newly published novel. He grabbed a copy of the latest thriller written by Millie's favorite author. It was so heavy. So thick. Over 1000 pages he noted as he flipped to the ending. And such small print besides. He smiled.

Yvars left Barnes and Noble and quickly walked into the gourmet's candy store down the street, purchasing a five-pound bag of Millie's weakness, Bassett's Allsorts. Hopefully, between her fancy licorice and her lengthy read, she'd leave him be. Let him do what he felt he had to do. He hoped his bribes would be sufficient.

Ten minutes later Marchov pulled up to Mort's apartment. Yvars was in the midst of paying the fare when he heard the peel of his cellular phone in his jacket pocket. The voice at the other end of the line was Simons.

Doug recounted what he'd uncovered in Demarest. Three minutes later Mort, stunned, speechless and still gripping the phone, stepped from the cab.

*　*　*　*　*　*

Yvars turned the key and was greeted by the unique aroma of his favorite food, meatloaf. His mouth watered in anticipation of the pleasure of swallowing every morsel of his last remaining vice. He knew he'd inhale it all, regardless of how confused Simons conversation had left him. If Carlin hadn't killed Webster, and Rollins was now dead, who then was behind all the killings? He gulped hard trying to regain his composure before Millie suspected anything else was wrong.

Mort placed the shopping bag from Barnes and Noble next to the front door. Millie raced from the kitchen. They embraced in silence for several minutes. He felt so good. She so warm and firm. They remained in each other's arms.

"How are you feeling?" Mort finally asked.

"Couldn't be better, especially now that you're home." Suddenly she looked at him. "What's the matter?"

"Nothing. Why?" Yvars asked.

"Mort your face is an open book."

"Simons called. He found Rollins in his house. Judging by the condition of the body, Doug believes the guys been dead for over two weeks."

"Mort enough already! Call Butler," Millie commanded.

"I'll call Butler right after dinner," Mort replied.

He walked into the bedroom, slipped out of his creased tuxedo, and put on a bathrobe. He met Millie in the middle of the living room. "Did Feinstein find out anything?" he asked.

"Yes. Nesbitt is a legitimate company. They aren't a giant in the pharmaceutical industry like Merck or Hoffman-LaRoche, but he's dealt with one of their sales representatives from time to time. They specialize in vitamins and various generic drugs. They even have their own brand of diazepam. I guess since Roche lost its patent on valium. All the drug companies are producing the tranquilizer."

"Feinstein looked through his PDR and several of his other pharmaceutical reference manuals. The company has a location, as you know, on 233 Duane Street in the city and a second facility in Leadville, Colorado. According to one of his books, their main office is the one in Leadville."

"Who's their CEO?" Yvars asked.

"He doesn't know. None of his drug reference manuals listed the names of any of the company's officers. He said, if you'd like, he would call his sales rep from Nesbitt Monday morning. The fellow is on vacation this week, otherwise he would have had that information for you by now. Feinstein said to call him Monday and he'll have the CEO's name."

"Damn. That won't do. I can't wait until Monday," Mort replied frustratedly.

Yvars walked back into the bedroom and pulled a handful of

crumbled papers from his pocket. He then quickly returned to the living room. "Here's some of Mary's notes detailing Webster's daily movements which she gave to Carlin. Several are missing."

"Where do you think they are?" Millie asked.

"In Leadville, Colorado at the Nesbitt Headquarters," Mort replied. "According to Carlin, he mailed Mary's notes each week to the Nesbitt Company's office on Duane Street. My guess is Rollins then sent them to Leadville."

"So if Carlin didn't kill Webster, and Rollins is dead, who's responsible for all these killings?" Millie asked.

"Most likely someone at Nesbitt's Headquarters in Leadville," Mort replied.

"Such as?"

"I don't know yet. I first have to find out who works there."

"You've done a great job. I'm proud of you. Call Butler and tell him everything. Let the FBI do the rest."

"I told you I'd call him after dinner," Mort replied

Millie's eyes darted to the Barnes and Noble package by the front door. "My goodness, what do we have here?" Millie asked eagerly.

"It's a surprise," Mort began. "Don't look! Let me get them."

"Them!" she lifted her eyebrows in anticipation.

Yvars lifted the heavy Stephen King novel and the five-pound bag of Bassett's from the plastic container. "For you. For being so understanding," he said.

Millie eagerly thumbed through the mammoth book and peeked inside the bag of assorted licorice. "We've been married for eight years. I think by now I've gotten to know you very well. One thing is certain. You are not from the surprises. I do surprises. You always give beautiful, thoughtful presents, but always for a special occasion. My birthday, our anniversary, Valentine's Day. You've never done something like this before Mort." She placed her hands on her slim waist. "What gives? Why the gifts?"

"Because you're you. Because I love you."

Millie didn't respond. She walked to the Barnes and Noble bag. It didn't look empty. It looked as if there was still something else. She reached inside. "You're not serious!" she exclaimed. "A map and a guide-book to Colorado. So that's what these surprises are all about. They are to soften me up for what's coming next." Millie paused briefly. "You've decided to forget Butler and Simons. You're going to be John Wayne. You're going to Leadville. You're going to go to the Nesbitt Company and find out who killed our patients. And then what will you do? Mort, get a grip on yourself. Wake up. This isn't the movies. This is real life. You were shot at twice. One bullet meant for you almost killed me. Three of our group therapy patients have been murdered. So was FBI agent Jackson and now this fellow Rollins. Mort, no more! I've had it. I can't continue living this way. I married a nice Jewish psychiatrist from New York with all the angst and neuroses that comes with that package. I went into our marriage with both of my eyes wide open. I knew what I was getting. I liked what I was getting. I've liked our eight years together. But now this! Is this your midlife crisis! Mort face it. You are Clark Kent. Not Superman. If I wanted Superman I'd have found a Superman. It's Clark Kent I married. It's Clark Kent I love."

Yvars didn't respond.

"It's that damn Webster woman isn't it. She won't let you off the hook!"

"Millie, we've been through this countless times already. I under-stand how you feel. I also know that what you say is logical. However, I can't stop now. I honestly thought once I went to the Nesbitt office I could. I found out I can't. I have to go to Leadville."

"What if after going to Nesbitt's headquarters in Leadville, you find more unexpected reasons to continue your one-man crusade. What if you discover the killer has a secret office hidden away in some remote part of Alaska. Will you then be heading there? Mort, this has got to stop!"

"I promise this will be it. If Colorado doesn't provide the rest of the answers, I'll turn everything over to Butler. I'll feel satisfied. Whatever it is that is driving me, whether it's Jane Webster, my concern for her son William's safety, clearing my name, finding out who killed our three patients, my inner demons, whatever, I promise you I'll stop."

Millie sighed in resignation. "What are you going to tell Butler and Simons?"

"I'm not. When Butler calls, tell him I left the city, that I wouldn't tell you where I was going."

"And Simons. What should I tell him?" Millie asked.

"He'll be busy answering the police's questions about what he was doing at Rollins' house. But if he asks, tell him I went upstate to press Mary Hargrove and find out if she knows more than she's told us," Mort replied.

"Simons and Butler are both very smart. They know you tell me everything. They'll never believe I don't know exactly where you are," Millie replied.

"I know. Just keep putting them off. I'll deal with both of them when I return."

"When are you planning to go?" Millie reluctantly asked.

"As soon as possible. Hopefully, tomorrow morning. Since this isn't the skiing season, I don't think I'll have any trouble getting a flight."

"You really promise this is definitely going to be the end to all this madness?"

"Scout's honor," he kissed her warm neck. "While you check on the meatloaf, I'll call Jane Webster to find out if she's uncovered anything else I should know about."

A few minutes later Mort reemerged into their living room, his feet sinking into the thick, peach-colored carpeting.

"Another five minutes or so and the meatloaf will be ready." Millie smiled. "What did Jane Webster say?"

"She thanked me for continuing to trust her."

"For what?"

Mort explained his temporary paranoia concerning the senator's widow.

"You definitely are a piece of work. Jane Webster is as likely to be involved in this as I am. Did she find out anything that might help?"

"Unfortunately not," Mort replied.

"Did she say anything else?" Millie persisted.

"She told me to be careful," Mort said.

"Ah, see. Even she is worried about your safety and she isn't even Jewish." Millie reached into the closet in the foyer and pulled out Mort's dusty, black, medical bag.

"What are you doing now?" a puzzled Yvars asked.

"Since you're obviously hellbent on this Colorado pursuit, I may as well join in and be, as they call it these days, your enabler. She opened the old leather bag. A stethoscope, sphygmomanometer, otoscope. Looks quite professional. You'd better take your medical bag with you."

"Why?" a perplexed Mort asked.

"Haven't you considered how you were going to gain entry into Nesbitt's headquarters? You really didn't expect you'd simply announce your arrival and they'd willingly open their doors so you could find the killer did you? Be real! This way you'll look like a doctor."

Millie then picked up one of the pieces of paper Mort had retrieved from Duane Street. "After dinner I'm going to do some cutting and pasting. I'll remove the Nesbitt letterhead, tape it to another sheet of stationery and run the paper through our copier in the den. Then I'll type a short note introducing you as a physician employed by the Company's executives."

"What on earth for?" Mort, still confused, asked.

"Because the Nesbitt Company is going to most likely have some form of security system you'll have to bypass. With your black bag and a letter stating you're there because you were called for a medical problem, you'll be let in. Being a doctor gives you certain advantages. Parking illegally is one. This is another."

"You are an enabler!" Yvars chuckled.

"Furthermore, you'd better think of a medical problem serious enough for someone to have summoned you so urgently."

Mort nodded his head in disbelief. "While we are at it, how about my bringing along a gun?" Mort said sarcastically.

"That's not funny. I'm trying to be helpful. Don't forget your cellular phone. If you run into unexpected trouble use it. I want you back in my arms safe and sound." Millie paused. "There is one other minor matter."

"Which is?" Mort asked.

"You'll be driving a rental car. You'd better remember to tell Nesbitt's Security Personnel that your car is in the shop being serviced."

"Pray tell why?" Mort asked.

"Because your rental car won't have an MD license plate. That's why! Now," Millie walked in the kitchen, "the meatloaf will be burnt soon. Let's eat."

32

The strong gust of wind swept the swirling sand in all directions, making visibility practically nonexistent. "Shit," Mort exclaimed, as his Ford Escort crept along the narrow two lane road off Interstate 70 at Exit 161. The one hundred miles of unexpected driving from Denver to Vail had been a minor annoyance, but the beauty of the deep blue sky and high peaked mountains on both sides of Interstate 70 made the ninety minutes relaxing and the time passed quickly. However, the same could not be said for the thirty miles he had driven since leaving Vail, especially once the sudden sand storm erupted.

Beth, Mort's travel agent, had explained to him yesterday that the United Express for Denver to Vail didn't operate during the off season. The passenger volume of the commuter line was not sufficient to make the route economically viable. She said it wouldn't be a big deal. He'd love the drive at this time of year. Beth had been right. The trip had been lovely. The scenery reminding him of those late night westerns on cable TV he enjoyed watching while munching on popcorn. That was until the violent sand storm erupted.

Mort glanced at his Rand McNally Road Map spread out alongside the driver's seat. According to his calculations, he should have reached the small town of Leadville by now. But how could he know if he had. Nobody could. Visibility was less than five feet in every direction.

Whoever heard of Leadville anyway? Even the Hertz agent at the airport gave him a surprised look when she inquired about his destination. She shrugged her shoulders. 'In the ski season we occasionally rent a car going there, but during the summer months, never!' was her comment.

Out of the corner of his left eye he saw what looked like a Texaco sign. Thank God. Civilization. He must have finally reached Leadville he thought. He carefully wound his way off the road, reached the   gasoline station and turned his motor off.

A tall, lanky, older man slowly lumbered up to his rental car. "The storm will blow over in five minutes. Wait inside and have a cup of coffee while I fill you up."

Mort begged off. He squinted through the bombardment of sand trying to make out where the Nesbitt Company was located.

"That'll be ten dollars and forty cents. Cash or credit," the man asked.

Mort handed him eleven dollars and poured the change into his blue blazer.

The man peered through Mort's window and noticed Mort's black medical bag. "You a doctor?"

"Yes," Mort answered.

"I have a niece. She's my sister's kid. She's also a doctor. She lives someplace in Boston. I can't imagine letting a woman, even if she is a doctor, examine me. The world's certainly changed since my day," he said. "Anything else I can do for you?"

The wind had died down considerably. Mort scanned the street. A general store, a post office, a church. That was about it. Nothing that resembled industry, let alone a pharmaceutical company. "Ever hear of the Nesbitt Company?" Yvars finally asked.

"Don't tell me you're one of those doctors who's driven through this storm just to get some free drug samples."

Mort felt relieved. The man had obviously heard of the Nesbitt Company.

"They employ many of our year-round residents." Mort wasn't about to ask for numbers. Looking at Main Street gave him enough information.

"Don't look so high and mighty," the older man said. "Our town's a hell of a lot bigger than she looks. While we're not in the same league as Aspen or Vail, we get quite a crowd during the ski season. There's a group of luxury condos, a large hotel and huge indoor shopping mall half a mile down the road." He pointed to a small road to the left of the gas station. "Our population during the summer months is only about one thousand or so. However, during the winter we can get up to twenty to twenty-five thousand on a busy weekend."

Yvars couldn't believe one thousand people lived anywhere in the surrounding area, let alone twenty-five thousand. However, he wasn't going to pursue this conversation any further.

The old man continued. "The Nesbitt Company's been very good to us locals. They built our new community center two blocks east of here. They have also donated most of the funds for a nursing home and a day care center that are in the process of going up. Both should be completed by Labor Day."

Mort continued looking around. He still could not see anything that could even remotely be construed as a commercial building. He took a deep breath. Breathing at an altitude of 10,188 feet above sea level was harder than he had anticipated.

The man burst out laughing. "No wonder you think I'm crazy. You can't see the Nesbitt Company from here. Their complex isn't on Main Street. It's on the road I pointed out to you. About two miles past our shopping mall. You can't miss it. It's at Mt. Elbert. You'll love our mountain. It's retained its natural look. The developers haven't gotten to it yet. You'll see what I mean when you get up there."

The sun, starting its evening descent, had reappeared after the sandstorm.

"What do you mean by 'up there'?" Yvars asked.

"You mean you don't know. Well, doc, you are in for a wonderful treat. The Nesbitt Company is located on top of Mt. Elbert."

Mort gulped. "How high is Mt. Elbert?" he asked.

"Another four thousand feet."

$$* \quad * \quad * \quad * \quad * \quad *$$

Yvars parked his grey car rental in the nearby lot sandwiched in between two high priced foreign imports. A black Mercedes and a green Jaguar with Colorado plates NESBITT. His spirits were lifted when he realized the green sports model most probably belonged to the CEO. The CEO would hopefully lead Mort to the killer.

Mort approached the burly security chief for the Nesbitt Company, his newly polished black medical bag firmly clutched in his left hand. His eyes focused on the ground, hoping to minimize the fear that had now begun to stir within him. Once again he dared not stare at the towering mountain peak directly above for fear of completely decompensating, blowing his cool and thus alarming he guard. Somehow, he had to swallow his fear. He had to get to the top of Mt Elbert. All four thousand feet of it. But first he had to convince the security officer he was for real. For that he needed to maintain the veneer his psychiatric mentor had taught him years ago. Forget your inner turmoil, your confusion, whatever your anxiety might be, his mentor would continuously preach. Those feelings are for you and your own therapist to resolve. Stick to the issue at hand, totally focusing on your patient and his or her problem. Patients are often incredibly perceptive, his professor would frequently say. It's a necessary tool for their imagined dangers. If you let on in either a verbal or non-verbal way that you are a nervous wreck yourself, all hope of getting the patient's confidence will be lost. It's essential for your patients to feel you are a master at coping with your own anxieties. If they sense otherwise, their fears will intensify. You'll lose them.

If ever there was an opportunity to practice his mentor's preachings, this was it.

"Hi. I'm Doctor Mort Yvars," he said to the guard. "I'm the personal physician for several of your officers." He reached inside his blazer and pulled out Millie's perfectly typed letter introducing Mort as a Nesbitt medical consultant. Mort marveled at the excellent job Millie had done in photocopying the Nesbitt Company's letterhead on a blank sheet of paper and then typing in her message. Incredibly authentic looking he thought. Mort waited until the clean shaven guard read the carefully typed letter. Mort worried about the lack of any executive's personal signature. Millie reassured him it wouldn't be necessary. It better not be, Mort realized. The stern looking guard glanced up at Mort before continuing to read the note. Mort's eyes scanned the guardhouse and he felt another surge of anxiety returning. Behind the office ran a long chain of empty chair lifts and gondolas that seemed to reach into clouds. He realized it wouldn't be long before he'd have to board one of those contraptions himself. He forced his mind not to run away with itself. When the time came, he'd deal with the trip to the top of the mountain. For now, he had to convince the guard of the urgency of his visit.

"The boss looked fine this morning. What happened?" The crisp, curt voice asked.

"Stomach pains. Last week I ran some tests to rule out the possibility of an ulcer. I received a phone call two hours ago that the pain was still there. The pills I prescribed are apparently not working. I'm going fishing for the weekend with some buddies, you know for some male bonding. I thought I should come over and do a physical examination before I left. I don't think it's anything serious, but I want to make sure. I wouldn't want to have given my reassurance over the phone and then find out a bleeding episode occurred over the weekend."

"Where are you heading for your fishing trip?" Brown, the guard, an envious look in his eyes, asked.

Mort paused. Shit, another story to create. "I don't know. The fellows are picking me up at 10 p.m. Bob, one of the guys is taking care of all the particulars. I'll let you know where we went the next time I see you."

"Sounds great," the guard beamed gleefully. "Fishing is my passion. I never could get into this ski stuff." He motioned Mort to walk over to the chair lift area. "Well, what's your poison?" the suddenly friendly guard asked Mort. "An open chair lift or one of our enclosed gondolas."

"One of the gondolas," Mort blurted out.

"I figured as much. That's why I asked you which poison, not preference. I use it on those who don't look like skiing is their thing. Where are you from anyway?"

"Do you mean where do I practice?" Yvars asked.

"No. Your accent. I'm a retired member of the Marine corps. During my career I met people from all walks of life and from all the States. I got darn good at being able to pinpoint exactly where people were from by their accents."

"Where do you think I'm from?" Yvars asked.

"New York. No doubt about it whatsoever. The tone of your voice. The inflection. That certain nasal quality. Your pale complexion. You're definitely one of those city slickers," Brown proudly replied.

"Right on," Mort said.

The guard pulled hard on the gondola door. It was stuck. He kicked it hard with his thick shoe. The door swung open. "These gondolas don't get much use during the off season. The boss and all the employees of Nesbitt prefer to take the chair lift to the top of the mountain. They love the crisp fresh air. The freedom the lift gives you. They don't like the gondolas. They tell me it reminds them of that closed-in feeling that they felt in the cities they left behind."

"I prefer feeling closed-in," Yvars quipped.

"You look like you would." He motioned for Yvars to climb inside the newly painted, royal blue gondola. "You never did tell me why you came out west?" Brown asked.

"I got sick of the rat race. Everyone back east is so competitive. No one realy cares about anyone but themselves. All they care about is becoming successful and making money. My wife and I wanted more out of life. We love it here. Sure we miss the excitement that New York City provides, but life is a constant series of trade-offs. All thing considered we are glad we made the move."

"How long have you been in the area?" Brown asked, opening the door to the gondola.

Mort paused searching for a response. "Three years," he finally said.

"Where do you practice? I know it's certainly not in Leadville. We have four doctors in town. I know them all."

"Vail," Mort said.

"Ah, that figures. Lots of your type have relocated there. Jetsetters. The glitz crowd as we refer to them. The place reeks with money. It's too rich for my blood. Maybe you know my cardiologist. His name's Michael Wolk. He practices at 280 Vail Road right in the center of the village."

Mort paused briefly. "Of course," he replied. What else could he say without arousing the guards skepticism. Vail might be larger than Leadville, Yvars thought, but even Vail wasn't New York City. In New York he could easily admit he never heard of Wolk and get away with it. But in Vail? He dared not gamble. Yvars glanced at this watch. It was 7:06 p.m. His fear of saying the wrong thing and blowing his cover had caused his dread of ascending Mt. Elbert to decrease. He grabbed his medical bag tightly in his clenched hand. "Would you mind if we continue our conversation some other time? My patient is waiting. I'd better get going."

"I'm sorry. I didn't mean to burden you with my chatter, but it gets incredibly boring working here during the off season. We hardly ever get tourists. Even our hotel on the top of the mountain is closed until Labor Day. You're the first person I've talked to, other than those who work for Nesbitt, in over a week. I must have gotten carried away with myself. Accept my apologies," the guard replied as he ushered Mort in the waiting gondola and slammed the heavy metal door shut.

*　*　*　*　*　*

Yvars, his eyes tightly shut, had been sitting in the gondola for five minutes, with both of his hands firmly holding onto the metal seat when suddenly he realized he wasn't feeling nearly as frightened as he had expected. The ride up the steep mountain wasn't all that scary after all. The gentle, slow swaying back and forth of the gondola conjured up childhood memories of climbing into his family's hammock in their backyard and rocking himself to sleep. He wondered if the same calmness sweeping over him now was similar to the feelings a fetus floating in the womb experienced.

He felt braver. He slowly opened his eyes. He glanced at the overhead pulleys; whirling, grinding, propelling his gondola up the mountain. He allowed himself to take in the natural beauty of the landscape surrounding him in all directions. Rocky terrain, meadows with wild yellow daisies, cacti jutting into the cool air, twisted vines enmeshed in gnarled tree trunks, tall thin evergreens reaching into the sky, and patches of greenery interwoven like a quilt with reddish brown soil calmed him. The descending sun, sliced through the thick leaves of tree branches, casting shadows over the terrain. Feeling relieved, he was able to bask in the marvel of it all.

The rising gondola passed a brook that transected a valley with two back packers and a lone bearded man on a bicycle peddling down the mountain against the encroaching darkness that would soon engulf them.

The peaks of the shorter mountain tops were now well beneath him. He couldn't believe how cozy and warm he felt despite the chill in the air. How was this possible he wondered? Here he was, thousands of feet in the air, yet he felt tranquil; so serene and peaceful that he actually found himself contemplating a winter vacation with Millie to Vail or perhaps Aspen. Not to ski. Perish the thought. However, a winter vacation spent enjoying the scenic views from their comfortable room, lying in Millie's arms cuddled next to a warm, crackling fire, reading, making love might be fun. Suddenly, a severe jolt rocked the gondola causing Yvars to lunge forward in his seat. He glanced out the window. The gondola had come to an abrupt halt. Damn, he should have realized the ride was going too smoothly. That the trip had been too good to be true. His calmness was only a temporary respite. His heart began pounding in his chest, his palms started sweating profusely. Silence. The whirling and the grinding of the pulleys

275

had ceased. Everything had stopped. The gondola began swaying in the brisk wind. What had happened? What had gone wrong? He noticed a sign in the distance. Elevation twelve thousand four hundred feet. That meant two thousand four hundred feet remained. Two thousand four hundred feet he was helpless to do anything about. He shut his eyes again.

He was seven. Mort and his father were alone in an elevator on the way to the top of the Empire State Building. It was to be a special occasion. A rarity. An actual father and son event. A surprise for his birthday. Then came the eighty-seventh floor and abruptly the elevator stopped. The lights went out. It was pitch black. Mort began crying, screaming hysterically. His father started yelling at him. 'Grow up, you little sissy. Don't be a baby. It's time you were a man.' The more angry and impatient his father became, the more scared Mort grew. 'Stop it. Shut up you brat. You little mamma's boy.' He felt a firm palm smash him on his jaw causing him to cry even more . . . to become more terrified. He shut his eyes tightly hoping, praying the fear would stop. That he'd calm down. That his father would stop raging at him. However, the harder he tried to quiet himself, the more fearful he became. More tears, further tirades from his father. 'I said shut up. Don't you listen? Do you want to grow up and be a man or a woman. Men don't get frightened. Now cut it out.'

It was useless. Why was his father so angry? Then it grew worse. He began sobbing uncontrollably. His father began smashing the walls of the metal enclosure and stamping his feet on the metal floor. The noise was deafening. The elevator began rocking, shaking, adding to his panic.

Suddenly, Yvars felt a lurching forward followed by the whirling, grinding sounds of the pulleys overhead. The gondola had resumed its ascent up the mountain. It was moving again. After several more stops and starts the ride smoothed out. Yvars kept his eyes shut tightly.

Another seven hundred feet or so. If there was a God, he needed him now more than ever. He took a deep breath. Beads of perspiration drenched his collar. He had to somehow calm down, regain his composure. He needed all his energies for what awaited him once he reached the top of Mt. Elbert.

*   *   *   *   *   *

"It's Brown," the Security Guard said, the receiver in his thick hand. "I'm terribly sorry for Dr. Yvars delay. Unfortunately, we had a minor mechanical difficulty with his gondola. However, the problem has been cleared up. He should be arriving in a few minutes, the ex-Marine paused briefly. "Are you feeling any better?"

"Better! From what? I'm fine," the high-pitched voice said.

"Dr. Yvars told me you called him. He said you were having severe stomach pains. He wanted to examine you before he left for his weekend fishing trip."

The voice at the other end of the line said nothing.

"Are you still there?" Brown asked.

"Oh yes. Forgive me. I practically forgot. I took two Maalox tablets and a Donnatal twenty minutes ago. I'm feeling much better now. Thanks for asking."

"I'm sorry I didn't call and find out how you were feeling before sending the doctor all the way up to your office. I would have saved him an unnecessary trip."

"Not at all Brown. I'm glad Dr. Yvars is coming anyway. I'll feel more relieved after he examines me and tells me I'm really fine. Otherwise, I might very well have worried I'd have another attack over the weekend and he wouldn't be around."

After hanging up the phone, a sense of relief welled up within. The doctor would soon be arriving. The final threat would finally be eliminated.

*   *   *   *   *   *

The loud, abrasive clanging of the pulleys suddenly ceased. "Not again," Mort groaned. For the past seven minutes Yvars attempts at putting into practice relaxation techniques to overcome his severe anxiety had been effective. He'd successfully transported himself and Millie to the Caribbean. He was lying on a beach chair, listening to the serene sounds of

277

the surf washing ashore. Coconut trees were swaying gently in the warm trade winds. A pina colada was by his side.

However, the sudden unexpected pitching forward of the gondola brought him back to the present. Mort tried forcing his mind back to the deep blue waters of the Caribbean. It was no use. He couldn't. He kept visualizing being trapped, dangling high in the air at the mercy of the god damn gondola. He once again began feeling his anxiety mounting, his fears resurfacing. The elevator, his father, the screaming.

He forced himself to slowly open his eyes. He couldn't believe it. Two buildings were directly ahead. On his left, a five story modern building with large picture windows; the name NESBITT PHARMACEUTICAL COMPANY posted in large block letters above the entrance. On the right, a twenty story highrise glass and steel structure with a sign prominently displayed in front of the hotel. CLOSED. WILL REOPEN LABOR DAY.

Mort sighed in relief. He had made it. He was actually perched on the top of Mt. Elbert.

Yvars quickly snapped open the hatch on the side of the gondola and climbed out. For a few moments he stood and stared at the star-studded, moonless sky and took a deep breath. He felt ten feet tall. He had succeeded in conquering his lifelong fear, had forced himself to master his inner demons. His father couldn't hurt or limit him again.

Mort began the thirty yard walk toward the brightly lit, five story building. His thoughts shifted to Siegfried, the mortal son of Siegmund and Sieglinde, his idol – the operatic figure he admired for his extreme courage and fearlessness.

He now was Siegfried. He reached the door to the Nesbitt Drug Company and pressed the buzzer that rested directly under the dimly lit floodlight.

Slowly, more thoughts about Siegfried began flooding his mind. He envisioned the fearless, valiant Siegfried standing before him; guiding him, directing him. Then he saw Siegfried innocently and rapturously describing to Hagan how he finally won Brunnhilde's love, in the opera Gotterdammerung, the fourth and final part to Wagner's 'The Ring.' Then Mort watched as Siegfried's attention was diverted by two ravens, messengers to Woton, as the two birds flew from a nearby bush across the Rhine. Siegfried kept staring at the two ravens oblivious to Hagan as he raised his spear and stabbed Siegfried to death.

Yvars shuddered. He had to hope his newly found courage wouldn't lead to a similar ending.

33

The Nesbitt Company's wooden door opened. "Come in," a high-pitched voice called out.

Mort stepped onto an oriental rug. His shoes sank into the thick carpet. The bright, overhead, fluorescent lighting illuminated the room. He didn't see anyone. Where did the voice come from? Yvars wondered.

He glanced around the brightly lit, spacious, oak-paneled office. He didn't see anyone in the room. His eyes took in a black leather couch on the wall nearest the door. A dark, mahogany desk and a cluster of armchairs sat against another. Opposite the entrance, a floor to the ceiling stone fireplace stood with its highly polished brass set of poker, anvil and tongs perched alongside a stack of neatly piled wood. Yvars imagined the crackling sound of the red embers on a cold, snowy night. He noticed there was neither a floor nor a desk lamp in the entire room. Whoever the Nesbitt Company hired to furnish the office obviously didn't care about creating an aesthetically warm environment in which to work. If Millie had decorated the office, she'd never have installed fluorescent lighting. The look was too cold, too uninviting.

Maybe the voice came from outside. Yvars walked to the large picture window on the wall adjacent to the fireplace and looked out. The sparkling stars, the sole source of light on this moonless night, cast dim shadows on the overhanging pine trees in the distance. There was nobody out there. "Where are you?" he called out.

Suddenly the voice replied. "Turn around. See for yourself." The figure slid from behind the door and faced Yvars.

Mort stepped back in disbelief. He blinked once and then again. It couldn't be. It wasn't possible.

"You aren't imagining anything Dr. Yvars. You are seeing me. You are clever. Very clever indeed. How ingenious to introduce yourself to the security guard as my physician. You had him so concerned he called and alerted me you were on your way to examine my poor aching stomach. I hear you're off on a fishing expedition afterwards. I under-estimated you. I never realized you possessed such a creative imagination."

Yvars was stunned and speechless. He couldn't believe his eyes. Standing directly in front of him was Ruth Webster, Judd's sister. Ruth was supposedly the only member of the Webster clan who cared for Judd, Jane and William. She was the one who had comforted Jane through the most difficult days following Judd's death. The woman who had personally traveled to Seattle with Judd's body to protect Jane from the Webster's at the funeral. The woman who had convinced her brother to seek psychiatric help for his depression. The woman Mort and Millie met at Jane's home in Washington, D.C. and had believed to be genuinely caring and concerned for Jane and her son William. How could this be?

Slowly Mort's shock turned to anger. "What the hell is going on?"

Ruth walked to her mahogany desk, pulled open the top desk drawer, grabbed her empty automatic and inserted six .44 caliber bullets into its chamber. "These are for you," she said. "As a doctor you'll be fascinated at the progression of your symptoms once you're hit by one of my bullets. You'll experience first hand what the others felt."

Yvars gulped hard. "You killed Judd? You killed your own brother?"

"Yes," Ruth replied. "He left me no choice. He was Evil. The voices insisted all evil had to be eliminated. Judd was evil. The voices demanded he be killed. That only the Good shall inherit the Earth."

"What are you talking about?" Yvars asked.

Ruth, her automatic at her side, walked back to the entranceway, locked the door and slipped the key into her pocket.

Yvars' anxiety resurfaced. He was trapped on the top of Mt. Elbert. Fourteen thousand eight hundred feet above sea level. He took a deep breath. Perhaps, if he remained calm and talked Ruth down the way he had learned to talk down acutely violent patients in the psychiatric ward at Bellevue, she would relent, would let him live. What if he couldn't convince her otherwise? He shuddered. He had to push those thoughts to the side. They wouldn't help. He had no choice. He had only one option. He'd do what he did best. He'd verbally draw Ruth out. Get her to keep talking. Hopefully, in the process, he'd somehow figure out a way to overtake her. "Why did you kill Judd?" he asked.

"I told you. He was evil. All evil must be destroyed. The voices speak the truth. Can't you hear them? They're telling you this right now."

Yvars' forehead broke out in a cold sweat. He was dealing with a crazed woman, someone who heard voices. Ruth was exactly like the paranoid schizophrenic patients he'd often confronted in Wentworth's emergency room. In the hospital he had orderlies who'd protect him if the patient, despite his efforts, became violent. He didn't have that option now. He'd have to pray his technique would work. He slowly moved towards the black leather sofa.

"Tell me why Judd was evil?" Mort asked in a calm tone.

"What difference does it make? He was evil. Evil is evil," Ruth replied.

"I was Judd's psychiatrist. I never thought of him as evil. I want to know why you thought otherwise."

"I didn't think otherwise. I knew otherwise," Ruth replied angrily.

"Forgive me. I didn't mean to upset you. Tell me why he was evil," Mort softly said.

Ruth sighed. "I don't understand what purpose my telling you will serve. You're not leaving here alive."

"Because I'm curious. I'd like to know why Judd was evil."

"If it's that important for you to know, I might as well tell you. After all, neither of us is going anywhere. Nobody is going to bother us.

282

I have all night. Where would you like me to start," Ruth asked, flipping her gun from one had to the other.

"At the beginning," Yvars replied.

"Things were not bad until Judd was born," Ruth said.

"What do you mean by not that bad?"

"I was supposed to be a boy. Father never wanted a girl. But for seven years he was stuck with what he got. He'd occasionally play with me, but most of the time he'd ignore me like I didn't exist. I'd constantly ask my mother why he didn't love me. I'd ask her what I did wrong. She'd always tell me he loved me. That was just the way he was. I began believing her. That is until Judd was born. All of a sudden, I saw a different father. A warm, affectionate, loving man. He'd hug and kiss Judd all the time, take him with him to work, have him sit in his golf cart while he played golf. He took him everywhere. They were inseparable," Ruth said.

"Unfortunately, many fathers are like that. They prefer sons to daughters," Yvars replied.

"That's what my mother would tell me. It didn't help. I'm no psychiatrist, but I do know all children need to feel loved. That's why I've been so close to William," Ruth said.

"But your mother loved you," Yvars said

"In her way, but she wasn't the affectionate type. I never remember her ever hugging or kissing me."

"You became jealous of your brother?" Mort asked.

"Of course, I was very jealous and envious of all the love and attention he received. However, it was more than that. My father started treating me like I was nothing but Judd's servant. I had to clean up after him, feed him, baby-sit. I was thirteen. He was six. I wanted to be with my friends. My father wouldn't allow it."

"Didn't you have a maid?" Yvars asked.

Ruth laughed. "Two live-in maids and a butler."

"Then why did your father force you to take care of Judd?" Yvars asked.

"Because he hated me," Ruth replied.

"You killed Judd because you hated the way your father treated you?" Yvars softly asked.

"I grew to hate Judd because of my father. Wouldn't you? It's what you shrinks call sibling rivalry, isn't it? But I wouldn't kill Judd because I hated him. After all he was still my brother. I killed him because he was evil. Listen to the voices. They'll tell you," Ruth said.

"But you only killed him two and a half weeks ago. If he was so evil why did you wait so long."

"Because I didn't know he was evil until two years ago. Until then, I just felt angry at him. However, I never blamed Judd. I always blamed father. That was until two years ago when I finally found out the truth. That's when the voices told me he was evil. That's when they said he had to be destroyed. Before then, I lived my own life as best I could. I went to Wellesley, did very well and made the only true friend I've ever had." Ruth started crying. "I'm going to miss him."

"Who are you talking about?" Yvars asked.

"Jerry Rollins. We were seated next to one another at a fundamentalist rally in Boston. The minister was mesmerizing. He talked about the need for purity of the mind and the soul because of the evil that sex, power and greed had caused mankind. He emphasized one needed to live a life on a higher plane. A life devoted to goodness. To chastity. That only through depriving oneself of the despicable appetites of the human condition could one truly live a good life. After the talk, Rollins asked if I'd have a cup of coffee with him. I was reluctant at first. I eventually agreed. If it wasn't for him, I don't know what would have happened to me. Now he's gone." She began crying again. "We must have talked for hours. We shared so much in common. The same values and beliefs. Both of us embraced the minister's message and vowed to live our lives accordingly. Purity. Chastity. Without power or greed. We'd laugh at how ironic it was that two people from such different backgrounds, he as poor as could be, on a scholarship to Harvard, and me, from one of the country's wealthiest families could be so alike. Yet we were clones. Identical on all levels.

"After college I wanted to go to graduate school. I always loved science, especially chemistry. Rollins wanted to make millions and then shove all that money in the faces of the rich and powerful, who'd scorned him throughout his childhood, by giving all his wealth to the poor. Fortunately, he was very successful. Otherwise, I'd never have gotten anywhere in my career."

"Why not? You had your own money."

"No I didn't. My father had it all. He refused to give me any until I married. Then he'd turn over my trust fund and give me anything I wanted. But not until then. He believed women were meant to be mothers and not take up positions in the work force intended for men."

"You mean to tell me he wouldn't pay for graduate school?"

"Exactly. He refused," Ruth said.

"What about your mother? Surely she had money," Yvars asked.

"She never went against my father. She also refused."

"And Judd?" Yvars asked.

"He was too young at the time," Ruth replied. "Fortunately, Rollins had made contacts at Harvard with some wealthy classmates whose fathers were willing to give him seed money for a venture he'd conceived."

"Which was?" Yvars asked.

"It's hard to believe it today, but when Jerry and I graduated college, Vail and Aspen were nothing but a spot on the map. Jerry was the one who envisioned combining the northerners love of skiing with the beauty of Colorado. He was one of the first who built skiing resorts both in Vail and in Aspen. The rest is history."

"Jerry Rollins paid for your education?" Yvars asked.

"Yes. All of it. Initially I refused. I felt funny about taking his money. However, he reminded me of our pact. The money he earned was meant not for materialistic pursuits, but rather for the altruistic purposes we discussed throughout college. He insisted he pay for my PhD. I eventually agreed. I applied to Boston University's program and seven years later had my PhD in pharmacology. The following year I began teaching chemistry at the University in Denver." Ruth paused and walked to her open bar near the desk. "Care for a drink?"

"No," Mort calmly replied, his words in direct contrast to his desire. He'd love nothing more than a glass of alcohol to lull him into a false sense of security. A spurious feeling of mastery over Ruth. A feeling he knew he wanted, but one he realized he could not afford. He had to maintain control over all of his senses, all of his thoughts. He had to be as alert as possible. Whether in the end it would matter he didn't know. He could only hope it would.

Ruth placed her gun down on the black counter top, mixed herself a martini and took a long sip. Then, holding her cocktail in one hand and the gun in the other, she walked to her desk and sat down.

"And Judd? Had he gotten into politics by then?" Yvars asked.

"Yes. Immediately upon graduating Yale Law School. Father pulled some strings and landed Judd a job as assistant to then Congressman Carlin of Colorado."

Yvars eyes brightened.

"I stood outside New York Hospital watching while you helped Carlin get into that ambulance. What was that all about?" Ruth asked.

"He almost died the other night. I arranged for Carlin to be admitted to Wentworth Hospital for a heart transplant."

Ruth smiled. "That was awfully kind of you. Very Arrowsmith like."

"Not exactly. We both needed something. I promised him a new heart in return for his telling me all he knew about what was going on," Yvars said.

"Good. So you know everything I was about to tell you." Ruth raised her gun into the air. "Then I guess we can get this over with."

Yvars started to panic. He had to gain a grip on himself. "No. That's not true. Carlin didn't know many of the details. He certainly didn't seem to know you were the one who killed Judd. He basically filled me in on his role, which I'm starting to realize was a very limited one." Yvars paused. "I'm helpless. You can kill me whenever you want. You know that. Hopefully, you'll decide to satisfy my curiosity first."

Ruth took another sip of her martini and put the gun down on her desk. "You must be a very good shrink. I'll tell you whatever you want to know if it's that important to you. After all Jesus had his last supper. This will be yours."

"Judd worked for a few years in Carlin's Denver office. The next thing I knew he announced he was going to run against Carlin in the primary. I couldn't believe he was that out of touch. I mean Carlin was loved in his district. I'd always thought Judd to be logical. Very ambitious, but rational. I couldn't understand why he'd decided to run against such a formidable and popular opponent."

"Did you ask him?" Yvars asked.

"Yes. He told me he was entering the race because he'd win. When the primary votes were counted Judd did indeed win. I was amazed. At the time, I figured he won because he was handsome, young and charismatic, while Carlin was getting on in years. I didn't know the truth then. The voices hadn't yet told me. Then when Judd went on to win the general election and became a congressman, I actually felt happy for him. I still hadn't seen the light. Jim Carlin regrouped quickly, spent the next two years campaigning for a senate seat and won his election. Both were happy in their respective positions.

"Then one evening, five years later, we were all in Washington celebrating Judd's birthday when father announced it was time for Judd to run for Carlin's seat in the Senate. Jane and I looked at each other like father had lost it. However, Judd loved the idea. History repeated itself again. Judd defeated Carlin in the primary and won the general election. He was now senator. Again I was thrilled for him. Again I thought he won through a combination of hard work and personal qualities. Again I had yet to discover the truth. The voices still hadn't appeared," Ruth said.

"What was your relationship with your father like during these years?" Yvars asked.

"The same as always. He constantly criticized me for wasting my time teaching chemistry. He insisted if I was hell-bent on teaching, I should get married, have children and spend my efforts teaching them."

"How did you feel about that?" Mort inquired

"You are good aren't you? Your questions seem to flow so naturally. I'm glad I convinced Judd to see you. Of course it was already too late. By then he was beyond redemption."

"What do you mean by beyond redemption?" Yvars asked.

"We'll get to that. I didn't know it at the time. The voices hadn't told me. I didn't have any reaction to father's comments. I had long ago learned I didn't count. This was simply another example. However, one night while I was in Washington for Judd's swearing in ceremonies, Jerry Rollins, who'd moved to the East Coast years before, and I went out for dinner. By then he'd made millions building Industrial Parks throughout the Northeast. We spent part of the evening laughing at how those who'd bullied him in his youth now begged him for favors. He'd tell them to fuck off."

"What did he do with all his millions?" Yvars asked.

"He kept building more Industrial Parks. He was eventually going to give all his money away. However, before he could, he lost it all. Fortunately, by then the voices had prepared me for what had to be done," Ruth said.

"You mentioned you only spent part of the evening discussing Jerry's career. What else did you talk about that night?" Yvars asked.

"He asked how my work was going. I told him I was getting bored teaching the same material year after year.. I'd love to do something more with my chemistry background, but didn't know what. He suggested I start my own drug company. I told him I'd love to, but as a teacher it wasn't a feasible option. He asked about my trust fund. I explained to him how father had set up a condition that I couldn't touch any of the trust until I was married."

"Is that legal?" Mort asked.

"I had no interest in finding out. Father earned the money. If those were his rules those were his rules. Jerry offered to bankroll the entire operation. I thanked him, but I refused. Over the next several months he'd call frequently and plead with me to accept his offer. The pact we made together in college demanded that I agree. Needless to say, his persistence eventually paid off. The Nesbitt Pharmaceutical Company opened its doors four and a half years ago. Jerry was the ideal partner. He put up all the money and didn't want any say in how I ran the company. In fact, he didn't want anybody to even know he was at all involved in anything having to do with my creation. He was truly one of a kind. It's too bad he had to go," Ruth said.

"Does your company specialize in any particular type of medications," Mort asked.

"We basically manufacture vitamins and generic brands of most of the frequently prescribed medications. Drugs whose patents have expired such as valium, tofranil and most of the other tranquilizers and anti-depressants. Last year Forbes listed us as one of the nation's best run small drug companies in the country.

"However, my passion was always elsewhere. I wanted to discover new drugs. I set up a research laboratory and poured a great deal of both manpower and money into trying to find medications that would hopefully cure cancer and AIDS. Our labs are located downstairs on the bottom three floors. They're underground. They were actually built into the mountain itself. It was quite a project hauling construction equipment up fourteen thousand feet in order to build what I wanted. We had to blast through lots of rock. It was really quite something. Our labs are a marvel of modern high-tech. Harvard and MIT would envy our equipment."

"What made you decide to build your company all the way up here? I drove from Vail. There seemed to be lots of land you could have used to build your facility that would have been incredibly more convenient for everyone."

"I'm basically a loner. I wanted a place as far away from civilization as possible. I love it here," Ruth replied.

"What did Judd think about your company?" Yvars asked.

"He didn't know anything about it. I never told anyone in my family. Not even Jane. Nesbitt is my baby," Ruth replied.

"What did your family think you were doing?" Yvars asked.

"They never asked. I assume all of them still think I teach chemistry at the University of Denver," Ruth said.

"Does the name Nesbitt have any significance?"

"Yes. Nesbitt is my mother's maiden name."

"Then she surely knows about your company."

"No. I named the company after her in the hopes she'd somehow find out and tell father. That he'd finally feel I counted. However, miracles occur in movies, not in real life. The truth is she doesn't know and father died two years ago without ever finding out. But that's the past. Father's death turned out to be my awakening. That's when the voices came. That's when I learned the truth. That's when I decided to forget trying to discover a cure for either cancer or AIDS and instead accomplish the ultimate. The only truly important thing in life." Ruth paused

"Which is?" Yvars asked.

"To rid the world of evil! The Good shall inherit the Earth. I finally had my mission."

"You've lost me. What's the connection between your father's death and your mission?" Yvars asked.

"Mother asked me to clean out father's vault. It was there that I first heard the voices. They've given my life a meaning. A true purpose. The ultimate purpose."

Yvars, his legs weary, sat down on the black leather sofa. Ruth finished her martini, stood up, poured herself another and pointed the automatic directly at Mort's chest.

How long can I keep her going, Yvars wondered, his anxiety mounting. "What happened in the vault that so profoundly affected you?"

Yvars asked.

"In the vault were my father's personal diaries. I began reading them. Father described in great detail all he had done on Judd's behalf, listing all those he had bribed, how he'd gotten to the head of the election board and made it worth his while to rig the election . . . to toss out many of Carlin's votes to ensure Judd would win both the congressional and then the senatorial primaries." Ruth paused. "However, the entire plan was conceptualized not by father, but by Judd. Father had the necessary clout. But the idea was Judd's. I couldn't believe it. I was horrified. I expected it from father, but not from Judd, not from my own brother. It was then that the voices came and told me what I had to do. That Judd was evil. Evil could not be tolerated. Evil had to be eliminated. I asked the voices what to do to carry out this mission. They told me to be patient. That 'it will come'. For several months the voices kept reassuring me 'it will come'. Nothing came. Then one morning I awoke and it 'came'. The voices had provided the solution."

"What was it?" Yvars asked.

"It was the vehicle I'd create to destroy Judd, all Judds, all evil. With my knowledge of chemistry, I'd develop a substance that would kill on impact, without bloodshed, without arousing suspicion. Death would occur within minutes. The chemical wouldn't be detectable. It would be concluded that Judd, all Judds, had died from natural causes, from sudden heart failure. The more I thought of my concept, the more excited I became. I began spending 18 hours a day, 7 days a week in my lab devising the perfect chemical for my mission. The voices kept me going whenever I'd get discouraged or exhausted. They kept stressing the importance of my mission. They wouldn't let me rest until I had come up with the correct chemical combination.

"Three months later it finally happened. The chemical reaction I dreamt about finally occurred. I had succeeded in creating a substance which, when injected into mice and cats caused instantaneous death. What made this chemical all the more enticing was that whether I injected the chemical into their stomach, skin, limbs or even their ears, the results were identical. Immediate and complete heart failure. I drew innumerable vials of blood and countless urine samples looking for traces of the chemical in their body fluids. It was amazing. Absolutely astounding. None of the blood or urine samples showed any remains of the chemical. All of the material had been metabolized so as not to be discernible by modern medical technology."

"You killed Judd and the others with this chemical?" Yvars asked.

"Yes. However, the chemical in and of itself wasn't sufficient. I had to devise a way to get my chemical into Judd, into all the Judds, into everyone who was evil. The voices once again came through. They whispered the method to me." Ruth paused and pulled out two bullets from her desk drawer. "This was how I'd do it." She then tapped her gun. "There are six of my beautiful, chemically coated bullets in here waiting for you.

I purchased this automatic and several others from a gunmaker in Wyoming I've dealt with over the years. Then I contacted and bought several cases of .44 caliber bullets from a small company in rural Montana. I soaked the bullets in my new liquid chemical formula, retrieved several unwanted strays from a dog pound in Denver, and shot all seven in various parts of their bodies. The results were identical to those cats and mice I injected with my chemical. All seven died instantaneously from acute heart failure. I was now confident I had exactly what I needed. Evil would be eradicated. The Good shall inherit the Earth."

Beads of sweat cascaded down Mort's face.

"I had produced the perfect bullet. A bullet that killed on impact, regardless of which part of the body was hit. However, I needed to perform one final experiment, this time on a human guinea pig. One night I picked up a homeless young man on a street outside a bar in Denver and drove him here. We took the gondola to the top of this mountain. In fact we might very well have taken the very same gondola which brought you to me."

"Once in my office, I juiced him up real good with lots of Jack

Daniels. When he was totally drunk, I shot him in the left arm. Within thirty seconds he went into cardiac arrest. Within two minutes he was dead. I drew blood and took urine samples. The results were identical to those in the various animals I'd previously experimented on."

"I dragged the poor fellow from my office and dropped him into our large garbage disposal in the backyard. I turned on the machine. Bones splintered and cracked. Then all was quiet. I had cleverly eliminated any possible incriminating evidence." Ruth stopped and stared at her gun.

Yvars heart began racing. He was dealing with someone possessing an irrational psyche locked inside a brilliant mind. All thoughts of escape were illusionary.

Ruth swiveled in her chair and laughed. "I was euphoric. I had complete confidence in my product. The voices were immensely proud of me."

"Do you recognize these voices?" Yvars asked.

"Yes. They all belong to the fundamentalist minister Rollins and I listened to while we were both in college. Sometimes his voice is deep, sometimes higher pitched, sometimes he sounds as if he's in an echo chamber. But I know it's always him. All of the voices are him."

"You've had these bullets for a year and a half?" Yvars asked.

"Yes. The voices told me to be patient. That the time would come. Until then, I was to wait. I'd know when the time was right. The voices would tell me."

Yvars tried to stay calm. He had to keep Ruth talking and hope he'd figure out a way to disarm her before it was too late. "What caused the time to come?" Mort asked.

"One day last October, Rollins flew here. He told me how Judd was using his powers as head of the Senate banking committee to force banks to call in all of his loans and mortgages. He faced certain bankruptcy unless he caved in and submitted to my brother's demands that he build low-cost housing rather than more Industrial Parks. Jerry knew Judd didn't give a shit about the poor. It was all part of the public image he was creating that he hoped would eventually lead him to greater glory . . . perhaps the presidency. Another example of Judd's evil nature. He was doing this to my best friend. My only friend. That's when the voices told me the time had come.

"I had read in the paper that Carlin was very ill and probably didn't have more than a year to live. I knew he hated Judd and now, with nothing to lose, would probably love to see Judd die before he did. I knew Carlin's bank account wasn't sufficient to allow him to be as philanthropic as he'd like. Rollins had served on several boards with Carlin. He knew Carlin wanted to have a pediatric wing of a hospital named after him that would symbolize his concerns for children. I came up with a masterful plan. However, I was afraid to let Carlin know I had anything to do with it. I knew he hated Judd. He might therefore hate me and refuse to participate in my plan. I couldn't take that chance. Rollins agreed he'd arrange everything. I needed someone to find out my brother's daily schedule. Carlin would be that man. I knew Judd was seeing you. All Rollins needed to do was convince Carlin to wait near your office after your Monday evening group sessions ended and select a woman from the group who seemed timid and needy. In return, Rollins worked out the financial arrangement that would allow Carlin to fulfill his final dream. I supplied Rollins with the necessary money to entice Carlin."

"How did you know Judd would want anything to do with someone as timid and needy as Mary Hargrove?" Yvars asked.

"You're not serious are you," Ruth replied.

"I'm quite serious. I'd never think of the two of them as having anything in common," Mort said.

"You didn't really know my brother. I did. I knew him very well. Too well. Remember, I was forced to spend a great deal of time with him until I went to college. Judd had another side. A hidden side. A side he'd share with me. A warm sensitive side. A side Webster men are forbidden to have. A side that unfortunately was no match for his evil side."

"This side made him prone to feeling very lonely and isolated. I'd seen other women tap into it. Jane never could. Those whores he had sinned with never could. Only those who were weak and needy brought out that side. Judd had several Mary's in the past. I always hoped he'd marry one of them. That was years before I knew he was evil. I just thought a Mary would make him a warmer and nicer person. Looking back at it now, I see how mistaken I was. He had always been evil. The problem was, that until that day when I was cleaning out father's vault, I hadn't seen it.

"After Carlin selected Mary Hargrove, he told her he knew Judd and that he was a lonely man despite his fame and would enjoy having somebody like her to talk to. She was thrilled. Carlin gave her Judd's phone number on Capitol Hill and made her promise never to tell Judd about their connection.

"Carlin, in turn, asked her to do him a small favor and jot down all she and Judd discussed during their conversations. Each Monday, after group, Mary and Carlin would meet and she'd hand over her notes for the week detailing Judd's daily routine. Carlin mailed Mary's weekly notes to the Nesbitt Company on Duane Street. Rollins had a key to the office. He'd pick up the envelope and either mail or fax the notes to me."

"He must not have always followed that procedure. I found some of Mary's weekly notes at your office," Mort said.

"I know. Jerry had a tendency to forget now and then. However, it didn't matter. After several months I had more than enough information to work with," Ruth replied.

"Why was Judd's routine so important for you to know?" Yvars asked.

"I needed to know exactly how he spent his days. The voices told me it would make eliminating him far easier. They were right. They are always right. I knew he always left Capitol Hill on Tuesdays at about noon to have lunch with several congressmen from Colorado in a restaurant in Georgetown. The day the voices told me it was time to kill Judd, I followed his car. I was surprised when he drove onto the beltway instead of going to Georgetown as was his routine. However, I kept my car several yards behind his. I eventually realized he was probably going home, pulled up alongside him and shot him. Within less than a minute, all evil had left him. He was dead."

Ruth stood up and began pacing around the brightly lit room. "Enough talking. It's time to get this over with."

Yvars gulped. "Just a few more questions," he blurted out. Why? What did it matter, he thought. Five minutes, fifteen minutes. He was only delaying the inevitable. He'd never see or touch his wonderful Millie again.

"All right, but only a few. I'm getting tired," Ruth replied, her automatic still fixed at Mort's midsection. "What else would you like to know?"

"Did you also kill Tyrone Sawyer?"

"Yes, " Ruth replied

"Why?" Mort asked.

"Years ago Judd told me about Tyrone. He made me promise never to tell Jane. I agreed. However, once I realized Judd was evil, I had no choice. Tyrone too was evil. Born out of sin. A creation of Satan. The voices demanded he also be killed. I wanted to kill Judd first. The voices persuaded me the order of the killing wasn't important. The only importance lay in destroying all evil. I was to be in Manhattan that Monday anyway. The voices told me to start with Tyrone. Judd mentioned to me how much Tyrone loved music. That he wanted to become a recording star. I called up several music stores, picked up the necessary equipment and personally decorated our small office on Duane Street so it resembled an actual recording studio. I was a set designer for two shows while I was at Wellesley. My cleverest coup was finding an old sheet rock set that replicated exactly a recording studio control room. It was made for an Off-Broadway show that had recently closed. I paid fifty dollars for it. It was quite a bargain.

"Judd had also mentioned Tyrone's agent's name. I had it written down. I called the agent and pretended to be the head of the Philmont Recording Company, I said we had listened to his demo, liked it very much, and wanted to set up an audition that evening at six p.m., with the possibility of a lucrative contract to follow.

"After killing Tyrone, I waited until I knew the building would be empty and the street deserted. I then dragged his body down the three flights of stairs, out the door and plopped him against a garbage pail by the side of the building," Ruth said.

"What about Eileen Matthews?" Yvars asked.

"That sinner. Of course I had to kill her," Ruth replied.

"How did you know Judd was having an affair with her?" Yvars asked.

"I didn't initially. It was actually Mary who made me curious. She mentioned in several of her notes that Judd and Eileen Matthews had had dinner together on several Monday evenings after your group ended. One evening I followed Judd and Eileen to a small, out of the way hotel. Then I knew. The voices insisted she had to be killed."

"Did you break into my office?" Yvars asked.

"Yes. I didn't know where Eileen lived. I figured you'd have Eileen's address somewhere in your records. That afternoon I made a mold of the key hole in your office. I had a key made within the hour. That night I went to your office. The key fit perfectly. I copied down Eileen Matthews' address."

"Why did you try to kill me?" Yvars asked.

"Because you were Judd's last hope for salvation and you failed. I persuaded him to see a psychiatrist, wishing redemption was possible. The voices insisted evil was incurable. They were right again. They are always right. Unfortunately, my first attempt in Central Park was unsuccessful when a goddamn woman ran in front of me as I fired. The bullet struck your bicycle tire instead of you. Then, at the parade, your wife got in the way. She was very fortunate that those two doctors were nearby.

297

Otherwise, she'd never have lived. That wasn't the case with that asshole FBI agent Jackson. He was snooping around. Those agents are really quite dumb. They are so easy to dupe. I called him, pretended to be your patient, the investigative reporter Doug Simons. I told him I had the evidence he was looking for linking you with the murder of Sawyer, Webster and Matthews. It wasn't difficult to convince him to meet me at the small park near the Hudson River at 97th Street. He almost wet his pants he was so excited. He was the easiest of them all."

"Are you also planning on killing Jane and William?" Yvars asked.

"Of course not. How could you think I'd harm either of them? I love Jane. She made a mistake falling in love with Judd. I forgive mistakes. I can't forgive evil. And William, he's such a dear boy. Fortunately, he takes after Jane. He's escaped his father's evil."

"What about Rollins? He was your best friend. Did you also kill him?" Yvars asked.

Tears welled up in Ruth's eyes. "I didn't want to."

"Then why did you?" Yvars asked.

"Because Rollins flew here shortly after the voices told me it was now time to kill Judd. He had changed his mind and insisted I shouldn't kill him. Rollins believed that Judd should live because his soul would spend eternity in hell and damnation. I agreed with Rollins. However, within hours, the voices became furious with me. They became relentless. They refused to let me change their decision. Furthermore, they demanded I now had to kill Rollins. I begged and pleaded with them for days. It was useless. You can't fight the voices. They are far too persistent. Far too persuasive. They made me see the light. Letting Judd live was siding with evil. Rollins was now evil. He also had to die." Ruth yawned. "That's it. No more talking. Stand up."

Yvars' heart skipped a beat. There were no further delays possible. No more questions to be allowed. No more questions left unanswered. He knew his time had come. He slowly lifted his frame from the leather sofa adjacent to the front door.

"Now turn around," Ruth ordered. "I don't shoot people in the back. It's too cowardly," she laughed. She cocked the automatic. "I think as a physician, you'll be fascinated observing your own death. You'll feel a slight sting. Any preference where you'd like me to aim?"

Yvars said nothing. His eyes bulging. His temples throbbing.

"If not, I'll shoot into your left thigh. After the prickling sensation, you'll feel a warmth travel through your entire system. That will be your capillaries and veins dilating. Then you'll feel hot and start perspiring. That will be the signal your large arteries are now widening. A lightheadedness and fainting sensation will follow, signaling your heart is on the verge of failing. That will be your final conscious moment."

Yvars didn't want to see what was about to happen to him. His eyes darted to the large picture window. He stared at the sky dotted with its sparkling, pulsating, shining stars.

Suddenly, it came to him. Why hadn't he thought of it sooner? Stars. Lightness. Darkness. Ruth. Judd. Judd came to see him because of a depression brought on by advancing retinitis pigmentosa, a gradual deterioration of his vision which made seeing at night almost impossible. Shadows, blurred figures perhaps, but nothing clearer. His vision in the dark was practically nonexistent. Retinitis pigmentosa was a genetic disorder that was inherited as a dominant trait. That meant if Judd had the illness, there was a seventy-five percent chance Ruth also was afflicted.

Yvars moved to the nearby wall, pressed down hard on the light switch, plummeting the large room into virtual darkness: shades of grays and blacks replaced the glaring white of the bright fluorescent overhead lights.

"You bastard!" Ruth screamed out firing wildly into the air; the bullet blasting into the oak paneling and propelling fragments of wood in all directions. "I can't see a thing. Where the hell are you?" She fired again. The shell exploded into the ceiling; jagged edges of plaster caromed off the mahogany desk and onto the thick carpet.

Mort sighed in relief. Ruth indeed had the same disorder.

Ruth began squinting, trying to decipher Mort's contour through the blurred dark shadows. She fired a third shot. The bullet narrowly missed Mort's right shoulder; lodging in the thick walnut door.

Yvars moved away from the wall and accidentally struck his knee on one of the steel legs of the nearby couch. "Shit!" he blurted out.

Ruth turned in the direction of Mort's voice. She squinted harder. The doctor's frame dim, but now visible through the grayness. She fired again. The bullet ricocheted off the wall.

Yvars began to panic. She had seen him. His sole advantage had been lost. How would he now escape?

His eyes darted around the spacious room, finally focusing on the poker next to the fireplace at the far corner of the room. If only he could get to the poker.

Suddenly, he heard the clicking sound of the automatic. He had only seconds left. He had to do something. She wasn't going to keep missing.

Mort bent down and began crawling as fast as he could, his eyes riveted on the poker. He grabbed the tufts of the thick wool carpet, pulling himself forward inch by inch towards the brass object.

"Where the hell are you?" Ruth yelled out, her voice becoming frantic. "You coward." She fired again.

Mort realized that was her fifth shot. That meant there was still one bullet left in the chamber.

Ruth suddenly jumped up. This was her office. She didn't need to be able to see. She knew the layout of the room perfectly. She'd simply feel her way around the various objects in her path. She knew exactly where the light switch was located. All she had to do was find the light switch and turn it on. Then Yvars would be hers.

Mort kept inching closer to the poker, streams of sweat burning his eyes, blurring his vision. He had no time to wipe his eyes. He had to press on.

He finally clawed his way to the stack of wood, grabbed the poker with his right hand, pulled himself up and quickly dashed behind the nearby desk. Mort stared at Ruth as her hand blindly canvassed the wall. Her fingers were only inches from the light switch.

Yvars, with the poker raised in the air, raced from behind the desk toward Ruth, his eyes focused on her fingers as they crept closer and closer to the switch.

Yvars had run out of time. If he waited any longer the fluorescent lights would be back on. He'd be an easy target. He had to strike now.

Yvars took a deep breath. Holding the poker tightly over his head with both hands, he hurled himself directly at Ruth, crashing the heavy brass object into her skull.

A terrifying scream resounded throughout the room. Then silence.

Yvars stood over Ruth Webster, watching for any movement, the poker still firmly held in his hands.

One minute passed. Then another. Then a third. Still no sounds. No groans. Nothing.

Two minutes later Yvars bent down and pressed his fingers on Ruth's wrist, feeling for a pulse. There was none. He placed his hand over her nose and mouth. She wasn't breathing.

Mort slowly stood up. He flicked on the lightswitch and stared at Ruth Webster's lifeless body. It was all over. It was time to go home to Millie.

EPILOGUE

Two and a half weeks later.

"How did you think our group went tonight?" Mort, standing in their living room, asked.

"Far better than I expected," Millie replied. She walked over to her husband and held out a chocolate-filled donut. "I bought this earlier today. I figured you might want a lift after this evening's session."

Mort smiled broadly. He bit into the chewy dough. "You are the greatest." He walked over to the built-in stereo system in their bookcase and put on Act II of Siegfried. He adjusted the volume. "I also thought the meeting went quite well. I was pleasantly surprised at the way in which all five patients handled their feelings. Mary Hargrove really was incredible. I never thought she'd be strong enough to reveal everything about her relationship with Webster. Her fury at Judd's secret life really made her come alive. Imagine her promising everyone in the group that by next Monday's meeting she'd have had it out once and for all with Max and, if he didn't start shaping up she was going to boot him out."

"Doug Simons was also very impressive," Millie began. "I thought he expressed his feelings of being tricked by you in a very understandable way. I never believed he'd return to the group after the way you used him, asking him for his help and then keeping him away with those white lies."

Mort broke in. "Maybe our group meetings are helping him come to grips with his anger."

"No. I don't think that's it," Millie replied. "I believe his behavior tonight has more to do with what he's personally getting out of what happened. I've read he's signed a book deal that could eventually be worth

302

two million dollars if it's picked up, and it probably will be, by a major movie studio."

Mort nodded in agreement. "The session was very reassuring. I was extremely apprehensive before we started. Therapy is based on confidentiality and on our patient's opening up when they are ready. However, what's gone on has completely undermined that. I was doubtful we'd be able to reestablish any trust. I thought they'd decide to quit the group."

"They still might. Only time will tell," Millie replied.

"I also didn't want to relive the nightmare I've just been through and feel those painful emotions again. But I knew I had to. I had to take them through everything from Tyrone's murder to my killing Ruth Webster. I almost lost it a few times. I kept seeing Ruth. The poker in my hand cracking open her skull. I don't see how I'll ever stop visualizing that scene. I keep thinking there must have been a way I could have stopped Ruth without killing her."

"There wasn't. You know that," Millie replied.

"I hope you're right," Mort replied.

"I am. Eventually, you'll accept the fact you had no choice. Until then, we'll do as we do with our group. We'll keep talking about it."

Mort finished the donut and licked his chocolate covered fingers. "I still think we should have read Judd Webster better."

"We've agreed we messed up. In the future, while I'm sure we'll do our best to screen our referrals more carefully and confront our patients when we sense something odd might be going on, we have to remember we are still human, and being human we are prone to making mistakes," Millie replied. "You've frequently said psychiatrists aren't mind readers."

"That's true," Mort said.

"Judd withheld so much nobody really knew him. Not even Jane. Ruth only learned what her brother was all about when she went through her father's diaries," Millie began. "We can only help our patients when they reveal their innermost thoughts and feelings. Judd never did. He never told us Tyrone Sawyer was his son, or that he had had an affair with

Eileen Matthews. He never even once discussed his childhood." Millie paused. "Besides, did you see the look on Bass's face when you had to admit you were at a loss to explain Judd? That it took his sister for you to understand him. He looked relieved. It was as if your not knowing made you more human. I have the feeling it will allow him to be more tolerant of his own limitations. Hopefully, the others will be able to do the same." Millie paused. "Now do me a favor and lighten up."

"You're right. I'll try my best. However, don't forget you've always been more accepting of the human condition than I have. I preach a good line, but you actually live it," Mort replied.

Millie planted a kiss on Mort's forehead. "I'm very proud of you. I bet you don't realize that since returning from Colorado, you haven't even congratulated yourself on going to the top of that mountain and facing your fear of heights." Millie paused. "If our group continues, when do you think we'll be able to bring in new members?" Millie asked.

"Not for at least a few months," Mort replied. "Healing, as you just reminded me, will take time." He smiled. "By the way I spoke to Jane Webster today. She's quite a mess. She's completely devastated. She thought Ruth was her one ally in the entire Webster family. I recommended a therapist in Washington D.C. for her to see. She sounded receptive. She doesn't know how she'll ever trust again. However, William is safe, and for now, that's all she cares about."

"How did your talk with Butler go?" Millie asked.

"He's still pissed as hell, but at least he's decided not to charge me with obstruction of justice."

Suddenly, the telephone rang. Mort picked it up. Five minutes later he turned to Millie. "That was Lance Wagner. Carlin's doing fine. He hasn't had any symptoms of rejection. It looks like he's going to make it. It doesn't seem fair that he's been given a new lease on life while the donor teenager lies buried."

Millie nodded. "I know. Life's not fair. We can't change that." Millie moved to the bookcase, pulled out a textbook on elementary

304

criminal law, flipped through several pages and felt a sudden surge of adrenalin stirring within her.

"Millie, please put down the book."

Millie smiled and slipped the thick book back into its space.

Mort moved toward her, bent down and lifted her into his arms. "How about some good, old fashioned sex?"

"Now you're talking!" Millie beamed.

*　*　*　*　*　*

THE END